RESILIENT LOVE

SECRET TRIALS
BOOK 1

GIULIANA VICTORIA

TABLE OF COCKTENTS

CHARACTER KEY

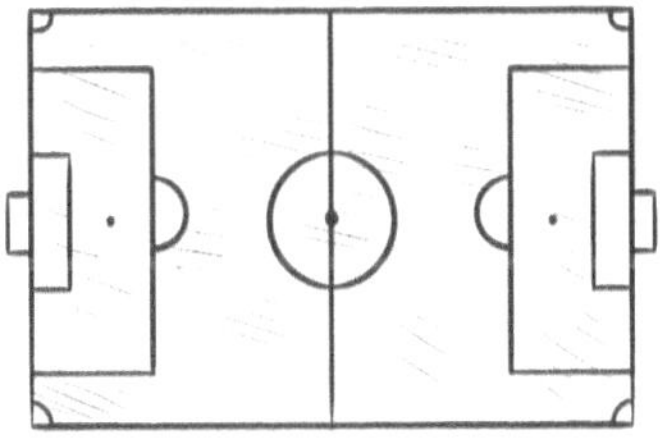

Elise Auclair (pronounced El-ees Awh-clare) Blaze's #9
Adhira Shah (pronounced Ah-deer-rah Shaw) Blaze's #6
Chelsea Lane (pronounced Chel-see Layn) Blaze's #8
Letty Dominguez (pronounced Let-tee Doe-ming-gez) Blaze's #1—Goalkeeper
Rafael Romero-Castillo (pronounced RAHF-eye-el, nickname "Rafa" pronounced RAH-fah) Wyvern Warrior's #2—Hooker
Nakoa Kawai (pronounced Nuh-koa Kuh-Vai) Wyvern Warrior's #15—Fullback
Jelani Hazzel (pronounced Jay-la-nee Huh-zel) Wyvern Warrior's #9—Scrum half

ALSO BY GIULIANA VICTORIA

Philia Players Series

Quiver

Tremble

Quake

Shiver

Secret Trials Series

Resilient Love

Rosa Ranch Series

Something Tangled Something True

Standalones & Novellas

Mistletoe Misconduct

SIGNATURE FRAGRANCES

Elise Auclair
Lavanila Vanilla Blackberry eau de parfum

Rafael Romero-Castillo
Bleu de Chanel eau de parfum

CONTENT WARNINGS

- On-page panic and the alluding to the loss of a loved one(s) (Prologues)
- On-page manic episode and financial loss as a result
- Mention of past mania and subsequent consequences
- On-page and descriptive consensual sex with elements of BDSM
- Sex w/ characters who are not MCs (no cheating)
- Loss of a parent by cancer (in the past)
- Loss of a sibling by suicide (in the past)
- Injury and guilt related to an accident involving a sibling (in the past)
- Scenes that may be difficult for readers with a severe fear of heights

DEDICATION

For anyone who's ever felt their battles weren't worth sharing because they can't be seen. Sometimes, the things we can't see are the hardest to overcome. Your struggles are valid, as are your dreams for a better, more joyous future.

FOREWORD

I have several notes for this book, the first of which is that this story takes place in the very fictional town of Embershire, UK, and other very fictional versions of real countries. This means that places mentioned are entirely fictional, but this is the location I chose to allow for the popularity of rugby, a challenge to myself to write in British English (to an extent), and the ability to include characters from many backgrounds with more ease and believability than I might have if written in the US.

That said, when I refer to "football," I mean American "soccer," unless otherwise noted. And when Chelsea, a side character (for now), calls the sport soccer instead of football, that is because she's from the Southern US.

The Spanish spoken in this book is Argentine Spanish; this means that if you learned Spanish elsewhere, it will not necessarily look correct to you. I had sensitivity readers born and raised in Argentina help me with this aspect as well. When a character not from Argentina starts learning Spanish, the dialect is not Argentine-specific until later as this character was later taught some Argentine Spanish while in Argentina. There's a certain nuance that went into this, and I promise I did my best, but I'm not perfect, so I ask for some grace.

It's also worth noting that while both Elise and Rafael live in the UK now, neither of them were born there, so the level of British slang/terminology they use varies based on the proximity to the country they were born in to the UK and how I envision their voices.

There are also going to be times when certain aspects of both sports (football/soccer and rugby) are written with changes that made parts of this book possible. I'm aware that football and rugby teams do not have the same number of players, but for one key scene in this book, they had to. That said, the actual on-page written scenes are as accurate as possible.

This book was an incredibly fun challenge to write, as has been the rest of this series, and I couldn't have done it without the incredible sensitivity readers who helped make it possible. I'm not an authority on football/soccer, rugby, bipolar 1 disorder, loss of a loved one as a result of suicide, spinal cord injuries, cultures, traditions, languages, backgrounds, etc. outside of my own lived experience, nor do I claim to be. This is where my sensitivity readers have come in, and I thank them very much for sharing their experiences with me, and in turn, with all of you.

It's truly an honour to have the opportunity to learn about different ways of life outside of my own and to be taught with such grace and love by the people sharing their time with me to ensure these books are written with intention and respect. I could have never envisioned my writing career to look like this, but the bookish community is a wonderful place, and I'm so thankful to be a part of it.

My last note is that while I do mention that a character has a spinal cord injury, I also mention "new and innovative treatments" that are not a reality right now. This is why in marketing this book, I do not mention "spinal cord injury or paraplegia representation" as this element was written with the storyline and a lot of hope for the future in mind and is not an accurate representation of the progression of illness nor the treatment and management of spinal cord injuries. I did my best to allow this element to ring true in some ways like the immense amount of work needed to make progress, the small improvements that may be possible with various treatments such as continuous physical therapy and occupational therapy efforts at home, but ultimately, this is not a part of the story that represents the lived experiences of those with a spinal cord injury and is not intended to. If this portion of the story will upset you or make it difficult to read, I absolutely understand and recommend skipping this book or emailing me for additional details.

I hope you love ***Resilient Love*** as much as I do because, for as much difficulty as this book gave me, I really love these grumpy, horny assholes. <3

PS. I also refuse to spell groin as "groyne." Fight me)

ELISE

PROLOGUE ONE

THE CAR DOOR slams behind me as I bound to the door following Dad. His brows are pinched, but otherwise, nothing seems amiss. I've done my best to ignore the unfamiliar feeling niggling into my stomach ever since *Maman* and Rachelle missed our call last night after the game, but with everything going on at home, they were probably just tired.

"I can't wait to show Rach the size of this trophy!" I say, excitement and pride whirling through me as I hold up the giant hunk of metal.

"Your *Maman* and Rachelle are going to be *thrilled, mon petit chou.*"

The door unlocks with a *snick,* and Dad pushes it open. I bull-doze inside, shouting, "Mom! Rach! *On est à la maison.*"

When they don't answer, that feeling burrows deeper, anxiety climbing up my throat.

I look at Dad, his shoulders tense, spine rigid, and his usual relaxed demeanour is nowhere to be found.

"They're probably still sleeping. Maybe they stayed up watching movies." I nod, but his words don't set me at ease. They would have answered the phone when we called if they were awake last night.

My heart pounds a little harder with each passing second, and the air is thinner and harder to breathe. I move through the house, footsteps quieter now, trying to hold it together. The stillness settles around me like a suffocating fog, and I swallow against the lump rising in my throat.

I swing our bedroom door open and find both of our beds untouched. My heart hammers against the walls of my ribcage, threatening to fly out of my chest. I push past Dad, sprinting to my parents' room. He yells something behind me, but I can barely hear him over the sound of my heartbeats growing louder in my ears, his words hitting me too late. I push the door open, and time stops.

Nothing makes sense anymore. My stomach free falls to my toes and I crumple to the floor, my knees smacking against the hardwood—I don't feel the pain, my entire being giving way to numbness.

We were too late.

PROLOGUE TWO

"*COME ONNN*, CARLITO," I beg my brother, all but getting on my knees. I'm filled with restless energy, the need to do something reckless taking over, causing me to pace. "This is what we've been waiting for all these years. *This* is our big moment! Tomorrow, we get on a flight out of here and start living our dreams."

"*Si, hermano.* And I don't want to *die* before I get to live out those dreams, so my answer is *no*," he says with a huff. "And you do realise that *I* am the older brother? Stop calling me Carlito, and respect your elders." He scoffs.

"You're seven centimetres shorter than I am; therefore, you are *Carlito*. And I do respect my elders! Just this once, *viví un poco*!" I'm flat-out begging now, and if I'm being honest, it's a little embarrassing. I promised Carlos and our parents that I'd give up seeking adrenaline rushes once we move to Embershire and start playing football at the college level, but that's not until tomorrow and I intend to use every second of my freedom.

"I *am* living, Rafa. Cut it out." He swats me away, rolling his eyes as he stomps toward the living room.

"I swear, this is the last thing on my list! After this, I promise not to do any more thrill-seeking. I'll give you anything you want, Carlos. *Please* do this for me."

"Will you shut up if I agree?" he asks, his voice gruff as he throws his hands up in defeated annoyance.

"Yes!"

"Then *fine*, let's go before I change my mind."

If I'd have known how this night would end, I'd have never pressured him to take the leap with me.

Fútbol. Uni. All of our shared dreams. *Washed away with any semblance of my will to live.*

RAFAEL

CHAPTER ONE
WEDNESDAY, MARCH 19

I TEAR through the locker room, fists balled as I make my way to Coach's office. Yanking the door open, it slams against the wall at my entrance. Coach leans back in his chair, his head supported by his forearms, as he eyes me with a smug smirk stretched across his lips.

"What the fuck is this about?" I challenge.

"What*ever* are you talking about?" he asks, his tone dripping in sarcasm.

"You know good and well what I'm referring to."

At that, he sits up in his chair, wiping the smirk clean from his face. He levels me with a flat expression before saying, "You want my job when I retire. Do this for me, and it's yours."

The wind is knocked from my lungs, a rebuttal on the tip of my tongue, but it never makes its way out of my mouth.

Coach Auclair relaxes back into his seat, crossing his arms over his chest. "I don't do ultimatums, so the job is yours regardless of whether you accept the position or not, but I really hope you will. I plan to retire in the next two years, and I don't want to have to worry about what I plan to do with this team."

I can barely think past the throb of my heartbeat against all of my pulse points as my mind works to figure out what his intentions are. "What's so special about this women's football team that

I, *of all people*, am being requested as their interim coach? And why would you suggest *me* in the first place? I haven't competed in a football match in years."

Coach Auclair knows all about my painful past with football, and if that wasn't reason enough not to include me in whatever plan he has, I'm not sure what is. *This isn't adding up.*

He lets out a sigh, placing his hands on the desk in front of him. He squeezes his eyes shut and pinches the bridge of his nose, steadying himself.

"It's my daughter's team."

My brows scrunch together. "I'm still not understanding," I answer plainly.

His eyes finally open, and the pained expression chiselled into his features has my heart clenching in my chest. I know desperation when I see it—it's an emotion I've grown entirely too familiar with.

"My daughter's team has won the National Championship the last two years. Elise plans to make it onto the Olympic team, and that can't happen without a coach. Her previous one was caught in a scandal, and no one wants to take the team on right now because they don't want their name involved."

Shaking my head, I ask, "What kind of scandal would deter potentially hundreds of available coaches, especially if the team is as good as you're suggesting?"

"It was with the players," he reluctantly admits, rubbing the space between his brows where the skin is wrinkled, his lips pulling taut. "The coach was sleeping with the players."

A chill runs down my spine as his words sink in. I blink, the weight of them pressing against my chest, and slowly nod, my mind racing as I trace the quiet tension in the air. My fingers curl into a fist at my side, but I don't move, standing here, assessing the shift in the space between us. "And you think it's a good idea to send one of your players, who hasn't played football in years and has definitely never coached, to act as interim coach, in the middle of the season? I'm genuinely curious where the hell this idea came from."

"I can't say I trust you to keep it in your pants, okay?" He rolls his eyes. "But at least you aren't old enough to be one of these girls' fathers. That said, I'd really prefer it if you kept your dick to yourself."

"Okay," I answer slowly, "let's say I agree to this, how do we plan to make this work with my practice and game schedule?"

"I'll rework practice times to be immediately before or after the Blaze's practices, and I've already arranged to have all of ours on their campus so you don't have to travel between locations. They're a sport-oriented school with a lot of money. Their facility is as nice, if not nicer, than ours. It won't be a downgrade. Besides, their season is nearly halfway through."

Shaking my head, I release a grunt. "Fine," I tell him, turning to leave.

"Wait! 'Fine'? You're saying yes?" he asks, dumbstruck as his hands grip the armrests of his wooden desk chair, his ass halfway out of the seat as he stares at me with wide eyes.

"Sounds like it," I say, calling over my shoulder as I stride out the door.

This is a terrible idea.

ELISE

CHAPTER TWO

FRIDAY, MARCH 21

"ELISE," the massive Brit purrs as he swipes the head of his engorged cock through my slick heat, "will you be a good girl and accommodate us both at the same time?"

"Yes," I moan.

Leo chuckles, lining his swollen tip up with my mouth. "It's really poetic, isn't it, mate?" He pauses, laughing again. "The good little French girl is about to do her first Eiffel Tower."

A laugh squawks out of me, hiding my disdain for the ignorant comment. Leo is often brash, leaning into certain stereotypes about Australians, never one to hold his thoughts in, which is something I usually enjoy about him, so I brush the comment off. "When did I say it was my first?" I challenge.

Noah smacks my ass from his position behind me. "He should've known better."

The sting sends a zap of electricity down my spine, and a moan slips past my lips. "Shut up and fuck me already," I instruct, letting the sass seep into my voice.

"Don't have to tell me twice," Leo responds before plunging his cock into my mouth.

"Oh, we've already started, huh?" Noah comments from behind, pushing into me, causing my mouth to drive forward, meeting Leo's hips.

Noah's pounding thrusts and the slap of his pelvis against my ass causes heat to pool in my core. My eyes are watering with the effort to remain on all fours with Leo's length threatening to suffocate me.

Noah's hand snakes around my bare abdomen, his thumb stroking over my clit. Another moan escapes me, and my thighs clench together as the firm pressure starts to coax my orgasm out of me.

Leo's position changes, his hips angling himself even further, burrowing into my throat.

I look up at him through my lashes and see that he's extending his arm over my head, presumably reaching for Leo's behind me. *A real Eiffel Tower. Well, I'll be damned.*

It takes everything in me not to laugh with his cock impaling my throat. If I did, he'd likely wind up with teeth marks.

Drawing in a deep breath through my nose, I focus on two things. Not choking and having an orgasm before I have to make it to practice.

Leo's callused hand grips my chin, then drags across my cheek. His fingers dig into my scalp, his groans of approval growing louder.

"Fuck, Frenchy, your mouth is fucking delicious," he says with a moan.

"She's gagging for it," Noah murmurs, his thick British accent sending another jolt of pleasure through me.

My walls are clenching around his length, the methodical rhythm of his thumb driving me wild. Tension builds throughout me, my muscles aching for release.

Leo's body goes rigid. "I'm about to come."

The hot, salty taste of his release fills my mouth, sliding down my throat. A satisfying moan escapes me as Noah pulls himself out entirely before plunging back in. I bounce my ass back into his hips, taking him to the hilt as I come undone around him. My body writhes against him as he fills me, tendrils of pleasure licking up my spine.

Once they've both pulled out, I collapse on the bed. "Fucking hell," Leo groans.

Noah's arousal trickles out of me and down my thighs. I'm spent.

Noah slumps beside me, angling his face to peer over at me. He's wearing a contented smile as he says, "Sorry 'bout that, love." He nods his chin toward my coated thighs.

A laugh escapes me as I roll over, smacking a hand to his chest and using it to push myself up. "Alrighty, boys, stay as long as you'd like, but I've got to get going."

"Your new coach starts today, right?"

I nod, heading to the bathroom to clean up.

Neither of them moves to stand, but I leave the door open so we can continue talking while I freshen up.

"Know who it is yet?"

I shake my head before realising that they can't see my response. "Not yet."

"Hopefully they're not a wanker like the last one," Noah drawls.

"He wasn't a wanker." I chuckle. "He was a slut. But so are we, and I'm not judging either of you."

"The man was old enough to be our father." Leo groans.

Grabbing a pair of shorts, I work them up my thighs. "Different strokes for different folks." I shrug. "Not my cup of tea, but I can't fault the man too much. If I looked like him at nearly fifty, I'd be sleeping with whoever I wanted too."

"You already do that," Noah jokes.

"Yep, and I've no plans to stop anytime soon."

"And why is that exactly, Elise?" Noah asks, a light brow raised at me.

Oh, here we go again. Why can't he leave well enough alone? I don't have the time, nor the desire, for more than what we're already doing, and with Noah's incessant questioning, I'd never be open to anything serious with *him*, anyway. Of course, I don't say any of that and opt for a kinder, more rehearsed version of the same sentiment.

"I don't have time for a relationship right now, and I have no reason to settle for just one cock. Maybe one day when I find one that satisfies me, I will, but lucky for you"—I wink—"today is not that day."

Noah chuckles, but the sound is tense. He sits up to get dressed, and my shoulders sag with relief. "Fair enough, but I'm not sure there's any human cock that could satisfy you. Hell, this bloke and I have been trying for months now."

I roll my eyes at that. "Don't act as if it's some hardship." Sex is the only time I can afford to feel anything besides the constant weight of loss. Sure, I might've let go of the resentment I used to carry around, but it doesn't mean it's not impossible to miss the two people I once counted on most. Without them here, focusing solely on my career is a necessary evil to ensure my success.

Bending forward, I double-knot my trainers. "Alright, let yourselves out, I'm gonna be late." I catch sight of the alarm clock on my nightstand. "Again," I groan, heading out with a noncommittal wave in their direction.

"The French, *always rushing everywhere*," Noah chides as I sprint down the steps.

I slam the door shut behind me, bolting down the rickety wooden porch steps and to my rideshare. I slide into the backseat, introduce myself, and luckily, he gets the hint that I'm in a hurry.

The drive doesn't take more than fifteen minutes, and the moment he's slowed down enough that I won't get killed, I fling myself from the car, sprinting to the locker room to throw my things down and rush out toward the field.

"I'm here!" I shout, sprinting past the water bottles lined up on the edge of the turf. I expect to see my teammates already stretching, getting ready for our first official practice with our new coach, but that isn't what I find at all.

My team is huddled together, staring at the field as I approach. I catch sight of the familiar blue streaks running through one of my best friend's hair and immediately steer in her direction. "What are we all looking—" The words get caught in my throat, my mouth running dry.

Chelsea makes no move to face me as she breathes the words, *"Rugby players."* As if that answers all of the questions suddenly racing through my head.

My eyes zero in on the massive men on the field, each of them in a different position as they stretch out their colossal, toned thighs. *Jesus Christ,* I'd pay to be crushed between a set of those things.

Some of the men are utilising resistance bands while others have their asses in the air, stretching their legs. Several of them are wearing what Chelsea refers to as "hoochie daddy shorts." The number of strange terms Americans use will never cease to amaze me, but this time, the phrase feels rather fitting.

Another familiar face catches my eye, and I see the broad smile belonging to my father stretch across his wrinkling face as he waves at me.

"What the hell is a professional rugby team, my *father's* team, doing at our school?" I question anyone within earshot.

"Not a clue, but I can't say I'm not enjoying the view," Adhira comments dryly.

"Are you back on your poetry kick, or did that rhyme come out by accident?" Chelsea asks, snickering beside me.

"That time, it was an accident. My comment still stands."

"Can't say I disagree," Ruby, another one of our teammates, comments.

"Alright, men, practice is over. Get off my kid's pitch."

I groan, unease rippling through me as he draws unwanted attention to me.

The men stand, heading past my drooling teammates as they take us in, wiggling their brows and sending winks in every direction.

All except one of them. *My father's team captain.*

The giant standing beside my father is facing us with his

hands on his hips, unwavering as his gaze sweeps over us slowly. My dad claps him on the back before jogging toward the locker rooms, averting his gaze as he rushes past me.

I don't have time to go after him before Rafael Romero-Castillo opens his sexy mouth to speak the words that are bound to wreck the rest of our season.

"Listen up, ladies, I'm Rafael, and I'll be your interim coach for the remainder of the season. I know this might come as a shock to some of you, but prior to playing rugby, I actually came *here* on a football scholarship." We all watch him with rapt attention. *How could we not?*

"And you think because you played soccer over a decade ago that you're qualified to coach us?" Chelsea challenges from beside me, her arms crossed over her small chest.

"No." He shakes his head, his shoulders rigid, jaw set in a sharp line. "I don't think I'm even a little qualified for this job, but *my* coach is making me do this because apparently without *me*, none of *you* would even have a coach this season. So, how about we all work together to get through this season and make the most of this?" he chides sarcastically, not looking hopeful. Wow. *Isn't he delightful?*

We each look to one another before levelling him with a stare. "Fine," I tell him. At that, each of us makes our way onto the field, ignoring his sceptical expression.

What he doesn't realise is that we've all been playing together for long enough to know what the other is thinking without having to speak about it. And luckily for him, we've decided on a silent truce. *For now.*

RAFAEL

CHAPTER THREE

FRIDAY, MARCH 21

WELL, *shit.*

Coach was right. These ladies are the real deal. They train hard and play even harder. Their form and attention to detail is beautiful, and they're so in sync that it's like they share one mind.

On one hand, it's helpful that they don't seem to need much coaching, but on the other, they're highly competitive athletes with a new coach that they haven't decided if they like, let alone trust. Working as one cohesive team with an outsider might be more of a challenge when there *are* things we need to change, and if one of them decides to make my life hell, I'm confident they all will.

It'll definitely be a new challenge for me, but I'm happy to face it if it means making *my* coach happy and securing my position taking over for him when he retires.

Well, *happy* isn't quite the right word, but I'm not nearly as pissed about it as I imagined I'd be.

I'm trying to do something that's extremely out of character for look on the bright side. It pains me to even think that sort of thing because it feels cliche and *wrong*, but the positives are the only things keeping me from totally spiralling down the dark hole where the ghosts of my past and self-loathing reside.

It certainly helps that these young women are fucking

machines on the pitch, and that makes it a touch less painful to be here. Nearly a decade ago, I was in this same place for very different reasons.

I watch them closely silent glances, barely noticeable shifts in posture—signals that would fly under the radar for most, but not for me. I know this language, the one my team and I speak without words.

Every team has their own cues. It's a part of what makes us work so harmoniously without having to shout at one another mid-game or give away our next moves, but these particular gestures? I know them well, and I have a hunch as to why that is.

"Auclair, come here for a minute," I shout over to the dark-haired woman. Her head whips in my direction before she nods, jogging over to me.

It takes everything in me not to stare at her perky tits as they bounce over the top of her tight sports bra. *This* is going to be a problem. It'd be helpful if she were younger because there wouldn't be any blurred lines. But I know from Coach celebrating her birthday that she's twenty-one.

Which means she's legal, but still every bit off limits. Even if I wasn't technically her coach now, it would be in everyone's best interest for me to steer clear.

Maybe if I refer to her as a girl in my head, my dick will get the memo. Nope, that won't work either because I fucking hate it when people, especially *men,* act as if young women are merely children.

These people out here are athletes. They're earning an education and working toward their dreams. They don't deserve to be thought of as less because my coach's daughter is too damn pretty for my own good.

She stops a couple feet away, standing tall and locking eyes with me. Her hands plant firmly on her hips, like she's ready for whatever's coming next. "What's up?" She huffs, appraising me. My eyes catch on the small bead of sweat sliding down her neck, making its way to the centre of her breasts.

She chuckles humourlessly, drawing my attention back to her pale-blue eyes. They're like glaciers, as chilling as her demeanour. She wears a smirk that tells me I've been caught. "Careful now or we'll be down *another* coach for inappropriate behaviour." Her quirked brow looks like a challenge, and I'm reminded of a version of myself from a decade ago, someone long gone who would've *loved* to accept her provocation just to feel alive.

My nostrils flare at the insinuation, but she's right. I need to get my shit together.

I ignore her comment and clear my throat before asking, "Who decided on those signals you use?"

"Me," she deadpans.

No surprise there.

"Your dad teach you those?" Clearly he had. I'm not sure why I'm goading her as if she's done something wrong. She's merely using the resources she's had available to her, and I'm only curious, but the words leave my throat like an accusation, leaving me bristling beneath her heavy glare.

A tight, forced smile pulls at her lips as she lets out a short, dismissive laugh, her eyes briefly glancing down at her feet before meeting mine with clear frustration. "No, *I* taught *him*," she informs me.

I'm taken aback by this. My brows pinch together, and my head tilts as I appraise her. "*You* taught *him*?"

She rolls her eyes at me. "Yes. That's what I said. You're welcome, by the way. You should be thanking me for my creativity at the ripe age of seventeen. *Really,* I'm partially to thank for your team's success," she says with a wink. The action has a knot buried deep in my chest tightening and burning from a frustrating combination of desire and annoyance. Neither of which have any business being there. Before I can get another word in, she turns on her heel and jogs back to the centre of the field to meet up with the rest of her teammates.

This is already going poorly, but it could *always* be worse.

ELISE

CHAPTER FOUR

FRIDAY, MARCH 21

THE WHISTLE CUTS through the air, sharp and unforgiving. I bite back a groan. My legs ache, my lungs burn, but there's no way I'm showing it. Not with Rafael prowling the sidelines like a disappointed predator. He hasn't looked up from his damn clipboard all practice, but that hasn't stopped him from barking orders like we're pawns in some messed-up chess game.

"Elise! Quit wandering and stay in position," he snaps, his voice dripping with irritation. I clench my teeth, my jaw tight enough to crack. I *am* in position, but it's not like he'd know; his eyes are glued to the paper in front of him. The rest of the team is just as drained, shuffling around with the kind of muted resentment that comes from spending two hours being treated like we're barely competent.

The ball lands at my feet, and instinct takes over. I flick it out to Ruby in the right midfield, threading it through two defenders like a needle through fabric. It's a good pass, clean and sharp, and I hear Ruby shout, "Nice one, Elise!" as she takes off down the line. But before the satisfaction can settle in my chest, Rafael's voice cuts in.

"Sloppy," he says without even looking up. "That should've been quicker."

The whistle blows again, and just like that, practice is over.

Coach Dickwad doesn't offer a word of feedback, let alone encouragement, before turning on his heel and walking off the field. No "Good work, team," no "See you tomorrow," just the sound of his grumbles as he saunters away. I stare after him, fury and exhaustion tangling in my chest, and then turn and slam a ball into the back of the net. It thuds hard against the netting, but the weight in my chest doesn't budge.

I'm not sure how I feel about Rafael yet. He hasn't been around long, so I'm doing my best to give him the benefit of the doubt, but with every passing minute, the doubt creeps higher.

What he does have going for him is that he's a beast on the pitch from every match I've seen him play, but that's not really an accomplishment when you're a rugby player. They're *all* beasts.

Luckily for him, there isn't much coaching that needs to be done. We are by no means perfect, and we take well to constructive criticism, but overall, we work together seamlessly. If there's an issue, we're good about pinpointing it and making the necessary changes.

These women and I have a silent understanding. If he doesn't get in our way, we won't make his life any more difficult than it already is for being thrown into this position. *One he clearly doesn't want.* There's nothing positive that could come out of that, but if he thinks we won't push back when he's being a tosser, he's dead wrong.

We never hesitated to tell Coach Lyon when we didn't agree with him, and as a result, we kicked ass together—that is, when he wasn't *eating ass*. The latter *probably* had something to do with his lax demeanour.

Thankfully, I never got myself into that mess. I'll admit that he was hot. I'll even admit that, within reason, I find older men attractive, but he was old enough to be my father, and that never sat well with me, particularly because my father is one of my best friends. To each their own though.

I head into the locker rooms, my teammates' expressions matching that of our new coach's. Would it kill him to stop grimacing all the time? *Wow, Elise, you're one to talk.* How many men have I snapped at for telling me to smile more? Likely more than I can count.

I strip out of my clothes, unashamed of my body, which allows me to continue playing the sport I love, as I grab a towel and head to the showers.

"Your dad didn't mention that it'd be one of *his* players taking over?" Chelsea asks, everyone's eyes panning toward me for the answer they've been waiting to hear all practice.

"Nope, I was as out of the loop as all of you," I tell them, my tone sharper than I'd intended as frustration at our situation bleeds into the words.

They take that at face value and all get back to showering and changing. *Thank god* because I sincerely hadn't the slightest fucking clue. Though I know if I had, there isn't anything we could've done about it. And frankly, I'm just happy to have a coach to continue the season with. It does feel a little like my father is babysitting me, and that causes the smallest trickle of resentment to trail down my spine.

I enter the shower and turn the knob to heat the water just below scalding. A reminder of hell, where I came from, according to Noah. If he wants sunshine and rainbows, he should look elsewhere.

We finish up in the locker room, then Adhira, Chelsea, Letty, and I head toward the parking lot, climbing into Letty's Ford Fiesta.

I can't say squeezing into her car is more comfortable than the rideshare I took to get to practice, but it's better than walking.

"Any idea why your dad picked him?" Chelsea asks, sitting beside me in the back.

I shake my head. "He's the team captain, but if anything, I'd think that would make him the least likely option."

"Yeah, wouldn't he want his captain fully focused on his own team? I mean, I know your dad loves you, but rugby pays the bills," Letty points out.

"Or maybe he wants the best for you and knows his captain will keep it in his pants?" Chelsea offers but laughs. "Though I'm not sure about that last part. His eyes were practically glued to your tits."

"I'd prefer it if you refer to them as 'incredible tits' but agreed, they were absolutely burning holes straight into my nipples." I let out a shaky laugh; the unfriendly reminder of Rafael's lust-filled eyes on me has my nipples pebbling, the reaction surprising me. I quell the sensation, rushing to redirect my inappropriate thoughts. "He did mention being a footballer at one point, so that's likely why." I wonder why he'd made the switch. I enjoy both watching and playing rugby, but I wouldn't trade football for the world.

"He seems like he'll be a decent coach. Not overbearing, and so far, he's mostly let you take the reins, which I appreciate. I don't particularly love that we couldn't find a female coach, but he'll do," Adhira says, always the voice of unerring reason. It's no wonder she's going into medicine after graduation.

"At least he's nice to look at," Chelsea adds.

"Can't argue with that," I joke, turning my attention to the small shops we pass outside my window as we head back to our shared house. When my emotions feel like they're becoming too overwhelming and complex, I've learned to pull back and redirect my focus. It's something that has come with years of therapy and practice, but even now, as my emotions teeter too close to the edge of annoyance, frustration, and confusion, I'm finding it hard not to over-analyse my actions. Maybe I shouldn't have taunted him earlier? Could I be making things worse for my teammates as a result of my childish behaviour?

Letty's smooth, melodious tone drags me from my thoughts. "You guys wanna grab lunch before we head home?" she asks.

I groan, my shoulders sagging. "I can't. I have to study for that sports policy exam I have on Monday." If it wouldn't absolutely kill my dad, I'd have dropped out of this program to join the premier league already. I owe him *everything* after he helped me pick up the pieces despite his whole world crashing at the same time mine had.

"You're going to do fine; you always manage," Adhira assures me.

My eyes slide to her. "Only thanks to you. If it weren't for the three of you drilling me on practice questions before every exam, I'd fail every bloody time. Whoever the wanker was that said sports management was an easy degree was dead wrong, and I'd like to hang them by their bollocks."

"Maybe if you weren't being drilled by—"

Adhira gets cut off by Chelsea. "It doesn't matter now. You're almost graduated, and you won't be using the degree anyway. You're here for football, and that's all you need to focus on outside of maintaining a passing grade. When we get home, I'll make us lunch and we can study," Chelsea tells me with finality in her voice.

"Yes, ma'am." I chuckle.

We arrive home a few minutes later, pulling up to the two-storey maisonette with brick siding and the completely out-of-place white-painted wooden porch. It's a bit of an eyesore in the centre of a long line of converted flats and Victorian-style homes, but it's all ours, and the bay windows are a cheeky addition that I adore, even if they are a right nuisance to clean.

I grab my duffel, rushing up the steps. Once inside, Chelsea gets to work putting together her dodgy grain bowls for everyone, forcing us all to eat a well-balanced meal. *What a cunt.*

Unfortunately for me and my desire to consume nothing but candy all day, I guess she has a point. She preaches about our bodies being our temple, and I guess I *would* feel like rubbish if I ate that garbage instead of real food. It doesn't make me want it any less, though, and she's really one to talk with the high fructose corn syrup-filled products her mum sends in her care packages from the States.

After we finish eating, I slide down onto the floor, resting my head against the cushion as the girls take their seats around me on the dingy couch.

Dad offers to buy us a new one at least once a month, but I can't part with it. It was the first real adult purchase I ever made, and the worn-out green fabric reminds me of a dress my *maman* used to wear for every special occasion when I was growing up. Though her dress was a hell of a lot nicer, and this couch isn't making my knockers look nearly as good as that dress had for her, but *c'est la vie*.

"Alright, let's get started. I have big plans to drag you *putas* out to that new club tonight," Letty says.

"What part of 'I have an exam on Monday' didn't you understand?" I ask, rolling my eyes, but knowing damn well I won't be here, studying all night. Not on a Friday. Especially not one of the only free Fridays we get during the season.

"You've got three whole days to study. We're going out. A little relaxation will do you good," she says with a nod as if it's confirmed. No one says 'no' to Letty, so it might as well be. That's the perk of being the goalkeeper.

"Fine," I grumble for the sake of being a brat. I love clubbing, so it's no real hardship.

Chelsea heads to the kitchen. "I'm grabbing some water. Y'all need anything?"

We all tell her "No thanks," but her gaze meets mine with a seriousness that crinkles the edges of her eyes. "You take your meds today, or do you need me to bring them to you?"

I wince at the question. I forgot, *again*. The guilt gnaws at me, a reminder of how I've let it slip too many times. Someday, I'll get it together. *I hope.*

"I had a busy morning," I explain, my voice quiet, though I know she's only asking to check in, not to judge. Still, the weight of it hangs over me. I feel like a burden, like I should be better by now. She shouldn't have to mother me, and neither should anyone else. It's *me* who's judging me. "Bring them over, please."

She nods, grabbing another glass of water and counting my

pills out for me. "A busy morning, huh?" she asks, her brow quirked, and a smirk plays on her lips.

"Yep, *super* busy," I tell her, my eyes dancing.

"By 'busy' you mean you were getting railed, right?" Adhira asks, blunt as ever.

"Yep," I quip, smiling broadly.

We all laugh in unison and fall into an easy rhythm of studying with practice questions and a speed round before getting ready for a night out.

"The black dress or the dark-blue one?" I ask, unsure of what to wear tonight.

"I'd say the dark-blue one because it brings out your eyes, but we'll be in a dark club, so it won't matter." Chelsea grabs the dresses from me and tosses a pair of leather pants, hitting me right in the face with them.

"*I'll* wear the blue dress, and you can wear the leather pants and matching corset. It brings out your ass and tits, which are *far* more important than your eyes." She chuckles, waggling her blonde brows at me.

"Can't argue with that," I tell her, working the skin-tight pants up my long legs. "Why a dress for you tonight?" I question, knowing she isn't dressing me for my benefit alone.

"A dress is easy access, and I fully plan on getting fingered on the dance floor tonight," she says with a wide, confident smile that shows off the single rhinestone glued to her right canine.

"You know, you own dresses of your own too," I say with a smirk, the words laced with a playful challenge.

"Yeah, but yours are better." She grins. "It's like shopping without spending the money. Plus, you're four inches shorter than me, which means your dresses are automatically shorter too."

She has a point.

"Will you ever learn to use the metric system?" I chide.

"Unlikely."

Once we're both dressed, we head out into the living room to meet the other girls. Joey and Ria are leaning against the kitchen counter, chatting with Letty and Adhira.

"Hey, glad you guys could make it," I tell our friends from the women's rugby team.

"And miss out on probably our last free Friday night for the next several months? Never," Joey says with a laugh.

"The Uber's just arrived, let's go," Letty says, ushering us out the door. You'd really think she would be our team captain, but while she loves bossing everyone around in her personal life, she has zero desire on the field. That's her time to play without any pretence clouding her fun.

The Uber pulls up to the club, its neon lights flickering like distant stars in the dark. We thank the driver and slip out, joining the line that curves toward the entrance. The air outside is cool; wind whipping past causes goosebumps to litter my skin. I focus my attention on the little bumps, smoothing my palm over my forearm, doing my best to block out the chatter of the crowd surrounding me. It feels too overstimulating, but I know that once we're inside, it'll be a nice reprieve from the heavy weight of my thoughts.

People-watching has always been something that effectively fills the spaces in my racing mind, allowing me to shut off the fire hose of too many emotions blasting me in the face.

The bouncer barely glances at us before stepping aside, letting us into the suffocating, dimly lit interior.

The club is alive with noise—voices, laughter, and the constant thrum of the bass that seems to seep into every corner. The air inside is stifling, heavy with sweat and perfume, and the crowd presses in from all sides. Bodies move to the rhythm, hands raised, faces lit by the unpredictable flashes of strobe lights. It's chaotic, like trying to navigate a dream that won't sit still—something I know all too well.

We make our way through the crowd, finally finding a booth in the back, where the noise dulls just enough to catch our breath. The air here is cooler but still thick, and the darkness wraps around us, a welcome contrast to the dizzying energy of the dancefloor. We pile into the booth, our laughter cutting through the haze as we settle in, trying to find our place in this madness.

"Hey, ladies, I'm Shamir. What can I get you to drink?" a handsome guy I recognise from campus asks us.

"I'll have a vodka martini, shaken," I say, forcing a smile that feels more like a stretch than anything genuine. I'm acutely aware of how standoffish I must seem, though it doesn't bother me much; I'm not looking to make friends outside of my inner circle. But Shamir's always been kind to me, offering a quick smile whenever our paths cross, so it feels like the least I can do to not outright glare at him.

He returns my smile with one that feels genuine, far more convincing than mine ever was, his cheeks darkening with a blush, and he quickly averts his gaze before moving on to take the rest of our orders.

Should you really be drinking? The nagging voice in the back of my head asks, a voice that sounds all too familiar to Rachelle's, so I welcome it with open arms despite the pang it causes in my chest or the way it twists my stomach in knots. I know I don't need to respond, it's not like she's here, but I start my rant anyway I like to have a drink here or there, but I promise, I avoid overdoing it if I'm with the wrong crowd. I don't love feeling out of control, as you very well know. *Especially since I already feel that way half of the time*, but I know my girls will keep me safe.

Between Adhira's no-nonsense attitude, Letty's ability to clear a room with a single look, and Chelsea's mama bear instincts, I know I have nothing to worry about.

"Oh shit," Chelsea whispers. "Is that the men's rugby team?" she asks, signalling toward the bar with her chin.

A groan slips past my lips. "It sure is," I whine.

"How is that a bad thing? I fully intend to be riding one of those juicy thighs before the night is over," Chelsea clucks, her Southern drawl making an appearance.

"I don't love the idea of a bunch of men who are essentially my dad's indentured servants watching my every move at a club and potentially reporting back to him about my...extracurriculars," I mutter, shifting in my seat.

"Your father is fully aware that not only are you an adult, but you're definitely not a virgin. I assure you, the man isn't keeping tabs on you. I'm gonna go dance, do as you please." She rolls her eyes, pushing me out of the seat and heading straight toward the dance floor.

My eyes land on Rafael, unable to tear my gaze away as I commit every inch of him to memory. His broad shoulders threaten to tear the satin material of his tight-fitting button down, the sleeves rolled to his elbows, and thick veins run the length of his tan and taught muscular forearms. I catch a glimpse of his firm, round ass and wide thighs stretching his black trousers, but the sight is gone too soon as he slides onto a leather barstool, dipping his head for one of his teammates to speak into his ear.

His posture turns rigid, and the teammate who I recognise as Jelani Hazzel flicks his gaze toward me. I'm quick to duck my chin and slide back into the booth, doing my best to focus on any one of the hundreds of people in the crowded club besides *him*.

The attempt becomes more and more futile as the hours pass by, my inhibitions lowering with every martini Shamir brings me.

I'm three martinis deep and absolutely feeling it. I hadn't anticipated drinking so much, but without the dance floor to keep me occupied, I fell into a pattern of drinking to keep my hands and mouth busy.

I've been watching my friends dance for hours now, sulking in this booth, not wanting to find myself too close to any of the rugby players. *Is that really what you're doing back here?* That same voice questions, and I roll my eyes, hating that my inner monologue sounds so much like my sister had.

Unfortunately, no, that is not the *only* reason. I'd prefer to hover back here than have my new coach running his mouth to my dad. It isn't that I'm embarrassed by my actions, it's more that if he's going to know about them, *I* want to be the one to tell him.

And on that note, I reach into my back pocket, tugging my mobile free, typing out a message to the man in question.

RAFAEL

CHAPTER FIVE

FRIDAY, MARCH 21

FROM THE MOMENT Jelani pointed out that the ladies, *my ladies*, are at the same club as us, I knew my night wouldn't have a shot in hell at being as relaxing as I'd hoped.

I've had so much pent-up energy with all the changes wearing down on me, the rugby season in full swing, coaching a team that I have no right to be involved with, and the upcoming charity event. I'd been hoping to have a couple beers, chat with my friends and let loose for the night.

But when I saw Chelsea, Letty, and Adhira sauntering out onto the dance floor, I had two immediate responses.

The first was that I should start praying to a higher power to convince the guys to leave so I don't have to watch my teammates flirt shamelessly, and the second was to look for *her*.

I knew where to find her, tucked away in a booth, sipping on a martini. As the night continued and my hopes of leaving here soon died, so had my resolve. I've been peering over my shoulder to steal glances at Elise, my jaw aching from grinding my teeth together. A woman as stunning and *off limits* as her shouldn't have tits I could bury my face in and an ass I'd love to take a bite out of. It's *wrong* of me to even think these things, but I have never been considered the moral one of any group. That's precisely how Carlos found his way into the absolute mess I'd created for him, and if I value my sanity, I'll keep my eyes trained *anywhere* but at her.

It's *wonderful* to know that despite my little pep talk about responsibility, I'm still finding myself watching over her. And after she'd finished her third drink, my brain glitched and my legs took over, dragging me toward her the moment the bartender personally came to ask her if she wanted something else.

"Would you like another round?" he asks her, his voice husky.

"No, thanks, I've had enough," she tells him, putting a hand up to emphasise her words. "Could I get a water please?" The buzzing in my skull starts to settle. At least she *knows* she's being irresponsible. And so am I for being here at all.

Her eyes flick up to meet mine as he heads back to the bar, unfazed by her lack of interest in him.

Fire blazes in her baby blues. "What do you want?" she asks with a groan, straightening her spine. *Well, hello to you too, princess.*

I slide into the seat beside her, but she stays rooted in place, refusing to budge. So, I nudge her over a foot with my thigh to make room for myself. As *Mami* would say, "No one is going to make space for you in this world; you need to do it yourself." Though I'm not sure a seat in a booth beside a woman over a decade younger than me is what she'd meant.

Elise's eyes narrow, shooting daggers straight through me. Something unrecognisable fizzles inside me at her attitude, and I push it back down, unwilling to entertain the feeling.

"Don't you think this is a tad inappropriate? You know," she says, sweeping her long, blue-black hair over her shoulder, "given how our previous coach was dismissed?" She's taunting me, and far be it for me not to play ball.

"I'm having a conversation with you, or trying to anyway," I grumble. "Not shoving my dick down your throat, Elise."

Her eyes widen, and a sly smile spreads across her plump pink lips. This woman is pure trouble. She shifts to face me, and the outside of her thigh slides against mine; the subtle movement has my body acutely aware of every inch of hers. "I think we could make that dream a reality," she purrs, leaning further into my personal space. Her breath tickles my ear as she whispers, "*Coach*."

I grab her wrist, holding the hand that she's just placed on my thigh from sliding up, feeling how affected I am by her. I *hate* that I'm so attracted to her. I haven't slept with anyone in a long while, mostly because everyone I've been with either wants more than I have to offer, or they don't like it as rough as I do. I'm not a man who's capable of "making love", and I've never claimed to be. Sex is a physical release, not a way to grow closer to my partner, and after several rounds of trial and error with both men and women, sometimes both at the same time, I'm resigned to the idea that I probably won't find anyone who matches my needs without wanting a switch or looking for an emotional attachment that I'll never be able to offer.

This leather-clad tyrant seated beside me has me thinking she might just be the exception to that rule, and I should never *ever* find out if that's true.

"Quit fooling around, Elise," I grunt out, dropping her hand into her lap. My gaze sweeps over the table for anything interesting I can use to keep my mind occupied, landing on her mobile sitting face up with a message to her *father*.

Her hand strikes at the same time my does, snatching the phone a split second before I can, but I'm not afraid to use my sheer size to my advantage. I've never claimed to be a gentleman.

"Give me the phone, Elise," I say, holding her fist in mine, our heated gazes just inches apart.

"It's *my* phone, Rafael. Stop acting like a brute," she hisses. A heady combination of her naturally sweet aroma and the vodka she's consumed has my mind whirling.

"I saw *my* name on your screen. I should be allowed to know what you're saying about me," I grit out, acting like an absolute ogre with no manners in sight.

Her eyes flash with something, an icy look crossing her face when I tug harder. She lets go at the same moment, sending me sideways with her mobile clutched in my hand. I huff out a breath, my nostrils flaring with annoyance as I straighten in my seat, my eyes catching on Elise's lips as the corners of her mouth twitch with amusement.

"What are you so bent out of shape about? You *said* you wanted my phone." She shrugs. "Now you have it." Her words act as a necessary reminder that I should be looking at her messages and ensuring she hasn't said anything that'll have me kicked off my own team.

I peer down at the message thread between her and her dad, my brows shooting up at what I find. I hate that I'm making myself so easy for her to read, but the contents of these texts are *not* what I'd imagined.

In our tussle, the message thread has moved up much earlier in their conversation than it should have, and I intend to read every word.

> **PAPA CHÉRI**
> Are you studying for your exam?

> Not quite.

> **PAPA CHÉRI**
> And why is that?

> Because I'm 21 and VERY busy making mistakes I can learn from. Obviously.

> **PAPA CHÉRI**
> As long as you're being safe, that's all that matters.

> Oh, is that so? Last I checked I had a new babysitter.

My brows pinch as I read. She thinks I'm babysitting her? I guess it does seem like I am, given our current predicament.

PAPA CHÉRI

ツ

I see my favourite trouble maker is bringing
the drama this evening.

Tell me I'm wrong.

PAPA CHÉRI

You're wrong.

You sure about that?

PAPA CHÉRI

Mon petite chou… YES! I'm sure! Rafael isn't
there to babysit you, he's there to make sure
you're able to compete and have everything
you want and deserve.

If you say so.

PAPA CHÉRI

I do. Now, give me the gossip. Is his grumpy
arse being good to you ladies?

My chest tightens, stomach threatening to bottom out as I read further, fear gripping me at the thought that she might have told him what an ass I've been. When I read through the next several strings of messages, I realise that couldn't have been further from what she's said.

Yes. He's a great coach and I think we're
going to go a long way with him. I have high
hopes for the season.

PAPA CHÉRI

Well, that certainly was anticlimactic. Tell me
how you really feel…

> 🙄 What I said is true, but he's an asshole and someone should get him to the hospital quickly to remove the three metre steel rod from his arse.

PAPA CHÉRI

I tried, but they said there was nothing more they could do. It was a very sad day for everyone indeed.

I refuse to laugh at the message, but the unfamiliar feeling bubbles in my chest, disappearing as quickly as it arrived. I notice a long pause between the last message he sent and the next one, her grammar giving her away

At lest yu trued

PAPA CHÉRI

Are you having a stroke or are you drunk?

Thee ladder

later

U knw what mean

PAPA CHÉRI

Tell me where you're at and I can come get you. I don't want someone taking advantage of you.

Im fin

I'm fine. food thn home

PAPA CHÉRI

Are the girls with you?

Yes coach 2

I groan loudly, scrubbing a hand down my face. It's been *one* day, and she's already causing trouble for me.

PAPA CHÉRI

I'm sorry, what was that?

Are you saying Rafael is too?!

Elise, please answer me.

I am but an old man with a weary soul and a daughter who's trying to KILL me. Please tell me where you are.

And confirm that my team captain isn't snogging you!

I was mostly kidding but now I'm not. Please just tell me you're safe.

I hand her phone back to her, tilting my head at the messages. "You better respond before he files a missing person report."

Her glacier-blue eyes roam over the screen, rolling at a few of her dad's overprotective messages, before she types out a quick message that I don't get to see, and then she turns her body away, shielding her phone from me.

When she's finished, she smacks the mobile down on the sticky counter and turns to face me. "Are you happy now?" she asks through gritted teeth.

"Not remotely, though I never am," I say, the admission shocking me. With any luck, she won't remember this tomorrow, but frankly, she seems to have made a full recovery. She'll probably remember every word of this conversation.

She searches my face, her lips pinched together. The attention leaves me feeling exposed.

"Let's get something clear, shall we?" she asks, a sharp brow arched in question.

I don't have a chance to respond before she's forcefully shoving me out of the seat, rolling her eyes at me. "You're my *interim* coach, not my *daddy*. Don't keep tabs on me, and definitely don't tell my father about anything I do outside of practice."

I'm too stunned to say anything as she heads out onto the dance floor, and for the first time tonight, I get the full view of her outfit.

Tight black leather pants hug her every curve. Her round ass bounces as she struts away, and her waist is cinched by a corset that I'd love to tear off with my fucking teeth. *If she were anyone else in this club, I just might.* My dick stands at attention for her, the combination of the venom in her words and the skintight outfit sending my body into a frenzy.

Nakoa catches my attention as he heads over to me, dragging me from my ungentlemanly thoughts. "You ready to get out of here? I hear Coach's kid is a handful, and I'd rather not be a part of that," he explains.

"Yep, good call," I answer, standing and adjusting myself in my pants before gathering up the guys and heading out of the packed club.

I have no explanation for why I drove back to the club after dropping my teammates off at home. I spoke to the bouncer to make sure they took an Uber home before finally making it home and crashing with Mrs. Purrito sitting like a comforting weighted blanket on my chest, her thunderous purrs lulling me to sleep.

RAFAEL

CHAPTER SIX

FRIDAY, MARCH 28

I KNEW JUGGLING COACHING the Blaze and continuing my duties as the Wyvern's team captain would be a challenge, but today I'm finding out how true that is.

I *want* to be upset about how tired I am, how my muscles are fatigued, and how I've already spent so much of my energy on a game that isn't mine to win, but I can't—and it's infuriating. I haven't been able to enjoy watching football in *years,* but Elise was on fire today. Every pass, every move she made—it was like watching a goddamn highlight reel.

With the way she teases me, trying to get a rise out of me, I shouldn't have enjoyed it as much as I did. The truth is that with every day I watch these young women train, it works to rekindle some of my love for the sport I once thought I'd spend the rest of my life playing.

The whistle blows, and the game kicks off. I move into position, lining up for the throw-in. I'm meant to be quick, but my body's not responding like it usually does. I bend to hook the ball, but there's a moment's hesitation, enough for the throw to go off-target, just enough to piss me off. My team keeps moving, but I feel like I'm stuck in place, sluggish.

One of the forwards gives me a look, waiting for a signal, but I don't have it in me to give him anything right now. I bark out the call, possibly sounding too harsh, but I can't help it. I'm annoyed at myself, at this feeling of being *off,* like I'm not where I need to be. The tension between us is thin, and I hate that I've let it creep in.

I push it down, trying to focus. But with every missed call and half-hearted push, it's like I'm losing more ground. I was supposed to be the one running the show here, the one making the game go my way. Instead, I'm second-guessing myself, thinking too much. I can't even get my timing right on the line-out; every throw feels like it's just a step behind.

And then, just as quickly as it came, the frustration hits a new level. Elise's perfect pass flashes in my mind again, how it made me feel alive in a way I haven't in ages. But I'm not supposed to care about that right now. This is my game, my pitch. I can't afford to be distracted.

I dig in, trying to push myself back into it, but I'm still fighting the fatigue, fighting the memories of that damn football match, and it's all bleeding into the way I'm playing. My legs are heavy. I'm not where I need to be. And I can't shake the feeling that it's all slipping away.

RAFAEL

CHAPTER SEVEN

MONDAY, MARCH 31

I STEP into Coach's office, per his request. "Take a seat, and tell me how things are going with my daughter's team," he says, leaning back in his chair.

I groan. "I don't think they like me." Not that I've given them any reason to. I should try harder. I *want* to try harder, but the way my heart seizes every time I see that damn ball and I'm reminded of the dream I stole from my brother, I can't muster anything more than a grimace and the occasional nod of approval. I don't say any of that though. "They play well. Hell, they're fantastic, but they can't stand me, and I'm not sure what the best way to navigate that situation is."

"Oh, I'm aware." He smirks at me. "Elise may have mentioned something about you being the biggest wanker of the century." He chuckles.

My eyes snap up to meet his, and I realise for the first time that they're the same blue as Elise's. *You don't exactly spend a whole lot of time gazing into Coach's eyes, dickhead. Of course, you wouldn't have noticed.* And I certainly shouldn't be doing it with his daughter either. He's goading me because unless Elise really hammered into me over the last week and a half, all she'd told him the night at the club was that I'm an asshole, which isn't wrong.

Judging by her apparent inability to open up, even to her father, I'm betting she hasn't broached the subject further.

"Don't worry," he tells me, dropping his legs from the lip of his desk and leaning forward onto his elbows. "I have a plan."

"Great, I'd love to hear it," I grumble, hoping anything he says will make my life easier somehow. Knowing him, it'll be a cluster fuck instead. He *is* the reason I'm in this situation in the first place.

"We'll have a team-building day. You and Elise can combine practices and pair up. One rugger to one footballer. Hopefully, by the end of it, everyone will be a bit more relaxed and get to see you've removed that stick you've got wedged up your arse."

Prick. Like father, like daughter. "I see where your daughter gets her *charming* personality," I tell him, and his brow quirks.

"Elise is many things, and frankly, charming isn't one of them. But I never taught her to be *charming*. I taught her to be kind and compassionate in her personal life yet ruthless and unyielding on the field. If you have a problem with that, well, I don't know what to tell you because nothing's going to change her, nor would I want it to." Kind and compassionate? I think he may have missed the mark with that goal, but I wouldn't dare tell *him* that.

"How exactly is this team-building assignment going to work?" I ask, confused and frustrated.

"You and Elise, since you're both team captains, will be paired together, and maybe after my daughter kicks your ass in a match, you'll be humbled and she'll be happy enough to tell the team to stop giving you such a hard time," he says, smiling smugly.

They haven't even made this transition all that difficult. If I'm being honest with myself, the hardest part has been keeping my eyes where they're meant to be and not all over Elise. That and the emotions it's dredging up and at the worst time of year for it. The upcoming fundraiser for people living with spinal cord injuries is both a blessing and a never-ending curse that always acts as an unnecessary reminder of how much I've fucked up. "Sounds lovely," I say, sarcasm tinging the words, as I stand, dragging my ass out of his office.

ELISE

CHAPTER EIGHT

WEDNESDAY, APRIL 2

I'M STILL TRYING to blink away the fuzziness in my eyes as I make it out of the locker room and onto the field. Most of my teammates are already out there with the Wyvern Warriors, Dad's team.

When I got the email about this little morale building field day, I wasn't thrilled, but I know that getting along with our coach will only help my team, and if this is what we need to do, we will. I would do just about anything for these women, and my dad has never steered me wrong, even if his methods *are* less than conventional.

Over the last three years, my teammates have become my extended family, and as someone who grew up with a sister and was suddenly thrust into the life of a pseudo-only child, that's meant more to me than I can properly express. More than I'd *care* to express considering I'm not always great at communicating all of the big feelings I carry around with me. My therapist has always said it's the nature of the beast that is bipolar 1 disorder, but I can't help but believe I'm just emotionally stunted from a sudden loss that left me feeling empty for so many years. Now, I almost wish the emptiness would return so I'm not forced to be swallowed by the heavy weight of stress, anxiety, and regret.

"Elise!" Chelsea shouts, waving me down to where she's stretching with Adhira and Letty.

I jog over to them with a wide smile plastered on my face, one that I know doesn't meet my eyes. *I'm exhausted.* Too exhausted to explain what's going on in my head, so a fake smile is the better alternative.

Chelsea waggles her blonde brows at me suggestively. "You didn't come home last night—must've been having a lot of fun with Leo and Noah again, huh?"

I smirk, unwilling to admit what I was *actually* doing last night. Running until I couldn't breathe. Collapsing into a heap of frustration and longing. Wallowing in my misery and calling my therapist for an emergency session that lifted a tenth of the weight I'd been carrying, but I'll welcome any reprieve. So instead, I mask my emotions, like I've become so accustomed to doing over the years. "I don't kiss and tell," I say with a wink for her benefit.

Adhira meets my gaze with a tight-lipped expression, and a chill skates down my spine. I swear, she sees right through my nonsense, and something tells me it's because she does the same things I do to protect my sanity.

Letty pats the turf beside her arse, motioning for me to take a seat.

We chat and stretch for the next several minutes as the rest of the players make it out onto the field.

My neck tingles with awareness, and when I look over my shoulder, I see Rafael heading my way, his eyes burning holes into my skin.

I fight the shiver working its way through me but can't help clenching my thighs together as he grows nearer. He crooks a finger at me and motions with his chin for me to meet him by the centre line.

I turn back around to face my friends, my brows climbing my forehead. "I guess that's my cue. Wish me luck, ladies," I tell them, getting up and taking my sweet ass time to make it over to Rafael.

Just by the way he shifts in place, rolling his shoulders back and crossing his arms over his chest, I can tell that he's fully aware of what I'm doing. Over the last two weeks, I've grown to crave the looks of annoyance I earn from him. I don't have a good explanation for it, but it's almost like chasing a high without the consequence because ever since that first night at the club, he's been doing his absolute damndest to avoid speaking to me.

"Hey, Coach," I say, smiling brightly and fluttering my lashes when I'm about two feet in front of him.

"Cut the bullshit, Elise," he grunts, rolling his eyes. Goddamn, this guy has *quite* the chip on his shoulder.

I level him with a stare, waiting to speak until I feel physically uncomfortable under his scrutinising gaze. "Alright, Rafael, you want me to cut the shit? Let's do it then. Clearly, you never wanted your position as our coach, and I'm not a huge fan of being an adult with a babysitter. That said, my chances of joining the Olympic team for twenty twenty-eight are dwindling with every day that my team doesn't trust you. So, let's get this day over with, play nice, and in a few short months, we'll be a blip on your radar."

When he first arrived, everyone kept it pushing the same way we always had, but with every grimace and grunt, it was effectively out of my hands as to whether my teammates like him or not. I don't blame them. He's been a complete jackass at every practice. When we do something he approves of, we get a nod. *A bloody nod!* As if we can even see that while in active play. When he doesn't like something, he shoots daggers at us but doesn't speak up. It's infuriating. Maybe *that* is why I make a point to get on his nerves. Because he *deserves* it.

A sly grin spreads his lips. He lets his arms fall to his sides as he nods, passing me. "Sounds good." Over his shoulder, he calls to me, "Oh, and princess? There won't be anything nice about how I plan to play with you."

My eyes widen, and my heart starts to pound at the insinuation. The grumpy asshole has jokes now, huh?

He stands in the middle of the field, clapping to get everyone's attention. When all eyes are on him, he starts discussing the plans we went over via email the other night.

"We've got a field day set up today. There'll be six activities, and you'll each be partnered up, one footballer to one rugger. At the end of the day, whichever team has won the most points will get to choose which sport we all play a round of. Anyone have any questions?"

I smirk because, of course, every rugby player on the field raises their hand while my teammates roll their eyes. Now *this* is on brand for us.

He claps his big hands together one time, wearing a lopsided smirk that deliciously twists my insides. *That certainly shouldn't be happening.* "Alright, then, I'm glad no one has any questions," he says, and it annoys me that he has a sense of humour on occasion. He entirely ignores his team and their raised hands. At least he's this crass with everyone and not just us.

Rafael starts calling out pairs, working his way down the list. "Letty and Jelani, Chelsea and Nakoa." His eyes lift to mine. "Elise, you're with me."

Everyone goes silent as their eyes flit between us, and the longer the awkward silence carries on, the more I squirm.

"Great!" I shout, my voice too high-pitched given the circumstances. "Tug-of-war first!"

I wave everyone down to the first station, where there's a rope in the middle of the turf with a pink ribbon tied, indicating the centre. "I assume you all know how to play. It'll be one pair on either side, and whoever wins each round will get a point."

They all nod, splitting off into their designated pairs, lining up on either end of the rope, awaiting their turn.

Rafael nudges his chin toward one end, and I follow, desperately wanting to go in the opposite direction just to spite him, but I realise how incredibly childish that is, so I refrain. I have no idea what it is about him that makes me want to defy him at every turn. I don't have a superiority complex. I've never struggled to listen to any of my coaches before, and in general, I'm capable of respecting authority, but there's something about this grumpy-ass, smug man that annoys me beyond measure.

We're at the back of the line, standing side by side, and when the whistle blows for Chelsea, Nakoa, Adhira, and Carson to start, a thrill rushes through everyone watching.

At our core, we're athletes, and that means we get rowdy for *any* and *every* occasion.

Carson and Adhira start tugging on the rope, digging their heels into the turf. How the hell did we get the school to agree to this shit? It absolutely shocks me when I see the little pink ribbon starting to edge closer to their side, but the moment my eyes land on Nakoa and Chelsea, understanding fully settles in.

A wide smirk stretches my lips, and warmth spreads in my belly, laughter bubbling up my throat, but I push it back down. I feel Rafael's knuckles accidentally graze the back of my hand, and sparks shoot up my arm. Nope, not sparks. *Definitely not* bloody sparks. He probably zapped me. He should rub his prickly arse down with a dryer sheet.

My gaze meets his, and those near-black eyes threaten to consume me. My throat grows dry. "What's so funny?" he mutters, quirking a brow at me.

I nod toward where Chelsea and Nakoa are standing, making little *real* effort to win. I can tell that's the case based on the way Chelsea winks at Carson, aiming to distract the poor bloke while Nakoa pretends to use all of his strength. Meanwhile, his muscles are as relaxed as they were before that whistle went off.

"Sneaky bastards," I whisper with a chuckle, hoping I don't have to give away their antics. Coach is a big boy, he'll catch on.

Rafael's gaze follows their every move, his dark brows furrowing, a flicker of tension crossing his face. He doesn't look away, his eyes locking onto mine again, intense and searching. "Are they?" He doesn't finish his sentence as I nod, grunting my answer.

Adhira's forehead drips with sweat, her deltoids twitching as she tires out. Carson looks slightly less fatigued, but he's still drenched in sweat as he digs his cleats into the ground, effectively using up all of his energy.

Everyone is shouting, clapping, hollering for their pick. The moment that pink ribbon is an inch from the designated cone on Adhira and Carson's side, Chelsea's bright-blue eyes meet Nakoa's, and with a curt nod, they tighten their grip on the rope. Their muscles flex; one swift tug and they pull the pink ribbon, along with Adhira and Carson, completely across to their side. The losing pair fall to the ground in a heap, Carson landing on top of Adhira, one of his hands meeting her tit as he scrambles to get off of her. He yelps, pushing himself up, and frantically shouts his apology. "Sorry! Sorry! Don't bloody kill me, I'm *so* sorry! It was an accident!"

Adhira rolls her eyes at him, standing and wiping her palms off on her shorts. Her eyes search for our roommate, landing on a *very* smug-looking Chelsea. Adhira points two fingers at her own eyes and then at Chelsea as she says, "You better sleep with one eye open, bitch." Her lips twitch, but she somehow manages to keep the serious expression on her face.

The men erupt in a round of taunting "whoops" and "oohs."

Chelsea smiles broadly, calling over to Adhira. "Don't worry, sweet cheeks, there's so much more where that came from. I know you like it a little rough," she says, winking. Adhira doesn't like anything, rough or otherwise. Chelsea knows that, which makes it that much funnier.

The laughter and clapping only grow with Chelsea's response, and I swear I see Nakoa's eyes nearly pop out of his head. He cups his chin, rubbing his fingers along the line of his strong jaw. I see the pad of his thumb dig into his hollow cheek as he swallows down his laughter, not wanting to spur Chelsea further into her antics.

The next several groups continue much more smoothly than the first, and eventually, we make it to the end with Rafael and I up against Letty and Jelani.

Jelani's a strong guy, no doubt. All rugby players have to be, but Letty's stronger than most women I've known. She's built like a brick shithouse and has endured a lot that's not only made her physically strong but mentally too. At least, that's what she tries to convey to the rest of the world. Deep down, I think she just needs someone to be soft and attentive with her. Her needs are *clearly* different from my own.

"Front or back, princess?" Rafael asks me as I approach the rope, tying my hair more securely to the top of my head.

"I'll take the back so you don't get distracted staring at my ass," I quip, smiling widely. If he weren't my coach, I'd tell him he can take me from either.

He scoffs, but a grin forms on his lips. "So, what you're saying is *you* are going to get distracted by *my* ass." He nods his understanding, and I *almost* laugh. "Got it. I'll keep that in mind for future practices. Wouldn't want my team's captain getting any funny ideas, so I'll make sure to wear the baggiest shorts I've got," he says, shooting me a wink as he takes his position in front of me. I don't even have a chance to retort before the whistle is blasting in our ears.

Good thing, too, because I'm not sure what I'd say to that other than *That's a damn shame.* Somehow, this man having found a sense of humour is proving to be more of a downfall than a redeeming quality. Whose downfall I'm not sure yet.

My fingers wrap around the rope, a scowl settling across my lips as it threatens to burn through my hands. As strong as Rafael and I are, we're no match for Letty and Jelani.

The competitive fire lit under my arse still leads me to dig my feet into the turf as they nearly drag my body across it, my fingers cramping, but at the last second, both Jelani and Letty drop the rope with wide smiles, sending Rafael and I flying to our arses. I land with a grunt, the backs of my thighs scraping against the ground, but it's nothing compared to the tumbles I take during our matches.

I look around us, confusion settling in as I realise *we won.*

I have no idea what their play is. Whether neither of them

wants to win, or they figured having their team captains and coach fall to their arses would be more satisfying, I'm not sure, but they both look extremely happy as they make their way over to us. Letty reaches down, and my hand clamps around hers, allowing her to hoist me up.

"You're welcome," she whispers, and as soon as I'm back on my feet, she takes off to sidle up to Jelani.

What the hell is going on with everyone today?

By the time we make it to the last station, we're all soaked with sweat despite it being eleven degrees. We honestly couldn't have picked a better day for this sort of thing because, for once, the sun has miraculously remained out the entire time we've been out here. That's not usually the case this time of year in Embershire, or well, *anytime*.

"Last one, and then we can take a quick break before our game," Rafael announces to the crowd of exhausted players. Spirits are high though, and as much as it pains me to admit, this *was* a good idea. However, I won't be telling my dad that.

Everyone's getting along well. Maybe our shot at closing out the year with a solid winning streak won't be as impossible as I'd thought.

I wasn't paying attention as Rafael explained our last activity, but I know what we're about to do, and I'm not thrilled about it. Whoever picked *this* particular event is going on my shit list, and it couldn't have been Rafael's stoic arse.

By the time we hit the third activity, it was clear we'd be here all day if we didn't change things up, and *fast*. Instead of the usual turn-taking, only the top three teams are racing to the finish line now, with a twist.

Which means I'm here, my right thigh plastered to the side of Rafael's, with Velcro straps holding us together. Chelsea and Nakoa stand to Rafael's right, and to my left are Letty and Jelani, who have repeatedly tried to fail at every activity today, but even *trying* to lose, they still couldn't manage. Talk about a bloody power couple.

"On your mark, get set, go!" Carson shouts, and we take off down the pitch. Or at least, we *try*.

"Pick up the pace, Elise, Jesus Christ," Rafael grunts out beside me, hauling my body alongside him. I can barely keep myself up straight, so I'm forced to retain a death grip on his thick bicep, and I absolutely *do not* notice the way his muscles ripple under my fingers. *Absolutely not noticing that.*

"You're the one with your good leg still in use, you asshat," I tell him through gritted teeth.

Anyone not tripping over their own feet with their legs tied to their partner is now standing by massive rubbish bins filled with water, armed with water guns.

"Who the hell came up with this in the first place?" I ask, my voice sounding shrill.

"Your *father*," he reminds me, his jaw ticking as he manoeuvres us down the field.

No surprise there.

I keep my eyes trained ahead, refusing to look at either team beside us. "Fuck!" I screech as ice-cold water splashes against my skin, goosebumps littering my flesh, and my nipples turn to hard peaks. First my father, and now my own body betrays me.

More sprays hit us, making it more and more difficult to stay upright as the ground becomes slippery. As if this wasn't impossible enough.

"We're going to get hurt, and then I'll be pissed," I mutter, and Rafael's eyes flit to mine before dragging down my body quickly. His eyes shoot back up to my face. Shaking his head, he winds an arm behind me, covering my shoulder blades. His fingers dig into my skin as he hoists me an inch off the ground and drags us to the end of the field. My eyes are wide as this hulk of a man carries both of our weight with only one of his legs in full use. When we get to the end, we're greeted by two big buckets of water being tossed over our heads.

My nostrils flare as I try to suck in enough air, working to calm my breathing as I push the soaking strands out of my eyes.

Rafael bends over, quickly working to undo our straps, my knee feeling like gelatine when we're finally separated.

I shake out my heavy limbs, and heat creeps up my neck. My eyes find Rafael's, but instead of settling on my face, they're on my chest.

I look down and realise I've made a grave mistake.

"Bloody hell," I groan.

At precisely the worst moment, a breeze skates across the field, chilling me to my core.

I can see a dark cloud in my periphery, a storm likely on the horizon.

My nipples pebble further, and if you couldn't see them through my soaked white sports bra, you sure as hell can now.

My not-so-subtle teammates start a chorus of catcalls, whistling and laughing at my expense. Normally, I'd brush it off— after all, it's just their usual nonsense, but it's not just anyone standing in front of me this time. It's Rafael, our new coach, the one my dad is so sure will help me land a spot on the Olympic team. And suddenly, their teasing feels a lot less funny.

I should really remember that the next time I'm thinking about his tight ass.

Rafael's eyes narrow, glaring at each of his teammates, several of whom are outwardly staring at my tits.

He grunts, whipping his shirt off over his head and tugging it over mine. I struggle under his hands. "What"—I spit, my hair stuck in my mouth—"the hell!"

RAFAEL

CHAPTER NINE

WEDNESDAY, APRIL 2

WHEN I FINALLY GET MY shirt over Elise's head, she's glaring at me with such fierceness, I can practically see her ice-blue eyes lit with flames behind them.

Her shrill voice is like an ice pick to my eardrums, but I don't give a damn.

"What, Elise? Did you want to stand here with your tits out for everyone to see?" I bark out, my tone not any nicer than hers.

She scoffs, rolling her eyes and crossing her arms over her chest. "They're *just* breasts, Rafael."

She says that, and yet, her cheeks were flaming the moment those *breasts* were getting attention from everyone around us. Though I don't bother pointing that out. Almost like I sure as hell won't be pointing out the fact that they most certainly are *not* "just breasts." Elise has an incredible rack, but as a grown-ass man who's over a decade older than her, I have to continually remind myself that she's also my coach's daughter.

Fucking Christ. You'd think I'd have got that through my head by now, but I can't seem to. Not when Elise is the most annoyingly stunning human I've ever met in my life.

Nakoa's booming voice cuts through the chatter on the field. "Elise, what're we playing?" he calls over to her, a small grin on his face.

"Football," I answer at the same time as she answers, "Rugby."

Her eyes cut to me, narrowing slightly. "He didn't ask you, *Coach*." She uses that word like it's a threat, and every time, it makes my dick jump to attention for her.

Again, my teammates manage to remind me how much more slowly men grow up compared to women when we're surrounded by their whistled responses.

I roll my eyes. "You sure you want to do that, princess? Rugby's a lot more physical than football," I remind her.

She exhales sharply, her eyes narrowing slightly, but maintains the smug smirk she wears so often. "I'm sure, *unless*"—her eyes flit to mine with mischief—"you're afraid of losing to a bunch of women?"

Thankfully, her voice isn't loud enough for anyone besides me to hear because if it were, I'd be fearing for my life right now. Truthfully, these women scare me.

"You know what? Rugby sounds *great*." The thought of playing football again makes me nauseous, so despite her intentions, this is to my benefit. My eyes coast over the players on the field, and with a clap of my hands, I announce the last part of the day. "We're playing rugby."

An eerie chill falls over the group as moods shift. The usually cocky, sometimes tone-deaf men are standing with their mouths ajar. Meanwhile, the women are grinning, their eyes darting to one another as if coming up with a hidden plan with not a single word spoken. Like I said, the women are terrifying.

I shake my head. "Absolutely not. I've been your coach for long enough to know you're formulating some plan that's bound to get me in trouble. This is *not* men against women. Split up with equal numbers of footballers and ruggers on each team," I announce, and much to my disappointment, the women don't deflate. They still look just as lethal as they had moments before.

This is about to be brutal.

Wordlessly, the women divide up equally, and it doesn't

escape me that the less experienced players, the ones who've recently sustained injuries, and those who generally don't play as well for one reason or another all end up on one team. Elise motions for Nakoa, Jelani, and several of our other strongest players to join her team. Her eyes meet mine, and she winks before choosing Elijah, our newest rookie player. I can't help but chuckle. She's strategic, and begrudgingly, I find it impossibly sexy.

No, you don't, you bastard.

I shake out the thought, running over to the side of the field with the players I'm now partnered with, and we get right to it.

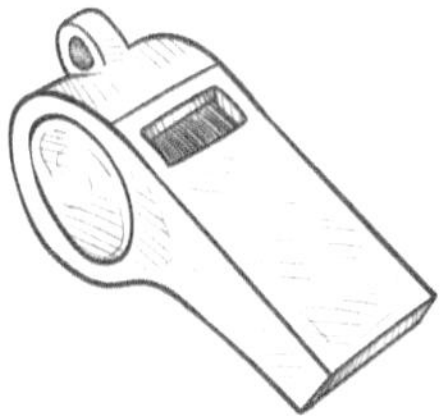

"I *knew* something was up when these women got 'the look' in their eyes," Trey says, making air quotes. He sighs, whining as we slug down water, desperately trying to recover from the back-to-back losses we've been suffering ever since this game started.

The dark clouds overhead are growing nearer, and it feels like an omen.

"Our team is good," I tell him but add, "they just happen to be better. They chose the most seasoned players. It was good strategy."

Trey chuckles beside me. "Yeah, most seasoned, *except for Elijah.* Anything not to have you, Cap," he says, still laughing as he jogs back into his position on the pitch.

It's more than clear based on how these women are leading the game that not only are they all *very* aware of how to play, but Elise has likely used rugby as a way to further hone their defensive tactics for use in football as well. I'll live a lot longer if I learn not to underestimate that woman. The end of their season can't come soon enough.

We all get into position on the halfway line, each team's forwards binding together. Our scrum half throws the ball into the middle of the tunnel, and we're off. Our hookers use their feet to manoeuvre the ball, each team fighting for dominance while simultaneously pushing the other team backward.

As much as my team tries, we fail, to absolutely no one's surprise. Jelani takes possession of the ball on their end, and we split off across the field. My feet carry me as quickly as they can down the pitch, but I'm not fast enough. Jelani tears by me, passing to Letty, who's basically the GI Jane of women. My teammates track her down, encroaching on her as she nears the goal line, but she swivels, throwing the ball to Elise, who jumps up high, gaining even more vertical height thanks to Nakoa, whose hands are digging into her hips as he hoists her in the air. A primal need to shout at him not to touch her slams into me, but I reel it back in. She's not mine to get jealous over. Her arms wrap around the ball, and the moment her feet hit the ground, she's off, tearing down the field at a breakneck speed.

She's so fast I practically miss her until she's past the goal-line, skidding across the turf, pressing the ball into the ground, and securing her team the win.

Her team mauls her, piling on top of her, screaming their heads off, and the fluttering feeling in my gut has absolutely no business being there.

And it's certainly not from the bright smile she's wearing that lights up the whole damn pitch through the grey English sky.

Shit, this woman is my personal nightmare.

RAFAEL

CHAPTER TEN

WEDNESDAY, APRIL 2

THANK *FUCK,* this seemed to actually work.

After Elise took over the field, making everyone do exactly as she wanted without a single word spoken, she and her team dominated the pitch. This only confirms my suspicions that she's previously used rugby during her team practices, and it's even more obvious that her father has taught her about as much as he's taught me.

Her speed, power, and sheer will to win is admirable and has my skin burning hot. It's warm today, I tell myself, but the lie doesn't stick as I peer down at the goosebumps lining the skin of my arm, the chill in the air cooling the sweat clinging to me. *Goddamnit.*

I *really* need to make more of an effort to remind myself that Elise isn't someone who could mutually benefit from a romp in the sheets. We're in two extraordinarily different places in our lives, and I need to get myself a pocket pussy or something because I'm starting to act like a horny fool.

I refocus my attention on the turf. The women are smiling brightly as they make their way to the locker room, and it settles a part of me that has been so consumed by anxiety these last couple of weeks.

I'm not sure that these ladies are really going to tolerate *me* more, but if they have any interest in drooling over my teammates' asses again, they sure as hell better try.

I make my way down the field, drenched in sweat, my shorts clinging to my thighs. I want nothing more than to shower and head home to my quiet apartment free of the noise these women seem to carry around with them. The only woman I need in my life right now is Mrs. Purrito. She's loud enough as is.

The light feeling of relief from the day nearing an end is disrupted as quickly as it came. My eyes snag on Elise and Chelsea huddled together, and I watch intently as Chelsea passes Elise something, which she takes and swallows.

Her gaze swings around the field, clearly checking for any prying eyes, but she's too late. *I've already seen her.*

ELISE

CHAPTER ELEVEN

WEDNESDAY, APRIL 2

I TAKE THE PILLS, swallow, and double-check that no one is looking, my stomach doing a little flip when I see our new coach storming down the field. His hands are clenched at his sides, and a furious expression mars his absurdly handsome features.

My jaw clenches, knees locking as if preparing for a physical impact. He invades my space, crowding Chelsea and me as he grits out, "What the hell did she give you?"

I roll my eyes, glaring up at him, doing my best impression of a cool, unbothered tone even though I feel anything but. My gut is a mess of emotions. "None of your business," I tell him simply, my throat bobbing painfully around the lump there.

His dark brows climb his forehead, and he crosses those thick, corded arms over his broad chest. "None of my business?" He scoffs, extending his arms wide. "Look around, Elise, for the foreseeable future, *you are my bloody business.*"

"Just drop it," I tell him, my voice climbing higher than I'd intended.

"It was an over-the-counter painkiller," Chelsea says, but her voice hitches with the lie, giving her away. She's the worst liar on the planet, but I appreciate her for trying.

"Chelsea, do you think I'm stupid?" he asks, pinning her in place with stoney eyes and pinched brows. "No one looks around for witnesses unless they're doing something dodgy," he grits out, turning his piercing dark gaze on me. Chelsea shrinks away from him but doesn't leave my side.

"Now tell me what the hell you took," he demands, glaring down, and I'm suddenly extremely aware of our difference in height.

My heart is racing, molars grinding at his insinuation. And the truth is that I'd rather he think I'm using recreational drugs than what I'm really taking. "Elise," Chelsea whines beside me. "*Just tell him.*" She's begging, and it *almost* has me explaining myself to this guy for her sake.

Almost, but not quite.

I shake my head in defiance. "Like I said, it's none of your business. All you need to know is that I would never do anything to risk my team's safety or chances at winning fair and square."

He puts his hands on his hips as he bores holes into my skull. "Looks like you made it my business, *Elise*," he says with venom dripping in his tone that has my hackles going up. "What you do on this field and while wearing that jersey is *absolutely* my business. So drink up, princess, you're gonna need to piss in a cup *very* soon."

He storms off, heading in the direction of the men's locker rooms.

There's a clap of thunder overhead followed by a bolt of lightning lighting the sky. The heavens open up, drenching us as we sprint toward the locker rooms while being pelted with fat drops of rain.

Fire must be shooting out of my ears with how pissed I am; my blood boils and my jaw aches.

"Elise, come on, you'll never pass a fucking drug test," Chelsea pleads when we get inside. Her blonde waves are high in her ponytail, and water dribbles down her temple as she pouts at me.

"It's not his business, Chels. I'm sorry, but you know as well as anyone that I try to keep my private life, *private*. I don't need to tell my new coach that I'm on medication for bipolar disorder."

"This is the twenty-first century, Elise. You shouldn't have to fear facing discrimination for something out of your control," she says, levelling me with an exasperated expression and a quirked brow.

I shake my head. *Clearly, she doesn't understand.* "You're right, I *shouldn't*, but I do. So please, drop it," I say, my voice sounding more harsh than I meant for it to.

She recoils before putting on a brave face that makes me feel like shit. "Fine, but we won't be dropping it for long when you're kicked off of the team for drug use," she says, rolling her eyes and stomping off toward the showers.

She's right. It shouldn't be something I'm worried about telling people, but *I am*. All the fucking time.

I make quick work of showering, eager to get home, but my hands are still shaking, and my heart is beating so fast that I'm lightheaded as I climb into Letty's car. The ride home with Adhira, Letty, and Chelsea feels long with how quiet it is.

Chelsea breaks the silence abruptly as we pull into the driveway. "Coach is about to drug test Elise!" she blurts, her cheeks tinged red, and her eyes flick rapidly between our roommates, judging their reactions. My shoulders drop, and there's a tingling sensation in the pit of my gut as I wait for their responses.

Adhira tilts her head in question, wrinkling her brow without a word. Letty chews on her plump bottom lip and stares at me with suspicion.

"The fuck?" Letty asks, breaking through the tension.

I sigh, sagging into the seat and pinching the bridge of my nose in annoyance.

Chelsea explains what happened, adding a little dramatic flair, which isn't unusual for her. "Does lithium even show up on a drug test?" Letty asks.

Adhira bobs her head. "It can. It depends on how thorough the panel is. Some look for opioids or marijuana, but others can be used to test for all of the most commonly abused drugs. Not that lithium is often abused, but it's still possible they'll check for it. Coach Lyon never bothered testing us, so it hadn't mattered, but why don't you just bring him your prescription information?" she asks, which absolutely *would be* the easiest option, but I'm stubborn, and more than that, I'm fucking *embarrassed*.

An unfamiliar thickness forms in my throat, and I swallow around it. "I can't," I say, my lip wobbling as I do.

Letty's eyes soften, and she unbuckles her seatbelt, climbing over the centre console. She appears almost comical as she squeezes her wide hips and thick thighs through the narrow space, collapsing into the middle seat between me and Adhira. She wraps her arms around my waist, tugging me against her chest, smothering me with her massive tits.

I wrestle out of her grip, taking an exaggerated gulp of air, and manage to dissolve any remnants of tension as we break out into a fit of laughter. "Christ, Letty, those things could suffocate someone!"

She smirks and shrugs her shoulders. "With the right angle, yours could too," she tells me with a wink. "Now get out of my car. I'm starving, and we have scheming to do."

RAFAEL

CHAPTER TWELVE

FRIDAY, APRIL 4

I HAD HOPED that Elise would go home, consider what she'd be risking by not telling me what she took, and think better of it today. But judging by the unfriendly welcome I receive at the start of practice, that couldn't be further from the truth. And more than that, all of the progress I'd made with the team has disintegrated.

She says nothing as she passes by my office and into the locker room, and neither do the other women. Instead, I get cold glares that threaten to freeze me to my core, and a chill skates down my spine at the eerie silence.

I shake my head, clenching my eyes shut, and let out a defeated groan. Pushing away from my desk, I stand and grab the stack of urine drug screen forms before marching into the locker room. I stop at the door, banging loudly on it as I shout, "Cover up! I'm coming in." I count down from twenty before entering to find that none of them have changed yet.

I steel my spine, refusing to be broken by a bunch of university-age women. "We have a routine drug screening today. Sign your forms quickly so I can get the medical staff in here. If you're fast enough, we should be able to finish the drills I have planned for the day," I announce to the room, my words bouncing off of the white-painted concrete block walls. *Please don't fight me on this*, I plead with anyone up above who might be willing to answer my silent prayer.

"Coach Lyon never made us do drug tests, so it couldn't be *that* 'routine'," one of the younger players says, her voice full of sass as she pops out a hip.

"This feels super invasive. Is there someone you're targeting?" another woman asks, her brow quirked.

How the hell did she manage to get the whole team on her side for this? Never mind, I probably don't want an answer to that.

I suck in a calming breath, realising how naive I'd been to think that Elise would be the only one with a positive screen. *You dumb fucker.* You were once a twenty-one-year-old athlete attending parties and smoking weed.

I ignore their protests, handing out the forms to each one of the women, and when they all have a sheet in their hands, they stare down the bridges of their noses at me as they tear them in half, pick up their duffel bags, and storm out of the building.

My gaze flicks to Elise, who I fully expect to be smirking, but instead, her eyes are glassy, and her chin quivers.

She looks away from me the moment our eyes meet, swiping at her cheek before picking up her bag and shoving past me. My entire soul aches as I watch her. I can tell she's being vulnerable right now, that this isn't some ploy to make me feel bad.

She keeps her eyes cast down, and a twinge of guilt ripples through me. I've never seen those blue eyes of hers anything besides passionate, but it nags at something deep in my gut that she looks so defeated.

Just tell me what's going on, Elise. I practically will her to comply, but naturally, the silence drags on, and soon, I'm standing alone in the women's locker room.

I played like shit at my match tonight, but my team carried us to our win with negligible help from me—the same as our last game.

My feet are propped up on the coffee table, and my limbs feel heavy as I sit here in the silence of my apartment.

I'm not sure why it bothers me so much that Elise is keeping something from me. I'd like to believe it's because she's making my job harder, but I know it's got to be more than that. I've been trying to tell myself that she's nothing more than a spoiled brat, but everything I know of her father leads me away from that conclusion, and it doesn't quell the unease brewing inside.

Speaking of *guilt*, I should call my brother.

I sink into the dark-grey couch cushions, propping my feet up on the marble coffee table and picking up my phone to dial him. It rings and rings, but before I give up, he eventually answers. "Rafa! *Che, hermano!*" he sing-songs cheerfully, never one to let life get him down. *Not that I've made that any easier.*

"Hey, Carlos. How's your week been?" I ask, hoping for better than last.

"Going great. I'm doing well in physical therapy, and you won't believe this," he says, pausing for a beat, "I was able to use my walker and take a full step today! By myself!" he shouts into the phone.

A mixture of emotions flurry inside dread, guilt, rage, frustration, sadness, elation, and lastly, *pride*.

"That's brilliant!" I shout, my voice choked as I hold back the sob threatening its way up my throat. *"Estoy muy orgulloso de ti, hermano."*

"I'm doing it, Rafa, *I'm really doing it!* I'll be back on the pitch in no time," he says, and my heart sinks to my toes, my throat constricting at the reminder of *why* he's in this position at all. He continues talking, giving me a play-by-play of his week, and it helps minimally to know that he's improving.

It's been over a decade since the accident, and I had lost all hope that he would ever walk again. You don't go from being paralysed from the waist down to suddenly walking, but he's never let that deter him. And finally, his determination is paying off, and so is the new physical therapist he's been working with.

When he lets me go so he can have dinner with our parents, I'm left with too many thoughts that are practically strangling me by the time I fall asleep.

ELISE

CHAPTER THIRTEEN

SUNDAY, APRIL 6

MY LEG SHAKES, bouncing my laptop as I balance it on my thighs. Everything feels foggy, and it's difficult to know if the words written on the screen make any sense at all. Much like my room.

I can't find my comforter. *Where could it be if not on my bed?*

My desk is covered in clothing; half-filled water bottles and old protein shakers litter the surface.

I've tried cleaning but I'm sure...

My eyes snag on a team photo from last season—it's tacked to the corkboard by the door.

My *team*. Right. That's what I was doing.

We have an away game on Wednesday, and as much as I appreciate my teammates standing by me, I can't let them down for my own selfish reasons.

So despite all reason, *I stopped taking my meds*. All traces of them should be out of my system by today.

None of my roommates know, because if they did, they'd be losing their shit. Rightfully so. I'm putting myself and my team in a really horrendous position, but it's just for a few days. As soon as I pass that test, I'll start taking them again. Problem solved. *I hope.*

Except, my thoughts are already feeling too jumbled, and it's becoming increasingly difficult to keep track of what I need to accomplish today. I chalk that up to withdrawal symptoms and push the thought from my mind, staring at my laptop screen, preparing to hit "send" on the email I drafted to Rafael. It takes longer than I'd like to steady my wavering hands and actually go through with it, but within seconds of sending it, a response stares back at me.

All the email says is, "Okay."

Who'd have thought that a single word would be capable of fuelling so much anxiety?

RAFAEL

CHAPTER FOURTEEN

TUESDAY, APRIL 8

I'M NOT sure what made her change her mind, but I'm glad she did. If they hadn't agreed to the drug testing, I'd have had to explain to Elise's father why they weren't going to their away game tomorrow. That's not a conversation I have any desire to have. I'm not her fucking babysitter, despite what she's previously accused me of. She's an adult, and I'm not here to snitch to her father about her actions, but she's been making that increasingly difficult.

It would've made sense to have them come in for testing yesterday, but there was a little part of me that wanted to give every one of them the extra day to get whatever the hell they needed to out of their systems. I'm pretty sure cranberry juice and saunas don't do a goddamn thing for a drug detox, but it's worth a shot when your future in sports is on the line.

I sit in my office, my fingers drumming over the oak desk, and a heavy weight sits on my chest. *I hate waiting.*

I'm far from a patient man, and not knowing what's going on out there is driving me wild.

Not to mention Elise's strange demeanour. She was entirely too excited about tomorrow's game, her voice a high-pitched shrill as she spoke rapidly. Chelsea tried to brush it off as a caffeine high, but I know in my gut there's something else going on. That in itself bothers me because I want to know what's going on with my team at all times, and I feel like Elise is such a wild card that I'll never be awarded that kind of peace.

There's a knock on the door, and Paige, someone on the medical staff for the university's sports program, pops her head inside, giving me a broad smile. "Hey," she says, waving a hand clutching a stack of papers, "they're all clear. You're good to go tomorrow."

A relieved breath exhales from my lungs in a rush, my body sagging into the plastic chair. I give her a tight smile. "Thanks," I say, nodding at her as I stand, collecting the papers and heading into the locker room to meet with the team.

My trainers squeak along the tile flooring; the sound makes me cringe, but nothing can dim the relief of not having to report anyone for drug use. I stand in the centre of the locker room, all of the young women seated or standing by their lockers as they wait for the verdict that decides tomorrow's fate. "You're all set for tomorrow. Make sure you're packed and ready to go by noon," I say, turning on my heel, but my eyes drag across Elise.

She jumps up on a metal bench seat, waving her hands over her head with a broad smile stretched across her lips. Her hair is a mess, with a pink feather tucked into her messy bun. It's such a contrast to the black-and-white ensembles she tends to wear, and no matter how leisurely her attire tends to be, there's a certain elegance about her. But today, she looks like she got dressed in the dark...at a thrift shop...with an eighties theme.

"Oh my gosh, such good news!" she shouts, doing a little dance, and my heart rate picks up, her teammates' eyes swinging between one another, brows quirked in silent question.

What the fuck is going on?

CHELSEA

CHAPTER FIFTEEN

WEDNESDAY, APRIL 9

MY HEART IS in my throat as I sneak down the steps and into the kitchen, moving as quietly as I can through the old house. The floorboards creak beneath my feet, and I halt my movements, holding my breath as I listen for any sign that someone's awake. The only sound is my pulse pounding in my eardrums.

When the quiet drags on, I open the wooden cabinet where Elise's medication sits in a small white plastic bin. I pull it down and then pop the top off of the lithium bottle first and pour them out on the counter, counting each one as quickly as I can. My brow furrows, my chest tightening. According to the date she filled this, she's only missed a couple of doses. That doesn't make any sense.

I recount them, coming to the same conclusion before placing the bottle back in the basket, repeating the process with the other medications she's supposed to take daily. Each time, I get the same number.

I hear footfalls from upstairs, my eyes widen, and I frantically turn my body away from the cabinet, doing my best to look nonchalant as I slump against it.

"Chels?" Adhira asks, her voice groggy as she rubs at her eyes, wearing her fluffy green robe and fuzzy socks as she makes it to the bottom of the stairs.

I blow out a breath, my heart beats slowing. "Yeah, sorry. Did I wake you?" I ask.

She shakes her head, pulling out a stool from the kitchen island. It scrapes across the floor, and we both cringe before she takes a seat. "No, I couldn't sleep," she says, stifling a yawn with the back of her palm. Her tan skin is mottled, with dark circles under her eyes, and a light sheen of sweat coats her forehead.

"You feeling okay? You look a little rough," I admit, fiery acid burning up my throat and new anxiety mingling with the thoughts of Elise's strange behaviour.

She waves me off. "Yeah, just tired from bad dreams." She nods to the cabinet behind me with her chin, a question in her gaze.

"I counted them a couple times, and she's only got two extra days' worth in those bottles," I say, keeping my voice down. "Do you think she's been taking them out of the bottle in case we counted them?" I ask her.

"It's possible, but at a certain point, she wouldn't be in the right frame of mind to even think of doing something like that. There's definitely been a shift the last couple days, so maybe that's when she stopped hiding them," she says. "I've never witnessed a manic episode, and I'm certainly not an authority on it, but something doesn't seem right."

There's a loud bang from the front porch. My spine stiffens as I swing my gaze to the front of the house. My poor heart needs a break after this night.

Jingling keys and laughter greet us a moment before Elise bursts through the front door, and my eyes grow wide, panic slipping under my skin. "Elise?" I hadn't realised she wasn't home.

"Hey! This is Trev and Tina," she says, waving between the couple who look drunk off their asses. Her eyes are unfocused, darting around the room as she introduces these complete strangers.

"Hi, what are they doing here?" I ask, doing my best to keep my voice light. My tense jaw doesn't help me in the endeavour.

Elise leans forward, cupping a hand in a c-shape around her mouth as she whisper-yells, "They're swingers, and I'm about to get swung." She giggles loudly. Even drugs and alcohol couldn't account for this kind of behaviour. *Not from Elise.*

The couple looks at each other with an inscrutable expression but says nothing.

"O-kay then," I say, waltzing over to them. I open the door wide, extending my arm out. "It was nice meeting you both, but you've gotta go."

Elise's head rears back, her eyes narrowing. "They're *my* friends! You can't kick them out!" she wails. She has bright makeup all over her face, shorts that leave nothing to the imagination, and absolutely nothing besides a lace bra covering her chest.

"Yes, well, maybe they can come play another time. But we have a flight in a few hours, so they've gotta leave," I say. Blessedly, Adhira calls over to her from her seat at the kitchen island.

"That's right, Elise. Aren't you so excited for our away game tonight? We're getting on a plane, and you *adore* flights," she tells her, and Elise's eyes widen. I clench my eyes shut, bracing for an argument. Elise *does not* like flying because she has a tremendous phobia of heights. But again, she surprises me as she claps her hands together. My eyes burst open to see her bounding into the kitchen, which gives me the perfect opportunity to usher the drunk couple out of our house. How they find their way home is none of my concern.

Letty stammers down the stairs in nothing but an oversized white Wyvern Warriors t-shirt. My brow quirks at her, my eyes travelling down her muscular goalie thighs, all the way down to her white high-topped socks. "Chels, what's going on? It's four in the morning," she says, her voice low and thick with sleep.

My gaze swings from Letty to Elise in a silent answer. Letty drags in an audible breath, plastering an easy smile on her full lips before she joins us downstairs.

Adhira, Letty, and I spend the next few hours getting Elise's luggage packed and helping her shower and change. She finally crashes when we board the plane, and it's an incredible reprieve. As the oldest sister of five with a single mom, I'm no stranger to caretaking, but when the person you're caring for is not in the right frame of mind to listen to reason, it's far more exhausting than chasing around four energetic siblings.

I'd love to take a nap for myself, but with Rafael's questioning gaze swinging between where Letty and I flank Elise, purposefully creating a barricade around her unconscious body in the middle seat, I can't chance her waking up and doing something stupid.

Coach's brow furrows before he looks away, slumping back in his seat, and each time he does it, I release a loud sigh. Acid churns in my gut, and I'm even more thankful than ever that you can get anywhere with just a short flight on this continent.

It's so different from where I grew up in rural Tennessee, and my stomach sours further with the reminder of everything I left behind.

I shake the thought away, focusing my attention on Letty, who conveys a whole conversation in her soulful brown eyes without a single word needing to be spoken.

What the fuck are we going to do? We are so unbelievably screwed, Chels. There's no way she can play like this.

I look up at the seatbelt light above our heads and blow out another breath before meeting her eyes again.

I know, but we'll figure it out.

She nods, facing the window, staring out over the city we're about to land in, but her shoulders are rigid, and her jaw is clenched, giving her unease away.

I hate everything about this.

CHAPTER SIXTEEN

WEDNESDAY, APRIL 9

NUMBER 9

Come on, Letty. Just one night.

THAT'S *what we'd said the first time, and look where it's gotten us.*

I chew on my lip, staring down at a message from Jelani that I've been avoiding responding to all morning. I know I'll eventually have to answer, but I'm not used to men who actively work for what they want.

I'm even less used to men who want *me* the way he seems to, but after the decision I had to make, I can't handle his endearing demeanour, and I'm even less thrilled about the lie of omission I've been letting corrode my heart the last two years. *It was the right decision for you, Letty. Stop it.*

Shoving my phone back in my bag, I clench my eyes shut, trying to centre myself, but when I sit up, finding Elise's eyes cracking open, my heart pounds violently against my expanding rib cage.

"Hey," I say, and she sits up abruptly, her gaze swinging around the plane. Rafael turns in his seat the same way he has over and over this entire flight. His eyes narrow on Elise, the unrelenting excitement pouring out of her a clear sign to anyone who's ever met her that something isn't right.

I give him a tight smile, clamping my hand down on Elise's thigh as she tries to stand. *Gracias a Dios.* She doesn't fight me. She just fidgets in her seat and starts blabbering on about some plans she has that make no sense.

Honestly, I have practically zero understanding of what a manic episode is supposed to look like, but this is so far from her baseline grumpy-assed self that I have to believe that's what this is. Or at least, it must be something similar.

Jesus Cristo, we are so fucked.

ELISE

CHAPTER SEVENTEEN

WEDNESDAY, APRIL 9

MY LEGS ARE BOUNCING as we sit on the bus, my body bouncing from the bumpy ride. My face feels tingly. I bring my hands up to my face, pressing the pads of my fingers into my skin and revel in the way sparks zap over my cheeks. I let out a little squeal, and the curious gazes of my teammates meet mine. I smile broadly at them, so excited to get off of this bus.

I like buses. They bring me to new places. I like new places.

Looking out the window, a brightly lit building that shines even in the daylight stares back at me. The word "Casino" is written in purple and red neon over the top of the building, and a large sign beside it reads, "Come be a winner today!"

"I wanna be a winner." I breathe, my eyes never leaving the sign.

"What was that?" Adhira asks from her seat beside me.

I don't take my eyes off of the building until we've passed it entirely, and I jump when I feel someone poke my side. My eyes swing to Adhira's.

"What'd you say?" she asks, and I tilt my head in confusion, unsure of what she's talking about.

Rafael's deep voice is behind me, sending a chill down my spine, and heat pools in my core. He's so sexy, it should be impossible to look that good while being that grumpy.

"Yeah, well, most people would say the same about you, I'm sure," Adhira deadpans. *Had I said that out loud?*

I hum, and the driver turns the radio up. I dance in my seat, and it isn't long before we're parked and I'm sprinting out of the bus. *Or has it been long?* Unsure.

We pile into the locker rooms, and there are so many people talking it's hard to make out what they're saying. *None of it matters.*

I'm about to be a winner. I slip past my roommates, heading down the hall, bobbing my head as I wander until I see a sign that reads, "Exit."

I make my way out through it, wind whipping past my face as dark clouds roll in. *Huh, that's not good.*

ADHIRA

CHAPTER EIGHTEEN

WEDNESDAY, APRIL 9

MY STOMACH TWISTS in knots as I search frantically for Elise. My heart is pounding too fast, and I feel dizzy from being bent over, looking for any sign of her under the bathroom stalls. I probably look like such a creep, and when Ruby asks me what I'm doing, I lie and tell her I lost an earring.

I don't even wear earrings anymore. They'd just get torn out on the pitch.

Nausea roils through me, bile climbing up my throat as an image pops into my mind. Elise's wide-eyed expression staring out the window of the bus, her attention caught on the casino across the street. *Bloody fuck.*

Rafael ends his speech, and my teammates give him a less-than-thrilled clap before making their way to the tunnel. Chelsea and Letty meet my worried gaze, their lips pinched as they realise the same thing I have.

She's gone.

RAFAEL

CHAPTER NINETEEN

RAFAEL

THE WOMEN PILE out of the locker room. All of them except the three troublemakers, who are looking between one another with frantic eyes.

Elise is nowhere to be seen, and that rock in my gut is now a boulder of despair.

"Where is she?" I bark out, not caring which one answers so long as I get some damn answers.

Chelsea closes her eyes briefly before meeting mine, her fingers toying with the edge of her black-and-fuchsia shorts. She swallows hard, and when she opens her mouth to speak, I swear there's a high-speed train rushing past my ears because her words barely register past the blaring sound of panic coursing through me.

"I'm gonna need you to repeat that for me," I grit out, and she gives me those big doe eyes that would probably work on someone with a bigger heart than mine, but after years of stomping on my own, there isn't much left to salvage.

"We don't know," she says again, her voice small, and her words choppy.

"You don't know?" I ask, enunciating each word.

"No." She shakes her head. "We lost her," she says, the words a quiet, watery whimper, her lips trembling before she slumps onto the bench behind her, tears soaking her sun-kissed cheeks.

I run a ragged hand over my face, disbelief and frustration humming inside me. "Fuck!" I shout, unable to hold it in any longer. The three women startle, their eyes widening, shoulders shaking, and I instantly regret my tone. I pinch the bridge of my nose, tensing my jaw as I aim for a more even tone. "Do you have any idea where the bloody hell she could be?"

Letty and Chelsea shake their heads, but Adhira whispers, "I think I might."

I tug on the roots of my hair, the strands long from days of anxiety that I haven't been able to pinpoint, my appearance falling to the wayside as I've grappled senselessly for control. I stare at the ceiling with barely controlled rage simmering in my blood. My eyes meet theirs before barking out instructions for them to follow if they know what's good for them. "Go tell the assistant coaches that there's been an emergency. They're taking over, *and Elise won't be back tonight.* If they ask for more information, say she was sick and I've got it taken care of."

They nod, rushing out to do as I ask. Adhira comes to stand in front of me, holding her ground. "Before you go after her like a madman, there are a few things you need to know first," she says, and I can already feel the pounding headache forming behind my temples.

"I don't have all day, Adhira," I grit out.

"Elise has bipolar 1 disorder," she says, and suddenly so many pieces of the puzzle that make up Elise Auclair come snapping into place. "Those were the meds she was taking when you saw her. She's still too embarrassed about her diagnosis to tell anyone about it other than the three of us, so I guess she quit taking her meds in order to test clean, but instead of restarting them, she started edging into mania. We don't have all day to talk about this, and frankly, it really is none of your business, but you need to know what you're walking into so you don't run the risk of her panicking and fleeing."

She gives me a rundown on what not to do when I see her, how to approach her, and where she's banking on me finding her. Apparently, there was a casino a few minutes away, and according to Adhira, people with bipolar 1 who are experiencing mania have a tendency to make impulsive decisions like gambling and seeking out sex.

The thought of finding Elise with another person pleasuring her has the edges of my periphery going black for reasons I can't even begin to fathom.

When Adhira's told me everything she can think of, I take off out of the building and down the road to the casino.

It's hard to miss, especially with how gloomy the weather is. The building shines like a beacon, and when I rush inside past security, a cloud of cigarette smoke falls over me, burning the inside of my nostrils.

I cough loudly, ambling through the large space, cursing Elise for getting us into this situation. If she's not here, I have no idea what I'm going to do.

Panic surges through me, my heart lurching inside my chest, my pulse speeding up as I pass by yet another set of slot machines without Elise seated behind them.

My fists clench at my side as I make it to the last row.

I release a loud breath, and my shoulders sag when my eyes land on her. She looks completely out of place in her gym shorts and sports bra, but no one seems to care. There's a crowd gathered behind her, cheering as she excitedly stares up at the glowing board in front of her.

My eyes widen when I see the screen for myself, bright with the number seven thousand fifty-three. She's somehow won over seven thousand pounds.

Before she can click the button to keep going, likely to lose everything she's won the longer she sits here, I push past her onlookers and drop to her side, placing a hand on the top of her thigh.

Her eyes are wide, pupils blown as they meet mine, and I give her a small smile, pushing past every emotion I'm feeling because I know my internal response to this situation would have her bolting out of here. *Thank fuck for Adhira.*

My gaze flicks to the screen for a moment. "Wow, you've won a lot of money, huh, princess?" I ask, keeping my voice light.

Her brows pinch, sending another wave of anxiety straight to my gut, but her expression smooths, and she gives me a bright smile. "I did! I've got to keep going," she says, turning back to hit the button in front of her. I snatch her wrist, and she opens her mouth to protest, her eyes crinkling at the sides, and her lips pull tight. I improvise, bringing her hand to my mouth and pressing a gentle kiss to her knuckles.

This is so fucking inappropriate.

Yeah, well, so is threatening to drug test your coach's daughter based on a poor assumption and a massive chip on your shoulder. I'll be dealing with those consequences a lot longer than I will this one, so I stand, hoping I've distracted her enough to pull her away from the machine. Her eyes dilate, and she sucks her plump bottom lip into her mouth.

"Come on, sweetheart, I'm gonna take you somewhere fun," I whisper into her ear, dragging her alongside me and out of the casino to where taxis line the front of the building.

Those big blue eyes of hers are darting around as she lets me guide her outside. It's almost like she can't focus on any one thing, as if there's nothing tethering her to reality right now, and it breaks something deep inside me to see her like this.

Goosebumps scatter across her arms at the chill in the air as wind whips past us. I usher her into the back of the taxicab, waiting until she's slid all the way in before I tell the taxi where to take us.

I hope she's not too upset about all the money she just left there.

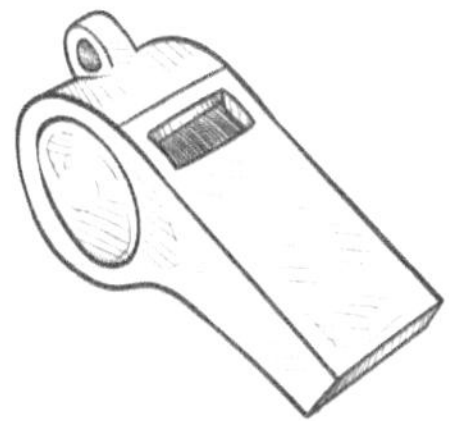

I continue pacing the hall outside of Elise's room. The sound of my trainers squeaking bounces off the linoleum floors and white walls, a harsh, cold reminder of the last time I was in a hospital.

The sound grates on my nerves, but I'm unable to stand still, walking from one end to the next and back. Over and over again, my heart battering against my ribcage as I wait for Coach to come out and give me an update. Kick me out. *Kick me off the team.* Anything would be better than the incessant worry clawing at my throat.

Anxiety thrums in my gut, churning with newly found remorse.

"Rafa," Coach's smooth, deep voice cuts through the rhythmic beating of the monitors in the rooms along this hallway.

My head snaps to him, blood rushing behind my eardrums. "Is she okay?" I ask, my tone thick like my tongue feels.

He nods, not speaking as he closes the door to her room with a gentle *snick.* "Come on, follow me to the cafeteria. I need a cuppa."

I walk aimlessly behind him, nerves coursing through my blood. My heart and mind feel heavy, like a thick layer of fog has settled over me. Memories of that day. *Of my mistakes.* They flood me, one after the other, rushing through me, gripping me by the throat and refusing to let go.

Coach claps a hand on my shoulder, levelling me with an earnest expression. "This is *not* your fault. I can only imagine what's going through your head right now, all things considered with what happened to your brother. But I'll tell you now what I told you after you'd confided in me about Carlos because it is *still* true, Rafa. Elise is an adult. She made her own decisions. Nothing that *you* did or said could have driven her to make those choices."

I try to cut him off. "But if I hadn't confronted her like—"

"Stop," he says, his tone terse and no-nonsense. "She should have told you what the medication was for. She could have handled that situation a hundred different ways, but *she* chose to stop taking her medications, not you. That is *not* your fault and not your responsibility."

I want to hear him. I *want* to believe him, but just like with Carlos, it all feels like it's just that.

My fault.

"I just—" I clear my throat. "I feel like I'm always bringing horrible shit to everyone's doorstep. Like I'm some harbinger for bad situations."

"And has Carlos ever told you as much?" he asks, pressing the button for the basement as we step into the elevator.

"Never."

"Well, here's a thought. Maybe you should start *listening* to him. I know it's hard to do with that thick skull of yours, but you should give it a go," he teases. The doors open, and my shoulders feel a little less tense, but then we get to the cafeteria, and all the anxiety is back with a vengeance.

"Who the bloody fuck thought it was a good idea to put the cafeteria next to the *morgue*?"

ELISE
CHAPTER TWENTY
SUNDAY, APRIL 13

I BLINK RAPIDLY into the pitch-black room, trying to get my bearings. I smack the nightstand beside me in search of my lamp, flicking it on when I feel the cool porcelain base beneath my fingertips. I have no idea what time it is when I finally open my eyes, but it must be late judging by how dark my room is.

I've had a day or so to come to terms with my actions and apologise to everyone involved. Everyone other than Rafael, anyway.

My friends are just thankful I'm okay now, but Dad was pissed. I explained that the whole incident had been entirely my fault and begged him not to take it out on Rafael, which turned out to be the wrong thing to say.

As it seems, my dad wasn't upset with Rafael at all. It wasn't his fault that I so selfishly avoided telling him about my medications or that he had to rescue me after the fact.

And he's right—it *is* my sole responsibility. *My massive mistake.*

I swallow several times, scratching at the base of my throat. I'm always making mistakes. My skin flushes, and sweat coats my brow, embarrassment mingling with the undercurrent of guilt and frustration.

I never should've stopped my medication. I realise that now

more than ever, but I'd genuinely believed that a few days off of it wouldn't be such a big deal. By the time we all got tested, I was already in the first throws of mania and unable to work myself back into taking my meds. Thanks to Rafael bringing me to the hospital right away, this hadn't technically qualified as a manic episode, seeing as it didn't fit the criteria of lasting more than seven days from onset.

Chelsea told me that when the rest of the team went back home while I was in the hospital, Rafael never did. He stayed the whole time, even after my dad got there to see me through the rest of my visit. I'd asked how she would know that, but he missed all of their practices and sent them an email saying he'd be away for a few days. It didn't take a genius to figure out why.

Dad only confirmed that theory this morning when he demanded I join him for breakfast. All I wanted was to stay in bed and sleep the weekend away, but he left no room for argument. I love my dad, and knowing I worried him for no reason has clawed at my insides ever since I found my way back to reality.

This morning, he made sure I was aware that Rafael is on my side, even if he might not seem like it. *He missed his Friday match to be there for my discharge from the hospital, according to my dad.*

That knowledge is something I really hadn't needed. It weighs heavily on my chest, and the emotions I'm feeling surrounding that concern me. I can't figure them out, and I'm not sure I want to.

I attempt to blink the sleep out of my eyes again, finally managing to sit up. My limbs feel heavy, as do my eyelids.

I move slowly, making my way into the bathroom that connects to Chelsea's room. When I've finished my shower and I'm back in bed, I roll over, grab my cell off of my nightstand, and open up my email. There's a message from Rafael already waiting for me, and luckily, he's just the person I needed to speak with.

His message reads, "I hope you're okay."

That's all it says. Four words, five if you count the contraction.

I think I may have finally met someone as shit at processing their emotions as I am. I click "Reply" and wait a beat while I figure out what I want to say. I keep it simple, saying, "I am. Thank you. Talk tomorrow?"

A text comes through, but my shoulders sag when I see the name "Noah" flash across the screen.

NOAH

Just let me take you out to dinner, Elise. I can show you what a good time we'll have and maybe you'll change your mind about your "no dating rule"

I clench my jaw, typing out a quick "No", and focus my attention back on my emails, awaiting a reply from someone I know won't bother me with questions about my dating life or lack thereof.

Minutes pass, and I'm ready to put my phone down and try to go back to sleep, but my notifications ping with an email.

"Yes. Be there early."

Well, alright then.

RAFAEL

CHAPTER TWENTY-ONE

MONDAY, APRIL 14

I'M convinced there are no words that could adequately describe the feeling of being back in a hospital, and with Elise Auclair, of all people.

It brought me back to that horrible fucking day, but I couldn't get myself to leave her. I know nearly nothing about her, and yet, I just *couldn't* leave.

My skin crawls with the memory.

When I called Coach and told him what was going on, he dropped everything to get there like a good father should. But even with him by her side, I holed myself up in the hotel next to the hospital and wouldn't leave until she had.

And now, as I sit at my desk waiting for her to meet me before practice, there's a lump in my throat I'm afraid I won't be able to clear.

She knocks at the door even though it's open, popping her head inside and giving me a small smile that doesn't meet her eyes. My heart clenches, and my head spins with her sweet, fruity scent swirling through the small space.

"Hey," I grunt out, motioning toward the chair across from me. "Have a seat, Elise."

Her fingers fiddle with the hem of her too-short shorts, and she bites her bottom lip, her cheeks flaming as she sits.

I clear my throat, getting ready to speak, but she leans across the desk, planting her forearms on it, and subsequently pushing her breasts together. My eyes linger between the cleavage of her full breasts before I can drag them away, and up to her crystal-clear blue eyes, heat clawing up my throat.

"I am *so* sorry," she says, unaware of where my eyes were only a second ago. "I was dumb, and selfish, and—"

I hold up a hand, cutting her off. "Stop it. I was a judgemental ass. I should never have confronted you like that. I didn't exactly make it easy to want to confide in me," I admit. My palms are sweating, and I resist the urge to claw at my throat, a sudden rush of heat overtaking me.

She casts her eyes downward for a beat before bringing them back up to mine. The emotions swirling in their depths have another breath caught in my throat. "Thank you for finding me," she says, swallowing, "and *staying*." Her voice is thick with emotion.

I'm not a fan of this little heart-to-heart because it means I have to actually feel things, and I'm not prepared to relive the absolute terror I felt while looking for her. So instead, I smirk and deflect. "You won't be thanking me when you find out how much money I made you leave behind on that slot machine."

Her eyes widen, and if she realises that I'm avoiding having a deeper conversation, she doesn't let on. She tilts her head and chews on her lip. "How much?"

"Over seven thousand pounds."

She falls back against her chair, shaking her head as she looks up at the ceiling. "Damn, I hope whoever won the fight for my empty seat had tons of fun with that money. God knows I could use it," she says with a low chuckle, but the comment strikes me as odd. I don't know *exactly* how much money her father makes, but it's definitely enough that she shouldn't be strapped for cash.

I ignore the comment, *for now*, allowing her to settle in further before my curiosity breaks through the overwhelming *need* to avoid getting any further into this conversation with her.

"In a party town like that?" I ask. "I could think of several fun ways to spend that money," I finish without thinking, but clearly, she catches on. Her eyes dance with mischief as she twists in her seat, crossing a bent leg over her knee. The hem of her shorts rides up, and the curve of her ass cheek peeks out, nothing concealing her smooth skin beneath the spandex.

I suppress a groan, and she says, "Could you, Rafael? Tell me" —she quirks a thin, dark brow—"how would *you* have spent that money?"

Considering the road surrounding the casino was lined with strip clubs, I'm sure she already thinks that's what I was getting at, and unfortunately, she's right. Though every other person on the planet has lost their appeal now that I've met Elise. A strip club would do nothing for me.

"I'll allow you to come to whatever conclusions you want to, *peligrosa*." *Trouble.*

That is what Elise Auclair is. Nothing but trouble, and I can't seem to stop coming back for more.

She lifts a brow in question, but she doesn't ask, and I don't offer the information. "Something tells me we would've spent it in exactly the same way."

I say nothing, holding my breath as I will my dick to settle in my shorts. She smirks again, and now would be a great time for my tongue to unglue itself from the roof of my mouth.

I relax back into my seat, blowing out the breath.

Such a tyrant.

"You mentioned needing the money for something," I finally manage to say, and before a question can pass my lips, Elise's entire demeanour has changed.

Gone is the relaxed woman seated in my office as if she owns the damn building, and in her place is the crumpled, wild-eyed shell of her, digging her nails into her thighs.

She slackens her jaw before I can change my mind and tell her to ignore what I'd said. "Yeah," she says with a tremor in that one word that has me almost desperate to turn back time and stop while we were ahead. *Before* I'd made us both so visibly uncomfortable that my muscles shake with tension. "Uh," she stammers, clearing her throat, "I'm not sure how it is for everyone with bipolar disorder, but from what I know, big purchases are sort of common, especially during a manic or hypomanic episode. I've got some debt to pay off," she explains, clearly skirting around the details, but I've learned my lesson. I won't push.

I'm not sure what to say yet, but I can't formulate a response because she's already talking again. "I don't talk about this often with anyone, not even my friends who know about my diagnosis. And yes, I am aware that I shouldn't be ashamed about it because it's out of my control." She squirms in her seat, shifting from side to side as if unable to find a comfortable position. "But no matter how much Chelsea preaches to me about it," she mutters with a groan, "I'm unable to move past just how fucking *humiliated* I am. It's less about my mental illness and more about my actions. Like *you*," she says with a pointed look in my direction. "I don't even know what I said to you that night, but I'm pretty certain my language must have been *colourful*."

My body chooses this moment to disregard each of my pleas, my dick going rigid in my shorts, a wholly inappropriate response to the conversation we're having. But with her words are the reminder of what she'd been saying in the back of that cab that night. The way her body had pressed to mine, how she'd flung herself over me, straddling my lap, whispering obscenely scandalous and deliriously sexy words into my ear as I refused her, focused on being a responsible person, *for once in my fucking life,* and getting her the help she needed. By the time we got to the hospital, I was sporting a painful erection that told me everything I needed to know about how explosive we'd be together. And that's exactly why nothing can ever happen between us.

In an effort to save both myself and her from the discomfort whispering through the room, *I lie.* It's a bald-faced lie and one I'm not sure I'll ever bring myself to regret.

"I don't know what you think you might've said, Elise, but I assure you that you said nothing like what you're suggesting. It was a quick drive to the hospital, and that was the end of it."

She assesses me slowly, her gaze moving from each corner of my face, and when she's satisfied, she slumps back into her chair again. "Thank you." She begins nibbling her lip, and I want to pluck it from her teeth, so much that my fingers twitch on my armrests. "I seriously can't say that enough, considering..." She doesn't have to finish the sentence. *Considering we both know she might have ended up much worse off had I not found her in time.* That thought combines with an unshakeable feeling that I'm getting too close to her despite everything that's conspired between us these last few weeks, and it has me scooting out of my chair, ready to fling myself across the room and out of the door to catch a goddamn breath.

"Yeah, no problem," I tell her dismissively. "We better go. Practice starts in five." And with that, I leave her to gather herself before making it out onto the pitch for her first day back since the incident.

ELISE

CHAPTER TWENTY-TWO

MONDAY, APRIL 14

I'M glad that Rafael and I cleared the air because practice went a lot more smoothly than it has in previous weeks.

I didn't intend to give him such intimate details about my past or my history with bipolar disorder, but it felt like I owed him an answer. And more than that, I still feel unsettled that he's letting me off the hook so easily, as if *he* doesn't want to dig further into the chaos my mind sometimes creates. It might not have been a controlled version of me that acted the way I had last week, but it *was* when I'd decided not to take my medication in the first place.

That's what leaves me feeling like there's more that I need to explain to him.

Though the smouldering looks he's been tossing my way today say otherwise. It seems he really doesn't think any less of me, and I'm not sure why it even matters to me, but that knowledge has my shoulders sagging in relief and a weight lifting from my chest.

Those deep brown eyes of his have also had a less-than-desirable effect. They feel flame-filled as they brush over my skin and have settled into my core. I'm going to need a solid hour with my favourite toy to move past the feeling, but then I should be able to rid my mind of him entirely. *Yeah, sure.*

I shake the thought out of my head and make it over to the locker room, changing before heading home.

A wide smile lights my face when I finish the godforsaken practice exam I've been working on for the last two hours.

How can you even call it a bloody practice exam if it's worth a grade?

It was brutal. Plus, the essay I had due last night, but luckily got an extension on, is going to be even more of a headache.

In the meantime, I plan to take a little break and reward myself for a job well done. Or at least, a job completed.

I shimmy my shorts down my thighs and kick them to the end of the bed, tugging the top drawer of my nightstand open and grabbing out my favourite toy. I turn the vibrator on and press the wide, silicone tip to my entrance.

My pussy is so slick, it takes almost no pressure to slide inside. My walls clamp down around it as I breathe a sigh, settling further into my mattress.

My eyes flutter closed, and as I work the vibe in and out, the mental image of Rafael hovering over me, his dick buried deep inside me, has my eyes snapping open. "No," I practically growl into my empty room, desperate for him not to invade this part of my life too.

I huff out another breath, settling back and picturing Leo instead. Except in this fantasy, when my breaths are coming out rapidly and I'm holding back a scream of pleasure, it's not Leo's voice that fills my ears. Rafael's stubble scrapes along my jaw, his warm breath coasting over my ear as an imaginary version of him rumbles, "You like that, Elise? Can you come like this?"

A frustrated groan leaves my lips, and my hand pumps the vibrator more vigorously, hoping to fuck away the mental image of that man, or at least to find my orgasm before he can make another appearance.

Just before I'm about to climax, my toes curling and my core clenching, *there he is again.* Rafael's corded arms frame my body, his thick dick spearing inside me as those onyx eyes sear into mine, nearly bringing me over the edge before I can stop it. I sit up, pulling the vibe out and throwing it across the room before I can come.

It hits the door with a loud *thwack* as I let out a frustrated scream. "Motherfucker!"

Chelsea bursts through the door, her eyes wide and the strands of blue hair framing her face plastered over her forehead. "What the fuck?!" she yells at me.

I collapse back onto the bed, my hands fisted at my side, and thankfully, my duvet stays put, keeping my lady bits covered.

Chelsea's eyes rove over me and down to the black dong, still vibrating at her feet. Her mouth splits into a grin, and we can't hold back the laughter that takes over.

RAFAEL

CHAPTER TWENTY-THREE

WEDNESDAY, APRIL 16

AS MUCH AS I appreciate my team for supporting me and my brother by participating in this fundraiser every year, it dredges up so many horrific memories and puts me in the worst headspace possible.

It's two weeks away and I'm already in a shit mood. I can't imagine anyone will want me around by the time the event starts, not that I could blame them.

None of it should matter because I have a job to do, and hopefully, pouring myself into that will be enough to keep me busy and the time will fly by. *Unlikely.*

Mrs. Purrito jumps up on the couch, swiping her little grey-and-white paw over my *cortadito*, nearly knocking it off of the armrest.

I grab for it before it can topple over, but of course, four little hairs are now floating in the foamy surface. "You're a freaking terror," I grumble, standing and heading to the kitchen to pour the coffee down the drain.

She jumps off the couch, meeting me by the sink and rubbing her long, chubby body against my ankles. I roll my eyes at her, grabbing a can of wet food from the cabinet, dishing some out into her tiny pink ceramic bowl, and setting it on the ground for her.

She purrs loudly, as her name would suggest, and decidedly, I've become another forgotten relic now that her salmon is in the picture. "Traitor," I whisper, grabbing my duffel bag from the hook by the door and heading out for practice.

By the time practice is over, I'm beat, but my shower will have to wait because the Blaze are already out here warming up. Jelani bumps into my shoulder and shifts to walk backward toward the locker rooms. A broad smile stretches across his face, dark eyes meeting my own. "What's up, Hazzel?" I ask.

"Just checking in on you, man. It's getting hot out here, and with the way you've got your eyes stuck to Coach's daughter, I wanted to make sure you weren't getting overheated," he says, his grin shifting to a smirk.

I shake my head at him. "It's not hot out here, and I glanced at her *once*. You're reaching, and you know it." *That's a total lie.* I can't seem to keep my eyes off of her, and Jelani is the most perspective person I've ever met.

"You can lie to me, but don't lie to yourself." He tsks with a deep chuckle, turning back around and sprinting off for the lockers. I need to get it together.

I shake myself out, sprinting over to where the women are getting ready for practice. Elise has these tiny pink shorts on, and I wish I could scream at her to cover up so it'd be easier to stop myself from looking, but my guess is that wouldn't win me any brownie points with the team, so I keep my mouth shut.

"Listen up, ladies," I shout, clapping my hands together to get their attention off of the asses of my teammates. These men are some of my best friends, but I want to strangle them sometimes. They've taken to wearing the shortest shorts they can fit their asses in, and it's all for the sake of the twenty-year-olds who can't keep their eyes to themselves.

"Yes, Coach," a few of them grumble, and Elise has the decency to cover her mouth, stifling a laugh. The motion has the corners of my lips twitching, but I shut it down, scowling instead.

"We're going to do some new drills today," I say, going on to explain what each component entails, and when ready, they line up with Letty at the goalpost. Chelsea starts the drill, moving around the mannequin at the centre line, pretending as if it were a defender. She checks the mannequin's shoulder, sprints in front, and pins it while calling the pass. Elise is up next. She plays a pass to Chelsea, who holds off the mannequin and maintains control of the ball.

I know that this is a drill, but it's still damn impressive to see how seriously these women take the sport they love. They're forces to be reckoned with.

And Letty, I swear, she's this high-spirited spitfire off the field, but the moment she's locked in as goalkeeper, she's in it. A mask overtakes her face, and there's not a single thought in or out of her head that you'll see coming.

Chelsea spins around the mannequin and into the penalty box, going head-to-head with Letty. Chelsea shoots the ball past Letty, but Letty still manages to throw her entire body into it, keeping it from her net by a breath.

Letty smirks at Chelsea, who tackles her playfully, and I look away on instinct, having seen first-hand how those two play-fight. It usually ends up with at least one of them missing an article of clothing, and I have zero interest in seeing that.

"Cut it out—Coach looks like he's about to be sick," Elise tells them, soft laughter slipping into her voice.

I look up when I hear the catcalls and laughter of the team, shaking my head.

Chelsea runs to the back of the line, and Elise starts the drill the same as she had. Her movements are maddeningly quick, and with every motion, her ass jiggles in those tiny spandex shorts I love so much. *Or hate.* I'm undecided. They're like a cruel form of modern torture.

When Elise gets to Letty, she fakes her out, hitting the ball in the opposite side of the net she had her body angled at. It's not a clean shot given the poor positioning, but it's enough to slip by Letty.

"Hell yeah, baby!" Elise shouts, pumping her fist in the air, and this time, I'm unable to hold back the smile that takes over my face.

Elise glances at me before I can school the expression, but before she can hassle me about it, Letty teases her with her hands on her hips as she shouts, "Back of the line, hotshot."

The rest of practice goes on like this. Some of these women have the speed and agility most professional players would kill for, and it's honestly unbelievable to witness. It's even more incredible to experience as their coach, though I know it's not forever.

It makes me miss playing football, but in the same way, it also makes me a little miserable because with that thought is the memory of *why* I'd wanted to stop playing in the first place.

ELISE

CHAPTER TWENTY-FOUR

FRIDAY, APRIL 18

IN A SICK TURN OF EVENTS, the bus for our away game broke down and we had to take a much smaller one. Which means I'm stuck beside Rafael. As team captain, it only seemed fitting, but I'm not sure breathing the same air as this man is safe when he's the one my thoughts turn to when I fuck myself at night.

I need to get laid.

Rafael's outer thigh is smooshed against mine, pulling my thoughts back to him. My breath gets caught in my throat as he turns to face me, and I watch with rapt attention as his Adam's apple bobs.

"Sorry, tight space," he says, but it's the wrong thing to say when I feel like a horny teenager.

My brows climb, and I clench my knees together, swallowing thickly, giving him a small nod. My mouth feels dry. "Nothing you can do about it," I say.

We cleared the air about my episode, but it doesn't mean things aren't still awkward. They absolutely are, and for a multitude of reasons. The first being that I'm sort of mortified over my behaviour, and I'm still trying to figure out how to pay off the debt I accrued while in my most recent manic state.

It's not like this hasn't happened to me before. It has, it's just never been because I was dumb enough not to take my meds.

Sometimes when I need a medication change or my dose needs to be adjusted, I'll spend an exorbitant amount of money on shit I don't need. It's impulsive and reckless, but I can't help it. One time, I even took out a loan. It's an unfortunate reality of bipolar disorder for many people, and I really try not to beat myself up about it, but it's hard. Especially when there are witnesses to the mania.

Witnesses I really wish hadn't seen me like that, because now every time I see him, I'm reminded of my mistakes, and my hands start to feel clammy with embarrassment.

The other major reason things are so painfully awkward is directly related to the number of orgasms I've had with this man's face, *and body*, in mind.

Yep, mostly his body. One specific part of it especially, though his deep voice is really what brings me over the edge.

I feel his eyes like lasers settle into the side of my face, and when I refuse to meet his gaze, he settles a hand on my knee, giving it a tight squeeze before releasing his hold.

"Everything okay?" he asks, the baritone of his voice barely above a whisper.

I nod, not offering any more information as the air gets sucked out of the space between us, suffocating me.

He clears his throat but says nothing else the rest of the ride.

By the time we get back home, it's late, but after an hour-long bus ride next to Rafael, I have some steam to blow off.

Leo and Noah are waiting on the porch when we pull into the driveway. I stifle a groan as I approach them. I'd texted Leo, but it seems he anticipated a need I didn't have and invited Noah along.

"Hello, ladies, how was the game tonight?" Noah asks.

Letty waves him off, passing him to unlock the door, her high cheekbones highlighted by the dim golden light hanging in the centre of the porch. "Enough small talk, Noah. It's late, we're tired, and we all know what you're here for. Just do me a favour and try to keep it down, yeah?" Letty asks, her words curt and condescending.

"Yes, ma'am," Leo says, saluting her with a wide smile.

I head up the stairs, knowing they'll follow me. Cutting to the chase, I strip down and wait for them to do the same. "Getting straight to it, then," Leo says, chuckling deeply.

"Noah, on the bed. Head at the end," I instruct, wanting to get this over with so I can enjoy the orgasm-induced bliss in my dreams.

"As you wish," the Brit says, stroking himself when he's positioned at the end of the bed.

Leo sheaths himself with a condom, tossing one to Noah as I climb over Noah's face, positioning my centre over his mouth.

He swipes a finger through my slickness, and I keen, arching into him.

"Already so wet, love," he muses.

"Mhmm," I respond, lowering myself further onto his face, hoping to suffocate him so he doesn't speak for the rest of the night. He's an alright bloke, but he gets on my last nerve with all the talking he does and his insufferable mentions of relationships.

"Shut up and eat, mate," Leo says, smacking my ass harshly. Glad I'm not the only one who thinks he needs to keep his mouth shut.

A grunt leaves my lips, the sting in my backside subsiding quickly as Noah wraps his lips around my clit. Leo positions the head of his cock at my entrance, edging forward.

"Hold on, mate. Aren't your bollocks going to be smacking me in the mug?" Noah whines, and I can't help but roll my eyes.

"Well, mate, we're about to find out," Leo says with a deep chuckle.

I plant my hands on the sides of Noah's hips, hovering my mouth over him, and ignoring his grumbles of disapproval. I really bloody hope Leo's balls are unshaven. This wanker gets more annoying by the day.

When Leo fills me up, it isn't either of these men I'm thinking about.

RAFAEL

CHAPTER TWENTY-FIVE

SATURDAY, APRIL 19

HAVING the day off should be a treat, but it's anything but.

I feel even more drained than usual. My muscles ache from the unnecessarily long run I took this morning, and my thoughts are threatening to strangle me.

I've tried to nap, but each time I do, I wake in a panic, my brother's screams filling my mind and crushing my soul repeatedly.

He's doing better, I try to remind myself, but the voice in the back of my head moves to the forefront with a megaphone in hand, shouting, "No thanks to you!"

Truly, it *is* "no thanks" to me.

Sure, I offer to send him money for his physical therapy and anything else he needs, but he wouldn't even be in this situation if it weren't for me, and he refuses my money anyhow. He's successful all on his own, but I still wish he'd take something from me *like I took everything from him.* But nothing I give him could ever compare to what my reckless thrill-seeking cost him.

Worse yet, I don't think I'd even be here if it weren't for rugby.

Or at least, not without the guys who introduced me to the sport.

When Carlos made me move here to follow *our* dreams of

playing football professionally, I thought I could do it. Really, I had tried. I didn't want my scholarship to go to waste, but everything I did felt like a disservice to him, and it dragged me down to the very pits of hell.

I haven't considered ending my life in a really long time, but the closer we get to this fundraiser, the more my mind takes me to that horrible headspace I was in when I first moved here.

If it hadn't been for the group of guys playing rugby that day in the park, looking for an extra player and willing to teach me, I wouldn't be where I am today.

Hell, I probably wouldn't be *anywhere* but six feet under.

I'm thankful every day that I'm not, but my chest still aches from the thought of everything Carlos has had stolen from him.

And it's all because of me.

CHAPTER TWENTY-SIX

SUNDAY, APRIL 20

THE COUCH DIPS where Letty takes a seat beside me, a giant cup of coffee in her hands as she tucks one leg under her.

"You called it an early night the other day," she remarks, eyeing me speculatively through thick lashes.

"Guess so," I say, peering back down at my laptop with the blank screen still in front of me, unchanged from how it was an hour ago.

"*Mija*, you know you can't play those games with me. You've got something on your mind; the least you can do is let me help you with that homework assignment you've been staring at all morning," she says, scooting closer to me.

"It's fine, really. I just don't know what to write about."

She quirks a dark brow at me, pulling my laptop out of my hands and settling it on the armrest on her side of the couch.

"Is that because a certain coach is on your mind?" she asks, her full lips turning up in a smirk.

"You know, it's not, but thanks for asking," I say sarcastically, rolling my eyes.

"*Ajá!*" she shouts, jabbing a finger at me. "So you admit you *are* thinking about him!"

I slump into the cushions, clenching my eyes shut and shoving a throw pillow over my face to scream into it.

"Yes! Alright?" I shout, tossing the pillow between us, frustration leaching into my words.

My jaw aches, and I can feel my pulse pounding in my temples as the grin widens on Letty's annoyingly flawless face. It should really be illegal to look that fucking pretty all the time.

Hell, she's one of my best friends and *I'd fuck her.*

"And you want to sleep with him, right?"

I narrow my eyes at her, pinching my lips together in defiance.

"Answer the question, Elise," she says, crossing her arms over her chest, making her enormous tits look even more luscious.

"Would you put those things away? They're distracting," I say, nodding my chin at her chest.

"Stop changing the subject. You have a thing for our coach. Now admit it."

"Fine. Yes," I say, my voice sounding whiny and annoying. "I want him to fill every one of my holes and make me fucking beg for it. *Now,* can you help me with this essay?"

She smiles broadly, moving the laptop to her lap, and gets to work, typing away happily now that she's gotten the answer she wanted from me.

RAFAEL

CHAPTER TWENTY-SEVEN

FRIDAY, APRIL 25

THE WHOLE WEEK has been absolute rubbish.

It's gotten worse with each passing day, but I hope that once this event is over, I'll feel better and be able to pick myself up. I do it every year, and this one's no different.

I've got to get through one more night like this, and then it'll be in the past.

Not that that'll matter much, but I'm really banking on it since I haven't had a solid night of sleep in weeks.

I lie on the sofa, with Mrs. Purrito making biscuits on my chest as hers rumbles with a mechanical purr. My mind threatens to wander back to that day, but I reel it in.

I turn on the telly, flicking through channels, but nothing catches my eye. My chest squeezes again as another ripple of anxiety tears through me, stealing my breath away. My phone vibrates in my pocket, and I stare down at the screen, welcoming the distraction.

THIGH DADDIES
JELANI

You alright?

Yeah.

I hate being vulnerable with anyone, even my closest friends. I feel stripped bare, and the idea that they can see through me enough to know that this event is particularly difficult for me makes a piece of my pride wilt.

NAKOA

Enough of that. You can talk to us if you want to.

Does it sound like I want to?

JELANI

Wowww, mate. So defensive!

NAKOA

Someone's got your knickers in a twist...

JELANI

Is it those girls again? Giving you a run for your money?

I know they won't let it go until I give them something to redirect their attention.

Those young women are arguably the least frustrating part of my current circumstances.

I just want to get through tomorrow and then I should feel more at ease.

NAKOA

I knew they'd be good for you. You're a great captain, Rafa. I'm sure that extends to how you coach them.

JELANI

Assuming he's dislodged the massive stick from his bum, I'm certain you're right.

NAKOA

Really, J? He was just opening up to us. Way to squash it!

JELANI

Cap needed a breather from the heavy stuff. I
could feel it through the phone.

How did I get stuck with these two idiots as best friends?

NAKOA

Yeah? Well, I can feel him wanting to break up
with us through the phone.

JELANI

An over the phone breakup? That's so crass!
Our boy would never.

> I'm not your boyfriend. We can't break up.
> Now leave me alone.

JELANI

We love you too, luv. See you tomorrow.

NAKOA

Let us know if you need us.

I'm blessed to have these guys in my life. They goof around a lot, but deep down, they have hearts of gold.

> Sure. Thanks.

Mrs. Purrito's kneading stops, and when I look down at her, her wide blue eyes are peering up, assessing me slowly. I gaze back at her, officially in some sort of staring competition with my damn cat, but I refuse to look away until she does. Her ear flickers as she tilts her head to the side and nuzzles into my chest, resuming her soothing vibrations.

It's annoying that this cat seems to understand me better than I understand myself sometimes.

ELISE

CHAPTER TWENTY-EIGHT

SATURDAY, APRIL 26

"I KNOW we all agreed to come for charity since it's both your dad and our coach's team, but could someone please explain why there's a massive table with fruit lined up over there?" Adhira asks, her brows pinched as she squints over at the white plastic banquet table.

"No idea, but I guess we'll find out soon enough," I say, heading toward a white-topped tent covering a table with baskets for auction. My dad's team does this event every year, but I've never gone. It always tended to line up with a game or practice of my own, and I don't have a job or any stable form of income, so I'd just be here for moral support, which no one's asked for. I'm not exactly the kind of person anyone *would* ask for moral support from.

"Ooh, I'll sign up for this one!" Chelsea chirps, leaning over the table to scribble her name on a ticket and pop it in the corresponding jar.

"What's it for?" I ask, reading the framed slip that outlines what the company donating the basket is offering.

"Food, duh," she says with a loud laugh. "It's for this restaurant downtown that offers private tables in the kitchen where you get to watch the chefs cook, and they give you samples of everything they make the entire night for the rest of the restaurant."

"Such a bloody foody," Adhira says, grimacing.

"As if you aren't? Just because you prefer food from vendors on wheels doesn't mean you aren't a foody," Chelsea chides.

Adhira crosses her arms over her chest, not dignifying Chelsea's assessment with a response because she's *right*.

One of the announcers who works at the Wyvern's stadium is here for the event, and whatever they're doing this year to raise donations is starting.

"Come on, children, let's go," Chelsea says, ushering us like her little ducklings in the direction of all the people gathering for the first event.

My eyes immediately find Rafael's through the crowd of people. His are darker than usual, hidden under thick brows and framed by dark circles.

He looks haunted by something.

A chill skates down my spine, and bile rises up my throat, but I swallow it back down, looking over at Letty, whose eyes are glued to Jelani.

"You thirsty?" I ask her, bumping her shoulder with my own. Her large brown eyes cut to me, and she narrows her gaze.

"Ha, ha, very funny," she says, crossing her arms over her chest, stretching the fabric of her tight white top.

It's interesting that she's so defensive. Usually, if she wants something, *or someone* for that matter, she has no qualms about going out and getting it. So I'm unsure as to why that doesn't seem to be the case here.

We're standing on the pitch near the centre line, surrounded by tons of potential donors as we wait for the first activity.

Robert, the announcer from earlier, is standing by the table covered in fruit, wearing a wide grin on his tan, wrinkled face.

"Hello, everyone, and thank you for being here!" he says, projecting his voice across the crowd despite the microphone in his hand. "As you all know, we're here today to raise awareness for a cause near and dear to the hearts of the Wyvern Warriors," he says, pausing for emphasis. "An estimated twenty-point-six million people worldwide are living with some form of spinal cord injury. The ways this impacts these individuals vary, as everyone's experience with any condition will be vastly different, but today, we're here to raise money for those living with paraplegia so that they are able to access life-changing resources that could improve their overall quality of life substantially. Our hope is to raise one hundred thousand pounds today. We have all the confidence in the world that this is possible with your help, and we hope you'll enjoy the day ahead!"

The crowd claps wildly as the men on the rugby team line up, each standing behind a plate of what looks like papaya sliced in half.

"To get the festivities started, these young men will be entertaining you all with a papaya eating contest!" The players groan, shaking their heads, and the sound is audible even over the crowd.

I can't believe this was actually chosen as a competition.

"For those who are unfamiliar with the way this works, each player has been assigned a number, which correlates to a percentage of the funds raised during this activity. You all have been sent a link to donate for this contest. The Wyvern Warriors will match the donation of whichever player wins based on the percentage they have been assigned. The players don't know who has the highest percent, but you all will as it's included in the link."

Everyone fishes their phones out of their pockets and handbags, opening the link they were all sent upon check-in today. The link will update with each event and allow us to keep track of our goal as the day goes on.

Robert allows everyone a few minutes to get their donations in as my dad steps out behind the guys. He smiles brightly as he gathers their wrists behind their backs, tying them. He's clearly taking too much enjoyment in this particular part of the event. I imagine he's wanted to string each of these men up with that rope on more than one occasion, and definitely not in the way that I've been thinking about doing the same to my coach.

"What the bloody hell is going on?" Adhira asks, her voice a whisper.

"I think I'm gonna like it, whatever it is," Chelsea says, her American Southern twang making another appearance.

I shake my head, directing my attention back to the men, but my eyes can't help but snag on Rafael. His snap up the moment mine land on him, as if he can *feel* my stare.

A blush creeps over my cheeks, and I avert my gaze.

"Alright! On your mark, get set, go!" Rob yells.

The players hunch forward over the fruit, each of them with a full papaya cut in half, seeds still intact, and something so strange happens.

My body tingles, my nipples pinching at the sight of these men eating that goddamn fruit! Some of them choose to eat the seeds, and others start by gathering them in their mouths and spitting them out on their plates. The sounds they're making are fucking erotic, and I feel a little lightheaded.

Chelsea reaches out, gripping my forearm tightly. "Babe," she whispers, "why the fuck is that so sexy?" she asks, her voice awestruck and hushed.

"I-I'm not sure," I stammer. My heart is racing though, and I can feel my bounding pulse between my legs.

My traitorous eyes land on Rafael again, and they remain glued there as he slurps and chews, taking large bites of the fruit, the juices coating his face. He looks up, keeping me in a chokehold as he continues his onslaught, with his eyes remaining on me the entire time. I feel my neck and ears burning, my throat constricting, and my nipples most definitely have a mind of their own as they peak so tightly I think they're trying to slice their way through my top.

My mind fills with the thought of me splayed out on that table as he absolutely devours my pussy.

"I'm chalking this up to nearly two years without sex. What's your excuse?" Letty asks me, chuckling.

Adhira scratches at her throat, her brows twisting, lips pursed.

"I don't get it. This is gross," she says. *Clearly,* this event isn't having the same impact on her as it is on us. "You lot are a bunch of freaks."

Rob is shouting excitedly into the microphone. "Rafael Romero-Castillo takes the lead, with Jelani Hazzel following quickly behind!"

Letty's knees practically buckle beneath her, but I'm too focused on Rafael to do anything about it aside from keep tabs on her from my periphery. Adhira wraps an arm around her waist and grits out, "You're pathetic."

"And you're an *angel,*" Letty says, her voice dripping in sarcasm, but she allows Adhira to hold up her weight as her legs fail her. The woman needs to get laid, and I'm not sure why she hasn't in so long. As a group, we're all very sex-positive, though Adhira tends to be less interested.

The moment Rafael breaks eye contact with me, my shoulders sag, and I take in a desperate gulp of air, filling my deprived lungs.

Several onlookers are shouting, yelling out the names of their favourite players, encouraging them to eat quicker. Among them are several women with drool practically spilling from the sides of their mouths. Guess I can't fault them, all things considered.

"The pot is up to ten thousand seven hundred pounds already!" Rob screams, his excitement contagious.

Rafael's dark gaze flicks up, and it's like I'm locked in again, unable to tear my eyes away from him even if I wanted to. His jaw works quickly as he takes large bites, swallowing them down. His Adam's apple bobs with the movement, and I swear to god I feel my thong soaking through. *What the fuck is happening to me?*

He finishes, standing upright, stomping his foot on the ground. His head rears back as he shouts up to the sky above, "Hell yeah!"

I turn my back to him, needing a moment to look away. I suck a strained breath through my nose, my chest heaving as I replenish the lost oxygen. Chelsea tracks my movements, bringing a hand up in front of me to fan me off. "Down girl, calm down," she jokes with a giggle.

I roll my eyes at her, swatting her hand away, and spin back around to face Rob, who's listing off all the stats for the event.

The next couple of hours go exactly as you'd expect for an event like this. Lots of random competitions, raffles, auctions, and finally, the announcement that the event significantly surpassed the goal of one hundred thousand pounds by nearly double.

I watch as Rafael slips past a crowd surrounding some of his teammates and hurries off toward the tunnel for the locker rooms.

ELISE

CHAPTER TWENTY-NINE
SATURDAY, APRIL 26

MY FOOTSTEPS ECHO off of the tile floors and white walls as I head down the hall toward Rafael's office.

I meant to email him last night but got caught up with another essay and forgot. We need to get the plan for this week's practices squared away, and as much as I hate to admit it, his drills have been helpful.

His office door is cracked open, and when I knock, it creaks, opening wider to reveal a distraught Rafael. He's hunched over his wooden desk, his elbows digging into the hard surface as he cradles his head in his hands.

"Coach?" I ask, chewing the inside of my cheek, my mouth going dry.

His head snaps up, his jaw clenched shut as he glares at me, sucking in a breath. He shakes his head, loosening his jaw, running a shaky hand through his overgrown waves.

"I can come back," I say, backpedalling. I'm not sure what's going on with him, but I don't think I want to find out right now.

He shakes his head again, grunting as he does. "No, it's fine. *I'm* fine. Have a seat," he says, his tone leaving no room for argument.

Against my better judgement, I shut the door behind me and

take a seat in the dark-red tweed chair in front of his desk. I've always been one for making questionable decisions, why stop now?

He scrubs a hand over his cheek, the stubble residing there much more prominent than I've previously seen it. The dark circles I'd noticed earlier look even worse in the crappy overhead light of his office, and a heavy weight settles in my gut.

I scoot my chair closer to his desk, unable to stop my body's response to him. I *want* to comfort him, I realise, the thought foreign to me. I give into the feeling, settling my hand over his, my whole body tensing as his gaze lazily travels from my hand to my face. I give his hand a quick squeeze, but I can't seem to tear the offending appendage from him.

This isn't a man who anyone would describe as "sunshine" by any stretch of the imagination, but as someone who's been told I'm "too grumpy" about a million times, I recognise this isn't his baseline piss-poor attitude. No, this is something far beyond what I'd consider typical for him.

"Do you—" I clear my throat. "Do you need someone to talk to?" My thighs squeeze as his expression shifts to something more intense, verging on feral.

He stands abruptly, his hand remaining under mine as he leans across the table, planting his other hand flat, and he brings his face mere inches from mine.

Rafael slips the hand from under mine, pinching my chin between his thumb and forefinger, dragging my mouth closer to his. "No, Elise," he grits out, "I don't need to *talk* about it. What I need is a *goddamn distraction*."

His voice is rough and low, almost menacing, but my body betrays me. My chest heaves at the proximity between us, and my core spasms, all self-preservation flying out the window with my sanity, replaced by lust and driven by an obscene need to let this man use my body for his own whims. My lips part, and there's a flutter low in my belly.

This is what I get for listening to all those damn mafia romance books on audio.

Evidently, I'm *attracted* to unhinged men, like this one, who looks like he could simultaneously fulfil all of my wildest and most erotic fantasies as he tears my heart and mind apart, piece by dreadful piece.

I swallow thickly and do my best to sound confident, but the words leave my mouth like a whisper. "I could be that for you." *Since when am I this meek little girl?*

His nostrils flare, and he works his jaw. "A distraction. *Just this once,*" I clarify, pushing more conviction into my words this time.

I'm rewarded with a visual of the exact moment his resolve snaps. His warm, callused hand scrapes along my jaw, dragging down my throat, where his fingers dig into the delicate flesh over my pulse. He brings his lips to hover above my ear, his cool breath a tickle over my heated skin, and I clench my eyes shut, begging my pebbled nipples to relax.

"Just this once," he whispers, the words rough, scraping across my skin as if physically capable of doing such a thing. My breath hitches, getting caught in my throat. "We'll get it out of our systems and move on with our lives after this, you understand, Elise?"

God, yes. I want nothing more than to fuck this man out of my system.

I nod, realising he can only feel the movement. "Y-yes." I stutter my agreement.

"Good," he says, pushing me out of his grasp by my throat. I fall back into the chair as he rounds his desk, prowling to the door to lock it before returning. "Before this goes any further, we need to agree on a few things here."

I nod my agreement, worrying my lower lip.

"I don't do slow and gentle. We're not 'making love'." He says the last two words as if they're dirty and tainted. "We're fucking. Rough and fast, and I can't coddle you throughout. If we do this, I want to get lost in *you.*"

I groan loudly, my heartbeat pounding in my throat as he drags the chair back a foot before standing in front of me and dropping to his knees. "Is that alright with you, or do we need to pretend this never happened?" His words are gruff, and they scrape against my skin like sandpaper.

"God, yes, that's perfect. I have absolutely *no* desire to be treated like porcelain."

His eyes narrow, searching my face for any semblance of a lie, and when he finds none, I'm rewarded with an almost imperceptible quirk of his lips—it might be the most erotic thing I've ever seen.

"You might be in charge out there"—he flicks his chin to the door—"but in here? I'm the one in control. Now let me see what's for lunch."

Oh, Christ, this man and his sinful mouth. I *knew* he'd be a dirty talker. My head falls back, my gaze averted to the popcorn ceiling above us for a moment as I regain my composure, but it's a moment too long for him.

"Eyes on me," he grunts out, sliding his callused hands up my thighs. Our eyes lock as his fingers dig into the material of my spandex shorts. He drags them down my legs, along with my thong, pulling them off of my ankles and dropping them beside him.

He takes a deep lungful of air, and I find myself mirroring the movement, reminding me to breathe as I shake with need.

Rafael grips my foot and calf, bending it up and dropping it over the top of the armrest. He repeats the movement with my other leg, splaying me wide open for him. The cool, stagnant air in this small space both chills me to my core and suffocates me all at once.

He rests back on his haunches, scrubbing a hand down his face and clenching his eyes shut as he releases a long groan.

I bend forward as best I can, tapping the centre of his forehead with my forefinger, a sly smirk spreading my lips, regaining some of my usual bravado.

"Uh, uh, uh." I tsk. "Eyes on me," I say, my cheek quirking when he rolls his eyes, a hint of a smile playing on his face.

"Who's calling the shots here, Elise?" he asks, his deep voice dropping another octave as he sits up, bringing his face to mine. He dips his chin and drags the tip of his nose over my jawline, his mouth hovering an inch from where I want it.

The thought is so strange. I *never* kiss the people I have sex with, because that is *all* we're doing. Fucking and moving on. Kissing feels intimate, it feels like *more*. More than I can or even want to entertain giving to someone, but that doesn't put a stop to the needy way my body reacts to this man. A whimper climbs up my throat, and I'm half a second from begging him to shove his tongue down in my mouth. I wasn't joking when I told Letty I want him to fill *all* of my holes.

He drops a hand to my core, and I suck a breath through my teeth, the heat radiating off of him seeping into me as he strokes my wet slit. His other hand winds into the hair at the base of my skull, tugging my mouth to his. Rafael's full lips press against mine as he pushes a finger inside me. I buck off the chair, but his body keeps me firmly in place as his lips mould to me.

He pumps a thick finger into my cunt, my insides melting as heat radiates through me, starting in my core and spreading outward. I whine against his mouth, his lips pressing firmly onto mine. He swipes his hot tongue across the seam, and I open for him, allowing his tongue to slip inside and tangle with mine.

My muscles clench, tingles shooting through me. Strangled moans leave my throat, only to be devoured by Rafael. The heel of his palm rubs deliciously against my clit, and I wind my arms around his neck, digging my nails into his traps.

He groans loudly, tilting his head for better access as he presses me further into the chair, squishing me to the seat.

His hot mouth leaves mine, but only for a second. He nips my bottom lip, and I practically dissolve against him, whining as he smirks down at me. "I think I asked you a question, *peligrosa,*" he says, lazily pumping his finger in and out of my pussy.

"I don't remember what it was, nor do I care," I answer, earning a second finger slamming into me. I arch into his warm, muscular body, my head falling back, exposing my neck. He ducks his chin, nipping the thin skin over my pulse and scraping his teeth up to my ear. I love that he's not delicate with me. I *hate* being treated like stained glass.

"Elise," he warns, "who's in charge here?" His breath coasts over the shell of my ear.

"You're, *oh god*," I cry, his fingers spreading inside me, stretching me out.

"Sorry, what was that?" he teases with a dark, humourless chuckle that's as sexy as it is infuriating.

"I said..." I grind my molars, trying to overcome the pleasure building from his hands. "You're not going to like my answer," I say, purposefully taunting him. This little back-and-forth turns him on nearly as much as it does me, and I have a feeling he enjoys it when I talk back to him. *Masochistic fuck.*

The more turned on he is, the more he tries to punish me for it, and *I fucking love it.*

RAFAEL

CHAPTER THIRTY

SATURDAY, APRIL 26

THE SOUNDS this little troublemaker releases when my fingers are inside her delicious cunt are the perfect distraction. *Just like she'd promised.*

The problem? I haven't even had her sliding over my dick yet, and I think I might be addicted.

"You know as well as I do that you aren't the one in charge here." I tsk, gliding my thumb over her clit, revelling in the way she arches into me, her face twisting with suppressed appreciation.

"I'm *always* in charge, Rafael, whether or not—*yes, oh fuck, yes!*" She finishes on a scream. *What a good little slut.*

"Sorry, what was that?" I tilt my head, brows furrowed. "I couldn't hear you over your screams, practically begging me to keep fucking this needy pussy," I say, my cheek twitching with a smirk.

"The more you try to prove you're in charge," she says, panting, "the better you fuck me," she admits, applying pressure to my shoulders as she pushes me down her body, sending my face to settle right over her dripping cunt.

Fucking hell.

Just like she wants, I dip my head down, sliding my tongue

through her wetness, and a loud groan leaves my lips. *God, she tastes incredible.* Like everything she's not pure sunshine.

Her tugging on my roots as her lithe body vibrates under my touch is going to have me coming in my shorts. I hate that she might be right... Maybe she *is* the one in charge here.

I remove my fingers, sucking them into my mouth, moaning around them until every last delicious drop is cleaned from them.

My mouth hovers over her again, and I nip and suck on her clit. Elise writhes against me, her eyes watering as she gasps, holding back her screams. "What is it, *peligrosa*? You need to come?"

She nods, biting her lower lip, her brows knitted together, her perfect, beautiful fucking face a picture of anguish. "I can see this is painful for you, so why don't you go ahead and give us what we both want?"

She shakes her head violently. "Never," she gasps, her voice catching on a hiccup as I pinch her clit roughly.

"Just ask nicely, and I'll make you come," I tell her, taunting, waiting for the moment I get to watch her break apart for me, begging for what she wants, finally giving in beyond her stubbornness.

I duck my head, working my lower jaw like I had that bloody papaya earlier, scraping my overgrown stubble over her pussy as my tongue swirls and ravages her. I can tell the moment she's gone too far, her whole body tensing, and those delicious thighs start to shake.

"Beg for it, or I'll stop," I grunt, my mouth never leaving her.

"Fine!" she shouts, and a wide smile stretches my lips. "You're in charge! Now please, let me fucking come," she demands through gritted teeth.

A groan of approval rumbles through my chest as I finish her off, bringing my thumb up to her clit to apply the firm pressure I know she needs. I increase my movements and snake a hand up her abdomen, pressing her further against the chair, sliding my fingers under her hot-pink sports bra, finding her nipple and twisting hard.

"Oh, god!" she cries, shaking under me, her pussy becoming even wetter, soaking my face as I tongue fuck her back to hell where she came from.

As her mind comes crashing back to earth, I ravish her, cleaning up every last drop she has to give me. Shudders continue running through her, pleasure slowly subsiding. Her body still twitches with remnants of her orgasm, her head lolling to the side as she blinks rapidly before her gaze finds mine. "For a cocksucker, you eat pussy pretty well," she rasps with a lazy, satiated smile.

I bark out a laugh, the sound surprising us both. "Sweetheart, I'll show you who's a cocksucker." I stand, winding a hand through her dark ponytail, wrapping it around my fist and pulling her to stand in front of me.

I shove her to the ground, not allowing her time to catch herself on her way down. She lands with a smack against the hard linoleum floors. Elise glares up at me, her ice-blue eyes becoming stormy.

"Ow," she says very dramatically as she enunciates the word but curls her fingers around the waistband of my gym shorts, tugging on them.

"We should've spoken about this before we got started," I say, my voice hoarse, "but I don't 'sleep with' or 'make love to' anyone anyway," I explain, making air quotes around the two vile ways in which my partners have spoken to me about what we do in the bedroom.

She scoffs, her brows pinching. "Of course we aren't. It's disturbing that you think you'd have to say that. We're fucking, simple as that," she says, unknowingly setting my mind at ease.

"Excellent, then we're on the same page."

"Anything else before I resume the show?" she taunts, one elegant brow raised in question.

"Yes, Elise. I like it *rough*. The harder and more depraved, the better. If you don't want me to fuck that pretty throat of yours, you're going to have to tell me now."

She blinds me with a wide smile that shows off the top row of her pearly white teeth, her pointed canines the only thing grounding me to reality, reminding me that this woman will ruin me if I let her. "Look at that, something we can agree on," she says, digging her slender fingers into my shorts again, conversation officially forgotten—the way I prefer. I lift my ass, making it easier for her to slide them down over my thighs.

My dick is fully erect, bobbing forward. It nearly smacks her in the eye, but she dodges it by an inch. "Jesus Christ, all this time you've been walking around with a weapon capable of nuclear warfare, and you *still* have a piss-poor attitude?" she asks, shaking her head as she stares at my dick with a scrutinising gaze, wrapping a hand around the base. "If I were a man and had a cock this big, you wouldn't be able to pay me to wipe the smug smile off my face," she says, pumping her hand up my shaft and squeezing tightly.

I groan, my eyes rolling back in my head. Her tongue darts out, catching the bead of precum forming on the tip, and her moan nearly brings me to my knees.

"New plan get the fuck up and ride my cock," I demand.

A small smile plays on her pretty pink lips, and I know whatever she's about to do is *not* going to be what I asked for.

"No can do, Coach," she whispers, her voice soft and playful. "You said to suck you off, and I'm nothing if not a team player."

She opens her mouth wide, practically unhinging her jaw, swallowing me whole. "Jesus fucking hell." I groan, nostrils flaring, my balls tensing as I do my damndest not to shoot my load down her throat already.

She slides her tongue along the underside of my cock, cupping my balls in one hand and the base in the other, twisting her hand to apply the perfect amount of friction as she slobbers all over me. Now I *know* I'm addicted.

That's the last coherent thought I have as she sucks and swirls, bobbing her head as she moans around me, the vibration making me feel weak in the knees. Thank fuck I'm sitting.

My fingers dig into her scalp as I wrench her off of me, white-hot heat searing down my spine as she lightly drags her teeth up my dick.

She rolls her eyes at me, but there's a hint of a smile when she grips the edge of the desk, hauling herself up.

"So, Coach, how was that?" she asks, batting her thick lashes at me, swiping the back of her hand over her swollen lips.

I shake my head, gripping her hips, and spin her to face my desk before pinning her hands to it. She shivers as I bite her shoulder and run my lips up the side of her neck, nudging her entrance with the head of my dick.

"Good start, *peligrosa*, but practice makes perfect," I whisper.

I grip the base of my cock, swiping the engorged head through her slick heat, notching at the entrance of her tight pussy, but her entire body goes rigid. My eyes widen, and I pull out immediately. "What's wrong? Was that not okay?" I ask.

She huffs out a sigh, turning in my arms to sit on the edge of the desk.

"Do you have a condom?" She tilts her head to the side, hope lacing her words.

My stomach drops to my toes as I hiss out a breath. "Fuck, I'm so fucking sorry, Elise," I say, dragging a hand through my hair. "I got carried away, and I—"

She presses a hand to my chest. "No, it's fine, it's not that I don't want it—want *you*," she corrects, "it's just that I'm on birth control, but one of the medications I take decreases the efficacy of my OCP, and as you can probably imagine, I have less than zero interest in getting pregnant right now."

Understanding works its way under my skin, slowly seeping into my blood and making its way to my brain. I nod heavily, my dick pulsing to remind me that he's down there, waiting to be dealt with.

I run a hand up her arm, and my body sings when goosebumps erupt in a trail left by my fingers. I cup her jaw, dragging her eyes to mine.

"I understand," I tell her, the moment sobering us both. "I don't have a condom, but that's probably for the best. And for your peace of mind, I get tested frequently and haven't been with anyone since before the last time I was tested. I'm happy to send you that report as well. We just"—I clear my throat—"had a momentary lapse in judgement. It was fun, but it won't happen again. Anything more would be too intimate anyway."

She swallows thickly, running her hands up my chest. She cups my cheeks, drawing me in for a mind-blowing kiss that leaves me breathless.

I've never had a goodbye kiss, but there's no mistaking it. *That's exactly what this is.*

ELISE

CHAPTER THIRTY-ONE
SATURDAY, APRIL 26

I'VE BEEN CRAWLING out of my skin, doing my best to stay busy and keep my mind occupied. The fact that I can't tell my friends about what happened today is driving me up the damn wall. I want to be able to talk to *someone* about it. Anyone!

God, it's so frustrating.

What's worse is knowing it'll never happen again but that I really want it to.

As if to add insult to injury, my phone pings with the fourth text message Noah has sent me today. I groan outwardly, snatching my phone off the counter to stare laser beams into his contact name, hoping it explodes or something. I should really just block his number at this point, so that's exactly what I do.

I set my phone face down on the counter, busying myself with organizing Chelsea's mug collection. It's nothing more than a hoarder's paradise of mismatched ceramics with holiday characters, funny sayings, and my personal favourite a mug with nothing but a picture of her ex-boyfriend's cat. She dumped him and stole the mug, almost took the cat too.

My mind betrays me, leaving me to wonder if the fur sometimes stuck to Rafael's clothing is from a cat or a dog. *Definitely a dog,* I decide. He could never pass for a cat daddy.

Why am I even thinking about him at all?

I just hope that practice on Monday isn't *too* awkward. It would be my own fault if it were, and like Rafael said, it was a moment of weakness. A brief lapse in judgement.

The awkwardness of it all will pass as we both forget about what happened, and then we can move on with our lives.

RAFAEL

CHAPTER THIRTY-TWO

FRIDAY, MAY 2

I CAN'T SEEM *to move on with my fucking life.*

I *thought* I was joking when I said Elise came straight from hell, but with every passing day, that seems more and more like the truth. She's like a succubus, invading my every waking thought, and I can't rid my brain of her no matter how much I try.

My dick is rubbed raw, and I'm pretty sure I've got new calluses forming on my palms from the absurd number of times I've fucked my own hand to the thought of her dripping cunt, and god, *that mouth.*

My jaw is clenched shut as the team unloads from the bus, piling into the hotel after an excruciating game that ended with us winning, but only by one goal.

Us. Because these women and this team have become *mine* in every sense. I root for them the same way I do my teammates, celebrating their wins as my own because they *are.*

And that's the only explanation for why Elise's behaviour at the end of the game struck me as odd. She was unusually frustrated, kicking a rubbish bin as she stormed off into the locker room.

My godforsaken brain wouldn't drop the thought that maybe

she's got as much pent-up energy over what never happened as I do.

No, I don't want that. I can't, I remind myself, following after the team into the brightly lit lobby.

Elise is already leaning over the concierge desk as he hands her the room keys, passing them out according to the sleeping chart we set up this week. We try to rotate who stays with one another on these trips to keep everything fair, even if they all wind up swapping as soon as I head to my own room.

She saunters over to me as the rest of the ladies make their way up the stairs or take the elevators, hauling their duffel bags over their shoulders.

I swallow thickly, taking in the sway of her rounded hips and the way her quads flex with each step. Her dark hair is wrapped up in a bun, and tendrils of those silken strands frame her face. Her dark features are a massive contrast to her icy-blue eyes and light sun-kissed complexion.

"Hey, Coach," she says, sticking out a hand wrapped tightly around my room key. I try to take it from her, but she doesn't budge when my hand swallows hers. She glances down at it, one corner of her lips curving. "I see you sprung for the suite, huh?" she asks, her eyes glittering with mischief.

"Yep," I croak.

She smirks, loosening her grip, and drops her hand to her side, leaving me in the middle of this massive, limestone-walled lobby with cathedral ceilings, and a hard-on that would rival Big Ben.

ELISE
CHAPTER THIRTY-THREE

FRIDAY, MAY 2

RUBY'S SEATED on the edge of her mattress, chewing nervously on her nail as she eyes me warily.

"So," she starts, shifting to face me. "I, uh—"

I roll my eyes at her, flopping back against the pillows with my arms tucked under my head.

"We already know you and Meg are shagging," I tell her, rolling my eyes. "It's fine, go have fun." *At least one of us should,* but I don't utter that last part.

She blows out a breath, her shoulders sagging with relief. "Thank fuck." She stands, grabbing her bag. "I'll be back in the morning before we head downstairs for the bus," she assures me.

"Have a good night, Ruby," I say, chuckling as she legs it out of here.

I grab the remote, turn the telly on, and flip through channel after channel. After wasting what was probably ten minutes of my life, I turn it off and grab for my phone, searching for an audiobook.

Not a damn thing catches my eye, but without anyone here to talk to, I press play on my favourite mafia rom-com. I've read it an embarrassing number of times, and it never gets old.

Naturally, I left off on a smutty scene that has me rubbing my thighs together, and it's most definitely not helping my already horny mind.

Bloody hell.

I toss and turn, trying to get comfortable before succumbing to the fact that I won't be relaxing tonight. I reach over to turn off the lamp, hoping sleep will find me.

RAFAEL

CHAPTER THIRTY-FOUR

FRIDAY, MAY 2

IT'S BEEN over an hour since I last saw her, but my dick gives zero fucks.

My cock is rock hard despite the ice-cold shower I recently took. I practically froze my nuts off, but my dick isn't giving up the fight. Elise's round, incredible ass sashaying away from me continues playing over and over in my mind like a damn movie stuck on repeat.

My fingers twitch by my phone as I stare up at the ceiling, reminding myself of our agreement.

One time, we said.

It doesn't count if I didn't get to actually fuck her, does it? Hell, I didn't even get to come.

No wonder my mind's not right. I didn't work her out of my system, and now I feel *stuck*.

Yep, that's the only reasonable explanation for this.

I fight myself, wanting more than anything to march downstairs and finish what we started.

She's not alone, you buffoon, I remind myself.

Stupid, stupid, stupid.

I've never lost this much control with anyone before, and the idea of going any further with her both consumes me and threatens to drown me.

Two loud knocks against the door have me flying out of bed, wrenching it open without checking who's outside.

Elise is standing before me, wearing nothing but an oversized sleep shirt that hangs just long enough to cover the tops of her thighs.

She launches herself at me, wrapping her arms around my neck, climbing me like a tree. I slam the door shut, stumbling backward onto the bed as I grip her ass, clutching her to my erection.

Gratification floods me, a tingle expanding at the base of my spine. *She wants me just as bad as I need her.*

Our touches are frenzied. Moans and whimpers leave our lips as we devour each other's mouths. Her tongue dances so beautifully with mine, and the taste of her sweet mouth is goddamn delectable.

She slides herself over my groin, and I hum in satisfaction.

She's absolutely soaking my cock through the thin fabric of my boxer briefs.

I slide my hands down her waist, over her firm ass, giving each cheek a squeeze as she groans, leaning further into me. Our mouths break apart, and she buries her face against my shoulder. I push her shirt up over her ass, and my cock practically goes off like a rocket, right here and now, my fingertips met with completely bare skin.

"You were walking around the hotel like this?" I growl, a twinge of jealousy and annoyance hitting me square in the chest.

"I sure was." She pants. "What are you gonna do about it?" she taunts, and I answer by flipping her onto her back, settling between her thighs.

She smirks up at me through hooded lids, her light-blue eyes swirling like a storm on the horizon. Because that's exactly what she is. A storm. And we might just be in the eye of it.

I snake my hand up her waist, squeezing her breast and flicking the pad of my thumb over her nipple as she arches into my touch. I don't get a chance to further investigate the cool metal beneath my touch before her legs part further, giving me better access to her as I press our pelvises together. *She's too much of a distraction.*

My hand finds her throat, and my thumb presses down firmly over her windpipe. Her eyes grow wide as she tries to suck in a breath, a hand finding mine, lying over top of it. "So defiant," I tease. "Always pushing me with that disobedient mouth of yours, *begging* for a rise out of me but when I give it to you, you look—" I lower my mouth to her ear and whisper, "surprised."

My grip tightens as she rolls her hips under me. I release her throat, sitting back on my heels, allowing the change in position to relieve some of the blood flow to my aching dick. Hopefully that'll help me last longer because, as it stands, *I'm a goner.*

"What can I say, Rafa? I like it rough," she teases, her cheeks and neck flushing red as she recovers from a lack of oxygen.

"And how rough do you like it, Elise?" I ask. Nausea roils through me as I await an answer that'll either disappoint me or prove that we're the same kind of fucked up and desperate to feel *anything* other than regret. I hope like hell this woman is able to make every fantasy a reality, one that no other partner of mine has been comfortable with.

On the other hand, I hope she *doesn't.* I hope she likes it soft and slow so I don't have to think about her this way again.

But when those full, dusty pink lips of hers curve in a smirk, her eyes glittering, I know the answer. *And I've never been more fucked.*

She tugs on the waistband of my briefs, slipping her hand inside. Her slim fingers wrap around the tip of my cock, my head falling back involuntarily. I groan loudly as I try to focus.

She pushes up, touching the tip of her nose to mine. Her warm, minty breath dances across my lips as she says, "I like it as rough as you can manage. Rougher than anyone you've been with before," she adds, as if reading my every thought.

"What's your safe word, Elise?" I ask.

She taps her chin, grinning as she says, "cum dumpster." She's beaming as a startled laugh leaves my lips. I shake my head.

"Fuck off," I say, still laughing. "Cum dumpster it is."

"And if my mouth is *full*, I'll tap on you three times. Sound good?" she asks, and I nod.

"Same goes for me then, I guess," I say, really hoping I won't need to ever use the phrase "cum dumpster" in my lifetime.

Elise tugs her shirt over her head, tossing it at my face. I pull it off and am met with a sight I'm afraid I'll never get to scrub from my mind. Mostly because I don't have the strength to do so.

Elise has a hand between her legs, the other toying with her nipples, squeezing the taut bud. Two identical golden barbells pierce the pink flesh, with a rhinestone scorpion on either side.

"I'm a Halloween baby," she explains as if that should mean anything to me. When it clearly doesn't, she rolls her eyes and says, "I'm a Scorpio."

"Whatever, *peligrosa*. Get up," I demand, backing away from the bed.

She climbs out, her long, lean legs straightening as she stands there, her arousal coating her thighs.

"On your knees."

She falls to the floor without question, her eyes looking glassy as she shifts to her palms, already knowing what I'm about to ask.

"Crawl to me," I demand, my voice rough and low.

She does as I say, but I continue to back further away from her, increasing the distance between us. Frustration plays between her brows, but she doesn't complain. I take a seat in the chair beside the fireplace, tugging my briefs down as she makes her way to sit before me.

I kick them off, discarding them beside the chair. I lean back, spreading my legs wide for her to sit between as I wrap her slightly damp ponytail around my fist, still wet from her shower. I tug it tightly in my grip, making her yelp.

"Get it nice and wet, Elise," I say, nodding toward my dick. She opens her mouth to lower it over the head. "Not what I meant, trouble. Make it wet with those juices dripping from your needy cunt."

She nods obediently, slipping her hand between her thighs, rocking back on her shins. A moan slips past her lips, and I tug on her hair, gripping her chin tightly with my other hand as I glare down at her.

"Did I say you could play with yourself, Elise?" She shakes her head. "That's right. I fucking didn't. Do as you're told, and wet my cock before I make you in a much more creative way."

Her pupils dilate as she sucks in a haughty breath, biting on her bottom lip. Her hand, now covered in her slickness, wraps around me, coating my dick in her. I loosen my grip on her chin, letting my hand fall to my side as she strokes me.

"Harder, Elise. Grip it *harder.*"

Her hand tightens firmly around me, and my breathing speeds up, electricity throwing sparks up each individual vertebra as her other hand joins, twisting in opposite directions as she squeezes me so hard her nails dig painfully into my flesh.

This is exactly what I wanted.

ELISE
CHAPTER THIRTY-FIVE
FRIDAY, MAY 2

MY NAILS SCRAPE up his shaft as I pump my hands up and down it, squeezing the head and darting my tongue out to lick off the precum beading at the tip.

His dick is so thick, lovely, and fuckable.

"Do you like the taste of us together, Elise?" he rumbles above me, his hand twining in my hair, tugging even harder. My scalp burns, sending tendrils of pleasure licking down my spine.

"Yes," I moan, moving a hand to settle on his muscular thigh as I hold the base, gagging on him with a lurid sound that makes his next words tremble.

"You're such a good girl like this." He groans. "So damn obedient. If only you'd listen to me without my dick to tease you. Now be my *best* girl and use your teeth."

My molars scrape over his flesh as I choke and sputter around him, taking him all the way into my throat, as far as he'll go. My eyes burn, tears spilling over, and I'm rewarded with his hand loosening in my hair to slide over my ear. He rolls his thumb and forefinger over my lobe as his other hand cups my breast, toying with the barbell.

My thighs clench, and I whimper, desperate for more.

"Aww, baby." He tsks, his tone taunting as he lowers his face over mine. "Are you horny? Do you need to be filled up?"

I keep his cock in my mouth, nodding around it, my eyes pleading with him.

A grin spreads his lips, and he nods. "Lie down." He flicks his chin to the rug in front of the lit fireplace.

I hollow my cheeks, dragging my lips over him once more from base to tip before my mouth leaves him with a filthy popping sound.

My tongue darts out, licking my lips as I scoot back, crawling to the carpet a few feet behind me.

He leans further into his chair, his legs spread completely, and his hands rest on the armrests, wrapping around the smooth wood.

"Spread your legs, and finger yourself. I want a show," he demands, tilting his head to the side.

A whimper tumbles past my lips, need so potent I might combust, consuming my every action. It allows my knees to fall to either side obediently before trailing my hand down my abdomen, slipping my fingers over my clit, rubbing the overly sensitive bundle of nerves.

"Fingers *in* your pussy, Elise. Or can you not understand basic commands?" he asks, lazily stroking himself. His harsh tone makes my mouth water.

I roll my eyes at him, a heavy dash of defiance rippling through me, but I do as I'm told, slipping a finger inside, and then another when he quirks a brow at me. I know I'll be rewarded for my obedience, and I'm willing to do *anything* to feel something other than the gnawing hollowness or the all-consuming burden of too many emotions that run rampant inside me.

My core spasms around my fingers, my head falling back on a loud moan. "God, I wish it were your cock inside me," I tell him, my chest heaving.

He pushes out of his chair abruptly, the wooden feet scraping across the hard floors as he stalks toward me.

His dark eyes burn into me before flicking to the crackling fire to my left. I continue pumping my fingers as I track his every movement.

Rafael grabs a fire iron from the stand of tools on the hearth. He angles the pointed tip at me, trailing the cool metal over my heated flesh, a stark contrast from the smokey heat warming my skin from the fire mere feet away.

A trail of goosebumps follows the tip of the metal. He rests it over my collarbone, his eyes raking over me.

"Don't forget your safe word," he whispers, turning with the poker in his hand. He opens the glass doors, shoving the poker between the blazing logs.

Fear threatens to grip me, but the most deeply depraved parts of me are cheering in elation. He doesn't treat me like a piece of glass, ready to shatter at any moment. Not even after seeing how fragile my mind can sometimes be. Not knowing this whole arrangement could go horribly, horribly wrong for us both at any moment.

He pulls the hot poker from the fire and holds it carefully over my abdomen, allowing it to hover just above my left hip bone.

"You're so gorgeous, Elise," he praises, and my fingers slow as the heat from the hot metal grows nearer to my flesh. "You do exactly as I say, and the best part is that, *for once*, I know you *want* to. It's quite the sight to see, I'll admit."

My lips part, my eyes honing in on his face as my abdomen tightens, waiting for the searing feeling of my burning flesh to overcome me, but the moment never arrives.

He pulls the metal away, tossing it down on the brick hearth. It hits with a loud clatter, and he falls to his knees, reaching out to cup my cheek. His thumb strokes my bottom lip as he watches me, taking in every last detail of my face before his lips finally meet mine.

His movements are slow; there's nothing rushed about this kiss. His tongue flicks out to run along the seam of my lips, his angle on my mouth changing as he tilts his head, demanding entry.

My mouth parts, and I sigh into him; his tongue dips in to tangle with mine, swirling over the tip of my own. The taste of mint coats my mouth as I moan into his.

He pulls away first, his hands still cupping my cheeks as he pants above me. "That was a test," he whispers.

"I've always hated school," I reply, the words hoarse.

"Then you'll be happy to know that you passed. You really are happy to be at my mercy, aren't you?"

I gulp, uncomfortable with his words because they speak of a truth that I've not come to terms with yet. "I can't wait any longer," he says, his voice quiet and strained. "I need to fill you up."

I nod emphatically. "I need that too," I whine.

He lowers himself down my body, ducking his head and stealing a taste from between my legs. My thighs clamp around his head, and he chuckles deeply, the sound vibrating through my body.

His fingers wrap around my thighs, pulling them apart to release him. He's smiling now, and it's *brilliant.* His white teeth glimmer under the dim lights, the fire beside us reflecting in his dark eyes as he stares down at me, cataloguing every inch of my body as if committing it to memory for when this is over and we return to the *before.* Where neither of us is allowed to yearn for the other, where we have to find something or *someone* else to fill the void.

He draws in a ragged breath before pushing up and sauntering away. He calls over his shoulder before I have a chance to ask. "Just grabbing a condom."

Rafael rummages around in his bag before returning with the foil packet, tearing it open with his teeth, and my mouth waters at the sight. He sheaths himself in one smooth movement before tossing the packet to the ground as he stands between my legs and lowers himself over me.

The tip of his cock presses against me, my core tightening

with need. His broad shoulders loom over me, making me feel so small beneath him.

I'm by no means a small woman, but Rafael is massive.

His arms are wide and corded. He notches further into me, leaning in to plant a hand beside my head, the other wrapping tightly around my throat, his biceps bulging.

I wrap my legs around his trim waist, pulling him in further as his eyes latch onto mine. He pushes into me all the way to the hilt, and the air leaves my lungs on a moan.

"You're so fucking big," I cry, not meaning to boost his ego. It's just a fact.

He smirks down at me. "I am," he agrees, lowering all of his weight onto me, crushing me to the ground as he holds his hips still. "Tell me what you want, Elise." His voice is barely above a whisper, his lips tickling the shell of my ear.

"I want—" I try to answer, but his hand tightens around my throat.

"What was that?" he asks, condescension dripping in his tone like the arousal dripping between my thighs. He rolls his hips once, only enough for my back to arch and my lungs to burn with the need for more oxygen.

"I want—" I try again, but he only tightens his grip, a wicked grin curving his lips, and annoyance flares through me, heating my chest.

"I can't hear you," he teases in a sing-song manner that causes me to lash out. My hand on his chest works to push him away from me just enough, and when his face is hovering over mine instead of pressed against me, my other hand snaps out, flying across his face with a loud *thwack.*

My palm burns as his head rears back, his lips parting, but his grip loosens slightly. His eyes blaze, crinkling at the edges and narrowing, and his jaw slacks as he rubs at it. Revulsion stirs inside me—*I can't believe I just smacked him.* The initial shock wears off and he finds my face again, groaning loudly, ducking his head to capture my mouth with his, and all regret is wiped clean from my conscience.

I wind my arms around his neck, fingers twining in the short dark hairs at the base of his skull as his hips roll and swirl. He plunges into me; the slapping of our hips meeting is an erotic chorus sounding throughout the suite.

He sits up, biting his lower lip, taking my hands in his. He slides my palms over his tight muscles, his tanned pecs, and down his abs before leaning back over top of me. They're the definition of washboard, and if this were the nineteenth century, I'd have him out on the porch with soap and water doing my laundry. He pins my hands above my head, and I earn the immense pleasure of watching those abs as they tighten with his every movement.

Rafael drops his mouth to my chest, tugging a nipple between his lips. "Rafa," I moan, wriggling under him as his hips slow.

"That's it, sunshine. Take your punishment," he says, his voice low and smooth despite having my entire tit between his lips.

"Punishment?" I question, bucking my hips for more friction, the rough carpet scraping along my shoulder blades. "*Oh, mon Dieu*," I moan out, my neck arching, eyes rolling back.

"Did you forget you just hit me?" he asks, tilting his head with a raised brow.

"I didn't hit you!" I yell, desperate for more. "I *smacked* you because you wouldn't let me answer your question and wouldn't let me *breathe*!"

His chuckle is deep and humourless. He trails his tongue across his full bottom lip before answering. "I did, didn't I?" he asks, clearly amused with himself. "Fine, Elise. You want to be heard so badly, tell me, what is it you want me to do to you?"

I roll my eyes, but I know this game. And reluctantly, *I enjoy it*. I'd die before admitting that to him though.

"Fuck me hard and fast until there are tears in my eyes and cum dripping down my legs," I deadpan.

His chin presses to his chest, a low rumble of approval

vibrating through him, and when his eyes meet mine again, there's fire lit within them. But this time, it's not from the fireplace.

He doesn't waste any more time, crushing his body to mine, bringing his mouth above my bounding pulse, nipping the skin, and sucking it into his mouth. "I'm about to make you my depraved little slut. I hope you enjoy screaming my name because I can guarantee, whoever has you next won't be the one you're thinking about."

And with his last word, his hips plunge forward, burying himself in me. My tits are bouncing on my chest, my core clenching tighter as he pounds into me relentlessly, and if I weren't so busy doing exactly as he said I would, I'd have a smile on my face. *Finally,* one dick that can satiate me, *and I can't even keep him.*

"Rafa, yes!" I scream. "*Comme ça...*" I plead, my tone breathy as he stretches me, lighting every nerve fibre in my body.

"So fucking hot," he grits out. "The dirtiest little slut for me."

My mouth parts, and my head rolls back as I keen against him. Everything feels hot and too tight, like I could implode at any moment, a writhing mess of emotion-packed particles.

His movements don't slow as he thrusts into me, his dick curving enough to rub beneath my clit, making my legs tremble.

His grip loosens on my wrists, dragging down my arms before he tucks them under me, hoisting me up his body as he sits up. He clutches me to his chest, standing and pumping his hips into me.

The change in angle is *everything.*

My back hits a wall, and his relentless, punishing thrusts don't stop. I grip his shoulders, meeting his movements as I lower myself further onto him, crying out as he meets me every time, thrust for thrust.

It's too much.

My core winds tightly, tears spill down my cheeks, and heat

grips my throat as his hand snakes between us, palming my aching pussy.

Rafael's fingers wrap around my clit, twisting and driving me over the edge. "Rafael!" I cry out, my head hitting the wall behind me.

I feel like I've fallen over a cliff, and I'm hitting every massive boulder and sharp edge as I make my descent back to solid ground.

His teeth dig into my shoulder, my mind still hazy as stars burst behind my eyes, and my breathing begins to slow. His body tenses. and he groans, pumping his hips into me, his movements fatigued and erratic.

When he's finished, he doesn't pull out of me until he's dropped me into the centre of the bed, onto the deep-green duvet cover. Small beads are sewn into the fabric in beautiful swirls, pressing into my bum in the most uncomfortable manner, but I don't have the energy to get up. My limbs are nothing more than gelatine, my body useless for the moment.

I watch intently as he tugs the condom off, tying it and depositing it into the bin before heading into the loo. He leaves the door wide open as he turns the sink on, grabbing a washcloth from the shelf. I watch as he cleans himself up, his round, perky ass even more perfect from his side profile.

Fuck, I love rugby.

When he's done, he grabs another cloth and a towel, turning off the bathroom light and returning to me.

"Open your legs, *peligrosa*," he says, his voice hushed. After the first time he called me that, I asked Letty what it meant and was not the least bit surprised to learn that he was calling me trouble from the very start.

"Can't, no strength," I whine, making no effort to move my still-twitching muscles.

He rolls his eyes, rewarding me with a lopsided smirk as he grips my calf, lifting my leg and dropping it several inches over, opening me up to him. He takes a seat on the edge of the mattress, swiping the warm, wet cloth over my thighs and then between my folds. The action is tender, and something aches in my chest, but I can't pinpoint the cause of the offending reaction. He uses the dry cloth to pat my damp skin, dropping both wash rags on the floor before climbing in beside me.

"They should really rethink these beads," I grumble after a few minutes. Rafael chuckles beside me, lifting up to grip the top of the duvet from either side of my waist, wiggling it down under me. The sharp edges of the embroidered beads make me wince, but just as quickly as the pain comes, it's gone, replaced by the satisfying warmth of soft, smooth sheets and a pillowtop mattress beneath me.

He lies back down, and we continue to stare at the ceiling, catching our breath, and as the high of what we did dissipates, I'm hit with the swirling dread of many, much less enjoyable emotions. I try to work them out, untangling the frayed, knotted edges of each sentiment, much like my therapist had instructed over and over again.

The thicker, longer thread is more like a rope. It's the largest, most foreboding of the emotions warring inside me. I slide that one out from the rest, imaging it as if it were an actual rope. This one has a heaviness to it, making my chest clench, my stomach twist, and pins and needles stab at my limbs. I recognise it as anxiety, fear, and dread.

The next is a thin little thing, clear like fishing line, difficult to dismantle from the rest. It's transparent, ever-present despite my efforts, but it snaps easily after years of practice. This one is easy to identify guilt. I'm remorseful for getting involved with someone who I shouldn't have. Someone my dad cares for. Someone I have no place being involved with because it's selfish. Many things could go wrong. He could lose his position as our coach, the same way Coach Lyon had, and as much as Rafael seemed to hate the job at the start, there's been a clear shift. He's now the first person to cheer us on, unable to stand still on the sidelines as he screams at the top of his lungs during every game and practice, fighting with the refs when he thinks they've made a bad call.

Dad might be upset, maybe even blame himself if I get hurt because he was the one who pushed Rafael into the position. My teammates could be let down if they don't have a coach and the season is a wash. My career could be over before it even started if I'm caught in a scandal with my coach. And who knows what would happen to Rafael's career after something like that.

I take a deep, steadying breath, filling my lungs to their maximum capacity before releasing it as a slow, steady stream. The action calms me enough to work through the "what ifs." Rafael and I are adults, and what we *both* engaged in was completely consensual. I do not bear the weight of every decision for every person potentially involved in this scenario. People sleep around in sports all the time, and while it might be broadcast on the news for a week, everyone eventually moves onto the next big thing. And even though I'd thrown a fit about having a babysitter in the beginning, I realise that's not the case at all. I was looking for problems where there weren't any because I was afraid of change. I recognise that now and can appreciate how much my dad has done to make my dreams a reality.

That clear strand always takes the brunt of the weight off once I've managed to work through it, the ache in my chest nearly gone, with mere remnants of smaller, more manageable emotions left behind.

"Elise," Rafa murmurs.

"Mhmm?" I ask, unable to speak as a lump forms in my throat and begins slowly drifting to settle in the pit of my stomach. He's about to tell me to go back to my room, where I'll be alone and reminded of the fact that as much as I know this can't happen again, *I really want it to.*

"I don't—" he starts, clearing his throat. "I don't think I can pretend that never happened."

My throat constricts, and I remain silent, waiting for him to fill it with his rejection or to tell me it was a mistake. That *I* was a mistake.

"So I think we need clear boundaries for how we go about this," he says.

My mind is reeling, unable to dissect what he's saying, so I turn over on my side, assessing him. His expression is hopeful as he turns his head to meet my gaze, tilting his chin.

"You mean, you want to keep seeing each other?" I ask, and my ears burn with how needy that sounded.

"If you—" he averts his eyes, "if you want to."

The breath gets lodged in my lungs, and I'm unable to answer with words, so I just nod, awkwardly, feeling completely pathetic.

What is going on between us?

As of a few weeks ago, we could barely stand to be around each other, and now I feel so drawn to him I'm willing to lie to my friends to have time with him. *It's just the sex, Elise. He's got a great dick.* It's not often that I lie, not to friends and certainly not to myself, but I recognise that thought for what it is.

Maybe it's the fact that his grumpy, shit-ass attitude matches mine, or maybe it's that he has something so broken within him that my mind and soul recognise. I'm not sure yet, but I have a feeling I'm on my way to find out.

When I still haven't managed to answer, he squeezes my hand, his dark eyes boring into me as if digging into my mind to search through the files in my brain, searching for an answer.

I swallow audibly, nodding slowly. "Yeah, I want to."

He cups the nape of his neck, then scratches uncomfortably.

"Okay, good, well, what boundaries are important to you?" he asks.

"We can't tell anyone," I immediately blurt out without any thought as to how that might make him feel. Though I'm sure he's probably relieved, and the moment he breathes out a loud sigh and drops his hand on the bed, rolling onto his back again, I know I was right.

"Agreed. This is only sex, companionship without all the extra, time-consuming shit like dates," he huffs out.

My mind starts to settle a bit. *Good,* we're on the same page then.

"Sounds perfect," I say. "If this starts becoming inconvenient for either of us, we stop," I add.

"Okay. And we need code names or something."

My lips twitch, brows raising. "Code names?" I ask, my tone teasing. "Are we Spy Kids or something?"

"The things I'm planning to do to you are far from child-friendly, though parental advisory may be advised," he says with a deep chuckle that vibrates through my core.

I smack his bicep, rolling onto my back, in desperate need of a reprieve from his handsome face. He's too distracting to look at. "What are these code names for?"

"You live with your best friends—they're a bunch of nosy, oestrogen-driven women. We can't have them finding out because I text you to meet up and your phone is in the wrong place at the wrong time."

"No wonder you're single. Who the fuck wants to be with a testosterone warrior who thinks women are all looking for gossip? Jesus Christ," I grumble.

"Then it's a good thing all you want is my dick," he says, and thankfully, he's right. Some of the strange, awkward haze from earlier has lifted, and I think I'm realising I'm just bloody exhausted.

"Yep, good thing. So, nicknames."

"I'll save you as 'sunshine' since your personality is *so* sunny," he says, clearly joking. I've never been called "sunshine" or anything similar in my life.

"Great, and I'll name you 'Sunny D.' Because your dick is the only thing about you that makes me feel so *sunny*." I smirk.

He barks out a laugh, and I'm flooded with a pleasurable feeling whispering through me.

"I probably deserved that," he says. "Any other boundaries?"

"You can send me dick pics all you want, but they better not be from weird ass angles. And speaking of weird asses, don't send me pictures of your asshole either."

"What the fuck is wrong with you?" he asks, but he's watching me with a sort of disturbed smile that I kind of enjoy. "Christ. Well, the same doesn't go for me."

I raise a brow in question. "You don't want pictures for when I'm not around? Nothing for your spank bank?"

He rolls his eyes. "No, I meant you can feel free to send me pictures of your ass. Pussy and tits would be great too. Lips wrapped around a vibrator would also be stellar."

Now it's my turn to roll my eyes. "I'll keep that in mind," I say, chuckling.

We exchange phone numbers, saving our contacts under the designated code names, and when we realise the time, I'm about to head back to my room, but Rafael wraps his arms around my waist, tugging me against his chest. He reaches across me, flicking off the lamp, and tosses the duvet over us.

I suck in a breath, ready to flee as my chest starts to constrict, but when he whispers into my ear and says, "We said companionship too, Elise. Don't make it weird," I settle down, dragged into the most restful three hours of sleep I've ever gotten outside of a hospital.

CHAPTER THIRTY-SIX

THURSDAY, MAY 8

I'VE SEEN Elise this week at practices and games. I've seen a whole lot of her, actually, but not in the way I *prefer*.

Now that I've had her? She's all my dick seems to want. No matter how hard I try, my hand just isn't doing anything to calm the raging, horny beast within me.

It's unnerving, and I feel like a fucking teenager all over again, not a grown-ass thirty-two-year-old man.

We haven't had any time this week to get together, and it's driving me wild.

Neither of us has practice today, and I had a game earlier, so I'm free the rest of the night. With any luck, she'll want to come over.

I take out my phone, ready to snap a dick pic, but remember she said no weird angles. *What the fuck does that even mean?*

I think my dick and I will have to take our chances. I grip the base and smirk as I snap a couple of pictures, attaching all of them to our unused message thread.

> Jokes on you, sunshine. My dick looks good from every angle.

SUNSHINE

While your D does look rather sunny, I can't
say it's enough to lose my pants over.

I scoff, rolling my eyes at my phone.

Why don't you come over here and I can fix
that?

SUNSHINE

We're debating whether your dick is picture-
esque, not whether it's quality in the sack.

We wouldn't be having this conversation if you
weren't.

Jesus Christ woman, could you get over here
and put me out of my misery?

SUNSHINE

Ask nicely.

A groan slips past my lips, and I shake my head, blowing out a
breath.

Will you please come over and put me out of
my misery?

SUNSHINE

Not nice enough. Try again.

Will you please come over so I don't get any
more calluses?

SUNSHINE

Please explain how that was nicer than the
last message? You get one more try or I'm
fulfilling my needs elsewhere.

My nostrils flare involuntarily as images flash through my
mind of Elise with another man. *Absolutely-fucking-not.*

Sunshine, will you please come over to my place so I can please that gorgeous pussy of yours, and bow at your feet? It would be my honour.

SUNSHINE

Apology and pleading accepted. I'll be over soon. Send me your address.

And here's a little something as a reward for being such a good boy.

A photo comes through, the little circle spinning to tell me it's loading, and I'm becoming more and more antsy as the seconds tick by.

When the photo loads, my cock throbs and I have to pinch my eyes shut, unsure of how I'll ever recover knowing I now have a photo of Elise's dripping cunt beneath the skirt of her faux leather mini dress on my phone. I may form a porn addiction to this single photo, and I've never been so elated to be someone's *good boy.*

Thirty minutes later, Elise appears on my doorstep in said mini dress. Her blue eyes look stormy, and her dark hair is piled high on her head, with tendrils framing her creamy, heart-shaped face beautifully.

"Hey, there," she says, her lips curving in a playful smirk. "You planning to continue drooling in the doorway, or are you going to invite me in?"

I open the door wide for her to slip in. "Brat," I grunt out, not bothering to correct her because I'm nearly certain I *was* drooling.

She steps inside, shrugging off her black peacoat, giving me the most perfect view of that tiny dress in all its glory. *Dress* is a bit of a stretch. It's basically a mere scrap of fabric.

"I won't deny that," she says, taking off her combat boots and lining them up at the door. She makes her way into the kitchen, opening up the black cabinets one by one. I lean against the counter, watching her as she shamelessly searches for something. What, I'm not sure.

When she makes it to the mugs, she pulls one out and opens my fridge, filling it with the water pitcher inside before guzzling half the glass down. She then grabs the electric kettle beside the stove, filling it from the tap and turning it on.

"Someone's thirsty," I remark, a teasing tone in my voice. There's a strange sense of satisfaction tangling in my chest as I watch her rummage through my cupboards, making herself at home.

She peers over her shoulder at me, smirking and tossing me a wink before pulling down a box of lavender Earl Grey, closing the door, and setting her mug on the counter. She twists to face me, hopping up on the cool marble countertop, and crooks a finger at me.

I willingly oblige, stepping between her legs, and the heat between them warms my abdomen. Her hands slide up my chest, digging into my shoulders and wrapping around my neck, pulling my face into her. I nuzzle her neck, anchoring my hands on either side of her hips.

It feels like it's the most natural thing in the world to be with her like this. Kissing her neck, allowing the unfamiliar calmness she brings to wrap around me like a soft blanket. If I'm not careful, I may start to like this a bit too much. Hell, I already have.

Elise's fingers curl into my hair, playing with the ends, then rubbing soft circles in my scalp with her nails. I release a sigh, and just as I do, she jumps.

"Ah!" she shrieks, her wide eyes meeting mine before flickering back beside her.

She clutches a hand to her chest, letting out a relieved sigh, her breasts heaving beneath the tight squared top of her dress. "She scared the crap out of me," she says, shaking her head. The side of her lips turn in a lopsided grin that shows off her dimpled cheek. "I didn't peg you as a cat guy," she says, sinking her fingers into Mrs. Purrito's silky grey-and-white fur.

"I didn't exactly get a say in the matter." I try to sound annoyed by it, but in reality, Carlos's demands for me to adopt this damn cat were a small blessing. I'll never admit that, but I think I needed her more than she needed me, and he knew it.

Elise doesn't ask for anything further, and it's something I appreciate about her. "I like her. She's sweet. I'd have thought you'd be more of a Doberman kind of guy, but this sweet angel sort of suits you. Like the yang to your yin," she muses.

It's a frustratingly accurate assessment. One that makes me feel bare to her, and not in a way I'm comfortable with.

I clear my throat. "I'll tell you her name, but only if you promise not to laugh," I say, pinning her with my gaze. *God, I hope she laughs.* Her laughter dances into the darkest parts of my heart, somehow managing to restart the mechanics of it with the sound alone.

"That bad, huh?" she asks, tilting her head.

"Mrs. Purrito," I say, my voice as deadpan as possible under the circumstances.

Her wide eyes meet mine, a completely blank face taking over her expression. She blinks twice, slowly. *And then it happens.* That loud laughter billows out of her, catching her by surprise as her shoulders shake, and her eyes well with unshed tears. My cheeks burn from the involuntary smile I've been wearing since she arrived, and right now is no different.

God, she's beautiful when she laughs. Hell, she's *always* so beautiful, it makes my chest ache.

"Well, aren't you full of surprises?" she muses when the laughter has stopped and she's managed to catch her breath.

I wrap my arms around her waist and toss her over my shoulder. She releases a surprised yelp but doesn't even miss a beat, smacking my ass as I carry her into my room, ignoring the high-pitched wail of the tea kettle.

ELISE
CHAPTER THIRTY-SEVEN
THURSDAY, MAY 8

I UNLOCK THE DOOR, turning the knob slowly, pushing it open as quietly as possible. Once it's locked behind me, I hang my coat and toe off my boots, pulling my phone out to text Rafael that I got here safely, like he demanded when I left.

I'd told him I couldn't stay because I had an early run planned with Chelsea and they'd know something was up if I didn't go home now. But that wasn't even remotely true. The real reason I had to get out of there was because things were feeling entirely too... *real*.

I've never been in a relationship and have had no real desire to do so. Which means I'm not certain that this feeling even accurately resembles what it would be like to want that for myself, but just the knowledge that it *could* be, scared me straight back to my place. I had to get out of there and let myself breathe without Rafael's overwhelming presence weaselling further into my being. It makes me worry that the newness of our situation is nothing more than a mass dopamine rush that I can't quit chasing.

I shove the worry away and pull up our message thread, blushing when I remember how our last text exchange had gone.

Just got home. Thanks for a fun night.

> SUNNY D
>
> Anytime sunshine, thanks for coming.

My cheeks heat again, and a fluttering sensation erupts in my chest, that is, until his next message comes through.

> SUNNY D
>
> Literally ;)

> Goodnight.

> SUNNY D
>
> Night, trouble.

I click the side button, turning the screen off before heading to the staircase. The lights flick on, and a shrill shriek leaves not just my lungs, but Chelsea's too.

"Chelsea," Adhira says, pinning her with a glare, "are you bloody serious? You were the one who turned the lights on in the first place!"

"I know, but her screaming scared me!" she yells back at her.

I'm still clutching my chest, sucking in deep breaths as I recover from the ambush.

"What the hell was that for?" I grit out, and three sets of eyes land on me.

"Don't play dumb, little girl," Chelsea chides with her hands on her hips.

"Chels, would you stop? That's weird," Letty complains, shaking her head. "We want to know where you went tonight and why you're sneaking in like a burglar."

I roll my eyes, ignoring the way my gut twists at the lie I'm about to tell. "It's nothing. I was just with a guy."

"Well, no shit," Adhira says, waving a hand from my head to my toes, as if my mere existence is answer enough. "But it's clearly a new guy, and someone you don't want us to know about if you didn't make him come over here. You're usually too lazy to go anywhere, even for dick." *She's got a point.* An unfortunate one that doesn't make my life any easier, but a point nonetheless.

"I don't want him here because his place is nicer, and things feel—" I hesitate, trying to work out the right word for myself. "Different?" The fact that feels like the truth only sends dread dipping lower in my belly, but I mask my expression and work to not give anything else away.

"I don't buy it, but whatever. I'm tired, and as long as you're being safe, I'm heading back to bed," Adhira says, all but excusing herself as she trails up the stairs, wrapped in her mint-green fluffy robe, her dark-chestnut waves a wild, frizzy mess behind her.

Letty and Chelsea don't let up so easily though. Where Adhira generally comes across uncaring and sometimes even cold, her last boyfriend referring to her as "a frigid bitch," to which she never even batted an eye, it's not true underneath the facade she wears so well. She's kind, caring, compassionate—all the things you want in a healthcare provider. She's just not *warm.* Though, neither am I—which may be why we get along so well. Adhira is a no bullshit kind of person, and as a general rule, likes to stay out of others' business unless it directly impacts her.

The same cannot be said for Chelsea and Letty, who are still standing in front of the steps, blocking my exit as their eyes bore holes into my skull.

Letty crosses her arms over her chest again, and I let out a defeated groan, nearly sagging to the ground. "Could you stop doing that?" I plead. "You know I can't say no to those tits."

She rolls her eyes, but her brow quirks and she bites her lip, an idea rolling through her mind, and I'm sure I won't like it, judging by the excitement twinkling in her big brown eyes.

"Tell us where you were, *honestly,*" she emphasises. "And I'll let you motorboat these *tetas,*" she says, her smirk twisting into a wide grin.

Damn her.

"As much as I'd love nothing more than for you to finally give in and decide that pussy is just as great as dick (it is, by the way)," I remind her, "I'm not falling victim to a one-and-done situation. I'm liable to fall in love based on this one interaction, and then I'll never be okay," I tell her, sighing dramatically. "I'll be destined to live out the rest of my days, wishing my best friend would be my perpetual butt buddy so I could give up all the complications that come with *men.*"

She scoffs. "You're fucking ridiculous. Come on, spill," she commands, as if by telling me what to do, I'll actually listen. The only person that works with is Rafael, and the thought alone has alarm bells ringing.

"Bossing me around will get you nowhere," I say, watching as Chelsea's eyes bounce between us like a ping-pong ball.

"It was worth a shot. I've heard how you like to be spoken to in the bedroom. I figured I could at least give it a go," she says, chuckling.

"Mhmm, and the *bedroom* is the only place I like to be bossed around. Now, will you *please* get the hell out of my way so I can get to bed?"

"Come *on*," Chelsea whines, likely because she knows I hate the sound.

If I were to cave, it would be from that before anything else. *God, I hate that sound.*

"Chels, I love you, but no. All I'll say is things feel a little too real with this guy, and until I figure out what that means, I'm not willing to have him here. Besides, until I know for sure I'm safe with this man"—*I've never felt safer*—"I'm not risking him knowing where I live. Where *we* live."

She lets out a long sigh, hanging her head. "Fine, off to bed we go," she says, trudging up the stairs ahead of me and Letty.

Brats, they're all fucking brats.

ELISE

CHAPTER THIRTY-EIGHT

SATURDAY, MAY 10

RAFAEL'S GAZE snags on mine as I make my way across the field, heading toward the locker rooms to change now that we've won another game of the season.

He holds his phone up, indicating that I should check mine, and when I get back to my locker, my core floods with heat.

This man makes me want to scream.

> **SUNNY D**
>
> Do you know what good girls who win their games get?
>
> My sunny disposition, that's what.
>
> Now change quickly because I'm five seconds from accidentally showing everyone on this field exactly what it is you do to me. I need your pussy like I need water, and something tells me you're dripping and ready to quench my thirst.

> Big talk for a man named after a children's beverage.

SUNNY D

Sunshine, shut the fuck up and get dressed
so I can tear your clothes off myself. For the
love of fuck.

I smirk—an unexplainable wave of joy slips over me from driving him up a wall. I love it when he's about to lose his mind.

"What are you smirking at over there?" Adhira asks, a dark brow raised as she tugs her shirt over her head.

I shove my phone back in my locker and grab a change of clothes. "You don't want to know," is all I say, not wanting to lie any more than I already am. And that isn't a lie. She really would *not* want to know that I'm doing something so reckless.

And because it's Adhira, she lets it go, rolling her eyes and shrugging. "If you say so. I take it you won't need a ride back to the house?"

I shake my head and hope like hell she thinks I'm shagging with a fan.

As usual, I don't do as I'm told. Instead, I take an unnecessarily long shower, and when I leave the locker room, the parking lot has practically cleared out, and Rafael is leaning up against the side of the sports building, scowling.

"Elise," he barks out.

I smile broadly, jogging over to him. "Yes, Coach?" I ask, happy to goad him, but before I reach him, fingers are wrapping around my wrist, tugging me backward.

My wide eyes meet Noah's as I'm tugged into his side, his teeth grinding together, bared like a wild animal. "Get your hands off of me," I grit out, my gaze flitting to where Rafael is now stomping up to us.

"You have exactly three seconds to remove your hand from her before I *make you*," Rafael practically growls at Noah, who releases my hand and backs away.

"We need to chat," Noah demands. I rub my wrist, an ache present where his fingers were, but I feel nothing toward Noah but resentment and boredom.

"We don't have anything to talk about, Noah. You're embarrassing yourself. We agreed to a casual fling, but that's over now, and I've grown bored. Leave me alone, and find someone else to pull." I turn on my heel, the angry blood roaring behind my eardrums blocking out whatever he's shouting behind me.

I leave Noah to follow after Rafael, who leans against the side of his shiny black sports car.

He lowers his voice and peers down at me, his arms crossed over his chest as he says, "You okay?"

"Yep," I answer, and I am. I'm tired of Noah's games. I've never told him a single genuine thing about me, so I know he isn't interested in *me*. He just hates losing—that's been made evident in the two times I've seen him show his ass during swim meets. To be clear, I've never shown up, but the sports world is a tight-knit community and everyone stays informed. That should act as a reminder that what I'm about to do with Rafael would be a horrendous idea, but I've never been the best at following rules.

"Good. Get your ass to my apartment. You're about to learn a lesson about defiance." Without another word, he stalks off in the direction of his car.

God, I love it when he's annoyed.

I barely have the door shut from the rideshare I took here before Rafael is storming over to me, abducting me. He's got me slung over his shoulder in zero point two seconds flat, dangling here with a perfect view of his perky ass in my face.

"Hey, Terminator," I goad him, smacking his ass of steel as he marches us into his building and straight into the elevator. "You'll be lucky if that guy doesn't call the police after the way you manhandled me," I tell him, all the blood now pooling in my skull beginning to pound.

"They won't be able to find us even if he did," he tells me, sounding much less grumpy now than before.

"I'm pretty sure the concierge knows where you live, Rafa. Now will you put me down? I'm getting a fucking headache."

"Sure, if we were going back to my apartment, but we're not," he says as the elevator pings and the doors slide open.

He waltzes out, and I'm dead weight in his arms, resigned to the fact this may be it for me. I may have pushed this hulk of a man a tad too far. *Maybe he's taking me to the pool to drown me.*

"I'm not going to drown you," he says as if I'm an idiot.

Had I said that out loud? I forget myself too often with him.

He pushes open a stairwell door and climbs up the eight short steps, my body bouncing limply against his back.

A cool gust of air chills me as he flips me over his shoulder, setting me back on the ground.

The door behind us shuts loudly, and I swing my gaze around, my eyes bouncing between the wide-open night sky, the stars twinkling overhead, patio furniture beneath strings of café lights, large potted plants, and finally, the thing that might have me retching the impossibly low wall that surrounds us. My legs sway beneath me, the blood flowing from my brain, draining into my poor, helpless heart.

He grips my hips, steadying me for a moment, and when my legs stabilise, he releases me, taking a few steps back.

We're on the roof.

Apprehension floods my system, all other senses dulled to fear. This is *not* some fairytale where the prince shows the princess a good time, bringing her out to look far into the galaxy, waxing poetic about stars, suns, moons, and all that other sappy shit that makes me want to vomit.

No, this is the tale of a horny cow and the even hornier tosser fucking on a roof while the cow sobs because she, the poor bitch, is *terrified of heights.*

Rafael invades my space again. His eyes are narrowed as he reaches for me, gripping my face in his palms.

"I said you're learning a lesson tonight, Elise, and the lesson has just begun," he tells me with finality in his tone.

I nod my agreement, my frisky cunt getting the better of me.

"Strip for me," he demands, and I do, my body at war with

my brain as my pussy spasms at the command while my mind tells me to high-tail down those stairs and back to safety.

My hands shake slightly as I tug my shirt over my head, dropping my shorts, thong and bra one after the other, toeing out of my trainers. I refuse to take my socks off because, well, bird shit.

"Are we going to get arrested?" I've already been there, done that. Not one of my finer moments, unfortunately, but what's done is done, and I'd rather not have a repeat of the situation. My father would die of embarrassment, his anger holding his soul hostage long enough for his ghost to haunt me. And then I'd *never* get laid again. *Sigh.*

He rolls his eyes before spinning me around, one hand snaking to cup my dripping heat and the other curling over my chest. He sinks his teeth into my neck, tugging on the flesh, and I all but melt against him as goosebumps erupt all over. My flesh is chilled from the breeze.

"Just shut the hell up, Elise," he groans, slowly pushing us closer and closer to the edge of the building.

My spine goes rigid, and my chest tightens. My nails dig into his arms the closer we get, my heels digging into the brick. I close my eyes, turning my head away, and he continues walking us forward. "Rafael, I can't," I whimper, my eyes burning with tears.

He stills, pulling me tighter into his chest. "Tell me to stop and this ends, but I *really* don't want it to," he whispers into my ear, my tense muscles beginning to relax. "Do you trust me?" he asks, and I nod, biting on my lip. "I need you to say it, Elise. I need you to trust me because what we're about to do requires that."

"Y-yes," I say, my chin wobbling. "I trust you."

"Good," he grunts out, his hand leaving my chest to press along my spine in the space between my shoulder blades. He pushes me forward, and my eyes fly open, my hands scrambling in front of me, landing on the thick stone ledge.

Skyscrapers line the night sky, none close enough for anyone to see what we're doing, but that is the least of my worries.

My *fear* is toppling off the side of this godforsaken building all because I sent a snarky text message to a man with a big dick.

That would be unbelievably on brand for me, and I can't wait to make it out alive from this so I can start to reevaluate my life choices. This branding seems outdated at best.

It's Rafael's finger running along my seam that brings me back to reality, a reality in which my tits are as high in the sky as the bloody pigeons, and frankly, it's not a reality I'd like to be living in.

He snakes a hand around my throat, gripping it tightly, and I feel the tip of his cock run through my seam.

"C-condom?" I ask.

"Already have one on," he assures me. "Now, are you ready for your lesson?"

"Not really," I whine.

"Elise," he groans.

"Fine, yes, I'm ready," I snark.

He chuckles darkly behind me and then, *he snaps.*

This is no longer the man who was leaving his own fantasy to check in on my reality just moments ago. No, *this* is a feral beast, and if I *do* die out here? Well, at least you can't say I didn't go satiated.

His hips thrust forward, plunging his thick length into me, my knees buckling. His grip on my throat tightens as he pounds into me, clearly for his pleasure and not mine, though my pussy hasn't gotten the memo, and I'm already spasming around him.

"You don't ever fucking listen," he seethes through gritted teeth, tightening his hold even further, my breath stuck somewhere behind his fingertips.

Heat sears through my spine, and my throat burns.

"You think everything's a goddamn game," he says. "And I'm *tired* of it, Elise. I'm tired of you waltzing around—"

His hips smack against my ass, and his chest presses into my back as he leans us further over the ledge. *Oh god, no, no, no!* My spine turns rigid.

"Acting like nothing fucking bothers you," he grits out. "But it does, doesn't it? You're so caught up in that gorgeous head of yours, the only joy you manage to get is when you're driving me up a fucking wall. Isn't that right?" he asks, and I don't have the good sense to disagree.

Blame it on the lack of oxygen to my brain right now, but as my knees start to wobble, I bloody *nod* my agreement.

Who does that?!

He lets out a disbelieving huff of air. "You like it, huh?" he asks, bringing his lips right above my ear. He readjusts his grip on my throat, sliding his middle and ring finger into my mouth, pulling down on my jaw, and sharp pain ripples through me. I yelp, but the sound gets caught in my throat.

The pain subsides, but he twists my nipple, then plucks at it like the string of a guitar before finally setting that hand on my hip and releasing his hold on my jaw entirely.

I let out a breath of relief, which was *clearly* the wrong thing to do, because now his hips are pistoning into me as he smacks the side of my ass relentlessly. Shockwaves of pain ripple through me, and my traitorous clit pulses needlessly, begging for more. "Oh, god," I moan, falling even further forward. My eyes bug out of my head as I take in the cars, nearly fifty storeys beneath us, crawling along the streets like tiny ants on the ground. *I might faint.*

"You're such fucking trouble, Elise. Do you know that?" he asks, but for once, I have the sense not to answer his *clearly* rhetorical question. "Ever since I met you, you've got me doing and thinking things I shouldn't be." He tsks, his hot breath panting over the shell of my ear.

I arch into him, unable to stop my body's unfortunate reaction to this. *I'm naked and very fucking afraid,* and yet, here I am, seconds from an orgasm. I guess it's not the worst outcome.

"For once, you're going to listen to me, Elise. You're going to come around my cock," he demands. "I want you strangling my dick and begging for more by the end," he says, his body going rigid as mine follows suit, my nipples peaked and screaming as I near my release. "And if you ever defy me again, this ledge won't be here to save you," he whispers, his voice maddeningly low as my brain crawls to catch up to his threat. My body is already on the way, though, knowing exactly what those words do to me.

"Ohh," I moan, my fingers white-knuckling the stone as he pumps and rocks against me, his movements more erratic as they slow. He all but collapses against my back, and my knees officially give out beneath me. I fall forward, my tits pressing against the concrete ledge, scraping the delicate buds, and as fear strangles me, my eyes grow even wider at what's beneath me.

I wait until his body has become lax, spinning around in his grip. I smack his shoulder as hard as I can muster, a newfound energy swelling inside me. "Are you fucking kidding me?!" I yell, my voice shrill.

He chuckles deeply, pulling me against his chest as he steps us away from the edge. "Did you really think I'd put your life in danger?" he asks, his brow quirked.

The real answer is *no*, no I did not. Which is precisely why I let that happen in the first place. "That doesn't matter! You let me go on thinking that whole time that I was this close," I say, holding my thumb and forefinger up, a centimetre apart, "to falling off the side of this damn building!"

"Well, *clearly*, that wouldn't have happened," he says, rolling his eyes playfully. It's adorable, and I hate it. *Okay, fine, I don't hate it, but I absolutely do hate that I don't hate it.* Christ, even my internal monologue doesn't make any damn sense. I wish I would've known there was less than a foot drop off with another three-foot ledge just beneath me. I definitely wouldn't have been crawling over the side to test its limitations or anything, but maybe my heart wouldn't have been in my throat the whole time.

"Just be glad you came because that won't be happening again for a long time, jackass. You're on probation," I tell him, crossing my arms over my chest, but I think better of it, grabbing my shorts and top to cover myself. I don't bother with the bra and thong. I doubt I'll be able to hold out once he gets me back inside. *What?* At least I know my faults.

"Yeah, yeah, yeah. You liked it," he says, rolling his eyes again, but a hint of a smile presses onto his lips, and I feel my heart constrict. "Now come here," he says, grabbing a blanket from a stack inside a cabinet by the lounge set. He unfolds it, opening it up wide for me to step into. It's impossible to stay mad at him when he's this damn sweet with me.

I let him wrap me up in the blanket, and when I'm thoroughly rolled like a snug burrito, he lifts me up and carries me over to a lounge chair where he takes a seat and holds me against his chest.

It's... It's sort of nice. In a way I never would have expected given my general lack of desire for intimacy of any kind outside of sex.

RAFAEL

CHAPTER THIRTY-NINE

SATURDAY, MAY 10

AS I HOLD ELISE, the stars twinkle overhead, her breathing slows, and she melts into me. My chest tightens, and I fight the desire to nuzzle my face into her hair, but eventually, the feeling becomes overwhelming, and I give in.

I suck in a breath, her silky strands tickling my nose as my lungs fill with the scent of her own sweet, warm accord. "Stop sniffing me," she grumbles. "It's creepy." Her voice is laced with exhaustion. A yawn slips free, and she drags a hand up, the blanket still covering it as she covers her mouth and sinks even further against my chest.

I laugh, pinching her upper arm, and press a kiss to the top of her head. "Brat," I whisper, and she rewards me with a closed-mouth grin that makes my stomach twist. I've *never* kissed someone's head like that. And suddenly I'm doing it with Elise, and she *likes* it?

You deserve to be happy. Carlos's words ring through my mind, echoing until my heart has settled, and my fingers trail over her cheekbone. She peers at me dreamily, clearly lost in thought.

A few silent moments pass before it all comes down around us. "Why were you so upset that day? After the fundraiser," she asks, clarifying which day, as if I didn't already know.

I could lie or brush it off, but I have no desire to. What happened to my brother is a fact of life, and as wholly complicated as it's become to be with Elise, I *like* being with her. I've had many times in my life where I've had to learn that when you want to say something to someone, you should just do it. Because sometimes, you never get that chance before it's too late.

So instead of following my first instinct, to run from the thing causing me discomfort, I say, "Do you know why we have that fundraiser every year?" I'm asking not because I want to run her in circles, but because I *don't* want to. I don't want to explain something she already knows to some degree.

She shakes her head. "No, not really. I know you've always done it, at least as long as my dad's been the coach, but I have no idea why other than it being a good cause."

I nod, letting out a slow breath to calm my racing heart.

"Do you want the long answer or the short?"

She peers up at me, those stormy blue eyes swirling beneath thick lashes. "I want as much as you're willing to share."

I nod. "My brother, Carlos, is a year older than me. Our plan was always to apply for the same schools, and wherever we got in, we both would go."

I let that new information hang in the silence between us as I work through my thoughts, stringing sentences together that I hope make sense.

"He took a year off after graduating high school and worked with our dad. He's a car mechanic." She nods, urging me to continue. "We both got in here, to your university, actually. We each had a full football scholarship."

She tilts her head, her brows pinching as she works through this. She says nothing despite the questions piling up in her head. Through all the chaos and her unrelenting sass, *I see her.* I see Elise Auclair for who she truly is, and buried beneath the rubble of a difficult past and emotionally taxing mental illness is someone just fighting to get to the next thing each day. *She's resilient.* And through seeing *her*, I'm able to see myself reflected a little more clearly too. That's what drives me to open up to her.

She doesn't rush me or push me further, and I appreciate that because I'm about to recount the worst day of my life, a day I haven't spoken about in years, and I can't be sure how it'll impact either of us.

"I wasn't a great kid, honestly. I made a lot of mistakes, but Carlos made sure to help me clean each one of them up. I was sort of a daredevil, always looking for the next adrenaline rush. So naturally, the night before we were supposed to fly here to make our dreams a reality, I convinced Carlos to do something reckless," I tell her, my stomach twisting in knots as bile rises in my throat.

She wiggles her hands out from under the blanket and brings them up, resting them on my cheeks, rubbing the pads of her thumbs over my cheekbones.

"Carlos begged me not to do it. He *hated* all of the dumb shit I'd do for a rush. But it was our last hurrah, and I promised him it would be the very last dumb thing I did if he went with me. So he did. He wanted to get it over with, so when he jumped—" My words get stuck as I involuntarily grit my teeth, my jaw aching.

Elise lowers her hands to my chest, waiting patiently for me to finish.

"His bungee cord snapped," I finish, and I'm hit with another wave of nausea as overwhelming guilt sears through me and wraps around my throat like a noose, my words the bucket being kicked out from under me.

Her eyes well with tears, but she blinks them away, pulling herself closer to me, resting her forehead against mine. I allow her warmth to seep into me, filling in the cracks of my long-forgotten soul.

She doesn't try to tell me it wasn't my fault. She doesn't look at me with pity. She just lets us lie here like this, cloaked in a heavy silence as we both work to comprehend what'd happened.

I clear my throat. "He's mostly paralyzed from the waist down and lives next door to our parents in case he needs help late at night. And the only reason I'm here instead of rotting away somewhere is because of him. He wouldn't let me sit around feeling sorry for myself. He didn't want me to stay home when I could be here, living the dream we both had planned. He's good like that," I tell her, pride swelling in my chest as I think about the incredible man my brother's become despite every challenge he's faced. The man is the CEO of a major tech company, choosing to live a humble life because it's what he prefers and not what he's been forced into.

She speaks for the first time in what feels like hours. "How'd you wind up playing rugby then?"

A smile turns the edges of my lips as I think about that day. The day that changed everything for me. *The day that saved my life.*

"I was miserable playing football. The sport I'd loved my whole life had become a constant reminder of everything I'd lost and all the pain I'd caused my family. So in the beginning of that first semester, I was on a run by the public fields and a group of blokes had asked me to join their rugby scrimmage for the morning. They said they needed an extra player because their friend was too hungover to show up. They taught me the basics, and it was a shock to everyone that I was actually *good.*"

I shake my head at the memory of the guys, most of them off playing professionally, spread out across the UK and Europe. "They introduced me to their coach, and he worked out a way for me to play for them and maintain my scholarship."

"Does it hurt you to coach our team? Does it dredge up bad memories?" she asks, her voice small, brows knitted.

I shake my head. "No, Elise. It doesn't. I'd worried it would when your dad first demanded I coach your team. It took some effort, but after I quit acting like a ballbag, most of the sadness fled. It's because of you ladies that I'm relearning how to love the sport I grew up playing."

A small smile lights her face, and it sends a thrill through my whole being.

"It isn't your fault, you know," she says. "It took me a long time to learn that after what happened to *Maman* and my sister, but eventually I did."

I know her mum passed away from cancer, but I don't know any details beyond that. "What would you have to feel guilty about?" I ask, shifting our weight so we can both lie on our sides, facing one another.

"My dad supported us both. He loved us endlessly, but because Rachelle had no desire to play sports, or watch them, for that matter," she adds, a sad smile crossing her full lips, "Dad was always with me. The weekend our lives went to hell was during an away game. *Maman's* breast cancer had spread." Her chin quivers, throat bobbing. "It metastasized to her bones, lungs, liver, lymph nodes, and toward the end, her brain." Elise takes a moment, chewing on her bottom lip before continuing, and my heart aches for her. "Treatments weren't working, and they'd gotten to a point they weren't even slowing things down anymore. She decided that the chemo wasn't worth it anymore if it wasn't going to improve her quality of life or prolong the time she got to spend with us. She was feeling better, not because she *was* better, but because she wasn't pouring toxins into her body to kill something that had already decided to kill *her*."

She takes another pause, her eyes welling with tears that threaten to break me.

"She convinced my dad and I that she'd be fine while we went away for the night. It was just *one* night. She swore she felt better." Her lips pinch, her gaze shifting toward the sky as she tries desperately to hold herself together. "But when we got home, we found her in bed, cold, and with no life left in her." Her chin wobbles, and I want her to stop talking. I want her to stop feeling the pain I can see rushing through her like a tidal wave, the same as when it first happened. "And then we found Rachelle," she whispers, her voice cracking as tears spill down her cheeks. I swipe them away, but they keep coming. "She overdosed. She was alone and terrified, and we weren't there to help her through it," she says, sobs wracking her body.

I tug her to my chest, and she buries her face in my shirt. I stroke my hand over her head, allowing her to get it out, and wishing like hell I could take it all away.

I had no idea.

I'm filled with a newfound respect for her father, one even greater than I'd already had. He's endured one of the worst things a person could ever imagine happening, losing the other half of their heart, and he still manages to smile and tries relentlessly to make those around him smile too. Maybe if I weren't so busy trying to keep everyone at a distance, I could pick up the pieces of myself that used to do the same—make people smile, laugh, and feel emotion outside of disdain, lust, or annoyance.

When time has passed and she's stopped crying, she wipes beneath her eyes and looks up into mine. "You probably can't tell from all the crying I just did," she says, sniffling after letting out a choked laugh, "but I no longer blame myself. I had no way of knowing any of that would happen. None of us did. It was nobody's fault, but it was the cards we were dealt. Sometimes, terrible things happen to good people, and that's all there is to it."

God, this woman is so *strong.* It's no wonder her age has never deterred me. I'd expected to feel weird about being intimate with her like this, but so far, I haven't. She's had to grow up too fast. But I'm grateful she's here with me, safe in my arms.

"Thank you for sharing that with me," I tell her, kissing the top of her head. The same thing I'd done just minutes ago, an action so intimate, but it feels right.

"Thank you for telling me about Carlos," she whispers.

"Will you show me, sometime?" I ask, then clarify. "Can you help me figure out how to deal with the guilt?"

She nods, and I feel the movement against my chest as she squeezes me tightly to her. "I can't say I'm the best at it. I think I've managed to turn a lot of my guilt into the general shitty attitude I know you *love*," she says sarcastically, but the frightening thing is that *I'm not sure she's wrong*. Though "love" probably isn't the right word for it. "But I'm willing to try."

We spend the rest of the night like this, tucked away from the world in one of our own creations.

RAFAEL

CHAPTER FORTY

TUESDAY, MAY 13

ELISE HASN'T CONTACTED me since she left my flat the other night, and I'm afraid we may have crossed over into emotional territory she wasn't comfortable with. That wet blanket that grabbed her wrist the other day seemed awfully taken with her. Could she have given him another chance?

So early on in our arrangement, and we're already breaking rules. Jealousy was most certainly not in the terms of engagement.

A heavy sigh leaves my lungs as I sink into my couch cushions, propping my feet up on the coffee table. Rather than bottle my feelings up, thinking up the worst possible scenarios, I'm going to do the adult thing, the thing Carlos would urge me to.

> You seemed frustrated at practice today.
> Need to work it out?

Alright, I said "adult" but this is halfway there, surely.

> SUNSHINE
>
> Care to explain what the point of code names
> is if you're going to message me things that
> only you would know?

> Just answer the question.

SUNSHINE

I don't have time. This assignment is kicking
my ass.

What class is it for?

A better question would be what her fucking major is. I'm
such a shit for not knowing something so simple about her. I bury
my dick in her, make her relive the shittiest day of her life,
unknowingly exploit her fear of heights, and can't be bothered to
know what she's in uni for? I'm such a twat.

I'm also a soppy git; the fear that she was ignoring me dries
up. From the sounds of it, she's been busy, and I might have to
dwell on that a bit later to work through *why* I care.

SUNSHINE

Sports marketing.

Come over. I can help.

SUNSHINE

I don't think your dick is going to somehow
provide clarity on the topic of marketing
sporting events, but thanks for the offer.

Such a cheeky thing.

No, dumbass. I mean come over and I'll help
you write it. I do have a sports management
degree, you know.

SUNSHINE

Actually, I didn't know, but I need to get this
done and you'll distract me.

Like you are right now.

Besides, this is sex and companionship.

Count this as the companionship part, then.
And I'd rather not explain how the captain of
my team is failing her classes when she's
supposed to be graduating soon.

SUNSHINE

Touché. I'll be over soon. Order food, I'm
starving.

Feeding you wasn't part of the agreement.

SUNSHINE

Neither was supervising me doing homework.
I need brain fuel.

You're a pain in my ass.

SUNSHINE

If you wanna try pegging, all you have to do is
ask. 😊

I'm more of a top. Sorry to disappoint.

SUNSHINE

We'll see about that. 😏

This woman will be the death of me, and I can't be bothered to evade my impending damnation.

I scrub my hand down my face, shaking my head as Mrs. Purrito jumps into my lap, kneading my thighs before lying down. Her purrs come out like a motor engine as I stroke her smooth fur and order food for the last person on the planet I should be craving time and attention from.

ELISE

CHAPTER FORTY-ONE

TUESDAY, MAY 13

"OKAY, so what *exactly* are you struggling with on this assignment?" he asks, tugging on my calves, laying my legs across his lap. He absentmindedly strokes a trail up my shin as he waits for my answer.

"Everything," I groan, fighting the urge to fall back into the cushion dramatically.

He rolls his eyes at me, wearing a grin that sends sparks of pleasure zapping up my spine. *God, I love that playful smile.*

"The essay's about creating a strategic play for engagement and revenue growth for marketing sporting events. It could be about anything from grassroots promotion to large-scale digital campaigns. It just has to be an idea that could really be implemented in the real world, and I have to have some sort of data to back my stance."

He nods his understanding, tugging his full bottom lip between his teeth as he sorts through his thoughts. "Well, what about something like the fundraiser we do each year?"

I shake my head. "That's a fundraiser for a good cause though; it's not for gaining revenue for the team."

He pins me with a disbelieving stare, and he smirks. "Elise, it *is* for a good cause, but we'd be naive to think that the *only* reason the higher ups allow this fundraiser each year is for my benefit. It's definitely *not*. While yes, they are helping people, and I appreciate it more than I could properly express, they're also making a good name for themselves by doing so, and they're driving potential donors to our events where they can check out our team and our amenities and mingle. We make them feel special, and important, leading them to be more likely to want to be a part of it so they then donate to our team and not just the fundraiser we do each year."

My head is spinning. "That's genius!" I shout, never having thought about it that way *at all*.

He squeezes one of my calves. "It was actually your dad's idea to do the fundraiser after I told him about Carlos. He said if management wanted to use money for events to gain traction, we should at least exploit that for good too."

Warmth spreads through my chest at the thought. My dad really is the best.

"Perfect, that's what I'll write about!" I tell him, excited to get this over with. It's by no means my last essay I'll write before graduation, but it's the last one for this class.

"We," he corrects.

"We?"

"Yeah," he says, reaching across me, snagging my laptop from where it rests on my thighs. He places it over top of where my lower legs rest over his meaty thighs. "*We* will write about it."

A blush creeps up my neck before I can control it. "You don't have to help me write it. I can type," I say, chuckling. "I just get stuck on the idea because honestly, I don't want nor need a degree, despite what my dad says. He just doesn't want me to wind up injured and unable to play with no fallback plan. That's why I'm not already playing in the premieres."

He tilts his head to the side. "Why didn't you choose something easier then if you weren't planning on using it?"

I let out a frustrated huff. "Because I thought this *was* an easy A. I figured it wouldn't be hard, and it at least had something to do with sports, but as it turns out, a sports management degree is bloody *brutal*."

A loud laugh erupts from him, and I love the sound. That should worry me, but it doesn't. Something about how easily our conversations flow and the happy feelings he elicits in me sets my mind at ease. He makes me feel calm even when nothing else does, and instead of running away from that like I so often would, I'm giving into it.

You deserve to feel things. It's been a while since I last heard the whispering of my sister in my mind, but today, I welcome it more than usual.

He places my laptop on the armrest, planting his hands on my sides, clutching my waist as he hauls me into his lap. I melt into the warmth radiating off his strong body and wrap my arms around his neck, resisting the urge to press a kiss to his temple. He smells like cedar and oranges, the heady accord enveloping me.

"Did you like school?" I ask, desperate to steer my thoughts to more comfortable territory and out of murky waters.

"I did actually, but I think it was mostly because it was something to keep my mind busy. It gave me a distraction from the mess I'd left at home and from all the guilt I was living with. It gave me direction I knew I needed to get through it."

"And where's home for you?" I ask.

He squeezes me more tightly, his brow smoothing out as he relaxes. "Home is here now, but I grew up in Argentina. We lived in a small town where everyone knew everyone, which was good and bad. As an adult, I think I'd love it, but as a reckless teen, it made not getting caught really difficult," he tells me with a wry grin. "You were born in France, right?"

I nod. "Yeah, but after what happened with my *maman* and Rachelle, Dad and I were desperate for a change. Some people handle grief by wanting to constantly be around the memories and in the space they were most with their loved ones, but instead of making us feel closer to them, it only made everything worse. It was like we were suffocating and unable to truly grieve until we got out. And Dad couldn't sleep in my parents' room anymore, so for months, we were roommates," I tell him, laughing as I recall the memory.

"Wasn't that...weird?" he asks, no judgement in his tone, purely curious.

I shake my head. "We weren't home often, and when we were, it was just to sleep. We used separate bathrooms and stuff, but every night, he'd climb up that ladder, bump his head on the ceiling, grumble to himself, and climb in, shaking the metal frame like an earthquake."

"Why the hell was he on the top bunk?"

I avert my gaze for a moment, gathering my emotions before explaining. "Rachelle slept up there because I was, and still am"—I pin him with a pointed glare—"afraid of heights. And it didn't feel right for me to sleep in her bed. So when he was offered the job to coach rugby here, *your* rugby team, he jumped at the opportunity, and I was thrilled to leave."

"How old were you when you moved then?"

"Seventeen. They passed away when I was sixteen, so we were in that house for eight long months before we were able to move. Neither of us has been back to France since, but I'd like to. I want to visit all the places my *maman* used to go, everywhere she'd take my sister and me. Maybe it'd be healing for me too."

He nods and presses a kiss to the top of my head.

"I appreciate you opening up to me," he says, his face still buried in my hair.

"You make it easy," I tell him, and he meets my eyes, confusion swirling in his, dark brows pinched, his nose scrunched in the cutest way that makes his gold hoop nose ring glimmer under the overhead lights.

"How so?"

"You just...listen. Without pretence. Without judgement. You don't ask tons of questions or pressure me into telling you more than I'm comfortable with. You give me time to say what I mean so I don't wind up saying the wrong thing and dwelling on it later."

He cups my cheek in his large, warm hand and brings his lips to mine for a chaste kiss. They're soft and pillowy as they mould to mine, and my body sags into the feeling on instinct. When he pulls away, it's like he's replied to what I've said but without any words being spoken at all.

"Well, so much for not bombarding you with questions, because I have one now," he teases.

"Mmm, and what's that?" I ask, tilting my head, sighing into his warmth. Rafael is outstandingly dreamy when he isn't trying so hard to keep people out.

"That wanker that grabbed you the other day..." he trails off, refusing to meet my eyes. It's a shame, really, because if he bothered to look at me, he'd see the absolutely massive grin stretching my lips till my cheeks ache.

"Are you *jealous*?" I ask, eyes wide.

"No," he rumbles, voice low. "I'm merely a concerned citizen. I don't appreciate women getting snatched."

"Tell me you're jealous and I'll explain who he is and why you have *nothing* to worry about."

He drags in an exasperated breath, finally meeting my eyes. "Fine. I *was* a tad green."

I can't resist the urge, squeezing his cheeks until his lips pucker like a fish, giddiness spilling into my actions, my body vibrating with the unfamiliar feeling. He places his hands over mine, pulling them from his cheeks to settle in his lap.

"Go on then," he urges.

"That tosser was Noah. He's about the blandest person on the planet, with a less than satisfactory prick, to boot. We've shagged on a few occasions, never without someone else." His brows climb at that, but I continue, leaving no room for more of his prying questions. "He started pressing me about spending time with me outside of our extracurriculars, and I have no interest in doing any of those things with him." The unspoken part being that for some ungodly reason, I *do* have an interest in spending time with Rafael outside of sex—exhibit A would be our current predicament. "He's about as interesting on the inside as he is on the outside, and as you'd seen, he looks no different than the crumbs at the bottom of a box of crackers. Pale and unsustaining."

Rafa's smirk says it all, so instead of adding to my assessment of my past lay, he says, "Let's get this essay over with so we can do better things with our time, yeah?" He sets the laptop over my thighs but with the screen facing him, typing all of my ideas, running through every thought I have for the assignment. His fingers fly across the keyboard, and by the time the sun has set, we've had our fill of salmon, salad, and pasta, and I've submitted the essay.

Rafael shuts my laptop and sets it on the wrought iron side table, lowering himself further into the cushions and shifting my body so we're lying lengthwise on the couch, facing each other.

He tucks a strand of hair behind my ear and trails a rough hand down my side, settling it over my hip where the bottom of my sweatshirt has ridden up.

"Are you ready for your reward?" he asks, his voice quiet and husky. The sound sends a shiver down my spine, and I arch into his touch. His low answering chuckle is the only sound as he slips his fingers beneath the waistband of my leggings. "I take that as a yes?" he asks, his brow quirked, and I nod my agreement.

My lips part, resting my thigh over his as he works his fingers under my cotton thong and over my clit. I feel my pulse beating between my legs, and a whimper falls past my lips.

"You were so good today, baby," he says, and I preen under his praise. "You played so well and then got to work like such a fucking good girl." His words are barely above a whisper, and while I'm someone who doesn't tend to love the tender touches or soft, whispered words, I want all of it with *him*.

The way his dark eyes hold my gaze makes the moment even

more intimate, and when he slips a finger inside me, I'm already soaked.

"I'm *so* proud of you," he says, pressing his forehead to mine as I stay locked in his gaze. "I'm proud of you for accepting help, and I'm glad I could give that to you. But I'm not such a good boy," he whispers, his voice dropping an octave. I want to say something, but I can't manage through the blinding pleasure building in my core.

"H-how?" I stammer.

"Because," he says, lowering his lips to my neck, tugging the skin between his teeth as he slips another finger inside me and I cry out, loudly. The sound of my strangled moans startles even me. When he rests his forehead against mine again, he spreads his fingers wide, just the way he now knows I like, and I nearly shatter. But what really does me in is what he says next. "This whole time I've been helping you, I've been *so* selfish, Elise, baby. I've been waiting for this moment. For us to finish your essay so I could bury my fingers inside you, and the only thing better than that will be when I get to suck you off of them."

I buck against him, his fingers pumping inside me as he presses the flat of his thumb against my clit. A hot fire licks up my spine, and Rafael devours the sounds I make with his lips pressed to mine, his fingers stroking my walls relentlessly until I've spilled every ounce of my pleasure onto his fingers. My body sags further into the cushions, and he slides a hand around my back, tugging me to his chest before he removes his hand from my pussy.

My eyes flutter open, and I watch with rapt attention as he sucks those fingers into his mouth. He moans deeply, his chest rumbling as he cleans his fingers of my juices.

"God, you taste delicious." He groans.

And I die. Right here on his couch. I simply pass away from how annoyingly hot that was. My body burned to ash, or at least, *that's certainly what it feels like.*

RAFAEL

CHAPTER FORTY-TWO

TUESDAY, MAY 13

"AND YOU'RE sure you don't want to spend the night? Or I could drive you home?" I ask, reluctant to let her leave me.

She rewards me with a lopsided grin, her dimple winking at me as she leans in to kiss me, squeezing my bicep. "I'm sure," she says. "But it's not because I don't want to be here. It's because I have an early class in the morning, and frankly, I feel like I'm growing a little too attached to you, too quickly, and I need the space to gather my emotions and not run the risk of falling into something that neither of us is comfortable with. Does that make sense?" she asks, tilting her head to the side.

It does, actually, and something buried inside my chest that warms with her explanation. I hate being in the dark with people. "Yeah, it does. And that's okay," I tell her, pressing my lips to hers another time as I prepare myself to watch her walk out this door. "Thank you for letting me in on your thought process."

She gives me a small smile, her cheeks flushing a light pink. "I've lost too many people wishing I'd had the opportunity to tell them how I felt just one last time. That's why I'm often brutally honest, and unfortunately for those on the other end of it, I don't hold back. Though I'm pretty shit at putting the way I feel into the right words. I do my best, but lately, between my impending graduation, adjusting to having a new coach, trying to solidify my chances at having a football career, and realising I'm attracted to my coach, well, let's just say I've been taking the piss out of the whole open and honest thing."

I clutch her against my chest, her arms wrapping around my waist as she sighs against me. Her phone pings in her pocket, and she checks it, peering back up at me with those baby blues. "My ride's here," she says, grabbing her backpack.

"Goodnight, Elise. And for what it's worth, you're showing me that good things can come out of proper communication, and I'm glad we're on the same page," I tell her.

"It's worth a lot," she says, pressing onto her tiptoes, leaving a quick kiss against my cheek. "Goodnight, Rafa." She tosses a wink over her shoulder as she enters the elevator, the glossy metal doors shutting behind her a moment later, leaving me to stare at my reflection. A goofy grin is plastered on my face, and it's a sight I haven't seen since high school.

My shoulders sag as I let myself back inside, heading to the TV. Mrs. Purrito is curled up in Elise's spot, and I can't even blame her. I'd want to be anywhere she's set that perky ass too.

She texts me shortly after she's arrived home, and my heart pangs in my chest.

SUNSHINE

Thanks for your help tonight.

Anytime.

SUNSHINE

And Rafael?

Now who's diminishing the point of code names?

SUNSHINE

Shut it.

I think I really like you.

My heart swells, and I tuck my shoulders back; pride that we've somehow managed to move past our rocky start whips through me.

> I think I really like you too, trouble.

SUNSHINE

Don't break my heart, okay?

> I don't think you're the one who has to worry, sweetheart. So please, don't break mine.

SUNSHINE

I'll do my best. Goodnight <3

> Goodnight <3

This is unfamiliar territory for me, and for every ounce of fear I feel, I'm met with an equal amount of wonder.

RAFAEL

CHAPTER FORTY-THREE

FRIDAY, MAY 16

SUNSHINE

Open up.

I ANSWER THE DOOR, and my jaw nearly drops to the damn floor.

This woman is going to be the death of me.

Elise is standing in the hallway outside of my apartment with her silky dark strands cascading over her shoulders. Her athletic frame is draped in a short black trench coat, and her mile-long legs are lightly tanned and bare beneath the coat. Those cool blue eyes of hers are even more striking framed by thick, dark lashes coated in a thin layer of mascara, and the rest of her face is completely free of makeup.

She's stunning. Always is, but especially when she doesn't have anything covering the light dusting of freckles over her nose or her otherwise luminous complexion. She bats her lashes at me, stepping forward, and purposefully allows the bottom of the coat to gape between her thighs. Drool is pooling in my mouth, and I release a long groan, squeezing my eyes shut and dropping my head back.

"You're killing me, woman," I whine, my fingertips tingling

with the need to tug on the belt looped around her waist, undressing her like my very own present.

She steps past me, doing a little twirl before turning her back to me. She unties the coat, splays it wide open, and looks over her shoulder at me, clocking my expression. My cock twitches in my sweats, and it's killing me not to launch myself at her and fuck her right here over my coffee table.

But then she drops the coat, and my brain does a double take.

A loud laugh bursts from my mouth, and I keel over, my hands on my knees as laughter billows out of me. Her giggles join with mine, and when we've gotten it all out, she stands and straightens the oversized t-shirt she had tucked into hot-pink baggy sweatpants she has cuffed all the way up to the tops of her thighs.

"Sorry, unless you're willing to ride the red river, I'm not here for sex," she says, chuckling. "I'm on my period, and everything aches, so I'd rather not do anything tonight if that's okay."

I approach her, gathering her against my chest, and press a kiss to the top of her head. "Of course that's okay. I'm glad you still came. I like seeing you," I admit, nuzzling into her hair, her warm fragrance wrapping around us.

I hoist her up and enjoy how quickly she wraps her legs around my waist as I carry her into my bedroom, where Mrs. Purrito is resting on my bed, exactly where she's not supposed to be, but this damn cat doesn't listen to anyone. I set her down beside the offending fur-ball, and she rolls over, picking her up and resting her on her chest. Mrs. Purrito revs her engine, purring so loudly the sound is vibrating Elise's tits, which I gladly take note of through her thin cotton top.

"I'm going to make us something to drink. Want a snack?"

She nods. "Popcorn, please."

"You got it." I head into the kitchen, returning a few minutes later with two hot chocolates, a bag of cat treats stuffed in my pocket, and a massive bowl of popcorn.

We lie in bed, watching old reruns of some show called "Being

Human", which she refused to watch the UK version of, saying that while American TV is rubbish by comparison as a generalisation, the American version of this one show is far superior.

I think she might just have a thing for Sam Witwer and his strangely endearing butt chin. That said, I'm annoyed to say she may have been right.

"It's okay, Rafa. You can tell me I'm right at any time. I'll wait," she taunts, her lids growing heavy and her small smile beginning to slip.

I lean across her, grabbing the remote and flicking the screen off before turning the bedside lamp off and dragging her body against mine. She lets out a relieved sigh and curls into me, hooking a leg over my hip and burying her face in my chest.

There's light seeping through my window blinds from the buildings surrounding us. It's not enough to disturb our sleep but just enough to see the curve of her high cheekbones, the way her bottom lip juts out further than the top. How her thick lashes fan out across her cheeks, even now that she's washed the mascara off from earlier. I've studied her face so many times, I also know exactly what I *can't* see in my dark bedroom.

I can't see the tiny white scar in the corner of her mouth from when her sister, Rachelle, was trying, and *failing,* to learn to play football and shot the ball right into Elise's face. I can't see the dusting of minuscule freckles over the thinnest part of her nose or the small pink birthmark in her hairline which she swears is nothing more than a blob, but I stand by my observation that it's a tiny heart.

She tilts her chin up further, smacking her lips together, making an obnoxious kissing sound, showing me what she wants rather than telling me.

An almost crazed smile spreads across my face, and I cup her cheek, dragging her lips to mine.

She kisses me a dozen times, just quick little pecks, but this new development is an intimacy I've never experienced with anyone before.

Instead of being afraid of what that might mean, I'm actually afraid that I am *not* afraid. Because with Elise, it feels like I can manage just about anything so long as I'm with her. And what happens if she leaves?

I heave out a sigh and push the thought away, focusing on the stunning woman in my arms rather than the weight of the "what ifs."

"Goodnight, *mi vida*," I whisper.

"Goodnight, Rafa," she says, her voice thick with sleep as she latches onto me.

I stare at her until I'm unable to keep my eyes open any longer, finally whispering into the dark room, "You were right, but not about the telly." Sharing my emotions with someone *does* feel good, and it has me craving more.

ELISE

CHAPTER FORTY-FOUR

MONDAY, MAY 19

THE RED TIDE has officially washed away, and with it, my immense horniness has returned. Free at last!

I grab my phone from the edge of my dresser and whip my top off over my head. Squeezing my elbows inward, I angle my phone over my tits, snapping a few pictures, and sending the best one to Rafael, waiting impatiently for his response.

Good thing that man doesn't know how to make me wait, even if he wanted to.

SUNNY D

Jesus Christ, woman! I nearly crashed my
bloody car.

Your tits are fucking phenomenal.

Absolutely worth the collision and subsequent
casualties I may have faced had my reflexes
not been lightning fast.

WHY ARE YOU TEXTING AND DRIVING?!?!?!

That's not something I tolerate. Not ever. It's selfish and unnecessary. Even if my tits *are* phenomenal. Which they most certainly are.

A photo loads on the screen, and when it comes through, it's of his face as he rolls his eyes at me.

> SUNNY D
>
> I'm NOT!
>
> I had my phone up for the GPS when the pic came through. I pulled over. I am STILL pulled over.

My heart rate slows, and I let out a relieved breath.

> SUNNY D
>
> I'd never knowingly put people's lives at risk like that, baby. Not again. I promise.

The way he says "not again" is like a punch to the gut, but we're still working on him forgiving himself and recognising what happened to Carlos wasn't his fault. And I'm not sure when he started calling me "baby" outside of sex, but I think I like it.

No. I know I like it.

> Good, now come pick me up. Park a couple of houses down, and I'll meet you there.

> SUNNY D
>
> Dick pic incoming…

> While you're on the road!?

Sure enough, a photo loads of his monster cock. He's gripping it by the base, and there's a drop of precum already spilling out the top.

> I think I might be in love…

> SUNNY D
>
> Don't tease me, mi vida.

God, I love it when he calls me that *too*. It's a very new addition to the constantly growing list of nicknames he has for me, but after googling what it meant, too afraid to ask Letty's perceptive arse, it became my favourite.

Now, I just hope he means it.

> Shut up and get over here so I can lick it like an ice cream cone. Please, and thanks.

SUNNY D

Run red lights. Got it

Twenty minutes later, he's parked two houses away. I make my way down the side of the street, sprinting through the overgrown grass, with my backpack smacking against my ass as I run.

I yank the door of his sleek black Porsche Panamera open and toss myself inside, the backs of my thighs sticking to the deep-burgundy leather seats.

He shakes his head, a low chuckle rumbling past those perfect, dark-pink lips of his. His onyx eyes, that once looked so dark and void of life, are now anything but. They're bright and devilish as he takes me in, cupping my cheeks in his palms.

The line he shaves into his right eyebrow is sharper today than it was yesterday, and his face is practically glowing as he presses his lips to mine.

I melt into his embrace, and he pinches my chin between his thumb and forefinger.

"How tired are you?" he asks, gazing into my eyes.

"Not at all. It's still really early, and I've got a lot on my mind to be excited for," I say, winking before shifting my gaze to his lap, wagging my brows suggestively.

He laughs, leaning over to tug my seatbelt across my chest before clicking it in place. He straightens in his seat, and the engine roars to life as he pulls out onto the small side street.

"Then we're going on a drive."

We only make it ten minutes down the road before I realise I'd already forgotten something I promised Chelsea I'd do this morning.

"Can we take a small detour?" I ask.

"Sure. Navigate us there, and I'll take you anywhere you want to go, *peligrosa.*"

I'm not sure *want* is the right word. I dread this appointment, but I have to go.

We arrive outside of the small phlebotomy clinic a few minutes later, the tiny white building taunting me as we pull into a parking space, the lot so packed with cars we almost don't find a spot.

"You need blood work?" he asks, his voice curious but not judgemental.

"Yeah. I have to check my thyroid every few months because of the lithium, and I'm overdue. I promised Chels I'd get it done today. It shouldn't take too long," I tell him, unclipping my seatbelt. My fingers are on the door handle before he stops me with a hand on my bicep.

"Can I come in with you?"

Warmth tangles in my chest, and I meet his eyes with a small smile. "That'd be really nice. Thank you."

The appointment takes longer than I'd hoped, waiting in the stuffy lobby for the twenty or more people ahead of me to get jabbed.

The nurse who drew my blood was quick and efficient, so we finished in just a couple of minutes from the time I'd sat down, and this time, I didn't faint. Small blessings.

On our way out, Rafael stops at a small jar, grabbing something out. He holds the door open for me, leading us to the car.

The engine rumbles to life, and he turns to face me, a glint of mischief swirling in his eyes. "Close your eyes, Elise," he tells me, and I obey, despite my instincts. "Stick out your hand."

Again, I listen, and the sound of crinkling plastic tickles my ears in a way I hate.

I feel the rough edges as he presses something into my palm. "Open your eyes."

Blinking my vision clear, I inspect the item, and in my palm sits a blue razzberry lolly. "You were such a good girl, I figured you deserved a sweet." He smirks and I roll my eyes, sinking into the seat and tearing the clear plastic off the top, popping the lolly in my mouth. "You suck that so nice. I can't wait for you to do the same to me later," he mutters, his deep baritone hoarse.

I wrap my lips around the lolly, hollowing my cheeks, holding his eyes with mine. He groans when I pluck it from my mouth with a lurid *pop*.

"We're leaving before I can defile you in the parking lot of a blood clinic."

The next half hour passes with my restlessness growing by the second. "Okay, seriously, where are we going?" I ask for probably the tenth time. He's driven us so far out of Embershire we're on a scenic route, passing farms with silos, barns, and cows grazing the lush green land.

It's beautiful, but I'm confused because this is *vastly* different from the skyscrapers and bustling city streets of Embershire.

"We aren't going anywhere if you keep asking that," he grumbles, and even from the side, I can tell he's rolling his eyes at me.

Damn, this man has the nicest side profile. A straight nose, full lips, and the lightest dusting of scruff along his chiselled jaw that I'm convinced is capable of cutting through glass.

I love the rare occasions when he doesn't have a game or practice to attend, like today, because I catch a glimpse of his nose ring and the small gold hoops he wears in either earlobe.

"Someone's grumpy," I joke, crossing my arms over my chest.

He just shakes his head, turning the music down. His gaze flickers to mine for a moment before returning to the road ahead.

"So, your plans are to join the Olympic team?" he asks, and the question seems strange, out of place.

"Uh, yeah, why?"

"I'm just wondering. I want to know everything there is to know about you, Elise."

I relax into his leather seats. "That's always been my goal, with a World Cup under my belt first, obviously. I know I'm good, good enough to win, not just good enough to be there. But it's a team sport, so I also want to be on a team that's the best."

"You will be," he says, his voice oozing with a refined confidence that makes me believe it even more than I already had.

"Thanks," I say, pressing a kiss to his shoulder. "What about you? Do you have plans for after you retire from the league?"

He quirks a brow at me and gives me a lopsided smirk. "You trying to get rid of me already?" he jokes.

"Not yet," I say, laughing loudly when he purses his lips, clearly unhappy with the suggestion.

"I want your dad's job. That's how this all started. He asked me to take over for Coach Lyon and said he already planned for me to take over for him as head coach when he retires in two years, but this would be a big help to him."

"Hmm, never one for an ultimatum, but he somehow knows just the right thing to say to endear you to him," I remark, laughing.

"He sure does," Rafael grumbles. "But I'm glad he did it." He peers over to me, his soft eyes meeting mine for just a beat before returning to the winding road ahead. "He seems to know what's best for most people, even if we don't ourselves. I thought coaching football would break me, but it hasn't. It's brought back some of the joy I'd lost."

He rests his hand on my thigh and squeezes gently, goosebumps erupting over my skin, partly from the cool air pumping into the car from the air-con.

A few minutes later, we pull up to a little red barn surrounded by wooden fences containing cattle, a hillside boasting bright wildflowers, and a massive wooden cutout sign of a white cow covered in rainbow sprinkles. He parks in the dirt-lined driveway and shuts the engine off.

"Where the hell are we?" I ask, unable to put the pieces together now that we're *here*. Wherever "here" is.

He doesn't bother answering me, climbing out of the car and jogging around to my side to open my door, holding his hand out for me to take.

"Such a gentleman," I joke.

He clutches his chest. "No one has *ever* accused me of such a thing. How dare you, Elise?" he asks, feigning hurt.

"You're ridiculous," I say, smacking his chest as he pulls me from the car. He winds his arms around my waist, tugging me against him and pressing his forehead onto mine.

"I think I'm *ridiculously* in like with you," he says, his voice small.

I want to laugh, but I don't because I know that in the same way that I'm not usually someone who allows myself to be vulnerable around others, Rafael isn't either. There's a huge difference between speaking my mind and feeling safe to be truly emotionally transparent with someone.

"I think I might be too," I finally say, bringing my lips to his. The kiss is quick, but it still manages to make my head spin.

"Alright, come on, the ice cream's gonna melt," he jokes, smacking my ass to propel me forward.

"Ice cream?!"

"Yes, ice cream," he says, dragging me into the barn, which isn't really a barn at all. It's got a bakery to the left and an ice cream counter to the right, and I can't wait to have my fill.

CHAPTER FORTY-FIVE

MONDAY, MAY 19

"IF YOU KEEP LICKING your ice cream cone like that, I'm gonna have to pull over and teach you a lesson about teasing me," I groan, side-eyeing Elise as she sweeps her tongue from the base of her pistachio ice cream all the way to the tip with one languid stroke.

"It's not my fault you're a horny man with an insatiable appetite," she taunts.

"Actually, I'm pretty sure it is. I wasn't even this horny in first year," I admit, clamping a hand down on her thigh as I try to focus on the road and not the way she's tormenting me.

"Well, then I'm glad to be the one to help you raise your testosterone. I hear that shit plummets in your old age." Now I *know* she's just begging to get fucked.

I pull off on the shoulder of the empty road, nothing but farmland and the occasional car for miles.

She doesn't even have the acumen to ask me what we're doing. No, she just rolls down her window, tosses what's left of the cone out of it, and turns back to me, her finger pressing down on the button, rolling it back up as she smirks at me.

I unbuckle each of us before grabbing her around the waist and hauling her over the centre console and into the back seat. I climb over it next, my wide shoulders and long legs making the task nearly impossible, but Elise is already scrambling to get her shorts and underwear off, giving me the perfect incentive to hurry up.

"You should know better, Elise," I tell her, pinning her with a glare as I manoeuvre around the backseat, releasing my cock from my gym shorts and rolling on a condom from my wallet.

"Know better than to what, Coach?" Her face is a mask of innocence. Emphasis on the word *"mask."*

"Than to call me *old* or to taunt me into wrecking you and this sweet cunt of yours. All you have to do is ask," I remind her as I climb over, positioning myself at her entrance.

She bats her lashes at me, those blue eyes churning with mischief. "I'm sorry," she says, running her hands up my chest and bringing her lips to my ear, "will you *please* wreck my pussy, Rafa?"

A groan slips past my lips, and all restraint is long gone as I plunge into her tight cunt. She squeezes around me, and tingles trail down my spine as she moans, clawing at my back.

I pump my hips against hers, balancing a hand above her head. "God, I wish I could choke you right now," I admit, my fingertips itching to wrap around her throat.

"Then do it," she pants.

I shake my head. "Not enough room, and I'd break your fucking neck if I did at this angle," I grunt as she rolls her hips.

"I'd offer to get on top, but I'm already close," she admits, her chest heaving as she squirms beneath me.

"Oh, fuck me." I moan, resting my weight on her and burying my face in her neck as my balls tighten and her pussy spasms.

"Yes!" she shouts. "Oh, fuck, yes, Rafa, please," she cries out, winding her legs around my waist and clamping her thighs down on my hips. Her nails dig into my back; the bite of her clawing at my flesh has me tumbling quickly over the edge with her.

We lose ourselves in each other, and when we're both sated, *for now anyway,* I press a kiss to her neck, smiling against her skin.

"Hey, Rafa?" she asks.

I clear my throat. "Mhmm?"

"Thanks for the ice cream," she says, but hidden within her whispered words is an entirely different meaning, one that has my heart clenching in my chest.

"You're welcome, *mi vida.*"

I lift up off of her, ready to get us home, but when I look up, a scream rips from my throat. "Ahh! What the fuck?!" I shout, hitting my head on the roof as Elise rushes to sit up, her head swinging to where my eyes are.

Hers grow to the size of saucers as she stares at the big brown eyes looking back at us. A *fucking cow* is peering through our window. Its moist black nose is pressed against the glass as it chews the grass hanging out of its mouth.

"I hope you got a good show, perv," I tell the cow, and a startled laugh finally breaks free from her lips, and mine follows suit.

I shake myself out, smiling as I help her over the console and back into her seat before I get out of the car, opting to get back in the driver's seat the easier way.

"Alright, trouble, let's get you home," I say, resting my hand on her thigh.

She relaxes into her seat, humming along to the song now playing through my speakers.

I was reluctant to leave Elise at her place, but I have a game in the morning, and I recognise that it's easier this way. Doesn't mean I like it anymore though. I've rapidly grown to adore having her beside me at night, and the rate that my soul has begun to crave her is alarming.

Despite knowing that, it still makes it nearly impossible to fall asleep, missing her.

It's just before midnight here, which means it's eight at night in Argentina, so I pick up the phone and call Carlos.

"*Che, hermano,*" he says, answering on the third ring.

"*Che,* Carlos, *qué anduviste haciendo?*" I ask.

"Just watching a game, going to get ready for bed soon. What's up with you? You sound...different?" he says, phrasing it as more of a question than a statement.

"Yeah," I say, chuckling, "I guess I have been a little different recently."

He takes a long pause, processing my words, but when he speaks, I swear I can practically see the wide grin stretch across his tan face.

"*Uy!* It's a woman! You're dating someone!" he practically shouts into my ear.

"We aren't dating, but—"

"*But* you want to be!" he says, cutting me off.

"Yeah, I think I do," I admit, suddenly feeling sheepish.

He practically begs me to tell him every single detail about her and how we met, and by the time I get through it all, it's nearly two in the morning for me.

"She sounds great, Rafa." His voice is gentle in the way it always is when he's about to spill some sort of truth serum all over my head. "I think you've got to just tell her you want more so neither of you end up getting hurt in the end. Okay?"

"Yeah, okay," I grumble, and while my words don't sound convincing because truthfully, I'm nervous as hell with everything that's at stake here, I *am* confident in this. Because he's right. If I don't admit that I want to get to know her beyond "casual sex and occasional companionship" now, and she decides she wants more with someone else, it'll crush me. I've never felt like this with anyone else, and I don't plan to take that for granted.

"Good, because you're worthy of love, *hermanito*," he says and releases a long yawn. "I've gotta head to bed, but I love you, and I'm proud of you. Make sure to keep me updated on your relationship because you *know* I live for a good telenovela, and this sounds just like one," he says, tired excitement evident in his quiet, muffled tone.

"*Que descanses, Carlito. Yo también te quiero.*"

When I hang up, I find myself opening my message thread between me and Elise, and a big, goofy grin tugs at my lips.

I'm down so bad for this woman.

I shoot her a text, knowing she won't get it until she wakes up, but hoping it makes her smile when she does.

> Goodnight, mi vida. I hope you sleep well.

I roll over, ready to put my phone on the charger and try my hand at sleeping again, but my phone pings.

My brow furrows as I see the message from Elise waiting for me.

SUNSHINE

Goodnight <3

> Can't sleep?

SUNSHINE

It seems you've broken me. I haven't been able to sleep without you since that first night at the hotel.

> The truth?

> Me neither.

SUNSHINE

So, what do we do about that?

Instead of texting her back, I call her, plugging my phone in and setting it on my nightstand beside my head.

"Hi, baby."

"Hi," she says, her voice groggy, making me picture her fluttering lashes as she fights sleep, her dark strands piled high in a knot on her head. I imagine her arm resting between her breasts because she has a terrible habit of sleeping like a T-rex, and it's absolutely going to cause carpal tunnel one day, but it's too cute to tell her to stop.

"You good to talk until we both fall asleep?" I ask.

"That sounds nice," she says, and there's a smile in her voice.

"Good, because I missed you. I know it's only been a few hours, but I did, and I figured you should know." *Boludo*, that feels strange to admit, like my heart is a puppet with Elise tugging on the strings.

"I missed you too," she whispers. "And Rafa?"

"Yes, baby?"

"Thanks for telling me," she says, her voice growing faint.

"You sure you can't fall asleep?" I ask, and she grunts.

"I might be able to now," she finally says.

We stay on the line, neither of us hanging up, and when I wake up a few hours later, Elise is snoring through the line, a sound that mimics Mrs. Purrito's contended purr.

My heart aches, and as unfamiliar as this is for me, I think it's going to be good. *For the both of us.*

CHAPTER FORTY-SIX

THURSDAY, MAY 22

SUNNY D

Pack a bathing suit, and an overnight bag.

It's not even an away game, why would I pack an overnight bag? I already have my stuff at your place.

SUNNY D

Don't ask questions, please just do as I say.

For once.

Fine, but I have to be home by Sunday.

SUNNY D

Done. Now hurry up.

First you boss me around and stop me from getting out of my house and now you want me to hurry up? Can't have it both ways, mister.

SUNNY D

I can and I will. Hurry. Up. Elise.

Give me one good reason.

. . .

A PHOTO STARTS DOWNLOADING ALMOST IMMEDIATELY, and when it loads, it's not what I'm expecting, but I love it all the same.

Rafael's full lips are open in a perfect "o", with his tongue hanging out and saliva dripping off of the tip. His facial hair is a little longer than a five-o'clock shadow, and I can already picture it rubbing over my sensitive skin.

> Ope. Be there soon!

SUNNY D

That's my girl.

I've learned the trick to getting you to show up early to something for once.

> Now if only everyone else could too.

SUNNY D

They better fucking not. Now get over here before we run out of time.

> Sir, yes sir!

SUNNY D

Such a brat.

He's right; while I'm never *late*, I *am* French. Which means I'm always rushing everywhere, but only because I like to move quickly to the next thing.

And now that he's given me something to look forward to, I find myself tossing my clothes into a bag, running around my room to get to him for whatever reward he has planned for me. I'm addicted to his touch, his kisses, his *smell*. Everything about Rafael has me smiling to myself, overwhelmed with a content happiness I haven't experienced in, well, *ever*.

And that is precisely what drives me to work extra hard to get to his office for my reward before anyone else arrives.

"Remind me again how you managed to make it seem like a coincidence that *neither* of us had to drive back to campus with the rest of the team?" I ask, my brow quirked as I buckle my seatbelt in the back of the rideshare Rafael booked.

"Like I've already told you, stop worrying about it, *peligrosa,*" he says, shaking his head at me.

"Fine," I huff out but lean into his touch, resting my head on his shoulder. I focus on his warm hand gripping my thigh and the faint pop music playing over the speakers. I'm tired from exertion, but the thrill of excitement at what lies ahead is the only thing between me and a nap right now. That and the stop-and-go traffic jostling me forward and slamming me back into Rafael.

He wraps an arm around me, clutching me to his side as we sit in a comfortable silence for the next hour until I hear the tyres slowing over gravel before stopping. I pop my head up, peering through the windshield and up at the cutest cottage-style inn I've ever seen. The whole place is surrounded by wildflowers in bright shades of yellows and blues. The building is covered in a light stone exterior, vines climbing the sides, with small balconies on the second level.

I turn to Rafael, who's already watching me, taking in my reaction.

"What are we doing here?" I ask, breathless.

"Get out of this poor bloke's car and you'll find out," he says.

I unbuckle my seatbelt and scoot out of the back seat, thanking the driver. Rafael meets me on my side, opening the door and taking my bag from me. He clasps his hand in mine, leading me up the stone walkway to the intricately carved dark wood door.

He twists the heavy wrought iron knob, holding it wide open, letting me slip inside first. It shuts behind us with a loud thud. An older woman seated behind a small desk with her gold-rimmed glasses sliding down the bridge of her thin nose as she reads her book is the only person around. Her head snaps up when she notices us, slamming her book shut and tossing it in her bag on the ground. Her cheeks flush a light-pink colour as she clears her throat.

Damn, I wish I would've paid more attention to the cover. That book must've been steamy.

"Hello," I say with a curt wave.

"Checking in?" she asks, regaining some of her composure.

"Yes, ma'am, for Rafael Romero-Castillo," he answers.

"Yes, dear," she says, plucking a key from a drawer, leaning across her desk to hand it to him. "You're the only guests here for the weekend. It'll just be two nights, is that correct?"

"That's right," he says, squeezing my hand as my eyes widen to comedic proportions.

Two nights?

We're spending *two* whole nights away together? My heart beats a little faster, knowing I want to spend as much time with him as possible but also knowing that being with Rafael isn't something either of us could have planned for and our lives might blow up as a result. We should have a conversation about where we're going, but the press of his hand in mine as he leads me up the staircase and the promise of what's to come makes the world shrink away, and with it, all sense of responsibility.

Two nights. We can have two nights together without shattering the spell we're under and having the hard conversation I can feel us both avoiding.

He drags me along to a massive set of white doors with gold knobs. He slides the iron key in, twisting it to unlock, letting us inside.

The room isn't huge, and it's nothing particularly special at first glance, but the longer I stand here, dumbstruck as I stare at the peeling wallpaper, the wood-burning fireplace, and the queen-sized bed with the canopy top, the more my heart clenches and twists in my chest.

"This is the place." I breathe.

The place. The one I showed him in a video I'd seen online last week. Someone did a tour of the area, and with how close it is to Embershire, I wanted to go. I'd sent it to Rafael because truthfully, I'd wanted to go with *him.*

And here we are. Something so seemingly insignificant as a message I'd sent him in passing and here we are, living it.

"It is," he says, tugging me against his firm chest, pressing a kiss to the top of my head. I melt against him, breathing in his clean, woody scent.

RAFAEL

CHAPTER FORTY-SEVEN

FRIDAY, MAY 23

THE SUN IS STARTING to rise above the clouds, streaming through the thin white curtains hanging over the balcony doors.

Elise groans, scooting her ass further against me, plastering her back to my front.

My dick happily burrows between her bare cheeks, and a grunt rumbles from my chest.

"I'd think you'd be broken by now," I whisper against her cheek, nuzzling further into her warm, intoxicatingly sweet scent.

"Maybe broken *in* but definitely not broken. Though the same can't be said for Mrs. Greene's settee or the armchair," she says, reminding me that we've only been here a night and I already owe the owner of this small inn a large sum in damages.

"Worth it," I say, chuckling against her neck.

She rolls over to face me, slipping her hand between us, gripping me roughly in her palm as she teases my tip against her entrance. "You aren't going to come inside me now, are you?" she asks, her tone a gentle scold.

I shake my head. "I'm *not* going to come inside you," I say, biting my bottom lip when she slips me inside her, still lying on our sides. "Okay, well, now I might," I tease.

She rolls her eyes but settles her hands on my shoulders,

rocking her hips leisurely against me until I'm fully seated inside her.

"What are we—" Her eyes roll back. "Oh, god," she moans, swallowing thickly. "What are we doing today?" she asks.

"You sure"—I suck in a breath—"you want to have this conversation right now?" I bite down on my lip again, pressing my forehead to hers.

"Mhmm." She flattens her lips between her teeth, her expression twisting as she tries to deny us both what we want. *Such a tease.*

I blow out a breath, squeezing my eyes shut as I let it all out. "It's a surprise, *mi vida.*"

"Another surprise?" She appears breathless as she continues circling her hips with just enough movement to drive me wild but not enough to get me to my breaking point.

"Yes," I grit out, sliding myself out of her, but before she can protest, I have her on her stomach, ass up as I slide back inside. I bite down on the side of her neck, causing her to yelp before I say, "You'll get your surprise after we finish up here."

She moans loudly as I pump myself inside her, already grabbing for the box of condoms on the nightstand.

ELISE

CHAPTER FORTY-EIGHT

FRIDAY, MAY 23

MY NECK IS CRANKED ALL the way back as I stare up at the absolute monstrosity before me. It's stunning with its intricate architecture, carvings of angels and cherubs in the smooth limestone, and pillars to match. What I don't understand is why we're here at all.

I straighten my neck out, turning to Rafael. "You wanted to take me to… church?" I ask, my head cocked and my snarky tone not even remotely hiding my disbelief.

He rolls his eyes. "It's not *just* a church," he says.

I give the enormous building another quick glance before peering up into his onyx eyes. I pop my hip out as I say, "Well, yeah, it's a *Catholic* church. Cathedral, whatever. Big whoop. There's one around nearly every corner." My eyes widen as a lightbulb flicks on in my mind. Okay, it's more of an opportunity to be a pain in his ass, but same thing. I snap my fingers and lean into him, dropping my voice an octave as I whisper conspiratorially. "If this is because of what we did last night, I don't think even a priest, all the holy water in the world, and confessional could wash away *those* sins."

He lets out an exasperated sigh, gripping my chin and tilting my head back, forcing me to meet his disapproving stare.

"Elise, I'm not taking you for mass or even a confessional,

though the Lord *literally* knows we need it. And it's a basilica, not a cathedral, not that it matters. Just shut your pretty mouth and wait to find out what the surprise is, okay?"

I smirk up at him as he shifts his hand from my chin to cup my jaw, lowering his voice as he says, "And baby, I don't have a single fucking interest in washing away a goddamn thing that happened last night. In fact, I think we should do it again, *tonight.*"

A shiver trails down my spine as he presses a firm kiss to my lips, dropping his hand and resting it at the base of my spine, ushering me up the slippery marble steps.

My trainers make a squeaking sound as we walk up to the tiny reception desk covered in rosaries hanging off of jewellery racks. A thin man stands behind the desk, nodding as we approach. "What can I do for you?" he asks, a thick Kent accent lacing his words.

"Two tickets to the top," Rafael whispers, not wanting to disrupt the nearly three hundred people sitting in the wooden pews, listening to the morning service. I didn't even know churches had services on Fridays.

The man collects his payment and points over to a thick pillar with an open archway that's about four feet tall. "You can enter from there."

Rafael thanks the man, taking my hand in his and leading us toward the small alcove.

My heart starts to speed up as we step inside the tight space, and Rafael grips my hand firmly in his. He takes the first few steps up the winding brick stairs, and *very* reluctantly, I follow him. The space is so tight, if my tits were any bigger, I might not fit in here at all. And these tiny stairs are barely big enough to place the top half of my foot on.

"Why are we doing this, exactly?" I ask, following behind him, reluctant as ever.

"You'll see, *mi vida.* I promise it'll be worth the climb."

I'm not sure I agree, but I continue up the claustrophobia-inducing staircase, wishing there was a genie nearby to grant me a wish. I'd kick this fear of heights to the bloody kerb.

After a solid twenty minutes of climbing, the narrow stairs begin to widen, opening up to a large domed room with a wooden cross-bridge.

My eyes swing from the ground, which is quite literally the top of the mosaic glass ceiling that I'd seen when we first entered the building, to Rafael's smirking face. "Absolutely not," I huff out, shaking my head, fully prepared to turn around.

He tugs me to him, winding his arms around my waist and snuggling his face against my neck in just the way he's learned makes me melt. "Not fair." I breathe.

"What's not fair?" he asks, his breath tickling the thin skin over my thrumming pulse. He laughs softly, and I'm certain he's more than aware of his wrongdoings.

"This is manipulation, and I won't stand for it," I say, but the further his hands travel down my waist, the less determination my words seem to hold.

"Come on, baby," he whispers, cupping me between my thighs.

"Sir, we are in *church*. This is a place of worship," I whisper-yell at him even though we've just climbed three hundred steps, a fact I'm painfully aware of thanks to the number painted on the side of the last brick step I took, and there's clearly no one around.

He chuckles deeply, the sound vibrating through his chest and against my back. "If you do this, I'll let you take over tonight. You can do *anything* you want with me."

My mind floods with images of all the ways I could wield that newfound power, and I'm suddenly standing a little taller and with a renewed sense of resilience.

I nod, taking off ahead, but as the wooden beam making up this horrifying bridge over the stained glass beneath us creaks with my weight, I take a step back and push Rafael forward. This was his dumbass idea, which means he better be there to catch my fall if this shite goes down.

My knees wobble as I hold my breath; clutching onto the side rails with a death grip, my throat constricts and my heart hammers in my chest. We finally make it to the other side, a fact that shocks me seeing as I almost passed out from holding my breath, and I feel warmth spread through me from the accomplishment.

Rafael peers over his shoulder at me, wearing a knowing smirk, but it turns out he's suddenly on his best behaviour because he remains quiet, not calling me out.

We make it around a corner that reveals possibly the biggest obstacle yet. "How does it keep getting worse?" I squeak out, feeling a little lightheaded as I stare up at the hollowed-out tower. The architecture in this area is clearly not something that resources were focused on. It's merely an extremely tall tower with metre-wide steps, railings, *thank fuck*, that wind up the sides of the walls, climbing higher to a point I can't even make out yet. All I know is that the windows in here are small and provide minimal visibility, but there *is* a burst of light some-where at the top, and if I were anyone else, that might make me feel *better*.

But I'm not just anyone. No, I'm Elise Auclair, fear of heights extraordinaire and apparently a closeted baby-back bitch. So instead of relief, I'm filled with a thick sense of dread at knowing this trek to the top is likely to lead me somewhere *outside*, and I might just die if I have to face this same fear again so soon.

"Wasn't fucking me over the side of a skyscraper enough for you?" I ask, whimpering.

Rafael squeezes my hand, bringing my knuckles to his lips, pressing a warm kiss to each one. "You're gonna be fine, *mi vida*. What did I tell you that day on the roof?"

I joggle my mind for an answer, but nothing comes to the forefront.

"I said," he whispers, "I'll never let anything happen to you." I feel my chest squeeze and my legs nearly give out as he tugs me to his chest and presses his forehead to mine. "I'll protect you with my life, because you *are* my life, Elise."

Everything is buzzing as the meaning of his words burrows into my skin. I'm tingling as they absorb into me and wriggle their way into my blood vessels, searching for the very marrow of my bones to settle into.

I have to fight my natural instinct to pull away from him, to deny what he's said and slink into a place of self-destruction, but repeatedly, he's shown me with his actions that his words ring true.

Neither of us speaks as he holds me in his strong arms, my gaze enraptured with his. And finally, I manage a weak nod before heading up the first of many flights of stairs.

After what was a very sweet moment, my pliable attitude has not proven to last long. I've complained every hundred steps since then, and Rafael's smile has only grown wider.

I'm arguably very much an "in shape" person. I sort of *have* to be, but this church and its thirteen hundred steps are making me question my entire existence.

"We're almost there, baby," he promises for the tenth time today, practically carrying me as we go. It annoys me that much more that this man is over a decade older than me and he's barely broken a sweat.

"Yeah, yeah, yeah. Promises, promises. I'll believe it when I see it. Whatever *it* is." He cracks a smile, lifting me effortlessly and bridal carrying me up the steps. "If I weren't so damn tired, I'd argue because this doesn't feel safe at all," I whine.

"Good thing you're tired then. It's the only time you'll shut the hell up and relax," he says with no bite in his tone.

I pinch his cheek, but the moment we're *here,* I know it, and not only because he sets me gently on my feet to gaze up at the mural left behind by the thousands of sappy romantics with a death wish who've climbed here before us.

The destination isn't the bright light at the very top. *No,* it's the massive painted wall with thousands of names drawn together by every person who's made it to this part of the ascent. At least, every person who knew of its existence and brought a marker.

Imagine making it here only to realise you don't have anything to write with!

Rafael produces a gold marker from his back pocket, handing it to me. I take it in my shaking hands, feeling the weight of this monumental moment settling down around us.

Sure, from the outside it might seem like we're just a new couple on a little weekend holiday, doing something touristy in a small town, but that isn't all this is, and I think we *both* know that.

Do I love him? *I'm not sure.*

It's moments like this that make me wish more than ever that I had my *maman* and Rachelle around. I could talk to them about him, tell them everything, and they'd leave me feeling less confused and flustered. They'd also pick on me for sure, but I wouldn't care because they'd still be here.

I've loved many people in my life. I think it's what makes me such a hard-ass sometimes. Because I've loved my family with a fierceness that rivals all other forms of love. I've loved my friends enough that I feel the need to protect them all from everyone and everything, including the wounded and tormented parts of myself that I've never had a desire to burden anyone with.

If I don't let them into all the messy places in my heart and in my mind, they won't have to carry the weight of it all with them. But with Rafael, the love I *think* I feel for him is so different.

We had a terribly rocky start to our relationship, and even now, we aren't truly together, not in the way I think we'd both like. And maybe we'll never get to experience that, but there's something so freeing in two unbelievably scarred, messy, and beautifully broken people being vulnerable with one another.

I've never known romantic love, but if *this* is as close to it as I'll ever get, I'll never want for anything more in my life.

Rafael hasn't taken his gaze off of me since my eyes first landed on this wall, my fingertips trailing over the scribbles and scrolls of every person before us. "What's running through your beautiful mind, *mi vida?*"

I turn to face him, and he reaches out, cupping my cheeks. He runs the rough pads of his thumbs beneath my eyes, wiping at the errant tears I hadn't even realised I'd let fall.

This is what's so nice about Rafael and me. We both understand the importance of sharing what's on our minds with the people we care about because you never know when you might not have the chance anymore. The hardest part has always been *knowing* that I should share my feelings but being unable to put that into action a lot of the time. It feels easy to let myself speak my mind when I'm with him, and it's a novelty.

"I'm thinking that I want more with you than casual, that I want to tell my dad about us, and that I definitely still hate heights even if this *is* really cool," I say, ending on a watery laugh.

A wide grin stretches his lips, making a set of annoying, knicker-melting dimples pop out with the full force of the sun on a cloudy day. "Good, because I'm thinking all of the same things, minus the fear of heights."

If this moment weren't so tender, I'd make a jab at him about not knowing he had dimples before this, but that would break my entire philosophy about not telling people to smile more.

My chest tightens as I push past the immense feelings I'm suddenly being drowned in.

His eyes flicker to the wall, and he taps against an empty spot just off-centred to the right. "What about right here?" he asks.

Nodding, I shake the gold marker and uncap it. I write "Rafael + Elise", and instead of outlining it with a simple heart, I write the words "resilient in love" in the shape of a heart surrounding them.

I cap the marker, taking a step back to admire my handiwork, and I swear I see this man's eyes fill with tears. They don't fall, but I promise *they're there.*

RAFAEL

CHAPTER FORTY-NINE

FRIDAY, MAY 23

THE WORDS she's written surrounding our names have my eyes burning with unshed tears. My throat feels tight as I swallow around a lump of emotion, unable to fully clear the haze in my mind that's covering up the unfamiliar emotion.

But if this is what I think this is, if *this* is love, then calling it an emotion is a very poor sentiment. It sullies the word itself because I don't think this could be reduced down to something as simple as a feeling experienced based on hormones and external stimuli alone.

So instead of speaking, knowing the words in my head would come out all wrong, ruining the moment and potentially causing Elise to run for the hills, I pull out my phone. I snap a photo of the place where our names will sit side by side until the walls of this ancient building come crumbling down around them with *us*, and this moment buried beneath it, an encapsulated memory of this precious moment in time. A moment where two people, so burdened by the heavy weights they've carried with them, are able to help the other carry that struggle, even if only for a moment.

I suck in a breath, physically shaking the uncharacteristically poetic thoughts from my mind before emailing the photo to myself, *just in case.*

"You ready to finish this?" I ask, and she rolls her eyes, all but stomping up the next hundred steps until she makes it to the last three. They're rickety wooden stairs, the smallest ones we've seen all day. They sit beneath a slanted metal door flanked by two thin windowpanes that let in the blinding streams of light from outside. Her hands visibly shake as she reaches up, unlatching the door and pulling it open.

She teeters backward, and my hands shoot out, gripping her hips tightly as she peers down over her shoulder at me, a silent "thank you" written all over her face.

"I told you I wouldn't let anything happen to you," I quietly remind her. She lets out a little huff and climbs the last three steps, her fingers pale from her iron grip on the railing.

There's a small metal platform on the roof. It's settled firmly on top of the terracotta shingles with supports beneath it and four-foot-high fencing soldered around the perimeter.

She barely moves as I climb up behind her, stretching my limbs from the way we were both hunched over for the last several steps due to the limited ceiling height. I wrap an arm around her waist, resting my chin on her shoulder. I do my best to hold in the laughter threatening to break free when I realise her eyes are cinched shut, possibly with more force than her hands on these railings.

"Baby, you've gotta relax," I whisper calmly into her ear. "Loosen your grip, I promise, this isn't like the time on the roof, okay? We're a foot from the railing, and I won't make you move any closer than that unless you want to. But you've gotta release some of this tension and open your eyes for me."

She nods her head, and I feel some of the tension ease from her body. It's certainly not all of it, but we're making some serious progress.

"That's good, baby. Now open your eyes."

I know the moment she does because she sucks in a gasp, whipping her head around to catch all the beauty of this unassuming town.

From up here, we can see *everything*. From the field of wildflowers we'd driven past on our way here to the inn we spent the night at, and the city's centre filled with food carts, street performers, musicians, and artists celebrating some Catholic saint.

"It's beautiful," she whispers.

I bring my mouth to the shell of her ear. "And so are you."

She melts against my chest, and after standing up here for fifteen minutes, enjoying the light breeze, the faint sounds from the streets below us, and the sun peeking through the clouds above, settling into our skin, we're both ready to turn back.

"You sure you don't want to close that gap and step up to the railing?" I tease.

She turns in my arms, rolling her eyes. "Ha, ha, very funny. But no. I've had more than enough nightmare fuel for the day," she says, pulling out of my arms and white-knuckling it down the steps.

ELISE

CHAPTER FIFTY

FRIDAY, MAY 23

AFTER A LONG DAY of facing fears that I absolutely have *not* overcome, regardless of the extra special trauma I experienced today, and many hours of strolling through the small town festival, enjoying live music and eating our way through the day, I'm glad to be back in bed.

Though as much as I'd expected to be tired, and *I am*, my pussy has certainly not gotten the memo.

Rafael has me clutched tightly to his chest, his eyes lazily roaming my body, committing every piece of me to memory. His thick length is jutting out, rubbing against the now wet silk seam of my pyjama shorts, and the feeling of his fingertips drawing leisurely patterns over my skin has every nerve ending firing.

"Do you remember what I told you earlier?" he asks, his voice low and husky.

I nod because I've been thinking about it all goddamn day my reward for nearly dying today.

Okay, maybe that's a *tad* dramatic.

"And what would you like to do with that information?" he asks, his warm breath coasting over my lips, sending a shiver down my spine.

I push hard on his chest, effectively rolling him onto his back, as I swing a leg over his lap and straddle his waist.

A lopsided smirk curves my lips as I peer down at him, my fingers digging into the sculpted muscles of his chest, and his large, callused hands grip my hips firmly as I settle down over him.

"You were very bad today," I taunt, sucking my bottom lip between my teeth.

"I'd argue that I was actually very *good* today, but go on. I like where this is going," he says with a wry grin.

I slide a hand up his chest, wrapping it around the base of his throat. His Adam's apple bobs beneath my palm when he swallows.

"And now you're talking back?" I question, quirking a brow.

He sucks his lips in, poorly hiding his smile.

I release his neck, sitting up to whip my shirt off over my head, tossing it to the floor. Leaning down, I press my chest against his, the coarse, trimmed hairs littering his skin creating a delicious friction over my nipples.

The head of his cock flicks along my seam as I roll my hips, revelling in the sound of his tortured groan. "You know exactly what you've got coming tonight, don't you?" I ask. "I can tell by that little sound you just made."

He squeezes his eyes shut. "I'm afraid I'm in for a night of edging, and I'm suddenly really unhappy with this deal we made," he admits.

It's a good thing that I am most certainly *not* unhappy.

I climb off of him, shimmying out of my shorts, glad that I've been forgoing knickers when with Rafael—it saves on laundry. I take a seat on the last remaining armchair, crossing my right leg over my left knee, and relax into the chair with my fingers curling over the armrests.

"Strip for me," I tell him.

He rolls out of the bed, tugging his grey sweats down his thick, tanned thighs. I'm momentarily mesmerised by the deep V that points an arrow to his impressive length. He has a faint tan line from the tiny gym shorts the rugby players wear, and that thought only makes me wetter.

A few months ago, I never would've believed I could love a sport as much as I love football, but suddenly, rugby is fighting for a tie.

He strokes his cock, but I shake my head. "Did I say you could touch yourself?" And because I'm an asshole and can't help myself, I look him dead in the eye and add, "And tonight, you'll call me Mommy." I have to suck my cheeks in to avoid the snicker trying to slip free.

He groans, dropping his hand to his side.

"On your knees," I say, nodding my chin at him. He does as he's told, planting his hands on the smooth wood floors. "Now crawl to me."

When he's got his face mere centimetres from my centre, I lift my legs, settling them over his back. "This may be the last meal you're offered tonight." I run the pad of my thumb over his plump bottom lip, plucking it from its place between his teeth. "Show me what a good meal I am, Rafa," I whisper.

My words act as a command, and he obediently dips his head, sweeping his tongue through my seam and swirling it inside my dripping core.

"Oh, god," I groan, slumping back into the chair.

"Oh, god, is right," he says, slurping and sucking on my tender flesh, lighting fireworks through me. "You taste so fucking good, *Mommy*. I could have you for every meal and fucking *thrive*."

I grip the roots of his tousled black hair, tugging tight enough that I know from personal experience it's got to hurt. He doesn't seem to mind as he feasts on me.

Just as my vision is becoming hazy and dark spots start to blur the edges, I sit up, pushing his face back.

"That's enough," I say, but the words sound breathless as I pant back the building arousal.

"I disagree," he grumbles, his dark eyes swirling like a black hole ready to suck me into them.

"I'm sorry," I say, sarcasm oozing from my lips as I cock my head to the side, "did I ask for your opinion?" My brows pinch. "*No*, I did not. Now, get up."

Reluctantly, he drags his ass off of the ground.

Standing and sauntering past him, I make my way over to the end of the bed. The soft mattress dips beneath me as I scoot far enough back for what I have planned, my legs still dangling over the side.

"Come here," I demand, crooking my finger at him.

He heads over to me, a weary look written on his face that makes me smile. His lips are pursed, eyes darting between mine, and I think I fully understand why he enjoys this side of sex, not that I'm doing a great job at the whole "dommy mommy" bit.

I pat my lap, unable to hide the massive grin I'm sporting at the prospect of spanking this thirty-two-year-old man who looks like he wants to cry angry tears.

He sucks in a deep, steadying breath before lying across my lap, perky ass up. "I swear to god, if you shove anything up my ass, I'm returning the favour," he grunts out.

"Noted," I say. I rub a small circle over one firm globe, the initial contact making him jump and glare up at me.

This may not be making my pussy any wetter, but I'm definitely loving it nonetheless.

Just when he starts to relax, I rear my hand back, smacking one cheek with a loud *thwack*. It leaves a bright-red handprint as he yelps.

"Such a bad boy you've been," I taunt, trying not to laugh, but when he snorts, I lose it. I fight to regain my composure, sucking in a breath through my nose and blowing it out through my mouth. "Alright, let's try this again."

"If you say so," he grumbles.

I smack his ass again, really thinking about what I'm about to say, but when I do it one more time, enjoying the sting of my palm, I feel his cock twitch, and all bets are officially off. "You're enjoying this, aren't you?" I tease, already knowing the answer.

"No," he groans. I reward the lie with another smack that

sends a sharp pain stinging up my palm, and again, his dick twitches at the same time his ass cheeks clench. "Don't even say it, it's a pain boner," he swears.

I smack the other cheek, and there's no mistaking the breathy moan that leaves this man harder than a metal rod. "Go on, admit it. You *like* being disciplined almost as much as you like doing the disciplining."

"I wouldn't go *that* far." He groans. "I'm very reluctantly, sort of, kind of, maybe just a little bit, enjoying myself," he says. "Now spank me, *Mommy,* and get me off of your lap before I collapse. All the blood is going to my dangling limbs, my cock included."

That earns him a few more spanks, and when my wrist is aching and my palm is sore, as is his ass, I'd imagine, I let him get up. Yeah, no, I'm pretty sure if I took a class in "the art of spanking" I'd be breaking every rule in the book. Ten out of ten, will try again.

"Now go sit down in that chair," I say, pointing to the last one still standing after last night.

He shakes his head, looking defeated as he hobbles over to the chair with his beet-red ass cheeks lighting the way like a beacon in the night. I have to suck my lips into my mouth to contain the laughter. Being on the receiving end of this same kind of torture is beyond fun, but damn, if I were a journaling kind of woman, I'd definitely be writing about *this.*

I scoot further back on the bed, angling myself so that when I lean back, opening my legs wide for him, he can see exactly what he's not allowed to have. *Not yet,* anyway.

My hand slips between my spread thighs, and I swirl my fingers over my clit, arching off the bed. Pleasure ripples through me, reminding me how badly I want us to get to the finish line.

"You can look, but you can't touch. Do you understand?" I ask.

"Yes," he grunts, but just as I'd thought, when I look over at him, he's fisting his cock.

"*I said* no touching, Rafael. Do I need to make myself more clear?"

"Seriously?" he whines. "I thought you meant no touching *you*. Jesus, fuck."

I'd pay good money, money I certainly don't have, to see this man whimper. In fact, it's my entire goal for the night.

"Nope, no touching at all. Sit on your hands."

I can tell he wants to roll his eyes, but he holds back, lifting his ass and sliding his hands under his thighs like I'd told him to.

"*Un si bon garçon*," I praise with a smirk, pumping two fingers inside myself, greatly over-exaggerating the sounds it elicits from me, knowing I'm driving him wild. Hell, I'm driving *myself* wild. I want him inside me already, but I'm having too much fun to give in yet.

Rafael's twitching as he releases groan after frustrated groan, and when I spread my pussy lips and drive three fingers inside, *he whimpers.*

My eyes are wide as I shoot up, removing my fingers from my centre.

I wear a wide grin as I watch him squirm under my gaze, his cock fully erect, with a bead of precum leaking from the tip.

"Alright, your turn," I say and watch as the recognition flashes in his eyes. He immediately stands, practically running to pick me up, just to toss me in the centre of the bed.

"On your knees, *peligrosa*. It's time I repay the favour." And boy, *does he ever.*

Everything is sore, and I'm mildly convinced my ass is going to be red for the next week, but it was well worth it.

Rafael cleaned us up, and now that his arms are wrapped around me as he hums a song I don't recognise, pressing kisses to the top of my head, my lids are incredibly heavy.

I reach over, turning off the lamp before settling back against his chest. Several moments pass, my mind drifting in and out of consciousness, but before I can fully doze off, Rafael's soft voice falls around me.

"Baby," he whispers. "Are you okay?"

My ears perk, worry niggling at the edges of my heart. I turn over so our chests are pressed together, sliding a hand up his, resting it over his heart. "Yeah, of course I am. Why? What's wrong?" I ask.

Maybe he's overwhelmed by how quickly we're moving. I feel like I might be if I allow myself to think on it too long, but everything with him just feels so *right*.

He captures my hand, resting his over mine and squeezing gently. "I just wanted to make sure you were okay. I'm second-guessing taking you to the church," he admits.

My chest suddenly has a boulder sitting on it. *Regret.* God, I hate that emotion. It's arguably my least favourite of them all and something I've worked diligently to overcome in therapy.

"I can practically hear the wheels turning in your head, Elise," he says with a chuckle. "I don't regret taking you or writing our names on that wall, or any part of the experience. I'm worried that it was too much with your fear of heights."

An audible breath leaves my lungs, and my rigid muscles melt back into the bed. "No, Rafa. I hated the heights, so don't do that shit again, but I don't have any regrets. It was romantic in a twisted and annoying sort of way." I let out a soft laugh, the corners of my mouth curling as I speak, amusement dancing in my voice.

He chuckles, pressing a kiss to my forehead. "Deal, but only if you promise not to spank me again. That got me hard for no good reason, and as much fun as it proved to be, I think I'll stick to being the one doing the spanking."

My cheeks flush with the memory. "Sounds good to me. It was fun, but I don't really have an interest in being a switch. Sex is one of the only times I'm okay relinquishing control."

He strokes a thumb over my cheekbone, tucking a lock of hair behind my ear.

"And why is that?" he asks, his tone soft again.

I take a moment to think, reluctant to answer something like that without putting thought into it, and after a brief pause, the answer is clear "Having bipolar disorder has taken a lot from me, I think. Sure, there are worse things, and I've been very fortunate that with medication I'm usually pretty stable, but the fear of slipping into a manic or depressive episode is something that just ruminates with me at a baseline. It's not at the forefront of my mind, but it sits there like background noise."

He runs his hand along the back of my head, pulling my cheek to rest on his chest, but he says nothing, letting me speak and get the thoughts out at my own pace.

"It feels like there's always this little piece of me that could make me lose myself if I'm not careful." My cheeks flush as I recall my most recent manic episode, one that he helped me find my way back from. "I try to have as much say in my life as possible to repress that feeling of being out of control. But with sex, I'm able to dissociate from it a little and let pleasure override my thoughts with endorphins and the knowledge that my partners are all consenting, willing participants who want me to experience pleasure almost as much as they do. Even knowing that, I've never been able to fully let go even with sex, at least, not until you."

"Why me?" he asks, his words sounding thick on his tongue.

"Because," I say, cupping the side of his neck and pressing a soft kiss to his plush lips, "I trust you, completely, with every part of me, *even my heart.*"

Admitting that has a knot of vulnerability tightening in my stomach. I've never wanted to allow anyone else to see this raw and unprotected side of me before, but it's true. I trust him in every sense of the word.

"Thank you," he chokes out, pressing his forehead to mine. "You're the only person I've ever even wanted to trust like this, and fuck, *I do.* I want you to have every piece of me."

"Why?" I ask, like the idiot that I am. *Why?* Really, Elise?

He chuckles, unfazed by my apparent inability to read the room. "Because, *mi vida*, with you, I feel whole."

Butterflies swarm in my stomach, my throat tightening as I repress the sob that suddenly threatens to take hold of me.

I'm not capable of words, so actions will have to suffice. I grip his cheeks in my palms, pressing my lips to his again, allowing his warmth to radiate into me. I fall asleep in his arms and have the most incredible dreams.

RAFAEL

CHAPTER FIFTY-ONE

SATURDAY, MAY 24

I FEEL like one of those lovesick idiots you see in the movies. The ones that wake up before their girl does, only to stare lovingly at them until they *finally* grace them with the gift of their beautiful eyes landing on them—the first thing they see when they wake up each morning.

I'd definitely never envisioned this for myself, but I can't say I don't like it.

Waking up with Elise in my arms, and the knowledge that she feels the same way I do, is nothing short of liberating.

A warm, comforting feeling trickles through me, and my blood hums as my fingers trail through her silky roots, brushing the flyaways off of her forehead to avoid obscuring my view of her. She's beautiful.

Elise is easily the most gorgeous woman I've ever known in my life, and it feels like a privilege to have her like this. To know that we've both lived through horrible and traumatic experiences, and we're able to trust someone else completely in spite of them.

Her eyes begin to flutter, and when they open, landing on me, the edges of her lips curve into a smile that knocks the wind right out of my fucking lungs.

"Good morning, *mi vida*."

"Morning," she says, pressing a chaste kiss to my lips before rolling over, arching her neck to look at the clock on the night-stand. Her eyes widen, and she kicks off the covers, flying out of bed.

"Where are you running off to?" I ask, watching in amusement as she works to shove all of her items into her duffle bag.

"We have five minutes before we're supposed to check out!" she shouts, and suddenly, I'm out of the bed, packing my own bag.

"I trust that your stay was enjoyable?" Mrs. Greene asks.

"It was wonderful, thank you so much," I tell her, a knot twisting in my gut as I hand her the key. She takes it from me, nodding as she rounds the desk and makes her way up the stairs.

My eyes dart to Elise's wide ones, her cheeks flushed.

I grab my wallet out, pulling out all of the bills I have and tucking it inside the cover of the book the woman had been read-ing. I tug on Elise's elbow and drag her out of the doors just in time.

We know the exact moment she's entered the room we'd been in. It's not hard to tell from the shriek she releases.

We bolt out of the doors, laughing and gasping for air as we yank open the car doors and slide inside, thanking the driver as he pulls out of the driveway and heads toward the train station.

Elise peers over at me after a few long moments of silence. "I feel bad that we broke half of her furniture. That could've all been family heirlooms," she whispers.

I shake my head. "They weren't. I felt bad, too, and checked the furniture last night. Everything was from Cox & Cox."

She blows out a breath, slumping further into her seat, and rests her cheek on my shoulder. "Thank fuck."

I chuckle lightly, my hand finding hers as we near the railway.

ELISE

CHAPTER FIFTY-TWO

SATURDAY, MAY 24

"WHEN I WAS A KID, I loved riding the train," I tell Rafael, seating myself over his lap and resting my palms on his chest.

"Where would your family take you?"

"Everywhere." An ache settles into my chest as the memories start to filter through the cracks in the walls I've spent so much time building and repairing. "On the rare weekends when I didn't have a game, my parents would take Rachelle and I on a day trip or sometimes for the whole weekend. My *maman* would pull out a map and draw a circle around the area we were allowed to pick from. It was usually something just a couple of hours away. We'd take turns with each trip, one of us picking a random location within the boundaries."

Rafa smiles, his dark eyes glinting, crinkling at the corners as he listens to me. "What kinds of places did you end up visiting?"

"It was sort of a mix of everything. After we figured out where we were heading, *Maman* would start planning. She'd pick out a place to stay or a park to visit. Sometimes there were concerts or theatre productions we'd wind up at. As long as the weather was nice, we were always outside. *Maman* would bring her kit, and she'd set herself up wherever we were, painting an image of

Rachelle and I playing, reading, *arguing*," I tell him, a sad, wet sounding laugh slipping past my lips.

Rafael reaches up with both hands, pushing the fallen strands out of my face and tucks them behind my ears. "I wish I'd gotten to meet her," he admits, and my heart can't take it. It crumples, dissolving into dust in my chest.

"She would've loved you." My voice is watery, and my chin quivers.

"I hope so," he whispers.

We spend the next hour sharing stories about past family trips, and the little pieces of Rafael I've been collecting feel like treasures.

It's like when I was a kid and I'd collect shells by the shore or take flowers from a field home to press and dry inside books. It felt like I was taking these tiny bits of a whole experience with me to remember, setting them aside to look back at later and marvel in their beauty.

And as much as I want to believe we're good for each other, and that these feelings we have growing will last, it's really difficult to feel confident in that. I've never experienced anything like this in my life. Is it the newness of it all that's heightening these feelings? My heart says a firm "No", but what if my intuition is wrong?

It wasn't long ago that we were at each other's throats. My dad used to say that the best love is one formed from passionate flames that continue to burn like flameless embers. Low and slow. Always present but never dying.

I take a deep, calming breath, forcing the sudden jumble of anxious thoughts to clear like cobwebs from my mind, but the spider is quick to rebuild them.

I might not be confident enough in my own capacity for love to be able to give myself over to him, not completely, but in the same way that he's fighting his demons, I'll do the same with mine. He deserves at least that. *We* deserve that.

Fear is the only thing holding me back. Fear of about a million things, but the constant worry that my mental health could nose-dive for the worst and he'd be here to witness it, leaving him vulnerable to the ups and downs of my moods—it doesn't feel fair.

Most days, I worry that I can't even take care of myself, let alone nurture an entire relationship. At a baseline, I have an unsettled feeling that I'll lose myself in my mental illness, and with the addition of Rafael in my life, that feeling is threatening to drag me under in the same way I worry it might take him too.

No. That's not entirely true. When I force myself to reflect on how I've been feeling lately, I'm hit with a wave of warmth, like sitting on a beach under a golden horizon. Sure, there are still bad days, but having Rafael by my side has been *relieving*. I just hadn't wanted to fully admit that until now.

"*Mi vida*," he says, speaking in a low tone against my ear as he smooths my hair over my shoulders and drags me back to the present, "you've got that cute little line between your brows that you get when you're overthinking."

Heat crawls up my neck, pooling in my chest at the thought of him watching me, studying every flicker, every shift, every crack in the armour I've spent years building. And in that moment, I feel the weight of it all, the weight of this disorder that isn't just mine to carry, but his now too. He knew that this was what he signed up for the moment it started to feel *real* for him too. And who am I to make that call, to push him away when all I really want is for him to stay? He's free to walk away anytime, and part of me fears he will. But I know this silence won't save us. I have to start speaking, even if the words shake. Even if they're not enough.

Just not right now.

"Sorry," I say, clearing my throat. "I went off to a different place for a little bit."

"Do you want to talk about it? Because I want to listen if you do."

I shake my head. "Later. I promise. I think that right now,

we've done a lot of sharing, and while I *like* that, it's not something I'm used to to this degree. I need a little more time to ruminate with my own thoughts before I share them," I admit, wanting to be clear in my intentions without jumping into an explanation that might be too hard to sort through given the newness of the circumstances surrounding the thoughts. "But I *will* share them with you, Rafa."

"That's okay. Take your time. I'll be here when you're ready." He rearranges us so I'm seated with my back pressed to his chest. "Tell me what you need right now."

I rest my head against his shoulder, closing my eyes and settling in. "*You.* Right now, I just need you and some silence to dissociate for a while." I twist to face him for a moment, ensuring our eyes are locked before I agree to something that I hope I don't regret later. "I'll come back to you in a little, I promise."

A hint of a smile touches his lips before he says again, "I'll be here."

RAFAEL

CHAPTER FIFTY-THREE

SATURDAY, MAY 24

"WE'LL BE APPROACHING Embershire Station in three minutes," the conductor says over the speakers.

It took the majority of the trip, but Elise has managed to dig her way out of the trenches of some of what's plaguing her.

She shared some of her fears with me about halfway into the train ride, explaining that her father is one of her best friends and she knows he'll accept us but there might be some resistance. But her biggest worry was about the toll *her* mental health might take on *me*, and that the thrill of our new relationship might be clouding her true feelings.

Growing up, I was always looking for a thrill, so I understand the sentiment, but I can tell this is different. I know it as fact, and in time, I hope she will too.

The fact that she says she has more to think about both tightens her hold on my throat and sends tiny sparks dancing in my chest. Because for someone like Elise, for someone like *me*, it can feel impossible to share all that's in our heads. Her taking the time to sit with her thoughts before moving on impulse means more to me than she could ever know, so when I said I'd be right here waiting for her to work it out for herself, I meant exactly that.

And something tells me she could use a bit of a distraction.

A slow smile tugs at the corners of my lips, a thought flickering to life in my mind, warm and promising. "Hey, trouble, have you ever been fucked on a railway?"

She rolls her eyes and sits up, her hands finding the waistband of her spandex shorts, sliding them down her toned thighs. She smirks as she says, "Nope, but I think I'm about to be..."

ELISE

CHAPTER FIFTY-FOUR

SATURDAY, MAY 24

RAFAEL DROPPED me off at my house, and the moment he left, my gut started to knot up, but when I hear a mixture of laughter and screams coming from inside, that tension in my gut settles. I've never had such a desire to be with someone all the time, and it feels strange to want him nearby so often, but I've also missed my girls.

I push the door open, and the sight is definitely something to see.

Chelsea's sitting on the kitchen counter, eating one of those vile creations she always makes with a fruit winder wrapped around a dill pickle, and her camera is pointed at Letty and Adhira.

Letty's got Adhira doubled over in a chair as she screams her head off, clutching her robe around her waist.

"What did I just come home to?" I ask, already having an idea thanks to the pot of hot wax sitting on the counter beside them.

"Your friend is torturing me." Adhira groans from beneath a cascade of dark hair. And for the first time, I notice she's a lot thinner than she had been at the start of the year. *Probably just stress.*

"My friend?" I ask, smirking as I drop my duffle by the door and take a seat at the kitchen island.

"I no longer claim her," she says, her posh British accent blending with the sing-song lilt of the remnants of her Gujarati accent from summers spent in India as she grits out the words.

Letty dips a thick popsicle stick into the pot of wax, winding it around several times to cool the molten liquid. "You asked for this," she says, showing no remorse as she pushes the fallen strands out of her way, applying a thick layer of wax along Adhira's neck.

"You're right. I should really be blaming my mother for plaguing me with her hairy neck."

"It's okay, babe. I'll get Chelsea's unibrow next," Letty jokes, ripping the wax off and clamping a hand down on the red spot blooming beneath it to calm the sting as Adhira yelps in pain. "One of these days, I'll have my unibrow permanently lasered off because waxing this shit every month is ridiculous."

Our eyes fill with tears from a mixture of pain and laughter over the next thirty minutes as Letty finishes waxing Adhira's neck.

Adhira pays her back in kind, even requiring Chelsea and I let her wax our lady 'staches as payback for laughing at her.

By the time we're done, my cheeks hurt from laughing so much, and that little pang of guilt is encroaching again. I wish I could tell them about Rafael. I wish I could tell them about my weekend, but I can't.

Not yet.

RAFAEL

CHAPTER FIFTY-FIVE

SATURDAY, MAY 24

"YES, Carlito, she loved it, just like you said she would," I tell my brother, thankful for the idea to surprise Elise.

"Your good looks are wasted on you, Rafa. If I looked like you, I'd be getting all the ladies," he jokes.

"We're practically identical," I say, groaning. "People assumed we were twins until they learned of our age difference."

"Yeah, yeah. I guess hot rugby player still outdoes thoughtful nerd though, so I'll accept that as explanation enough. Now, tell me everything," he gushes.

Carlos is a romantic at heart. He's kind of awkward when he first meets someone, but he opens up quickly, willingly exposes every piece of his soul, and lives for thoughtful gestures. He's everything I hope to be for Elise. It's not in my nature, but for her, I'll make the effort.

I tell him about the church and how everything went, leaving out the less tasteful details, and by the end of it, he's giggling like a schoolgirl. "Little Rafa's in *love,*" he sings over the line.

My face heats as the truth of that lights me up and terrifies me all at the same time. Because when you love someone, it's that much easier to get your heart broken if they leave or *worse.* And as guilty as it makes me feel, I worry about her struggles with bipolar disorder. I'm willing to learn and take the time necessary to give us both the support we need to navigate that, but I'm afraid I'll fuck something up or say something harmful or triggering.

But we'll cross that bridge when we get there, because we *will* get there. *Together.*

"Maybe," I say, and immediately, he calls me out on it.

"No need to lie, baby bro. I can't wait to meet her! Speaking of, when are you bringing her here? You haven't come to visit in years, and Mamí won't stop talking about it."

My shoulders feel tense, guilt wearing on me. "I don't know, Carlos," I say, stalling as I search for a better answer.

"Come on. You've got a break coming up in a few weeks. Just come visit for a few days. Bring Elise with you!"

I groan, melting into my couch cushions. Mrs. Purrito hops into my lap, circling around to find a good spot before settling in.

I stroke her soft fur, closing my eyes and waiting for an answer, but for the first time in forever, I don't have a *good* reason not to visit. And it's not that I don't want to. It's that without Carlos ever having the slightest intention of doing so, he fills me with an overwhelming guilt I struggle to shake off for weeks after visiting.

Though I guess that if I don't visit when I actually have the time to, it might make me feel exponentially worse.

"Fine," I say, letting the word ring in the silence between us.

"F-fine?" he asks, disbelief clear in his voice.

"That's what I said, isn't it?"

"You'll actually visit?"

"Yep."

"Alright, then," he breathes. "Text me the details and I'll let Mamí know," he says, fully aware of why I wouldn't want to tell her myself. If it ends up not happening for some reason, I'll never hear the end of it.

"Thanks, Carlos. Now, tell me about how physical therapy is going."

Thankfully, he takes the bait, telling me all about the new PT he's seeing and the innovative treatments they've started implementing.

CHAPTER FIFTY-SIX

SUNDAY, MAY 25

MY HEART STARTS to take off at a sprint as I read his words, unsure of where this is going and if I'm ready for whatever *this* is yet.

Thankfully, he saves me from my anxious spiral before I have the chance to start shutting down.

Thank god.

SUNNY D

Head downstairs and open the door.

> Lol I'm not going to hitchhike if that's what you're suggesting. I think we can both make it one night.

SUNNY D

Speak for yourself.

And just do as you're told for once.

Like the smart man that he is, another text comes through immediately.

SUNNY D

Please, mi vida.

I climb out of bed, careful not to step on any of the creaking floorboards as I pad across the hardwood. I turn my light off so the girls won't wake up but leave my door open in case I'm about to sneak a boy—no, a *grown man*—into my bedroom. This is just like senior year of high school all over again.

I make it down the stairs and to the front door without anyone waking up, my heart in my throat as I recall their most recent intervention. The door unlocks with a snick before I tug it open and find Rafael standing on my porch wearing a cocky smirk that leaves me lightheaded.

He reaches out to tug my bottom lip from between my teeth, shifting his hand to cup my jaw and pull me in for a chaste kiss. When he withdraws, he grips my shoulders, spinning me around and swatting my ass. "Go on, *sunshine*. Lead the way." My heart suddenly feels like it's bursting.

The thing about that damn nickname is that with him, I sort of do feel like the sunshiny girls I grew up envying.

I don't have much time to reflect on that before I'm grabbing his hand and leading him up the stairs, careful not to make too much noise for fear of outing us to my best friends.

Once we're in my small, dark room, I find my bedside lamp and illuminate the small space in a soft, warm glow.

Rafael peers around, refusing to let go of my hand as he takes in every detail from the small wooden bed frame with the baby-blue quilt to the matching chest of drawers with photos of my parents, Rachelle, and my friends. He picks up each photo, studying them one by one, silent as he continues on through every last one.

His eyes finally meet mine when he says, "You look like them, you know." His voice is so gentle, and the words wrap around me like a plush blanket. "But I can still tell which one is you in these photos. I'd know my girl anywhere."

My girl.

He says it as if this is our thing now. As if we'd solidified that as fact, and that I'd somehow become officially his. It should infuriate me that he's staking some claim on me, but it doesn't. Not at all. In fact, it has the opposite effect, making me realise just how much I want that to be true.

"I'm not, you know," I say, peering up at him.

"Not what?" he asks, his dark brow with the freshly shaven line at the corner now arched in question.

"Not yours," I breathe but add, "but I want to be." I avert my gaze, my neck flushing with heat. "If you'll have me."

I've spent the better part of the weekend sorting through my feelings, and no matter what path I took, they all led me back to *him.*

Yes, we've spoken briefly about wanting to trust each other with our hearts, and that was sweet, but we need a full conversation, and I'm ready to have it.

His large hands settle on my cheeks, pulling my eyes to meet his before smoothing them over my hair and down my back to tug me to his chest. He winds his arms around me, and I feel so damn safe in his embrace.

"I most definitely want you, Elise," he whispers.

I hold my breath, my eyes burning as they fill with hot tears, waiting for the "but."

It never comes.

"I know this wasn't planned. That *we* weren't planned, but I don't think fate or destiny or whatever you want to call it, gives a shit about our plans. I don't know how either of us is going to learn how to be what the other needs without losing ourselves in the process, but I want to figure it out with you," he says, his words ardent.

"It'll be a mess," I remind him, but that doesn't deter him in the least.

He just smiles and says, "A beautiful mess."

My heart does this strange thing that I can only explain as cracking wide open after bursting at the seams, only to turn itself inside out and swallow me whole. *That* is what his words do to me.

I've never had anyone want to be a beautiful mess with me. Never had anyone I cared enough about to even want to try that with.

"We'll work it out, *mi vida*. We'll take it one day at a time, okay?"

I nod but croak out, "But we have to wait until the season is up. Recruiters are showing up to our games all the time now, and I don't want to throw the team's momentum off or act as a distraction. So we've got to wait."

"Then we'll wait. I have a feeling I'd wait forever for you, Elise. No matter what, even if you change your mind altogether, just tell me how you're feeling, alright?"

"The same goes for you," I say, pinning him with a hard stare.

"Of course, baby." He buries his face in my head, murmuring into my hair and peppering kisses to the crown of my head before tugging me toward my bed.

We settle in together, and his large frame eats up most of the space in my small bed. After a few beats of silence, I take a deep breath and ready myself for the part of this conversation I've been most worried about.

"What are your concerns?" I ask him, steeling myself for a few heavy blows to the heart, but this is important. I need to know, even if it hurts.

"I just want to make sure you don't hold back with me. I don't know a lot about bipolar disorder. I'm learning, I'm reading, and I *will* do right by you, Elise, but I need you to be patient with me," he says, whispering the last words. "I need you to tell me what you're thinking, and how I can help you navigate it because I have absolutely no idea what I'm doing, and I'm terrified I'm going to say or do the wrong things."

The blows never come. Not even a solid gut punch.

And yet again, he tells me not only what I *want* to hear, but what I so desperately *need* to hear.

"Rafael, you can't really do or say anything wrong when it comes to my mental illness because most of the time, I don't even know how I'm expected to feel about it or how I should be navigating it, but I think that's something we can learn together with time. It's something that's relatively new to me. I was diagnosed shortly after my eighteenth birthday, and if I really dig into my family trauma, it's probably added to my reluctance to lean on anyone else because it felt so shitty to have to add another thing to my dad's plate after my *maman* and Rachelle died." This isn't a completely new revelation, but it's certainly one I hadn't been able to put into words, and I definitely haven't shared it with anyone other than my therapist. It's scary but also freeing to have someone to help shoulder the burden.

"Then we'll sort it out together." And there we have it, ladies, gents, and everyone else the reason the age-gap trope works so well in both books and real life.

Because this man is grown, and I know I wouldn't be having this conversation with the likes of a Brad, Chad, or Brett.

I peer up at him, finding him working his bottom lip between his teeth as he stares at the corner of my ceiling.

"You're making me nervous with that lip-chewing nonsense. What's wrong?"

A startled laugh spills out before he can muffle it. I clamp my hand over his mouth and level him with a glare.

"Sorry," he says, fully recovered from his outburst. "I just feel like a dweeb for suggesting this, but I was talking about some of my fears with Carlos, and he suggested couples counselling."

My eyes widen, but I bite my tongue, remaining silent as I wait impatiently to hear what this could be about.

"And I know it sounds strange, especially because we've *just* entered our relationship, but he explained it as being something that's useful for couples who aren't yet having problems. He said that we currently have a brand-new car—" My brows knit together as I try to figure out what the hell that could mean. "Just bear with me," he says, chuckling. "He says we have this new car when we start our relationship, but couples counselling gives us the spare tyre, the tyre jack, electric air pump, flashlight, wet naps, and whatever else we might need along the way. That way, when problems arise, we already have ways to work through them and prevent our metaphorical car from breaking down."

"And to be clear, the car is our relationship, right?" I ask, unable to hide the humour in my voice.

"Yes," he says with another laugh. "If you don't want to try it, that's okay. But I think he makes a good point. Maybe after we've spoken to your dad and have worked through the first steps, we can give it a try?"

My lungs feel tight at the mention of my dad. God, he'd be so disappointed right now. Not because of who I'm dating but how I'm going about it. Knowing that has bile climbing up my throat, and my lungs feel tight.

I give his hand a squeeze, silently telling him that I just need a few more moments to process the suggestion. I think that's become something we do and haven't even been fully aware of it. And if something like this might be what a counsellor would suggest we put in our "new car", I'd be open to it. But there's another idea I've thought about off and on the last year, and I think now would be a good time to voice the thought.

"Couples counselling sounds like a good idea, but I also want to go back to therapy," I say, meeting his eyes again. "Alone."

He turns us over, pressing his forehead to mine. "Anything you need, and maybe I should put some thought into that for myself."

Butterflies dance in my belly, and such a strange, light feeling passes over me.

"I'm sorry I could barely tolerate you when we first met," I tell him.

His lips widen into a full grin. "Hopefully your dad still tolerates me after we finally tell him we're together," he says, and my heart feels like it's glued itself back together, twisting behind my ribs.

"Yeah, you and me both," I say, mostly joking.

A thought nags at the edges of my mind, my smile faltering. "What is it?"

"I want to tell my dad about us as soon as the rugby season is over." A heaviness settles on my chest, and my throat feels tight.

"We can tell him whenever you're comfortable."

I nod, and he runs the pad of his thumb over my bottom lip. "And to be clear, I don't give a damn about the consequences, Elise. You're an adult, and you're *mine*. That'll remain true regardless of what happens with your dad."

That weight starts to lift the smallest bit. "I'm not worried about him lashing out on you, in case that's what you're worried about. I'm only worried that he'll be hurt that we hadn't told him sooner."

"We've taken some time to get to know each other better, and in doing so, we've developed feelings. That's not something either of us can prevent, and I wouldn't want to even if we could. Your dad might need time to process, but he'll get there. I'm sure of it."

Tears well in my eyes, my nose suddenly stuffy. "I wish my

maman were still here," I whisper. "I'd be able to tell her, and she'd lighten the blow with Dad."

I settle down on top of him, allowing his strong arms to cocoon me in his comforting embrace, the rhythmic beating of his heart a steady sound that soothes some of the ache in my chest.

"I can't even begin to imagine how hard it's been for you to adjust to so many changes in your life these last few years, but I'm in awe of you."

"I don't understand. Why would you be in awe of me? I'm a brat to ninety percent of people, I can't cook to save my life, and I rely heavily on my roommates to make sure I stay alive. It takes three business days for me to sort through my emotions well enough to speak about them—"

He cuts me off, unwilling to hear my doom spiral. "The fact that you *know* it takes you a while to process your thoughts and have been giving yourself the grace to do so is something to be proud of. I'm used to acting on impulse or not speaking at all, and it's something I've been working on. Now, I didn't realise you couldn't cook, but that actually makes a lot of sense seeing as you've never even tried in my presence, but we'll hire a chef or get meals delivered, and I can teach you how to cook. *Mami* will too, I'm sure."

I lift my head, wide-eyed as I stare at him. "Your mum?"

He averts his gaze, looking sheepish with lightly pinkened cheeks. "Yeah, so..." He reaches up to scratch his neck, his eyes never meeting mine. "I was talking to Carlos, and he begged me to come visit with you, and I said yes. I hope that's okay."

I can't help the chuckle that escapes me at his sudden shyness. "Rafa," I say, but he still refuses to meet my eyes. "Rafael, look at me." I snicker.

When his big brown eyes meet my gaze, he's pouting, and it's unbelievably adorable. "I would *love* to meet your family. I'm absolutely going to fuck it up and embarrass you and probably throw up on the way there because I hate plane rides, but I want to go."

He grabs my cheeks and plants a sloppy kiss on my lips that leaves me bursting with happiness as he pulls away, his eyes squinted at the corners and a contented smile on his full, wide lips. "You can't fuck it up, Elise. There's no way for you to."

"Is that a challenge?" I joke, my brow quirked.

He rolls his eyes playfully, tugging me down onto his firm chest. "Thank you for agreeing to come," he whispers.

"Thank you for wanting me to go."

"I always want you with me," he says, making my heart grow three sizes in my chest with his soft-spoken words. "Now, let's get some sleep. We've both got games tomorrow, and you've gotta be on it."

"Am I ever *not* on it?" I snark, rolling my eyes and tugging my quilt up to my chin.

"No, *mi vida*. No, you are not," he says, kissing my forehead and leaning over to turn off the lamp, bathing us in darkness.

"Goodnight," I whisper.

"Goodnight, *mi vida*."

His steady breaths are the last thing I hear before drifting off, my dreams filled with a memory of my favourite birthday, before *Maman* got sick.

RAFAEL

CHAPTER FIFTY-SEVEN

FRIDAY, MAY 30

AS I STAND out on the sidelines of the pitch, watching the ladies take their places on the field, my heart swells with an unfamiliar pride.

A lot has changed for me since I first accepted the position as their interim coach, and as strange as it seems, knowing my teammates are here to support these women is really fucking cool too.

They don't *have* to be here, and if they didn't want to be, I know they wouldn't, but it's the final game of the season. Elise's *final* game, and while my friends don't know what she means to me, they at least know this team means way more than I'd ever anticipated it would.

So today, despite having a game of our own in just a few hours, my closest friends are here to cheer us all on.

Elise jogs toward me, the game not yet started. "Hey," she says, letting out a breathless laugh as she stops in front of me. "You see all the recruiters in the stands?" she asks, her eyes flitting over the crowd of people gathered in the bleachers.

"How could I not? You've been sending me pictures of each of them all week so I'd know who's who," I say, smirking.

"I'm glad you've been paying attention. Now, get ready to be amazed because *that*," she says, tilting her chin to a thin brunette woman who looks to be in her fifties, seated a few rows up, centre field, "is Lorelle Laurent, the UK women's football recruiter for the Olympic team. And I'm about to show her exactly why they need me." Her face is fucking glowing with excitement and joy like I've never seen it before.

"I have absolutely no doubt," I say, keeping our interaction brief because the longer she stands here, the more likely it is I'll kiss her. "Now, Captain, get your ass back on the field."

"Yes, sir," she says with a chuckle, turning and sprinting into position.

My palms burn as I continue clapping them together, screaming across the field. "Yes! Yes, Elise!" My throat is raw from the last hour of obnoxious shouting I've been doing.

We're more than halfway through the game, and these ladies aren't tiring out. Well, everyone besides Adhira.

She's been sluggish tonight, but judging by her ashen skin and sunken eyes, I'd say she's probably coming down with something. I'd pull her entirely, but it's her senior year, her last game, and frankly, we're still winning, so it hasn't made too much of an impact.

For someone who loves to be in control, rightfully so, Elise is a great captain. She trusts her own instincts and her teammates even more so.

Watching her play, silently nudging her teammates where she wants them to be while compensating when someone looks like they're struggling—it's fucking incredible. She thinks so damn fast on her feet, and when she sees Adhira having an even harder time than she has been the rest of the game, she gives the Mayhem the runaround, taunting their defensive midfielder, giving Adhira a moment to catch her breath.

And the moment I see that little wink she shoots Adhira, my fucking gut is squeezing tight, and my blood hums with adrenaline.

Elise feigns directions, shooting out the opposite side, just barely making it past the Mayhem's defence as she hauls her tight little ass down the pitch.

I'm not sure that she even realises she does it, but one thing that sets Elise apart from any other player I've ever known is her ability to just *act*.

There's no contemplation when she's playing. She moves on instinct alone, her body carrying her to where she needs to be. On the rare occasion that she misses a shot, she just moves the hell on with no dwelling involved. She doesn't think before she makes a play; she just does it, and it's goddamn *beautiful*.

My heart clenches in my chest watching as she makes her way to the goalkeeper, and just as I expect, she makes her move without anyone, including me, knowing what she's going to do or what part of the net that ball will be sailing into.

And fuck me, it makes all the blood rush to *both* of my heads the moment she sends it soaring through the air, the Mayhem's defence grappling for her just as it slips right past their goalie's fingers.

CHAPTER FIFTY-EIGHT

FRIDAY, MAY 30

MY KNEES BUCKLE beneath me under the weight of the Mayhem's fullback, but my smile is still fully intact when I hit the moist ground with a painful thud.

My gaze swings over to the stands, searching for the Olympic team's recruiter. I find her the moment the ball makes it into the net.

I don't see it happen, but I *know* it does because my teammates are screaming, Rafael the loudest of them all, and then there's the fact that Lorelle Laurent herself is standing, her eyes locked on the goaltender, and in that sweet, beautiful moment of victory, her clenched jaw unhinges as she whoops loudly, bending in half with a relieved expression.

I don't think recruiters are supposed to be this biased, but how could you not be? I'm about to be the best footballer of my fucking generation, and not only do I know it, but now *she does too.*

The rest of the game is much the same. I'm pushing myself further than I'd ever have thought possible, scoring goal after goal, making the last game of my university career the best it can be. Between Rafael cheering me on, Lorelle being in attendance, and the sheer adrenaline coursing through me, I'm on fucking fire tonight.

We're in the final seconds of the game, our score nearly double that of the Mayhem's, but it isn't enough for me. I have one more in me.

I know I do, so I drag my aching, tired muscles across the pitch, whipping past the defensive line as my heart pounds in my chest, threatening to explode behind my ribcage with the force of my movements. The Mayhem's players grab for me in a failed attempt to slow me down, but not today. *Today* I have my eyes on the prize, and absolutely no one is going to stop me.

I rush toward the goalie, and without a second thought, my foot connects with the ball for the last time before it sails through the air. The movement was so strong, and thanks to a midafternoon rain shower, the wet pitch landed me on my ass, but this time I get to watch from the ground as the ball makes it into the bottom left-hand corner of the net.

My cheeks burn from the smile causing my facial muscles to cramp as I flop on my back, staring up at the overcast sky, the sun peeking out from a grey cloud. My heart rate starts to slow down as my chest heaves from exertion.

Everything happening around me seems to slow to a crawl; the sounds of my teammates' cheers become muffled as this sweet, blissful moment washes over me.

It isn't until Rafael and my dad are dropping to their knees beside me, their faces lit up as Rafael physically shakes me, pulling me up into his arms, that I snap out of the quiet moment.

"You were stellar, Elise. Fucking stunning," he says, clearing his throat when he realises my dad is beside us, "performance. A stunning performance on the pitch for your final uni game," he finishes, releasing me abruptly. I have to bite my lip to contain the laughter bubbling up inside me.

"Thanks, Coach," I manage to choke out, turning toward my dad, whose brow is quirked, but his lips are still stretched in a wide smile. I wrap my arms around his shoulders, and he clutches me tightly.

"I've never been more proud, Elise," he says. "You were

unstoppable out there." His next words come out as a whisper, spoken into my messy hair so only I can hear them. "Your *maman* and Rachelle would be so incredibly proud," he says, his voice cracking.

My throat feels tight as my eyes burn with unshed tears. "I think so too," I croak.

The moment passes quickly as my teammates rush over to pull me up, still shrieking over the rush of our final win together.

Just as I'm headed to the locker room, I hear an unfamiliar voice call my name, stopping me in my tracks.

"Elise! Elise, I'd love to have a quick chat with you," she says, and as I turn, my eyes land on Lorelle Laurent. She waits until I jog up the pitch, stopping a couple feet in front of her and extending my hand. "It's nice to finally meet you, Elise. I'm Lorelle Laurent from the Embershire women's football Olympic team."

I shake her hand firmly, the goofy grin overtaking my face refusing to be toned down. "It's great to meet you too, Ms. Laurent. Thanks for coming out today."

"The pleasure was all mine," she says, her lips turning up in a wide smile. "Truly, that was an unbelievable match. I have a feeling I'll be telling my grandchildren about you someday."

A blush creeps up my cheeks. "Well, I certainly hope so."

"Me too. Listen, I'll let you get showered, but here's my card," she says, passing the small rectangular paper to me as if it's nothing. As if this isn't the day I've been waiting for my entire life. "I got your information from your coach, so you'll be hearing from me soon, but tryouts for the twenty twenty-eight Olympic team are starting soon, and I'd like you to be there."

"I'd like that very much. Ah, sorry, I mean, thank you so much for the opportunity." *Come on, Elise, stop being so awkward.*

"Hey, again, it was great chatting with you, and we'll talk soon," she says, giving me a little wave before she turns back toward the exit.

It isn't until I'm in the locker room that I allow myself to get lost in this overwhelming high.

My teammates are all completely silent as I enter, their eyes locked on me, waiting for something, *anything*.

"THEY WANT ME!" I shout, and chaos ensues. The locker room erupts in cheers and shouts, and once again, I'm being tackled to the ground, but this time, it's by their love and support.

I'm practically floating through the motions of showering and changing before we leave for the last time. It's so surreal.

"Alright, hotshot. What would you like to do tonight to celebrate our last big win together?" Chelsea asks, and I expected those words to hurt, to act as a reminder that while I've gotten almost everything I've ever wanted this year, I won't be playing the sport I love with the people I love.

But before I can take myself to that place, Letty speaks up.

"Look at the four of us," she says, slinging an arm over mine and Chelsea's shoulder. "We're all getting everything we want out of life. I'm starting my internship, Chelsea has her culinary school plans lined up, and Adhira got accepted at her top-choice physician assistant program. And we can't forget about our fearless leader who'll be playing in the premier leagues soon and is getting appointed for the Olympic team, where she'll allow the past three years of her education to wither away."

"I'll pretend I didn't hear that last bit," I joke, nudging her in the side with my elbow.

We're all getting everything we want for our careers, and there's almost nothing better.

"What do you say we celebrate by watching some perky rugby ass and getting sloshed at the pub after?"

"Perky rugby ass?" I ask, my brow raised in question.

"Yeah, Coach's team came out to watch us; I figured we could repay the favour," Letty suggests.

"Well, alright then, it's settled. Rugby thighs, on three!" Chelsea yells, putting her hand in the centre of our group with her palm toward the ground. We all roll our eyes but reluctantly join in.

"One, two, three," she says as we shout, "rugby thighs!"

Laughter fills the space as we make our exit, heading home to change just in time to make it to the Wyvern's match.

ELISE

CHAPTER FIFTY-NINE

FRIDAY, MAY 30

I'M CRUSHED between Letty and Chelsea because Adhira yelled at them about minding her personal space, which means that I no longer have any.

Chelsea shoves her plate of chips in my face, silently telling me to help her eat them. I take a few, popping one into my mouth as she starts with her usual bullshit.

"Do you think they wear those tiny shorts to distract each other?" she asks as the players get into their positions on the pitch.

"Something tells me they aren't nearly as distracted by them as we are," Letty answers.

"This represents the first match between the Embershire Wyvern and Wales Wolverines since the Wyvern won their second World Cup. It's certainly going to be an exciting day for rugby fans around the world."

The Wyvern's fly-half starts off the game, sending the ball sailing high in the sky and straight through the Embershire's ruck to the players' awaiting arms.

"Jelani Hazzel takes the ball, oh, and is immediately tackled inside the quarter."

Players from both teams pile on top of him, but as each player focuses their eyes on whoever's in front of them, the Wyvern's rookie blindside-flanker wiggles his way out between their legs and takes off.

"And here's a breakout! Elijah Elliot makes his way, tearing across the pitch toward the Wale's ruck. Oof, and down he goes."

"The match has *just* started. I'd appreciate it if you'd save the broken skin for the last few minutes, please," Chelsea tells me, nodding her chin to where my nails are digging into her thigh.

"Sorry," I say, extracting my hand from her. "Didn't realise I was doing it," I admit.

"There, there," she says, patting my shoulder. "I'm sure Coach won't disappoint us by losing tonight. Don't you worry," she says in a mocking tone, her eyes glittering with mirth.

"I wasn't worried," I grumble, and thankfully, she doesn't press further.

"It looks like the Wolverines' defence is taking a little bit of a nap as the ball goes to Nakoa Kawai."

"Damn, that torpedo was beautiful," Chelsea admires, stuffing her face with more food.

"Are they even trying?" Adhira asks, sounding bored despite the way her eyes are locked on the pitch, and she hasn't so much as glanced in my direction since the match started.

"I'd say they're trying judging by the buckets of sweat already pouring off of them," Letty tells her.

"Yeah, they're trying. They just aren't as good as the Wyvern," Chelsea says.

"It's an incredible sight to see as the Wyvern dominate the pitch, making their fifth try in the first nine minutes!"

My heart is pounding out of my chest as we watch every minute pass, the Wyvern absolutely pulverising the Wolverines. The way they take control of the ball, working together in a beautiful dance of strategy, is stunning. I've been watching this sport all of my life, and it isn't until now that I share the level of appreciation my father has for it. I can understand why Rafael would be almost as fulfilled by rugby as he was football.

Excited fans wearing the Wyverns jerseys surround us, their faces painted as they shout and clap, filling the space around us with an excited energy so strong it's palpable.

Letty's voice cuts through some of the tension. "How is it that Americans think they created football when both our sport and *this* exist?" she asks in apparent disbelief.

"It's a game of feet, Letty," Chelsea scoffs.

"And yet, their *feet* are hardly ever on the ball," I murmur.

"I won't argue that it's the lesser sport, okay? But us *Americans* don't use the metric system, so the game is quite literally about *feet*," she argues.

"It's technically yards, not feet. And that raises an excellent question in itself, Chels. Why *don't* Americans use the metric system? Everyone else does. It would be so much easier for all involved. And what really is the purpose of having names that mean practically nothing? An inch, foot, yard," Adhira chides, shaking her head. "Milli*metre*, centi*metre*, kilo*metre*. Now *that* makes sense. So strange," she finishes, effectively ending the conversation, one we seem to have entirely too frequently.

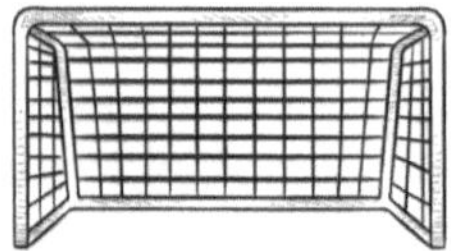

I shift for the hundredth time, trying to get comfortable in these crowded metal bleachers. "I have an even greater appreciation for our fans after this experience. I can't see how anyone would want to sit here when they could be on the field or even at home watching from the comfort of their sofa," I admit, raising my voice to be heard over the cheers of the crowd.

"I just don't understand why people leave their rubbish everywhere," Adhira remarks, looking around at the frilly silvery wrappers, crushed beer cans, and popcorn littering the stands.

"Can you both shut up and stop complaining? The game is almost over, and I can't see with how loud you're all being," Chelsea grunts out.

"You realise that makes no sense at all, right?"

Adhira shakes her head. "She's saying it's difficult to concentrate with too much going on around her. It's a distraction and makes it hard for her to focus on one thing when she's overwhelmed by the others."

Well, I've certainly never thought about that before.

I swing my eyes back to the pitch when I hear the announcer yelling Rafael's number.

"Wyvern's #2 successfully hooks the ball back through the prop's legs, winning possession of the ball once again!"

The scrum breaks apart with the Wyvern's second-row sprinting down the pitch. He passes the ball to the nearest player with just enough time before he gets mauled by two of the Wolverines.

My heart is in my throat as I track the ball, losing sight of it momentarily as the slow trickle of rain starts to come down harder. I cup my hands over my eyes, standing for a better view as the Wyverns make another try.

I blow out a relieved breath, sagging back into my seat.

"This is bloody huge for them!" Adhira shouts, sounding more excited in that one sentence than I've heard her in the last three months. "They're one try away from breaking a league record!"

I quirk a brow at her, and she rolls her eyes, crossing her arms over her chest.

"What? Can't a woman enjoy sports other than football?" she asks, her tone sounding accusatory.

"I had no idea you were such a fan, I'm sorry," I say, chuckling with my palms up in surrender.

She swings her gaze toward the field and then back to me. "You listen to porn," she says before shifting her gaze between Letty and Chelsea. "You watch porn, and *you* read porn. I watch rugby. I'm not ashamed to say that those thick thighs do it for me too."

A startled laugh passes my lips, and I'm joined by Letty and Chelsea, who can't seem to catch their breath. Chelsea's making a wheezing sound reminiscent of a tea kettle as her laughter dies down.

"I can't argue there."

"With only thirty seconds left in the game and one try left to break the premiership world record, can the Wyvern make it?!"

These last few seconds are the most hair-raising of them all.

My skin is tingling with electricity as I dig my nails into Chelsea's arm this time. The Wyvern are commandeering the ball, and the crowd is shouting, counting down every last second. All the while, my pulse is hammering!

The rain continues to fall, leaving the pitch slick as the players slide across the field, several going down, giving others the opportunity to slip in for a chance at gaining possession.

"Come on!" I find myself screaming, if not for any real reason other than to get some of the energy that's threatening to suffocate me out of my body.

"Step your pussy up!" Chelsea practically screeches, and if I had any idea what that meant, I might even adopt the phrase right now.

The sound of my heart pounding in my ears covers the voice of the announcer as I see one of the Wyvern's players kick the ball down the pitch before being tackled. My eyes ping-pong to the lock who's being hoisted up by his shorts in an effort to catch the ball.

The moment his hands make contact, he wraps his arms around it as he's quickly lowered to the ground. One of the Wolverines players tackles him, his fingers digging into his waistband, and as he takes off toward the goal line, shaking the other bloke off with complete abandon, he's got not a single care that the Wolverine's defence dragged his shorts so far down his arse that the crowd is getting an unobscured view of his untanned cheeks.

With every passing second that the Wolverines grow nearer and nearer to him, my chest squeezes, as do my lungs, but that beautiful moment as he falls to the ground, sliding over the line and pressing the ball firmly into the ground, is like nothing else.

The rush of adrenaline sweeping through me as the announcer shouts about their world record-breaking win; it's incredible. Simply bloody incredible, and the sore ass I've got from these seats was absolutely worth it.

Rafael and his team rush to the centreline, sprinting off to my dad and piling on top of him. They break away with wide smiles on their faces, a mixture of sweat and rain dripping down their foreheads. It doesn't take long before I'm honed in on Rafael's face as he searches the stands for me. If I thought his smile before was bright, I was absolutely wrong because nothing compares to how this one lights up his whole face like a ray of sunshine as our eyes meet.

Maybe that nickname is sort of fitting.

He tears his eyes away from me, turning to speak with Jelani, and heads toward the locker rooms, but I don't miss the sly smack he gives his own ass, instructing me to keep my eyes where they belong. *On him.*

I huff out a laugh as Chelsea makes a show of Adhira's current predicament. "Someone needs to get her some water—she's nearly fainted after seeing a set of perky cheeks!"

"Shut up, will you?" Adhira rumbles beside her, smacking her shoulder hard enough that Chelsea slams against my slide with more force than I'm prepared for.

"Sorry," I tell the guy beside me, pushing Chelsea off of me.

"Yeah, Chels. Let off on Adhira. I think the more pressing matter is what's going on with Elise and Coach," Letty taunts, leaning forward to focus her big brown eyes on my quickly reddening face. She wiggles her brows, a sly grin spreading her full, mauve lips.

"Nothing's going on," I say, choking the words out.

"Mhmm," Letty says, leaning back in her seat. Once the three sets of prying eyes are off of me, I can finally drag in a deep breath.

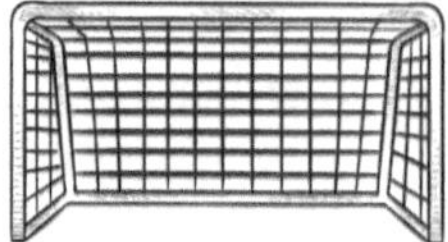

As nice as it feels to get to hang out with all of my favourite people in one place, it would be nicer if I got to be open with them about Rafael and me, but since I don't, not yet, this will have to do.

My best friends and I walk behind Rafael with his closest teammates, leading us into a small pub between campus and where we were for their game tonight. The place is clean but has the charm of a building that's been filled with people every night for longer than I've been alive.

The bar is in the centre of the large room with wood flooring and high-top tables lining the walls. The guys push a few of them together, giving us the space we need to accommodate everyone.

Nakoa and Jelani head over to get a round of beer for everyone, and as the table begins to buzz with conversation, it finally hits me that I'm about to graduate, and this is our last big hurrah.

The outside of Rafael's thigh brushes mine, dragging me from my thoughts. He leans on his elbow, his head propped up on his hand as he smirks down at me.

"Hey, Rafa, you want anything besides a water?" Nakoa calls over to him, dragging Rafael's attention away from me.

"No, I'm good, man. Thanks." As I've learned over the last few months, Rafael takes being the designated driver very seriously, which I can appreciate. There's nothing more selfish than putting yourself in a position to potentially harm tons of people for no one's benefit besides your own.

Getting behind the wheel of a car after drinking isn't something anyone should be comfortable with, in my opinion.

"Who's this?" Jelani asks, setting Letty's drink down beside her, swiping her phone from her hand.

"None of your business," she says, rolling her eyes and grabbing for her phone. He raises it high above her head, wearing an easy smirk as he chuckles deeply. "I'm serious—give me my phone back," she grits out with a pointed glare.

His shoulders drop, and all the laughter leaves his expression as he immediately hands it back to her. "I'm sorry, Letty," he says, leaning in to whisper something into her ear that I don't catch, and not for lack of trying.

I watch in awe as her tanned cheeks pinken and the smallest smile grazes her lips.

"I won't lie and say it's okay, because it's not, but you're forgiven." He gives her a small smile and tucks a rampant curl behind her ear, taking a seat at the other end of the table.

"So, who *was* that? I wanna know too," Chelsea says, smiling into her glass as she takes a sip of her beer, the froth coating her upper lip.

"Just someone I met online. It's nothing serious," she says, tucking her phone into her back pocket.

My eyes flick to Jelani, whose jaw is set, tension rippling through him no matter how much he tries to hide it.

"How's that going?" Adhira asks.

"It's fine," Letty says. There's a beat of tense silence before she slumps forward, shaking her head. "I'm lying, it sucks."

We erupt in laughter and spend the next half hour discussing the many failed prospects Letty's encountered while online dating, several of whom are apparently already dating at least three or four other people in our area.

"Anyone wanna play pool?" I ask, standing from the stool. The back of my hand grazes Rafael's, and I feel him stiffen beneath me before pushing out of his seat to join me.

"I'm game," he says.

We enter the side room, still in full view of our table, but with fewer people around, it's easier to actually speak to each other.

I wrack the balls before grabbing a cube of chalk and a stick.

"Clearly you've played before?" he asks with his cut brow raised.

"Sure have. You need a lesson?" I smirk.

"Actually, yeah. I could use a lesson," he tells me, grabbing the stick from my hand and positioning himself in front of the Q-ball.

My grin widens, my gaze flitting to our table of friends. They've all dispersed around the small stage, where a few patrons are belting out popular karaoke songs.

I slide around him, pressing my fingertips into the space between his shoulder blades, and push him forward as I plaster my body to his.

He shakes his ass against my front, and I can't help the squawk of laughter that leaves me. I smack his hip, shaking my head as I lean over his large frame, cupping his hand in mine.

I have to stand on my tiptoes to whisper in his ear, "Not like that, princess." He snorts as I reposition his hand on the stick, then the other on the table.

"Okay. You gonna show me how it's done?" he asks.

Warmth spreads through my chest, and I bite my lip, helping him mimic the motion a few times before allowing him to do it himself. He misses the ball entirely, spinning around and snatching me by the waist, twisting to press me into the smooth, glossy wood frame of the pool table, and whispers in a low growl against my ear, "Stop playing games with me, *peligrosa*. We're in public with too many prying eyes, and I can't punish you yet."

I flit my gaze around the room, catching Adhira's unimpressed expression as she rolls her eyes at me and looks back to the stage on the opposite end of the building, where Letty, Chelsea, Jelani, and Nakoa are now belting out the lyrics to "Dancing Queen" by ABBA.

I grab Rafael's hand and drag him behind the bar, pulling him into the restroom and twisting the lock as soon as we're inside.

His hands are on me in an instant, pushing me up against the door as his lips travel the length of my neck, nipping at my jaw before finding my lips.

My body burns under his touch, and my voice comes out rough and raw. "Is this the part where you teach *me* a lesson?" I ask.

He grips my jaw, pushing my head back against the door, and his lips descend on mine again, his tongue flicking at the seam of my lips before delving in and taking.

Our tongues tangle, heat licking up my spine as I moan into his mouth, sagging against the door.

He breaks the kiss, his dark eyes boring into mine. I watch in awe as his expression shifts from feral to amused.

"This," he says, unlocking the door behind us, "is how I teach you a lesson."

In the next second, I'm standing in the bathroom, mouth agape as I stare at the door swinging closed behind him.

RAFAEL

CHAPTER SIXTY

FRIDAY, MAY 30

I SWEAR TO GOD, leaving her when she sounded so goddamn needy and ready for my cock was nearly impossible, but I've got a team to lead and a promise to keep.

I make my way over to the bar, unable to contain the smirk I'm wearing as Elise strides by me with daggers in her eyes. I have the good sense to cower away, ducking my chin.

"Just a water, please," I tell the bartender, sliding a five to him as a tip when he hands me the large glass.

I feel the familiar buzz of my phone vibrating in my back pocket before pulling it out and glancing at the name on the screen.

I open the message thread when I see that it's Carlos. There's a video loading, and the moment it starts playing, my heart is bursting out of my fucking chest.

Carlos is in the middle of a room surrounded by equipment as he pushes himself out of his wheelchair, wobbling slightly as he makes his way into a standing position. He turns his attention to the camera and with a broad grin says something that I can't make out with how loud it is in here. He's got side rails bolted to the ground beside him, and he's gripping them tightly.

My pulse hammers against my skin as I watch him put one very shaky foot forward and then the next before Dad runs up behind him to grab him under the arms and help him back into his seat.

I don't make the conscious decision to do it, my body just drags me to her, abandoning all sense. I find myself dashing to where she's seated, gripping Elise's shoulders with wild eyes meeting her frightened ones before releasing her and shoving the phone in her face, playing it from the beginning. My chest heaves as I watch the range of emotions fall over her features, and when the video stops, her bright eyes swing to mine. She jumps from her seat, swinging her arms around my neck. I slide a hand around her waist and the other behind her head, pressing our mouths together in a frantic kiss before dropping my head to her shoulder. Relieved laughter spills out of us as we embrace, and the tight sensation coiling within me loosens slowly as we release one another.

My smile falters as I peer up, meeting the confused and shocked expressions of our teammates. My heart stops beating, plummeting to my toes as my jaw unhinges from how utterly stupid of a mistake I just made.

Worry simmers in my gut before they break out in applause, starting with a slow clap that turns to whistling catcalls and cheers.

Jelani smacks Nakoa on the shoulder. "Pay up, big guy. I called it."

Nakoa rolls his eyes, pulling his wallet out of his back pocket, and tucks a wad of cash into Jelani's hand.

I let out a loud huff, relief flooding me. "I'm glad we can all stop pretending to not notice. It's exhausting," Adhira says, sliding back into her chair and swirling her straw through her lemonade.

ELISE

CHAPTER SIXTY-ONE

FRIDAY, MAY 30

OF COURSE, they knew all along, and leave it to Adhira to point it out so bluntly.

It's not like we were particularly good about hiding the side-long glances and smirks, and frankly, I spent a lot of time on the field staring at his ass. I'd kind of convinced myself they really didn't realise we'd been together though.

"Yeah, it was honestly becoming painful to have to pretend we didn't know you guys were fucking each other. I mean, *we get why* you couldn't tell us, but it was difficult nonetheless," Chelsea chimes in, twirling a strand of blue hair around her pointer finger.

"I think we get it," I say, rolling my eyes at her, sliding into my seat. Rafael follows beside me, wrapping a thick arm around my waist and tugging me close before pressing a tender kiss to the top of my head. It feels *good* to be like this with him, out in the open with our friends. And even better not to have to lie to the people that matter most to me.

Save for my dad anyway. The reminder that I'm still lying to him leaves my gut twisting.

"If it makes you feel any better, we're telling Coach soon," Rafael tells our friends as they all get seated around us, his thoughts mirroring my own.

"And how are you guys feeling about that?" Jelani asks,

suddenly a bit more serious than he usually seems. From my limited time spent with him, I'm already gathering that he's someone who lights up every room, brightens the mood, and would give you the shirt off his back. And *apparently*, he's also able to match vibes and take things seriously when needed. I think I like him.

"Good," we answer simultaneously.

My cheeks flush with realisation over just how nice it is to hear him agree with that. "It'll be a weight off to finally come out and tell him. I haven't hidden much of anything from my dad since I was in high school, and it feels strange to do it now with someone so important," I admit, peering up at Rafael.

His eyes meet mine with an understanding expression that warms me inside out.

"We haven't told him yet because we didn't want either team to deal with the repercussions, but now that the Blaze's season is over, we're one step closer to telling him. We could do it now, but we figured waiting till the end of our season would be best," he says to the group, but his eyes never leave mine.

We break contact when Jelani speaks again. "Excellent, mates." He raises his glass high, and a wide grin spreads across his deep-mahogany cheeks. "Then let's celebrate," he says, tipping his chin and shooting me a wink before taking a big gulp of his ale.

"Thank you!" we shout at Rafael as he waves at us from his window before pulling to the end of the driveway. I know he won't leave until we're inside, but he should get going because this may take a while.

Chelsea and Letty take turns jabbing the key at the tiny hole in the door, huffing as they do. Adhira rolls her eyes but makes no effort to help, probably knowing she won't be able to do it either.

I stumble forward, snatching the cold metal from Letty's fingers. "O-out of the-e way," I slur.

I crouch down beneath the handle, bringing myself eye level with the keyhole, and press my fingers over it while using the other to guide it into the hole. Once it's in, the four of us burst into cheers, with Chelsea jumping, and then stumbling, into the side of the porch, steadying herself on the railing.

"I'm good!" she shouts, pumping a fist in the air.

The four of us clobber inside, making our way up the stairs and into our rooms. I pop my head out of my door and shout down the hall. "I love you guys!"

Three more heads appear from their respective rooms, one after the other saying the same, with Adhira sounding slightly less enthusiastic. As Letty and Chelsea shut their doors, Adhira fixes me with her warm brown eyes. "Hey," she whispers. "I'm happy for you."

You know that feeling when someone just says something that seems so damn *ordinary* but coming from them, it's *everything*? This is one of those moments.

I know because my heart swells in my chest, heat trickles through my limbs, and hot tears of admiration sting the corners of my eyes. "Thanks," I whisper, my voice giving me away with a watery sound that's foreign to my own ears.

She gives me a small smile before heading back into her room and closing it with a quiet *snick*.

I lie in bed for a while, waiting for the vibration of my phone alerting me to the text from Rafael letting me know he arrived home safely and that he misses me already.

The feeling is mutual <3

Before I can exit out of the messages and go to sleep, a new text comes through.

PAPA CHÉRI

I hope you had an incredible night of celebration, mon petit chou. Let me know when you get home.

Just got in, going to sleep. Love you!

PAPA CHÉRI

I'm proud of you and love you no matter what. Goodnight <3

His words sting, but I brush them away, knowing that very soon, we'll be able to let him in on our secret.

ELISE

CHAPTER SIXTY-TWO

SUNDAY, JUNE 1

"THANK FUCK this is the last time we need to help you with one of these essays because they're boring as shit," Chelsea complains, and not for the first time tonight.

"I know they're boring, but I need to do it, and like you said earlier, it's faster if you guys help me," I say, using her earlier words against her while batting my lashes.

She places a plate of toasted bread and veggie crudités with a whipped feta and truffle dip drizzled in truffle-infused honey and topped with crushed pistachios on the arm of the sofa beside me before setting two more plates around us and plopping down on the rug at my feet. "You need brain fuel," she says before shoving a piece of cucumber with the dip in her mouth.

"Clearly," Adhira says, leaning over to grab one of the plates from the coffee table. As much shit as she talks about Chelsea leaving a mess in the kitchen, she's usually the first one to eat whatever she's made, so long as it's vegetarian. Though recently she's been eating less and less, and it's starting to worry me.

"Alright, let's finish this shi—ahhhhh! Oh, fuck no!" Letty screeches, jumping up and onto the back of the couch, plate in hand as she continues pointing and shrieking.

"What?!" I yell at her and watch in horror as Chelsea's eyes land on the thing causing Letty's outburst.

Chelsea's massive blue eyes are the size of saucers as she stares down at a spider so fucking big, I swear to god it's making eye contact *with me.*

"Oh, hell," I say, pulling Chelsea up and into my lap.

Adhira shakes her head, rolls over the back of the couch, and sprints up the steps with her plate of food. "You lot can deal with that mess yourselves," she deadpans.

"Oh, great! Just leave us down here to be eaten alive!" Letty hollers at her, but her words are met with the sound of Adhira's bedroom door slamming shut.

I take a deep, calming breath before pushing Chelsea's bony ass, scooting her onto the centre cushion. "It's fine," I say, but I'm pretty sure my lip is wobbling as I do. I'm trying to put on a brave face.

"It's big, but it's not like, you know, cat-sized or anything, right?" I ask, trying to reason through this.

"We're going to die here, Elise. That thing is moving in, and we're going to pay its rent in exchange for our safe departure. *That* is what's happening here," Letty says, shaking her head at me.

"We're not. I'm gonna kill it," I tell her, climbing off of the sofa. It turns to face me, jolting forward a couple of inches as if it's a full-grown *human* man ready to compare the sizes of our dicks. *Newsflash* but this spider has a bigger prick than I do, even on my most courageous day.

I sprint around the coffee table, swinging the pantry door open and grabbing the broom before slowly approaching the spider. I raise the broom but before I can smack it over the spider, Chelsea shouts at me, putting a frantic hand out to stop me. "Wait! The fucking thing has babies on its back," she yells on a full-blown sob.

"What the fuck do you mean?!" I ask, shouting as I tiptoe backward and climb onto a barstool.

"If you hit the fucking thing, it'll explode with babies every-where, and she'll have an army to do her bidding against us in her honour!"

"Oh, Jesus Christ. New plan." I wiggle up onto the kitchen island and pull out my phone, dialling Rafael's number.

He answers on the first ring. "Hey, baby. Want me to come over?"

"God, yes!" I shout. "Get here fast."

"Everything okay?" he asks, his voice deepening with concern, any hint of flirtation now gone.

"Just hurry!" I say before hanging up to stare our assailant down.

A few short minutes later, a timeframe that should be entirely impossible given the distance from Rafael's place to mine, he's banging on the door, shouting for me to open up.

I hop down from the counter, bringing the broom with me for safety, and unlock the door, pulling it open.

Rafael's eyes are wild as he inspects my face. "Sunshine, what's wrong?" he asks.

I hear gasps from behind me. "I fucking knew 'sunshine' and 'Sunny D' were code names!" Letty yells at us, pointing a manicured finger in our direction.

Chelsea swats her hand down. "Doesn't matter anymore. He's here, and he's our saviour!"

"Saviour? What's going on in here?" he asks, taking a tentative step into the living room.

He looks down to where we all point, and he physically *jumps*. It looks like his soul just left his body, and I'm suddenly realising that he may not be the saviour we'd hoped he'd be.

"Excuse me, are you afraid of spiders?" I ask, sounding incredulous.

His dark eyes swing to mine. "Uh-uh. Don't do that," he says, shaking his head. "Don't make me feel like an idiot when you called me here because you're afraid of those creepy little bastards too!"

At precisely that moment, the spider lunges at him, sprinting directly toward his feet. Rafael jumps over it and crawls his massive bulk onto our kitchen island, which looks so much smaller with his giant frame lying overtop of it.

"I'll give you a blowy to kill the damn thing! Let that give you strength," I urge him, thrusting the broom into his hands, but he shakes his head adamantly, letting the broom clatter to the ground.

"You would've given me a blowy anyway!" he yells back at me. "*That*"—he points to the spider—"is *not* a spider, Elise! It's a small dog with rabies. You're better off burning the bloody house down!"

I stare down at the furry, wide-eyed spider. It looks like it's ready to chest bump me to show me it's the bigger woman here, so I do the only acceptable thing, catapulting off of the counter and running like hell out of the fucking house, slamming the door behind me.

I make it to the porch, letting out a relieved sigh as I take a seat on the bench and peer inside through the small window beside the door.

Each time the spider moves, Rafael, Chelsea, and Letty scream their heads off, and I can't help the laughter that spills out of me at the sight. Who would've known watching a big man like Rafa yell like that would be so damn funny?

I hear the stomping before I see her.

Adhira's back in her fluffy green robe with an empty plate and a look that could kill. She swings it around the room as she approaches the kitchen, setting the dish in the sink before bending down. When she pops back up, she's holding a can in one hand, grabbing the discarded broom I'd left with the other.

She glares at each one of us, including me, through the window before she leans over the spider and sprays a stream of something at it for several long seconds. I hold my breath as I watch with wide eyes, waiting for the thing to attack her, and when it doesn't, she slams the broom over it as we all shriek in unison, Rafa included.

She sets the items on the ground, leaving the spider to her very timely demise and grabs the plate of dip and vegetables from Chelsea's hand before climbing back up the steps without a single word.

Rafael takes a tentative step off of the counter, his big toe touching the ground before he waits another beat just to be sure the spider really *is* dead, and then makes his descent down.

He picks up the broom and spray can, and announces, "It's all clear. It's definitely not coming back from that."

After he's cleaned up the mess, I head inside and spend the rest of the night working on the essay, this time, with Rafael's help speeding things along, and I *do* give him that blowy, even if he didn't deserve it.

RAFAEL

CHAPTER SIXTY-THREE

FRIDAY, JUNE 6

MY ASS IS sore from sitting in the hard bleachers of the auditorium for the last three hours after the entire graduating class of spring twenty twenty-five walk across the stage, but it was worth the wait to see Elise in her gold-and-blue cap and gown, accepting the diploma she's worked so hard for.

Though she did try to convince me that neither of us had to come since she had no plans on using her degree. Obviously, I wasn't going to let that slide.

As the families pile out of the auditorium in search of their students, Coach stands and faces me with an inscrutable expression on his face. "You want to grab dinner with us?"

I shake my head, waving off the suggestion. It's actually a miracle he accepted my explanation that I felt I needed to be here for *all* of the girls on the team. The glances he shot me when Elise was on stage, or when I obnoxiously cheered for her but was slightly quieter for Letty, Adhira, and Chelsea, make me think we might not be fooling him either.

"Oh, no, I don't want to impose. I'm just here to, to uh, show my support for the Blaze."

He smirks, giving me a small nod as he assesses me, a breath stuck in my lungs as I wait for his response. "Those girls must've made quite an impact on you, considering you hadn't even wanted the position a few months ago."

"Yeah, you could say that."

"Alright, then, have a good night," he says, heading out to the parking lot, where Elise is now hauling ass in her tiny black heels toward his coup.

MI VIDA

Thanks for coming today.

I meant it when I said I wouldn't miss it. Proud of you, mi vida.

MI VIDA

Our flight is at six tomorrow, right?

Yep, I'll pick you up at four.

MI VIDA

Can't wait. Goodnight <3

Goodnight <3

ELISE

CHAPTER SIXTY-FOUR

SATURDAY, JUNE 7

"HOW MUCH LONGER?" I whine.

"I'm never taking you anywhere again," he says, chuckling. "You always do this."

"Invent a teleportation device, and maybe I won't have to keep asking."

"For you, I'd try, but unfortunately, I'm not sure I have the background for that sort of thing." Rafael's lips curve into a lopsided smirk that makes my cheeks heat.

"Well, you should really get on it because we've spent the entire day flying, and I'm over it," I complain again for good measure.

Rafael pats his thigh. "Come here, baby."

I crawl over the centre separating our seats in first class and settle onto his thick thighs, resting my chin on his shoulder.

The plane is comfortable with wide seats, flight attendants frequently checking if we need anything, TV screens attached to the back of the seat in front of us with a seemingly endless number of movies, and the air conditioning isn't too cold or too warm and stuffy. But we're still in a tin can soaring through clouds, and in my opinion, if you don't have wings, you're just tempting fate by flying.

"Have I told you how excited I am for you to meet my family?" he asks in a whisper, pressing a kiss to the side of my head.

"Only every hour since I agreed to come." My heart fills with a sticky warmth I only ever feel with him.

"Good, because I am."

"I'm excited too," I assure him. I'm also terrified, but I keep that part to myself. I've spent the last few weeks refreshing the Spanish I've learned from Letty, preparing for this day. I know his parents speak English, but he says it's a lot easier for them to communicate in Spanish, and I'm coming to their home, so I want to learn their language.

A few hours pass, with several more complaints from me that Rafael kisses away, deciding that's the easiest way to shut me up, *and he's right.*

The time passes slowly thanks to nerves rolling through me, and by the time we make it to his parents' home, my hands are sweating as we get out of the rental car parked at the end of the driveway. It's not his parents waiting at the doorstep though, it's Carlos. Thank god for that. Meeting Carlos first feels like a warmup to the main event because I've spoken to him over the phone countless times now, so it feels like I know him. His parents are a different story, despite both Carlos and Rafael working to convince me they'll love me.

"Carlitooo," Rafael sings as we make our way up the gravel walkway with his arm wrapped around my waist.

"My favourite little brother and his gorgeous girlfriend are home at last!" he says, his brown eyes shining with a glint as he greets me with a broad smile. He wheels himself closer to the edge of the ramp on the porch, but we get to him before he can start making his way to us first.

"*Hola, Carlos. Es un placer conocerte finalmente,*" I say with potentially the most butchered Spanish accent he's likely to have ever heard.

His lips pinch together, and his brows climb as he appraises me with an impressed expression. At least, I *hope* he's impressed.

"And it's nice to finally meet *you*, Elise. Though I now see why my brother wanted to hide you away for himself. He probably figured it was best not to let the more handsome brother try to win your heart until you were fully invested in him," he says, shooting me an exaggerated wink over Rafael's shoulder as he drags his brother to him for a crushing hug.

My sister used to give me the same type of hugs, and a twinge of sadness pinches my soul at the thought.

"Very funny," Rafael says, rolling his eyes playfully. "Let's go see Mamí before she finds us out here and drags us inside."

We follow behind Carlos as he leads us into the one-storey home with picture frames littering the walls telling of a happy childhood and beautiful memories. My lips twitch as we pass a photo of Carlos with Rafael in a headlock, big goofy grins on both of their faces. Rafael looked so carefree and full of life in that photo—none of his grumpy attitude to be seen. Not that I've seen much of that lately either.

"Are they here?" I hear a feminine voice ask from the kitchen. Nerves ricochet through me. We're really here. I'm *really* about to meet his parents! I've never dated anyone, let alone been in a relationship to know what meeting the parents is like, so I'm praying I don't disappoint them.

"*Sí, Mamí,* we're here," Rafael says loud enough for her to hear him. There's shuffling in the kitchen, and then an older couple with dark hair, warm brown eyes, and tan skin greets us with wide smiles.

Rafael's mum, Catalina, wraps her arms tightly around Rafael, pressing a kiss to both his cheeks before pulling away to greet me. "And you must be Elise," she says, smiling warmly at me, dragging me in for a hug. "It's so nice to meet you. We've heard so much about you." A sob threatens to choke me. It's a reaction I could've never expected, but Catalina's hug makes me miss my *maman* with every ounce of my soul.

"*Sí,* Carlos talks our ears off about you after his nightly calls with Rafa. He's such a *chismoso,*" he says, waggling his brows.

Butterflies take flight in my stomach, replacing the sadness, and my shoulders lower from their place beside my ears, my earlier nerves fizzling out. "Oh, really?" I ask, my eyes swinging to Rafael. "I didn't know you talked about me so much."

"You're the most important thing in my life, Elise. You're *all* I talk about," he informs me, and I swear, the whole room swoons, his father included.

"Awww," his parents and Carlos say in unison, and Catalina fans her face, preventing the tears welling in her glassy eyes from falling.

"So romantic, *hijo*," Catalina says.

"Who would have guessed?" Diego, his father, says with a smirk.

"Certainly not me just a few months ago," I say, trying to steer the attention away from Rafael a bit. His cheeks are flaming, and while it's adorable, I know he's been both excited and worried about coming home for the first time in years.

He explained to me that while he's wanted to come back, he has a lot of fears over his own reaction to being here. He was afraid that Carlos being around would act as a reminder of his perceived shortcomings nearly a decade ago, and he didn't want to deal with the extra stress, but said that if I came with him, it would help.

It's still so surreal to think about how far we've come in the last few months. I could absolutely believe I'd be fucking him, but falling for him? Developing real feelings? Definitely not.

"Oh, is that so? He's such a grump sometimes," Catalina says. "We'll have to hear all about how you met over lunch. I bet you're both starving. Follow me," she says, ushering us toward the kitchen with her.

I hover behind with Rafael, reaching for his hand. He squeezes it the moment his fingers slip between mine, bringing the back of my hand up to press a kiss to the thin skin.

"You okay?" I ask, my voice barely above a whisper.

"With you here? I feel like I can walk through fire," he

answers, bending down to give me a chaste kiss. My heart starts to settle, knowing he's not regretting having me here. For the rest of the night, I revel in the immense pleasure of finding out who the incredible people are who raised this wonderful man, and my heart feels so full.

RAFAEL

CHAPTER SIXTY-FIVE

SATURDAY, JUNE 7

I FLICK OFF THE LIGHT, pulling the covers up and over me and Elise before pulling her against my side to nuzzle into her hair.

"I didn't know you were learning Spanish," I tell her, keeping my voice low and quiet. The walls are thin here, and I don't want to keep my parents up.

Elise turns on her side, throwing an arm and a leg over my body. "I wanted to surprise you," she admits, her voice sounding small and maybe a little embarrassed.

"Thank you, *mi vida*," I say, kissing the top of her head and squeezing her gently. "That means more to me than you know."

Her voice sounds sleep-laden and thick. "It's the least I can do to thank them for welcoming me into their home, and hopefully someday—" She pauses for a long beat, but I don't rush her despite the way my heart is violently hammering in my chest. I wait, impatient as ever, for her to finally say what I hope she will. "Hopefully they'll welcome me into their family too."

Before I can get a word in edgeways, she adds, "I think that language is such an important and unique part of someone's culture, and I want to share that with you and your family. I'm absolutely horrendous at the pronunciations of everything, but eventually I'll get better."

"Especially after a few more trips to Argentina," I say, hoping that the insinuation will calm the nerves I feel vibrating through her.

She blows out a long breath, her tense muscles relaxing into me, and I know she's starting to calm down. I love that we can both be vulnerable with each other despite how scared we sometimes are when it's time to say the big things.

"Can you make a deal with me?" I ask, stroking her damp hair along her back before returning my fingers to her scalp to massage her roots, just how I've learned she likes. She starts to melt, her throat humming with a sound I can only describe as Elise's version of a cat's purr.

"Depends on the deal," she says with an airy laugh.

"I'd like to start learning French. I know you don't speak it often since your dad is really the only person around you who's fluent, but I still think it'd be a way we could connect on another level."

She reaches up, giving me an answering kiss on the cheek that warms my insides.

"And what's the deal?" she asks.

"I'll help you learn Spanish if you help me learn French," I tell her, shifting my hand to massage the lobe of her ear.

"I thought you'd never ask," she says, sighing dramatically. "I don't know what it is, but for some reason, my lips simply do not want to make the proper sounds," she whines.

"Don't worry, *mi vida*. I know *plenty* of ways we can teach your lips what to do."

She smacks my chest with a huff. The movement only makes my chest rumble with a laugh that I fight to suppress, knowing I'll get smacked again if I let it out.

"Rude." I can practically *hear* the eyeroll in her voice.

"I'm kidding, baby," I say, planting a wet kiss on her cheek that she rubs at furiously. "Teach me something in French."

She shifts again, lying on her back to stare up at the ceiling, effectively squashing my arm beneath her, but I'd be lying if I said I mind.

In the dark room, with nothing more than the light beneath the door from the hall to illuminate her movements, I see her tap her chin before peering up at me. "*Mon amour*," she says just a second before I answer with, "My love."

"Very good, student," she says, swatting my thigh.

"French and Spanish are both considered romance languages. They're descended from Vulgar Latin, so a lot of the basis for them is the same, which is probably why you've been able to pick Spanish up so quickly."

"Not quick enough," she grumbles.

"How long have you been trying to learn?" I ask.

"Letty has been teaching me here and there since we moved in together a few years ago, but it wasn't until we started planning this trip that I asked her to take her lessons seriously."

"Baby, that was *two* weeks ago," I remind her. "Of course you're going to suck at it."

"Oh, so you admit I suck at it then, huh?" she asks, her tone all sass, and I fucking love it.

Yes, she's absolutely terrible, but it's adorable and the most thoughtful thing anyone has ever done for me.

"Oh, completely," I say, and just as I'd expected, she rolls over on top of me, straddling my hips, and smacks my chest.

I reach out to grab her hand, placing it over my heart. Her bright, playful smile slips into an expression I'm sure I'm wearing too. One of awe that I get to be with her at all.

"We have a big day tomorrow, if you're still up for swimming."

She shifts her hand out from under mine, cupping my cheeks in her soft hands. "You're asking if I want the opportunity to ogle you while you're half naked?" she scoffs. "If so, the answer is always yes," she finishes with a chuckle.

I pull her face to mine, swallowing her soft laughter, her plush lips moulding to mine as she deepens the kiss, sliding her hands into my hair and tugging at my scalp.

I slide the tip of my nose up the bridge of hers, leaving one last kiss between her brows. "Goodnight, *mi vida*."

"Goodnight, *mon amour*," she says, and I can see the smirk and little wink she gives me, even in the dark room.

RAFAEL

CHAPTER SIXTY-SIX

NOT THAT IT'S even the least bit of a surprise to anyone, but my family adores Elise already.

She took her sweet-ass time getting up this morning, but when she eventually did, she made sure to shower before me so she could help Mamí in the kitchen.

As I enter the kitchen, I find Elise bent over the sink, trying to suck in air as she laughs a full-bellied laugh I've never heard from her before.

Mamí turns, facing me, and I see the flour handprint on her cheek as she does. She's got tears streaming down her ruddy cheeks and a smile so blinding I might need sunglasses to protect my eyes from it. Her shoulders are shaking with the semi-repressed laughter, and when Elise turns around, she and Mamí make eye contact for a brief second before sputtering out more laughter.

Elise is covered in flour, both of her pink cheeks coated in the substance with two handprints that mirror the one on Mamí's cheek.

"You two want to explain what's going on in here?" I ask, my cheeks starting to burn from the smile I'm unable to fully quell.

"*Tu novia cero en la cocina,*" she says, another laugh spilling out past her crinkling lips, more tears leaking from her eyes as she presses a hand to her chest, spreading the flour even further.

"*Che! Te escuche!*" Elise laughs, swatting at the air in front of Mamí, who grabs her by the cheeks and presses a kiss to her forehead. They each let the laughter die down, but the unadulterated joy I feel simmering in my blood never seems to follow suit. Their immediate connectedness makes me feel elated, and the way Mamí is nurturing Elise in the same way she always did with me soothes a messy part of my mind I haven't fully dealt with.

"Yes, Mamí. I know she can't cook," I say with a smile as I meet Elise's glare, but her little smirk gives her away immediately.

"That's why you taught him how to cook, right? So he could one day be a happy house husband to a wildly successful athlete," Elise says, beaming at me.

"*Exactamente*," Mamí answers, reaching up to pinch my cheek. Mamí wets a washcloth, cupping Elise's cheek and swiping at her face, cleaning her off as she asks about our plans for the day.

"I'm taking her swimming."

"Ooh, are you going to—"

"Ah, ah, no, Mamí. Don't ruin it," I chide, cutting her off before she can effectively ruin the surprise.

"Ohh, I see," she says with a knowing look, her smile wide and brows raised. "Well, you two have fun, but I expect you home for *Chinchón* and dinner tonight, yes?"

"Yes, Mamí. We'll be home by sundown."

Mamí cups my neck, giving me a quick peck on either cheek before doing the same to Elise, who looks over at me like my mother hung the sun, the moon, and all the stars in the sky.

ELISE

CHAPTER SIXTY-SEVEN

SUNDAY, JUNE 8

RAFAEL and I parked along the side of the road and have been walking in the heat for what's been at least ten minutes, and I'm roasting out here.

The views of the cliffs are gorgeous, but it's hard to see much of anything with the sun blinding me, even with sunglasses on. "I'm not even going to say it, but you know what I want to know," I grumble.

"Yes, princess. We're almost there," he says, his tone teasing as he smacks my ass.

We walk for a few more minutes before we approach a massive rock wall with striated layers throughout. The roaring sound of rushing water isn't far, and anticipation starts to sizzle through me.

I bounce on the balls of my feet as the sound grows nearer, and the moment it comes into view, I know exactly where we are.

I have a habit of watching travel videos, something Rafa has started to do with me. And a few weeks ago, I'd shown Rafael another video I'd found online about the most amazing places in the world to visit and told him I'd love to come to this waterfall in Argentina someday. It looks like today is that day.

My wide eyes swing to his, and I'm met with an irrepressible smile that fills my blood with honey. He takes my hands, dragging me along with him as we run together toward the entrance.

I'm stopped in my tracks when we get to the small alcove that opens up to where the frothy cascade of water falls into the crystal-clear pool below. There are three distinct falls with some smaller ones between them only trickling with water by comparison.

The lush greenery surrounding us combined with the distinct absence of people is awe-inducing. It feels like it's our own private oasis, and it's far more beautiful than in the video.

"Come on," Rafael says, gently dropping my hand and reaching behind his head to pull off his shirt.

If I thought my mouth was hanging open before, it's nothing compared to how I probably look *now*.

"God, you're beautiful," I admit, wasting no time running my hands over his chiselled abs, outwardly staring at every inch of him. I think I could spend every minute of every day with him and still feel disarmed by his beauty.

His warm brown eyes meet mine, and that bowed mouth of his tilts in a lopsided grin as he loops his fingers in the waistband of my denim shorts, tugging them down my legs. He releases a frustrated growl when they get stuck over my ass, his deft fingers working furiously to undo the button, slide down the zipper, and pull them the rest of the way as I use his shoulders for support.

"Come on, gorgeous girl, let's go for a swim."

In the next second, he has an arm cradling my back and the other hooked under my knees, carrying me toward the water.

He walks several feet into the glistening pool before sinking us down into it. My arms are wrapped around his neck, and when he releases his hold on me, I start to float with ease, my body bobbing to the surface of the cool water.

My brows crinkle as I let go of him, cupping handfuls of the water.

"I feel weightless," I murmur, slicing my hand through the surface. "Aren't waterfalls supposed to be fresh water?"

"The falls themselves are fresh, but they get their water supply from an entirely different stream than the pool they fall into. If we swim closer to the falls themselves, you'll sink more easily as the water toward the rock walls is more brackish." He takes my hand, guiding me toward the gurgling water.

Cool mist coats my skin, and just like he'd said, the weightless feeling dissipates the closer we get.

I stand with my arms out and my face toward the sky, soaking in the sun's rays, which are much less harsh here compared to our walk from the car. The tops of the cliffs are sprawling with lush, green-topped trees creating a shaded hammock over this space. It's not enough to make everything dark, but I don't have to squint my eyes or cover them with a hand.

This place is truly otherworldly, unable to be adequately described with words alone.

I feel his fingers tickle the base of my spine as he pulls me to him, my legs winding around his waist with ease.

"Thank you for bringing me here," I tell him, pressing a kiss to the tip of his nose just how I know he loves but never asks for.

His eyes glitter as I do, and a swarm of butterflies threatens to carry me away from their place in my stomach.

"This isn't even the most impressive part," he says, slowly walking us to the saltier part where large crystal formations are growing from the ground up, but he carefully manoeuvres around their sharp edges. "The person posting that video you showed me clearly hadn't done their research."

"Lie on your back and close your eyes, *mi vida*. Just float with me," he says, helping me untangle myself from him as he holds my hand while we lie back in the water. I don't close my eyes until he has, but the moment I do, it's like my whole world comes to a blissful stop for just a brief moment, and *it's heavenly*.

My whole body floats beside his, effortlessly being supported by the salinated water surrounding us. My ears are just beneath the water, blocking out all other sounds besides my own breath, the slow and steady beat of my heart, and the gurgling of the falls as it plunges into the pool at the cliff-side.

This sweet, calm version of euphoria is one I'm not familiar with. It leaves me realising just how much noise I'm surrounded by, making it more difficult to regulate my emotions. These passing seconds of solitude ease some of the overwhelming feelings I always carry around with me, sometimes without even knowing.

Rafael's gentle squeeze to my hand draws me back to the here and now. I slowly crack my eyes open, the edges of my vision erupting in an intense rainbow of prismatic beauty that steals my breath one last time before he tugs me to him. Rafael wraps his arms around me as I come back down to earth from this tiny piece of heaven he's shared with me.

RAFAEL

CHAPTER SIXTY-EIGHT

SUNDAY, JUNE 8

MUSIC PLAYS SOFTLY over the radio as we drive back to my childhood home. Elise has her forehead smooshed against the glass of her window, unable to take her eyes off of the beauty surrounding us.

"Would you ever want to move back here?" she asks, catching me off guard.

"Uh, I'm not sure. I love it here, but ultimately, I guess it depends on where you are and what kind of opportunities there are for your career and mine," I answer without much thought, and the sudden weight of the words that just slipped so effortlessly from my mouth has my stomach twisting as I wait for her response.

I hear her shift in her seat and chance a brief glance in her direction. She's got that full bottom lip sucked between her teeth as she looks at me, her gaze searing my skin as I wait on bated breath for her to say something, *anything*.

"I like it here, and Argentina does have a fantastic women's football team," she says so simply, as if she hadn't just flipped my whole world upside down.

I reach for her hand, pulling it to my lips, and press a kiss to each of her knuckles. "That's certainly something to consider," I murmur against her smooth skin, placing her hand on my thigh.

"It definitely is," she says with a confidence that calms me so easily. "Hey, do you mind if we cancel our plans for tomorrow?" she asks, suddenly changing topics, not that that's out of the ordinary for her. I've seen her at her highest, her lowest, and on an average day, she seems to live somewhere just toeing the line between a little low and a little high. I never know what each day will bring, but I'm flexible, and getting to be there for her in either is a gift she has no idea she's given me.

Today it seems she's riding a bit of a high.

"Sure, you have something else in mind?"

I catch her little smirk in my periphery before she tries to suppress it. "That's for me to know and you to deal with later," she says with a chuckle.

"Well, alright then."

ELISE

CHAPTER SIXTY-NINE

THIS IS EITHER GOING to backfire completely and blow up in my face, or I'll get to keep my promise to Rafael and help him understand that the guilt he carries isn't his to bear.

Either way, the moment I saw it from the window of our rental car, I knew it was just the kind of thing I've been searching for.

RAFAEL

CHAPTER SEVENTY

SUNDAY, JUNE 8

THE SHARP COUNTER edge digs into my hip as I lean against it, watching Elise dancing around the kitchen with my mother, apparently in her new element.

She's integrated herself into my family so well, it feels like it would be impossible to ever go back to a life without her. I'd never be able to move on. Never be able to bring another woman home without my family comparing them. Anyone else would fall short because Elise is the closest thing to heaven on earth I'll ever know, and I wouldn't want it any other way.

She's stunning in an unattainable way that makes my chest ache, and the way I feel about her makes me physically ill to think about living this life without her.

These thoughts sound dramatic, even to my own brain, but they ring true.

"You love her, *hermano*," Carlos whispers beside me, nudging my forearm with his shoulder.

I have no idea how he manages to know what I'm thinking even when we've gone years without seeing each other in person.

"I do," I whisper back, and the thought of saying those three little words has my chest fluttering and my hands sweating.

"Does she know that yet?" he asks, peering up at me with a

knowing look on his face. We've had a similar conversation to this before, but I haven't gotten myself to tell her since then.

I shake my head. "I'd hope she knows, but I haven't told her in so many words."

Carlos lets out a loud snort, reaching up to pat me on the back. "You're an idiot, Rafa. You better tell her soon. There's no reason to wait." He nods his chin to where Elise is leaning over the kitchen counter, rolling out dough for *medialuna*, her head tossed back as she laughs loudly at something Mamí is saying. Warmth spreads through my chest watching the two of them together.

Carlos's smooth, hushed voice draws me back to our conversation. "She's not going anywhere. Tell her how you feel so she can return the favour and put out that fire burning a hole in your chest with worry."

I don't bother asking how he knows this feeling because it doesn't matter. He's right. *He usually is.* "I will."

"Promise?"

"Yeah. I promise."

ELISE

CHAPTER SEVENTY-ONE

MONDAY, JUNE 9

"YOU'RE A SHIT DRIVER, you know that?" Rafael asks through gritted teeth, one hand braced against the dashboard with the other white-knuckling the "Oh shit handle."

I roll my eyes and stick my tongue out at him like the massive child that I am. "I don't have a car, in case you'd forgotten. I'm not a bad driver, I'm just a little rusty. Besides, there's no one on the road here anyway."

"With the way you talk about drunk drivers, I'm surprised you don't also consider *this* reckless."

"Listen here, big man. I'm not driving *recklessly*. I'm going the speed limit; I'm making turns at a reasonable speed and using my turn signals too. There is nothing reckless about the way I'm driving—*you* just have a control problem," I blurt out, not even a little afraid to call him on his bullshit.

"I'll give you that," he huffs out, "but in no world are you a *good* driver. Can we at least agree on that?"

"Well, duh, is anyone really a *good* driver? I think that's subjective," I say, nodding my head so he knows this conversation is over.

"Whatever, *mi vida*. At least if we die in this car, we'll die together," he says, his tone taking on a flirtatious quality that is more likely to get us in a wreck than anything else that's happened in this car the last half hour.

"Yeah, remember that sentiment later, okay?"

Rafael lets out a little growling sound that has me practically cackling from the absurdity. "Stop growling, you whiny baby. We're almost there."

And luckily, we *are* almost there. According to the GPS, I've got one more turn to make and then we'll be at the place that could either end our entire relationship and the fragile trust we've developed these last few months or make us even stronger. For Rafael's benefit, I'm willing to take the chance.

It's hard to tell whether he's upset or not because his body language has been on edge this entire drive, and I'm not sure that much has changed as we pull down the muddy trail, parking out front of the wooden treehouse.

I put the car in park, turn off the engine, and lean back in my seat, waiting for the big reveal of his emotions as bees swarm my stomach, climbing up my oesophagus and stinging their way up.

He releases his hold on the handle, but I can't say that "relaxing" into his seat is the right word for what he's doing. "Resigning" might be more accurate.

He turns to face me, his skin a touch pale, forehead already beading with a light sheen of sweat, and his lips are pulled taught in a straight line.

"Elise, no," he says adamantly, shaking his head. "We are *not* going up there. Absolutely not. How could you think this was a good idea?" he asks, his voice raw with emotion. I let him sit without saying another word for a solid two minutes as he has his moment to freak out. He slumps against the seat, and I unbuckle myself, climbing over the centre console to straddle his hips.

I press my warm palms over his cheeks, drawing his attention to my face before speaking. "*Mon amour,* do you remember when you asked me to help you deal with the guilt? To finally recognise that what happened to Carlos was never your fault?"

His silent nod is his only answer.

"Good, because that's what we're doing today. We can turn around at any point, just use your safe word," I tell him with a wink, doing my best to break through some of the tension thick in the air around us.

"Elise," he groans out. "I'm not saying cum dumpster in public," he whines. "Let's just go back home to my family where we'll be *safe*."

"You'll be safe *here*, Rafa. That's what I'm trying to show you."

He clenches his eyes shut, blowing a breath out through his nose, and rests his forehead on my shoulder as he winds his arms around my back. "Please, *mi vida*."

I run my fingers through his thick, dark waves, to his neck, and down the length of his spine a few times, waiting for the sounds of his heavy sigh. It's a sound I've learned to wait for, knowing that once it's left his lips, he'll be okay.

When that sound comes, I say, "Just let me show you something, and if you want to leave before we actually get started, we can. Deal?"

I feel his nod against my shoulder, and if this were sex, I'd require a verbal confirmation, but right now, I think this is all he's capable of giving me, so I accept it for the answer that it is.

I unlock the door, pushing it open before climbing off of his lap and holding out my hand for him to take it as he gets out.

He takes his sweet ass time walking up the wide pine staircase to the top of the round, canopied treehouse.

I recognise the thirty-something-year-old man leaning against the desk at the check-in counter from his picture on the website.

"*Che*. Santiago?" I ask.

"*Sí*, it's nice to meet you, Elise. And you must be Rafael?" he asks, extending his hand for him to shake.

"Nice to meet you," Rafa says, and I'm thankful he's retained his manners despite his anxiety.

"Well, let's go ahead and get started then, yeah? I'll start by giving you a tour of where we keep all of the equipment and go over the details with you."

We follow Santiago around the front desk and back down a short hall with wooden beams. He unlocks the storage space, opening the door wide, revealing an air-conditioned room with shelves along the walls, each with various pieces of equipment labelled on them.

"This is our storage room where we keep all of our equipment. It's weather-proofed because we want to make sure our equipment doesn't rot out or form rust. We keep the doors locked when one of the staff isn't in here to make absolutely certain no one could come in and tamper with the equipment." Rafael's eyes widen a hair, and Santiago must notice because he adds, "We've never had anything like that happen, and we have cameras all over the property, but we've heard some stories and want to make sure we don't wind up a part of some true crime podcast."

I'd definitely listen to that podcast but he's right—I'd rather not be featured on one.

"That sounds *very* responsible," I emphasise, and I'm rewarded with an eyeroll from Rafa.

He takes my hand in his, squeezing it tightly as Santiago shows us each piece of equipment from the harness to the gloves, helmet, and the individual components. He explains the weights they'll each support, how frequently they replace them, the routine testing they perform on them, and the statistics on failures, of which there are very, *very* few.

"Any questions about this part of things, or can I bring you to take a look at our rig?"

Rafael scratches his neck nervously, his grip tightening on my hand. "I think we're all set, thanks!"

Santiago nods, leading us out of the room and locking up before walking us up another set of pine steps that lead to the first platform built around a massive tree trunk.

"This here"—he waves a hand in front of a tall pulley system at the front of the platform facing the open expanse of water below—"is our zipline. One of the key features is a heavy-duty stainless-steel cable that is mounted to the platform on the other end. It can easily hold up to thirteen hundred kilos, but for safety reasons and due to the weight restrictions of our harnesses, we can accommodate up to two hundred kilos, which is about four hundred and fifty pounds."

The more he speaks, the more I regret this idea. My stomach roils, acid burning up my throat. Heights are a big fuck no, but with nothing besides a heavy cable and harness to hold me up? Who the hell was I kidding?

I suck in a deep breath, willing the elephant seated on my chest to lift its heavy ass so I can get some goddamn air and focus on Rafael.

The entire time Santiago speaks, Rafa is rubbing at his jawline, scratching his neck, or bouncing his foot. He's anxious, and it makes complete sense, *but that's why we're here.*

Santiago then shows us the mechanics of the system, explains all of the details and how he, his father, and brother, the owners of this company, maintain the system. "We run a daily check each morning to make sure it's safe to operate for the day and have routine checks with a local team that assesses the quality of the lines. You'll also notice that once you're clipped into your harness, you remain clipped in until you finish the course. This way, you're always attached to the line and won't risk falling over the edge of the platform in the event that something extremely strange happens like losing consciousness."

There are about fifteen other safety mechanisms he and his family have implemented, and by the time he's done explaining everything, I genuinely feel like ziplining is a million times safer than driving or flying. Not that it helps my fear of heights any.

"If you're ready to get started, I'll walk you both down to the desk, and we can get you fitted for your equipment and get your safety waivers signed."

After we've signed away our lives to this very nice man, who makes it seem as though having your feet firmly planted on the ground is *not* as necessary as I believe it to be, Santiago heads to the supply closet to grab our equipment, which leaves Rafael and me some time to talk.

I pull on Rafa's hand, dragging him alongside me to the wrap-around porch overlooking the lush green trees and a colourful mountainside striated with clay.

I run my hands up his arms, shoulders, and to his neck, staring into the warm depths of his brown eyes, even as they threaten to break me from the worry etched into the edges.

"Why are we here?" he asks, his voice so small it forcibly pierces through my heart.

"Because, *mon amour*, I needed you to see this. I needed you to see that what these people do every day isn't just to protect their livelihood, but it's to keep the people who come here safe."

His dark brows pinch further together, and I can't stand the sight of it. I run my thumb over the skin, smoothing it out as I take a deep breath and prepare myself for what I'm about to say.

"What happened to Carlos wasn't just an accident, it was a *tragedy*. But it was never *your* fault. That's not your burden to bear, Rafa."

His tense shoulders start to loosen, so I trudge on, hoping like hell I say the right things and don't fuck this up.

"Do you see everything Santiago and his family do each day to maintain their equipment, to make sure this activity they love and the business they've built remain safe for anyone who wants to come and enjoy it?"

He nods, but the movement is jerky and doesn't settle the swarm of bees still stinging away inside me.

"I need you to hear me when I say this, and then I need you to repeat it back to me. Say these words 'What happened to Carlos was not my fault.'"

His head rears back, and the muscles in his neck tighten. I feel his strong pulse beneath my fingertips as it speeds up.

"No, Elise. This isn't going to work." He grunts, looking anywhere but at me.

Time to try a new approach.

"If we get on that zipline and something happens to you today, would you blame me for it?"

His eyes widen with shock, as if the very idea of the words I've just spoken is so ridiculous he can't even believe I asked them. "What the hell? No, of course not. How would that be your fault?"

"Well, I brought you here," I answer.

"That doesn't matter, Elise. That guy just told us about a million reasons why that thing is saf—" And then the word dies on his tongue, as do the bees in my gut, each one having lost their stinger in the fight to be free before finding their demise as I watch understanding spread across his features. "It-it wasn't my fault," he whispers, and his eyes fill with tears that never fall.

I reach up on my tiptoes, wrapping my arms around his neck, and squeeze him against my chest. "What happened wasn't your fault," I whisper, reassuring him.

"It wasn't my fault," he chokes out. We continue just like this until he no longer feels the need to say it, until his trembling limbs have settled and the wet tears he's left on my shoulder have dried up.

When I loosen my hold on him, he pulls away just enough to rest his forehead against mine.

"Thank you, *mi vida.*"

I don't bother answering in words because the gift he thinks I've just given him is truly nothing compared to the relief he's given me. Knowing that he's been carrying that guilt around for the last fifteen years has weighed on me in a way I hadn't even realised until this moment.

The boulder I've unknowingly been holstering has lifted, and I can feel my chest expanding with every full breath I'm able to take.

Santiago opens the door, sticking his head out. He hollers over to us, "You both ready to get started?"

"Yeah, thank you," Rafael answers without a moment of hesitation, pressing a kiss to the tip of my nose before pulling me inside.

Santiago helps us into the equipment, explaining how we should feel once everything is secured, making adjustments as we go, and once ready, I stagger outside, my knees wobbling with each step.

My palms are sweating as we near the platform, this time harnessed and clipped in, except that now I don't have the distraction of Rafael's anxieties to keep my mind off of the distance between solid ground and my feet.

Rafael slings an arm around my shoulder, kissing my temple before tickling under my arm. "Stop it!" I screech, swatting at his hand, my eyes wide. "I'm not about to fall off of this thing because you thought tickling me was a good idea, you idiot!"

The colour has officially returned to his face as he tries to suppress his laughter. "Okay, okay," he says. "You know, we really don't have to do this." My eyes cut to his, narrowing. He puts his hands up in surrender. "I've already got your message, okay? We don't have to do it if you're afraid," he amends.

I put on my version of a brave face, lifting my chin as I say, "I made you face your fears today, now I'm going to face mine."

He playfully shakes his head, lowering his mouth just above my ear to whisper, "That's my girl." His words have goosebumps forming on my skin, and I have to shake off the sudden chill.

I suck a breath through my nose and turn to Santiago. "I think we're ready," I confirm, not missing the smirk he tries to hide. "If you two are done laughing at me, I'd like to get this over with."

"Yikes," Rafa says, but his deep-bellied laugh distracts me just enough that I don't exactly remember why I'd wanted to stomp on his foot just a second ago. Unfortunately, the moment is fleeting as I step onto the edge of the platform on shaky limbs, wishing I were on flat ground, at his parents' home making *medialuna* that would be entirely inedible if not for Catalina's skill in the kitchen, or swimming by the waterfall like yesterday.

RAFAEL

CHAPTER SEVENTY-TWO

MONDAY, JUNE 9

I HAVEN'T FELT this light in years, and I only have Elise to thank. Who the hell would've thought that Coach's spitfire daughter would also be the most tender and caring person I've ever known?

"Okay, Elise. The line has a steel spring brake toward the end so you don't come to an abrupt stop, so just remember that if you want to slow down, you just pull here, but don't do it too soon, or I'll have to go out there and push you the rest of the way. All set?" Santiago asks her, sucking his cheeks in as he clips her shaking body to the line.

"Y-yep," is all she manages.

"Can I talk to her real quick?" I ask him, and he nods, moving my clip so I can get closer to her. I wrap my arms around her waist and breathe in her sweet berry scent, nuzzling against her ear. Her quaking slows as she melts against me. I take the opportunity to whisper in her ear, keeping my words low and slow so Santiago doesn't hear. "If you do this, I'll make sure we find a nice place on the drive home for me to fuck your needy cunt, but if you don't want to, we can always leave now."

That gets her attention.

I don't love the fact that she demanded she go first to get it over with. She probably doesn't realise how similar this situation is to what happened to Carlos, but she swears it's to her benefit that she goes first. After seeing all the safety mechanisms Santiago and his family put in place, I'm finally able to let go of the past and recognise that these situations are completely different. The people are different, as is the activity and the level of attention put into ensuring everyone's safety.

Elise's spine straightens as she gives me one strong nod. "I'm ready," she squeaks out, and there's no hiding the laughter rumbling in my chest.

She spears me with a glare, but when Santiago has me safely clipped back to the starting point, he pushes her forward, and I swear, every woodland creature and bird in the sky shuts up to listen to the bloodcurdling scream that Elise lets out the entirety of her way to the next platform.

My cheeks ache from laughter watching as she makes it to the end, tossing a hand up at me. I'm almost certain she's flipping me the bird, but I couldn't care less. I'll pay for that later. All that matters is that true to Santiago's word, *she's safe.*

I expected my stomach to bottom out and my knees to feel weak seeing her make the jump, an unkind reminder of Carlos's accident, but I'm surprised to find that it never happens. It only took a second before I was confident she was fine, and then laughter took over.

When it's my turn, I take a deep, steadying breath, and as he pushes me over the edge, it's like flying.

Exhilaration floods my body, an ultra-awake feeling taking over as adrenaline washes over my senses. The water gleams hundreds of feet below, and I can hear a rush of water from the falls to my left. Wind tickles my cheeks, and the faster I go, the more alive I feel. By the time I get to the end, my eyes are dry from the cool air, and tears prickle at the edges.

I hold down on the brake, slowing and coming to a controlled stop a foot in front of the platform. Santiago's father greets me on this side, leaning forward to grab me by the harness and tug me the rest of the way onto the platform.

I grab Elise's cheeks as she meets me with wide blue eyes and a smile that could rival the sun in its intensity. My lips descend upon hers, and she sags into my embrace, opening her mouth on a little gasp that goes straight to my dick.

Her tongue swirls against mine, sending electricity zipping up my spine. When we finally pull apart, Santiago and his father are standing nearby, openly smirking at us.

"We're glad you enjoyed yourselves. Ready for the next part of the course?" Santiago asks, laughter spilling into his words.

Elise reluctantly completes the entire course, which takes seven sets of ziplines to get us to the bottom, where we're unclipped and led down a heavily tree-lined path to our cars.

"Did you two have fun?" Santiago asks as he helps me unbuckle my harness, but when he tries to move to do the same for Elise, my inner Neanderthal comes out to play.

"I've got it," I grunt, bumping him out of my way to unclip her harness.

Elise smirks, ignoring me as she says, "It was great, and thanks again for opening so early to give us a tour of everything."

She set this up *just* for me? I figured she called ahead but hadn't realised the extra attention and explanations were her doing. I thought it was standard protocol for them.

"It's not a problem at all. I'm glad you both enjoyed your-selves. I—" he clears his throat, shuffling a bit as I hand him her equipment. "I was actually wondering if you'd sign something for me," he says, scratching his head.

"Oh yeah, sure," I tell him.

He clears his throat again, his eyes darting nervously between us. "Sorry, I meant her," he clarifies, nodding to Elise. "My daughter is a huge fan, and even though you're not playing profes-sionally yet, she still begged me to pay for this subscription so we can watch your games. I've admittedly become a massive fan myself. I can't wait to see where you turn up in the premier leagues and beyond."

Elise takes this in stride, not even batting a lash as she gladly follows him to the desk to sign seven different Auclair items he's purchased over the last year. I'll have to help her look into trademark and licensing for these because I'm nearly certain no one is paying her any revenue for these things.

When she's done signing everything, she asks if he'd like to call his daughter so she can say hi, and I swear, this man nearly falls to his knees before her. I mean, I get it, but I'd rather be the only person on their knees for this woman.

His daughter, Rosalia, screams over the line when Elise introduces herself, and when we leave, I'm left filled with an overwhelming sense of pride for this incredible woman that I'm practically bursting at the seams with.

I hold the passenger door open for her, buckling her in before sliding into the driver's side. As soon as the doors are closed and it's just us again, I kiss her like my life depends on it.

And some days, *I think it does.*

"Let's go find that nice place I promised you, *mi vida*," I tell her, kissing the back of her hand and pulling out onto the main road.

ELISE

CHAPTER SEVENTY-THREE

MONDAY, JUNE 9

"THIS LOOK NICE ENOUGH FOR YOU?" Rafael asks, trailing his fingers up the inside of my thigh as he brings the car to a stop at the entrance to what looks like a private beach.

"For now." I look around the area, satisfied when I see no other cars or evidence that anyone else is around. "We've got to make this quick though because I don't know if I've ever told you this or not, but I've been arrested before, and I'm not thrilled at the prospect of adding anything else to my record."

He scoffs, throwing his car door open and walking around to my side. My fingers can't move fast enough as I work on getting my seatbelt unbuckled. Rafael pulls my door open, wrapping his strong arms around me, and pulls me out of the vehicle, setting me on the hood.

He wastes no time tugging my leggings and thong down, tossing them beside me, and undoing his belt. The hot metal stings at first but dissipates quickly.

I'm enraptured as I watch him pull himself out, stroking his rapidly hardening length. "Open wide, Elise," he says as he fishes a condom out of his wallet and rolls it on.

Birds crow overhead, their songs a loud reminder that anyone could drive by and see us. My skin is flushed, but chills erupt as the cool, damp air touches me between my legs.

His dark eyes narrow, gripping me by the hips and dragging me down the hood to meet him. He holds the base of his cock, swiping it through my wet centre.

My lip quivers, and my chest heaves as he enters me in one smooth thrust. "Oh, god," I cry, my eyes watering as I arch into him.

He pulls my legs up, helping me wrap them around his back as I dig my nails into his traps. He dips his head, stilling his movements and drawing my lobe between his teeth. "Hold on, *mi vida*," he growls against the shell of my ear.

And with those four words, his restraint breaks as he slams into me, drawing gasps and moans from my lips.

"You were so good today," he tells me, and my abdomen floods with a gnawing heat in response. "Facing your fears for me," he praises. "Such a good girl."

His words do me in, pulling every ounce of my arousal out of me as he slides his hand down my tummy, flicking my clit with his thumb and successfully creating fireworks behind my lids.

This might be the fastest I've ever come before, and I'm overwhelmed by sensation. The sound of distant water splitting across the surface of heavy stone, Rafael's murmured praise, the cool brush of the breeze of my skin, the sun's warm rays seeping into us. They all mingle with the feel of Rafael, the man that I *love* stretching me, pressing against the walls of my pussy, dragging out my pleasure as he meets his own. Sweat from what we'd just accomplished, and the pride that reminder breathes into me at *both* of us overcoming our fears mingles with the heady scent of our arousal, and a familiar, warm and citrusy scent that is so uniquely Rafa.

My nipples pebble as I hear his groan and the subsequent tightening of his ass under the heels of my feet before he stills, resting his bulk on me, my cunt still spasming around him as his release fills the condom inside me.

He licks a trail up the side of my neck, a shiver rolling through me, and my fingers scrape through his scalp. His soft lips press at the base of my ear, and his warm breath tickles me as he says, "Baby, let's get you home."

ELISE
CHAPTER SEVENTY-FOUR
MONDAY, JUNE 9

"HEY, I'm willing to try almost anything once so long as it doesn't end with me in prison or dead," I joke with Diego when he asks if I'd like to try *mate*.

His deep chuckle has easily become one of my favourite things in the last few days. It's hearty and comforting.

He prepares the dried leaves with hot water, allowing them to float to the top before handing it to me. "It's got an acquired flavour, so don't feel bad if you don't like it. The act of pouring and sharing *mate* is considered a gesture of love and dedication."

Rafael had told me about *mate* once when he was talking about his childhood. He said that *mate* is considered an integral part of Argentinian life. Sharing it with people is like a ceremony. It's tied to feelings of friendship and is shared with both friends and strangers.

It's sweet that something so seemingly simple as sharing a beverage with someone has such a profound meaning to an entire culture.

"*Gracias*, Diego." I thank him, wrapping my hands around the clay mug, the heat warming my palms.

Rafael runs a hand down my arm, eliciting sparks of awareness over my skin as he squeezes my elbow. "The straw has a filter, that way you don't drink the leaves."

I nod, breathing in a deep whiff of the earthy, almost grassy scent before pressing the warm metal straw to my lips and taking a sip. My eyes widen, and my cheeks pull taut, lips puckering. I swallow it down despite the bitter, almost astringent taste coating my mouth.

His family is seated around the dining table with us, sucking their lips into their mouths, and before I can even say anything, they burst into laughter.

"It's a little bitter," I admit, my shoulders quaking with suppressed laughter, heat blooming over the apples of my cheeks.

Rafael tugs on my hair tie, pulling it out and putting it around his wrist. He sinks his fingers into the base of my scalp, rubbing gently and then applying firmer pressure that makes me melt into the chair.

"You purr like a cat," Catalina remarks with a knowing grin, shuffling the deck of cards. She hands them to Diego to pass out to each of us and grabs a plate of *vigilante* from the stove and sets it in the centre of the table. The smell of sweet butter lingers in the air, making my mouth water.

I've learned that in Argentina, it's common to eat dinner at nine or ten at night, so having a pastry, or *facturas,* around five or six with *mate* or *cortadito* is what I've grown used to these last few nights.

"Speaking of cats, how's Mrs. Purrito doing?" Carlos asks, and the smirk he's wearing tells me there's a story behind that cat that I haven't heard yet.

I perch on the edge of my chair, trying to look like I know what the hell I'm doing as I stare at the cards in my hand. Spoiler alert I don't.

"She's with Nakoa and Jelani, so I imagine she's laughing maniacally while rubbing her ass on J's pillow since he's allergic to cats," Rafael says, dropping his hand from my head to pick up his cards.

It takes everything in me not to pout at the loss of contact.

"If he's allergic, why would he agree to watch her?" Catalina asks. She's the picture of calmness as she arranges her cards. Something tells me she's three steps ahead of everyone else. As the mother of two boys, I suppose she had to be.

"Because it's Jelani. It's not that he has a hard time saying no, because he doesn't. It's that he genuinely doesn't *want* to say no, and it wasn't until we got here that Nakoa texted to give me an update on her and also let me know that they shouldn't watch her again because J would never tell me, but he's been sneezing every two minutes and has had three nose bleeds so far. I feel like shit about it," he grumbles, and the regret in his tone has a dagger jabbing straight through the centre of my heart.

Diego waves a hand through the air, dismissing the thought just as quickly as it came. "Oh stop. You didn't know."

"He's right. How about we tell Elise how you came to have Mrs. Purrito in the first place?" Carlos asks, and I sigh because it's what I've been waiting for this whole time.

Rafael groans, sorting through his cards. He doesn't bother lifting his head as he says, "You can tell her yourself because I know you're dying to."

Carlos's smile stretches wide across his handsome face, twin dimples shining brightly as he relays a story about the time he hadn't heard from Rafael in weeks, but knew he was alive because he'd been watching his games. "I figured I'd get his attention one way or another, and this little cutie," he says, showing me a picture of a mud-covered Ragdoll kitten on his phone, "was just the right accomplice."

"Don't forget Elise's father," Rafa grumbles, grabbing a card from the middle of the table.

My brows knit in confusion. "I'm sorry, did you say *my father?*"

"He sure did. I got a hold of your dad and asked him if he'd help me with my plan to get Rafa's attention." My brows are at my hairline, and I'm hanging onto every word spoken from Carlos's mouth. "He picked Mrs. Purrito up from the shelter and brought her to the pitch for me. Let her loose after the game was over and made his team captain chase the little thing around on live TV. As soon as she was in his arms, he had a whole slew of cameras and mics in his face pressuring him on whether or not he was keeping her, and of course he had to. Who wants *that* bad publicity, right?"

My mouth hangs open, and I have to make the conscious effort to shut it, waiting for Rafael to confirm this is all true.

He's lazy with his response, simply saying, "At least she's stopped tearing my shit apart since then. I threatened to have her declawed, and that seemed to tame her."

I gasp, smacking his shoulder without considering what his parents might think, but his mum, who's seated on his other side, is smacking him in the back of the head at the same time as me. I huff a laugh but ask, "How could you?"

He rubs his shoulder, shooting me a playful grin before turning that same expression on his mum. "I *wouldn't*. I swear, but she took the threat seriously, and that was all I'd hoped for. I'm not about to chop her toes off. That's fucked up."

"Agreed," Carlos says across the table, lifting his cards to his face.

"You ready to lose again, Carlos?" Diego asks with a smirk that somehow manages to be both charming and a little intimidating. He effectively steers the conversation back to the game that I've just barely figured out how to play by watching them the last few minutes.

Carlos rolls his eyes so hard I'm worried they might get stuck. "Please, Papá. You got lucky last time," he taunts.

"Ah, but luck is just preparation meeting opportunity, *hijo*," he says.

I nudge his shoulder. "He's got you there, Carlos."

He shoots me a betrayed, mock-outraged look and says, "*Et tu*, Elise? My own future sister-in-law?"

My cheeks heat at the insinuation, but Diego cuts in. "It's not siding. Elise is just appreciating greatness when she sees it," he says, patting Carlos on the back.

Rafael snorts, taking a loud sip of his *mate* as he finishes his mug, slurping the last of the liquid. "You're talking a big game, Carlos. Let's see if you can even manage a meld this round."

"It's not about winning," Catalina chides. "It's about spending time with family."

"Eh, winning makes it better," Rafael says, sounding uninterested in the game.

The game continues, and I'm completely lost within two rounds. Rafael keeps trying to give me tips, but they mostly consist of vague advice like which cards not to throw away. He doesn't bother explaining why, and I'll enjoy teaching him a lesson about throwing his *highly competitive* girlfriend to the wolves like this.

Next time we come to visit, I'm spending months prior learning the rules of all these games so I can really play.

Halfway through the game, Carlos suddenly slaps his cards down on the table. "*¡Chinchón!*" he yells, throwing his arms up in victory.

The way his dad raises an eyebrow says everything. "Good, *hijo*. But let's see if you can do that again."

Carlos is practically beaming, clearly riding the high of his big moment, while Rafael mutters something under his breath. I bite back a laugh. I love it when he gets like this. When Rafael is annoyed and grumpy, all he wants later are cuddles. He's a lot like me on my period.

By the time we get to the last round, it's tense. Diego is sitting there, cool as ever, and Carlos looks like he's ready to burst a blood vessel, which is hysterical considering he's generally so calm and sweet. Apparently, he's got a mean streak when it comes to card games.

Catalina and I have already accepted our fates as losers.

Carlos slaps a card down with way too much force. "Papá, you're going down this time."

"Patience, *hijo*," Diego says smoothly, drawing a card from the pile. He looks at it, smiles, and then, in a move that feels almost theatrical, lays down his entire hand.

"*¡Terminé!*" he announces, throwing his hands up like he's just won a championship.

Carlos's groan is almost a growl as he throws his cards onto the table. "You've got to be kidding me!"

Rafael lights up for the first time in the past half hour, laughing so hard he nearly spits out his drink. "And he does it again! You really thought you had him?"

"*Cállate*, Rafa," Diego mutters, glaring at him.

I rest a hand on Carlos's shoulder, trying not to laugh at how serious he looks. "It's just a game."

"No," Carlos says dramatically, looking around the table. "It's not just a game. It's about pride. Legacy." He points at his dad. "You're ruthless, Papá. Ruthless."

Diego shrugs, gathering the cards with a little flourish. "That's why I'm the head of this family, Carlito. A true *Chinchonero* never lets his guard down."

Catalina gives Carlos a comforting look, but I can see the smile tugging at her lips. "There's always next time, *mi amor*."

Carlos shakes his head, muttering, "Next time, I'm taking you down, Papá."

Diego just grins and winks. "I'll be waiting."

The table erupts into laughter again, and I can't help but smile. This family, they're competitive and chaotic, but they're also kind of perfect.

There's a strange combination of sadness and nostalgic joy that curls inside me.

It's families like this that make the ache so much worse, reminding me how much I miss my *maman* and Rachelle, but it's also beautiful to know I get to be a part of this world with them too.

The rest of the night goes on similarly, with Rafael and Diego poking fun at Carlos while he gives it back to them ten-fold after taking a few minutes to sulk. Catalina and I wind up on the back patio, going through pictures of Rafael and Carlos as children and drinking a much less bitter version of *mate* that she served to me cold inside some sort of gourd with orange essence. The flavour has definitely grown on me, and I'm thankful for that because I want to share these special pieces of their culture with them.

It makes me feel like Rafa and I really belong not only *with* each other but *to* one another. It's something I've never experienced before but can't get enough of now that I have.

ELISE

CHAPTER SEVENTY-FIVE

WEDNESDAY, JUNE 11

I CLUTCH Catalina tight against me as we say our goodbyes while the boys load up the rental with our luggage.

We've barely had any time together, but it already feels like a whole chunk of my heart is being torn from my chest now that we have to leave.

"*Che, mil gracias por recibirme en tu casa,* Catalina," I tell Catalina, thanking her for welcoming me into her home.

She pulls back from me, sliding her hands up to grip the outside of my biceps as she looks up into my eyes with her dark-brown ones, the same colour as Rafael's. "*Gracias por devolverme a mi hijo, más feliz que nunca,*" she says, her chin quivering.

If there's one thing she can count on me for, it's that I will *always* bring her son home to her. This is where he belongs, surrounded by the people who love him most. And maybe we won't be here all the time, but I'm making it my personal mission to ensure he sees them at least once every three months.

Tears prick my eyes as I tug her back into my chest; the sweet, cinnamony scent of her skin from the pastries she helped me make this morning envelops my senses, and I reluctantly leave her embrace to say goodbye to Diego and Carlos.

"Thank you for coming with me, *mi vida*," Rafael says, pressing his warm lips to the top of my head, my cheek resting on his shoulder as the pilot takes off down the runway.

"I love your family, Rafa. They're incredible," I tell him, my voice sounding thick with emotion.

"They love you too, you know. How could they not?"

An ache stirs in my gut, and I die a little waiting for him to speak the words I've been too afraid to say myself.

Peering up into his glittering eyes, I cup his cheek and suck in a steadying breath as I prepare to say the words I want to hear from him. *How could I blame him for not saying them when I'm too chicken-shit to do it myself?*

"I love you," we say in unison.

Our mouths move at the same time, and my heart stops in my chest, my eyes widening as disbelief passes between us.

"I'm sorry, what was that?" he asks, his full lower lip hanging in bewilderment.

I shake my head, a closed-lip smile overtaking my face as I roll my eyes at him. *"I said"*—I enunciate each word—"I. Love. You, Rafael."

His wide-eyed expression morphs into one of appreciation as a smile curls his lips. He cups my cheeks, and his hot mouth meets mine in a tender but short-lived kiss.

"I love you too, Elise. Hell, I probably love you *more*. No," he says, running a hand through his cropped hair. "I *definitely* love you more."

His words whisper through me, warming me all over and

tugging at the heartstrings I've only recently allowed someone the capacity of breaking. Before Rafael, there was no one else I'd ever have let get this close to me, let alone to fall deeply, madly, *terrifyingly*, in love with.

But now that I have him, *I'm never letting go.*

RAFAEL

CHAPTER SEVENTY-SIX

SATURDAY, JUNE 14

"NO WONDER you hated this office so much, you never made it your own," Elise says, dropping into the chair behind my desk and swivelling around in it. Her dark strands wrap around her face as she spins faster.

She jolts to a stop as I grab the headrest to halt her movements.

"What, *peligrosa*? Did you expect me to put up pictures of my favourite girl in here?" I ask, tipping her chin up till our eyes meet.

She peers around the room, making a show of looking at the bare white walls as a smirk stretches her lips. "Yeah. I think that's exactly what it needed."

"Mhmm, and I'm sure that wouldn't have caused any problems for us, huh?"

I drop to my knees in front of her, gripping the tops of her thighs and sliding her toward me, running the tip of my nose up the inside of her thigh. "It seems it's too late now, but maybe we can make some last memories in here before we go. Yeah?"

It's been three days since we returned from Argentina, and it's like I've been floating on cloud nine, completely enamoured by the ease of my day-to-day with Elise.

I go to practice, and she and Adhira came to our game last night, making the game that much more fun for me to play. We've spent every night cuddled in bed together, and my heart has been absolutely bursting with love. It's a warm feeling, like honey and hot tea when you're sick, or any other time of the day really, according to the Brits I'm surrounded by. This feeling of being with Elise makes everything else slow to a crawl; it's all more manageable and less bitter with her around and the weight of Carlos's accident lifted from my shoulders.

I'll never get tired of her.

I swipe a finger over the seam of her thin athletic shorts, dragging it through the slickness that's already waiting for me, and her eyes swirl with grey clouds like a brewing storm.

"Fuck me," she says, her words a breathy whisper, "*Coach.*"

I swear to god, that word is like a trigger for my dick, so just like she demands, that's exactly what I do.

ELISE
CHAPTER SEVENTY-SEVEN
SATURDAY, JUNE 14

I SUCK Rafael's fingers clean, releasing them from my lips with a *pop* before standing and pulling my shorts back up my thighs.

He takes a minute to gather the rest of his things, and I take the larger of the two boxes because there's not a man on earth who's going to make me feel like a dainty princess, not even this absolute monster of a man.

"You about ready?" he asks, taking one last look around the small, windowless office where all of this started. The question feels heavy, like it holds more meaning behind those three words, but no matter the meaning, my answer remains the same.

"I am if you are," I tell him, and when he nods, I hold the door open for him. Except instead of walking through the door, he stops in his tracks, and his jaw sets in a hard line, the muscle twitching.

I peer past him, and who I see is the last thing I'd have expected, my stomach plummeting to my toes.

My nostrils burn as my throat tightens, a sudden wave of loathing hitting me with the strength of a monsoon.

"So much for never being satisfied with just one dick," Noah says, slowly shaking his head in that condescending way of his. "Seems to me that you were just waiting for an off-limits prick. Isn't that right, Elise?" He tilts his head in question as he leans against the wall, looking prim and proper in his dress slacks and loafers. Such a contrast to the slimy, uncouth individual under the clothing.

I steel my spine, grinding my teeth. "If you recall, I said I wouldn't settle down until just one satisfied me. Turned out yours was never in the running, Noah." My words ring true, and I know they have the desired effect when his eyes flash with rage. "Now get out of our way," I say, brushing past him in the tight hallway. Rafael follows behind me, grumbling something I can't quite make out.

"Just wait till I tell your father about this," Noah deadpans.

I spin on my heel, outrage scorching through me at the thought that this insolent man-child would threaten me as if I were a teenager again.

"In case you hadn't noticed, I'm an adult, Noah. You can't blackmail me to get your way. What is it that you want anyway?"

"You," Rafael says, answering for him. "He clearly wants what he can't have, and he's willing to do whatever it takes to get you. Well, whatever someone like him is able to."

"What's that supposed to mean?" Noah asks, his voice reaching a higher pitch, straining his thick Oxford accent as his cheeks grow pink and his expression more indignant than before. He puffs his chest, shoving up against Rafael, who rolls his eyes, treating him as nothing more than an annoying gnat.

"It means you never had a chance. Elise doesn't need any man, but what she *wants* is a *real* man. And that's something you sure as fuck are not."

Without a second thought, Rafael drapes his heavy arm over my shoulder, steering me out of the locker room as Noah shouts behind us.

"Leave him, Elise! Leave him, or I'll tell your father! I'm not fucking playing around, Elise!" he shouts, his shrill voice piercing my ears as dread seeps into my gut.

I hold it together as we make it out of the locker room, down the long hall, and into the parking lot. Rafael is quick to open his trunk, piling the small boxes into it as I do the same, biting painfully on my lower lip.

He opens my door for me, helping me into the car before running around to climb in on his side. He makes quick work of backing out of the parking spot, careful not to skid through the puddles left from the earlier rain shower, the dreary grey sky cloaking us reflecting my current mood.

My hands are shaking as I form the next words. "What are we going to do?" I ask Rafael, unsure of what he's thinking.

He looks so calm as he drives us toward his apartment building.

"We tell him." He shrugs.

He doesn't elaborate further. Doesn't try to qualify his statement. Just tells me the words I needed to hear to settle the demons swarming through me.

"What about your season? We agreed we'd wait until it was over before we told him."

He pulls off, parking a couple of metres from the road. The sounds of car horns and heavy traffic pass along the highway beside us, his tyres crunching through dew-heavy grass before he puts the car in park, turning to me and taking my trembling hands in his. "Yeah, but plans change, and frankly," he says, rubbing my wrists with his thumbs, "if your dad gives me any ultimatums, *which he swears he'd never do*, then we deal with it then. His reaction doesn't change anything for us, *mi vida*. That's not just a nickname, baby." He's always so quick to remind me of that, and it makes my heart pound even more intensely.

Tears prick at the corner of my eyes, and I swallow around the thick lump forming in my throat. "I've told you once, and I'll tell you again a million times more if that's what it takes to get through to you. You *are* my life. I love rugby, but I love you more. End of story, so stop worrying about an outcome that hasn't even happened yet, and call your dad to see if he's available for dinner tonight."

With a weak nod, I fish around for my cell phone while Rafael pulls back out onto the road.

"Hey, Dad!" I say, my voice sounding entirely too chipper, and he knows it judging by his automatic response.

"Wow, someone's happy. Must've *really* enjoyed the holiday, huh?" he asks, and I know he's mocking me. "Never mind that, I'm sure I'll hear all about it at dinner tomorrow, won't I?"

I clear my throat, a tether of apprehension tugging at my stomach. "About that…"

"Are you cancelling?" he asks, genuine surprise filling his voice. "You've never cancelled one of our dinners."

"No, no. It's not that, Dad. I was actually wondering if we could move it up. To tonight."

There's a long pause of silence before his usual playful tone is filling my ears. "Of course. I'll see you both at six," he answers before hanging up.

Both?

CHAPTER SEVENTY-EIGHT

SATURDAY, JUNE 14

MY PALMS ARE slick as I grip the steering wheel, turning into the drive of my future father-in-law's home.

I can honestly say I'd never imagined meeting my future wife's father like this. Not to mention the fact that I *already know him.*

The path to the house is lined with brick, leading up to a one-storey Victorian-style home with a large bay window in the front that boasts a brightly lit dining room that I can see clear through the drawn curtains. "Are you ready for this?" she asks, resting her hand on my thigh, giving it a tight squeeze.

"Never been more prepared for anything in my life," I lie.

She rolls her pretty blue eyes, smirking at my expense. "Such a liar."

"Maybe a little," I admit. "I'm going to fuck this up, you know. Inevitably I'm going to say something stupid, and he'll be mentioning it in our wedding speech."

"Our *wedding speech*?" she asks, her brows raised and eyes wide, but that smirk still dances across her pouty lips. She's beautiful, and I want to kiss the expression clean from her mouth.

"See?" I shake my head. "It's already started."

Her face turns serious as she grabs my cheeks in her palms, resting the tip of her nose against mine to stare directly into my eyes. "It doesn't matter what you say in there. I'm still going to love you, and even if he doesn't approve, *he'll get over it.* Okay?"

"Okay." I breathe, closing my eyes and revelling in the solace she brings me. "Ready."

When I open them, I'm met with hers, filled with such determination that all of my fears seem to melt away. *Even if he's pissed, it changes nothing.*

Because there isn't a world I want to live in without Elise. A life without her wouldn't be worth living at all, and over the last few months, I've come to realise that.

If there's one thing our love will never be, it's *selfless love.*

CHAPTER SEVENTY-NINE

SATURDAY, JUNE 14

I MIGHT TALK A BIG GAME, but that's just for Rafa's benefit. In reality, *I'm losing my shit.*

We make it to the door, my hand shaking as I raise it to knock, but it never makes contact.

The dark wooden door swings open, with my dad standing on the other side, his lips pressed into a thin line as he looks between us, making no effort to let us inside.

"What the hell is my team captain doing here?" he asks, his brows pinched together. If he wasn't referring to Rafael when he said "both of you" earlier, who on earth could he have meant? Had Noah got a hold of him and spewed lies about him and me?

Neither of us makes any move to speak, a sudden chill zipping down my spine at the intensity in my dad's glare. This is a man who is *never* upset about anything. Why did he have to choose *this moment* to take life so seriously?

He lets out a huff, stepping out of the way and opening the door wide for us to pass through.

Or, to let *me* pass through, rather. His foot shoots out, physically stopping Rafael as he halts in the doorway, his large frame shaking with suppressed terror. I don't even blame him. My father is a big man, and he can pack a punch, both literally and metaphorically, with his big personality.

I sidestep my father, whose grimace seems to waiver, but maybe that's just me being hopeful, and step back out onto the covered porch.

I peek up at Rafael, who has a bead of sweat rolling down his temple, tugging on his hand, I help him uncement his feet from the wooden planks.

He follows me into the main dining room in the front of the house. The table is set with a colourful red bouquet of *Ceibo* spilling onto the white tablecloth. *I've only ever seen those flowers in one place.*

Rafael must be thinking the same as he loosens his grip on my hand, letting it fall to my side as he bends over the table and lifts one of the waxy flower petals in his palm. He takes a moment to inspect it, working his jaw on a swallow.

"Beautiful flowers, aren't they?" Dad asks, his words spoken through gritted teeth, his arms crossed over his broad chest as he watches Rafa's movements.

Rafael's gulp is audible, which only serves to add to the way my gut is beginning to churn with bile.

"Very beautiful, sir," Rafa answers. Dad's lip twitches, but he says nothing as Rafael turns, pulling my chair out for me and taking a seat in his own.

His leg bounces, the silverware rattling on the table. He reaches for his glass of water, and it's painful to watch the way his hand physically shakes, water spilling over the top of his glass as he brings it to his mouth, guzzling the clear liquid as if it'll somehow save him.

Dad's deep baritone cuts through the unnerving silence. "I've heard they're a symbol of both bravery and *resilience* in Argentina."

Rafael's body stills beside me, a beat passing before he places his glass down and turns his full attention on my father. "You've known this whole time, haven't you?" Rafael asks, his words so quiet I can barely hear them.

I deflate, my shoulders sinking as I realise just how right

Rafael is, and based on this strange taunting he's doing, he's not really mad. Though Dad does have a flare for the dramatics.

Rafael manages to wipe the stunned expression off his face, resting a hand on my thigh.

"Rafael isn't great about logging out of his email when he works at my desk between practices," Dad deadpans.

It takes a second, but some memory must click because Rafael pulls his phone out of his back pocket and sifts through his messages. He leans across me, bringing the phone to my face, and all the air whooshes from my lungs.

It's the picture he'd taken of our names drawn on the wall of the church.

"I assumed something was going on between you two for a while before that, but I wasn't sure how serious it was until I saw that photo pop up on my screen. I didn't want to pry, so I just waited until you got around to telling me. I guess today is that day," he says, relaxing back into his chair and resting the back of his head on his crossed arms, his grimace now a taunting smirk. "Any particular reason why we had to move things up?" he asks, his greying brows knitting together, causing his usual relaxed expression to shift into something more serious.

"Noah found out about us and is threatening to blackmail us," I admit, my mouth growing dry and my cheeks heating.

Dad leans on his elbows, concern now marring his features. "What could he possibly have to blackmail you with? Better yet" —he shakes his head—"what does he want?"

Rafael clears his throat, and I feel the bounce of his leg as his black slacks slide against my calf. "He wants Elise to leave me for him, and his little plan was to tell you about our relationship if we didn't tell you first. Clearly, that didn't work because we had already planned to tell you. We were just waiting for the end of the season to do so."

"And because I have zero intention to leave him," I cut in, giving Rafael a sideways glance. "Ever."

Dad's posture relaxes again, and he releases an audible sigh, an easy smile sliding onto his tanned cheeks. "Well, I'm relieved to hear you've been planning to tell me either way, but that little shit Noah has another thing coming if he thinks he can try and manipulate *my daughter* into doing a damn thing. He acts as if he isn't just another nepo baby relying on his daddy's money," he says with a scoff and roll of his eyes. "Good thing I know his father. If he wants to act like a child, he can be treated like one."

And *this* is one of many reasons I love my dad. He sees things in their entirety and is always the first to work out a reasonable plan for how to deal with them while setting me completely at ease.

All the anxiety vanishes from my body as I slump against Rafa's shoulder. The tension from his muscles has disappeared too, and he wraps an arm around me, kissing the top of my head just how I love.

"So," Rafa ventures. "You aren't...mad?"

Dad squawks out a laugh. "What? No, of course not." He shakes his head. "It was just fun to see you sweat. My daughter is a woman, more than capable of making her own decisions. I'm her father, *a part* of her support system but not her entire world anymore," he says, and the words make the tip of my nose burn as he gives me a glassy-eyed smile. "If she chose you, then I will too. I'm not her owner, and she isn't my property."

"Thank you," Rafa says, the words passing his lips like a whispered prayer, sent straight to heaven.

I look back across the table at Dad, and his eyes practically have hearts glittering in them. The man is a true romantic.

"I just *love* love," he sing-songs, resting his cheek on his palm as he takes us in. "I'll admit this is weird, but I'm willing to bet it's a lot less weird than if this had happened with Coach Lyon," he jokes, and Rafael's choking laughter fills the small dining area.

I sit up and pat him on the back, my cheeks aching from my unrelenting smile. "Well, this conversation has been positively enlightening. Now, what are we having for dinner?" I ask as my stomach rumbles loudly.

Despite the formal setup of the dining room, Dad serves us *croque monsieur*, which is essentially a grilled cheese with Gruyère, ham, and béchamel sauce. It's one of my favourite comfort foods, but I'm entirely too lazy to learn how to make a bloody béchamel.

The time passes quickly as we discuss the trips we took together without Dad knowing, and I apologise about a million times because the guilt of not including him in so much has been gnawing away at me. Dad sets that to rest after the millionth and one time, all but shouting at me to quit apologising.

Laughter is wheezing from my lungs as Dad and I make jokes at Rafael's expense. "And then—" I suck in a breath. "You should've seen his face when Santiago admitted that he didn't want Rafael's autograph, he wanted *mine.*" My cheeks burn. "He didn't even know who Rafael was."

"And someday, everyone in the world will know who you are, *mi vida*," Rafael says against my ear, but apparently not low enough because my dad makes a mock-vomiting sound.

"Come on! Not at the dinner table. People are trying to eat here," Dad whines. "Save the sugary sweet crap for dessert."

Rafa's face has been glowing red the entire time we've been here, and I'm not sure that'll stop anytime soon.

After dinner, we all work together to clean up before crashing on the couch, where Dad demands we stick around for a movie, the time passing too quickly.

I stretch my arms over my head, yawning loudly as the romcom comes to an end. Dad swipes at his eyes watching the credits roll by. "That damn movie gets me every time," he murmurs. *Such a softy.*

He flicks the telly off and turns the lamp beside him on. "I guess you two should be heading home, huh?"

"Probably, but we can have dinner anytime. You know, now that you're in the loop," Rafael tells him.

Dad rolls his eyes, standing, and we follow suit, heading to the door. He wraps me in a crushing hug that's so comforting I don't bother telling him that he's ripping my hair out with his big arm.

"Goodnight, Dad. Thanks for having us, and for"—I look down at my feet—"for everything else."

"Anything for you, *mon petit chou*," he tells me. He turns his attention to Rafa, opening his arms wide, and that signature smirk is plastered on his face again. "Come here, big guy. We're family now."

Rafa reluctantly steps into his arms, and I *swear* I see him melt just a little bit.

"This day has been so fucking weird," I whine, stripping out of my clothes, leaving pieces littered on the floor as I make my way to the bathroom to brush my teeth.

"You're telling me. I was ninety percent sure your dad was going to kill me and the nice guy act was to throw me off so I wouldn't see it coming," he says.

"Yoo nefer know," I mutter around my toothbrush, "coot still hapfen."

I don't miss the way a shiver runs through him, but ignore it, fearing for his pride if I bring up his completely unwarranted fear of my father.

I spit out the toothpaste, rinse the brush and then my mouth, padding across the plush carpet with Rafael trailing dutifully behind me. I find Mrs. Purrito curled on top of Rafael's pillow when I crawl into bed. "Seems she's come to love having her own pillow," I say.

"Yeah, well, I hope you like sharing because I think that's

going to be our reality," he grumbles, climbing in behind me and tugging on the end of *my* pillow.

"Absolutely not, I refuse to share," I whine.

His hand lands on the base of my belly, rubbing soothing circles, and a sigh slips past my lips. He nuzzles against my neck, nipping at the skin, and blows a cool breath over my ear that causes goosebumps to erupt. "Sharing is caring, *sunshine.* Now get some sleep, and I'll show you just how much I care about you in the morning," he whispers, settling against me.

My thighs clench, but Mrs. Purrito distracts me from my trance. She stands to shift her ass right in my face, circling the pillow and plopping down, resuming her loud engine-like purrs.

As strange as sharing six inches of a king-sized bed with a man the size of a tank and a cat who won't shut up and is constantly trying to smother me with her arse fur might seem, I can't help but sigh into my new reality, drifting to sleep knowing *I've got everything I want, right here.*

The end.

ELISE

EPILOGUE PART ONE

"YOU KNOW, the little bromance the two of you have going on just doesn't sit right with me anymore. It was cute in the beginning, but it's starting to freak me out, and I especially don't appreciate being ganged up on," I say with a pout, crossing my arms over my chest.

"Don't be such a baby, Elise," my dad says, rolling his eyes.

"Yeah, get your big girl knickers on and stop whining," Rafael says, nudging my shoulder.

"It's almost my birthday and this is what I get?"

"No, it's almost your birthday and your two favourite people in the whole world are taking you on holiday in France. Now stop your complaining, we're almost there," Dad tells me, shifting his luggage into his lap as we prepare to get off the train.

"Ah, so I see her incessant need to ask *are we almost there yet?*" Rafael says, raising his voice in a mock interpretation of mine, "is not a new development."

"Definitely not," Dad says with a deep chuckle.

The conductor announces our next stop, and the train comes to a screeching halt a minute later, opening the doors with a puff.

Beautiful sunshine spears through the train cars as we make our way to the nearest exit. Stepping onto the platform, we're surrounded by passengers rushing by, pulling their children behind them or carrying their large shopping bags filled with designer items.

When in France, I guess.

RAFAEL

EPILOGUE PART TWO

ELISE STRETCHES AGAINST ME, pressing her ass into my erection. Heat smoulders at the base of my spine, but I groan into her ear. "Your dad is right next door, *mi vida*. And *you* are entirely too loud for this to go any further."

She huffs, rolling onto her back, but the pout on her lips doesn't last long before my mouth is wiping it right off.

She moans into my mouth, and I relish the sound, the taste and feel of her under me. Reluctantly I pull away, tugging her lower lip as I do. "Happy birthday, *mi vida*."

"It'd be a much happier birthday if you'd fu—" her words are cut off by the shrill ring of the phone on the nightstand.

I release a steadying breath through my nose, wrenching the corded phone off the line, and press it to my ear. "What is it, old man?" I grit out.

"Well, good morning to you too, Rafael! My most favourite future son-in-law who I just *know* is wide awake and ready for another beautiful day on the coast of France for my equally lovely daughter's birthday," he says, rambling on and on in that annoying sing-song way that he does. I don't know how he manages to lead a goddamn thing because all he seems to do is drive me up a fucking wall.

"We'll be ready in a half hour," I grumble.

"Make it twenty minutes—we've got some pedal boats to catch!"

The line goes dead and with it, my good attitude.

"Pedal boats, really?" I ask Elise, and the way her eyes gleam and that single dimple caves with her growing smile is all I needed to suddenly be equally excited for the stupid activity as her dad was.

The boat rocks gently beneath us, the water sparkling like something out of a postcard. It's a perfect day in France, the kind of day that feels like a love letter to life, or maybe I've just heard that kind of corny shit in one of the romcoms Chelsea's subjected Elise and me to.

This might even be peaceful, but naturally, Coach has turned our little adventure into a military operation. He has the energy of a man half his age and the patience of a caffeinated squirrel.

He's standing at the bow like he's captaining a yacht instead of a wobbly plastic boat. His voice booms across the lake, startling a few ducks nearby. "Come on, Rafael, use those legs. Stop being so lazy!"

I groan, shaking my head. This is not what I imagined when they said it would be a relaxing day on the lake.

"Where the hell do you even think we're going, Coach? It's a tiny ass lake with no destination."

He turns his upper body to face me, narrowing his eyes, though I think that's more from the sun and less as an intimidation tactic. The whole boat starts to wobble with the abrupt movement, and I'm starting to think I might be suffering from seasickness.

"Maybe I want to feel the wind in my hair today, Rafa. Have you ever thought about that?"

"Well, no. I haven't. Considering you don't have a whole lot of hair left anymore, the thought never crossed my mind."

He flips me off and says, "I've got more hair on my head than you, asshole."

He's not wrong. The annoying fucker has an infuriatingly thick head of hair, but any chance I've got to bring up his age, I'm taking it.

I look over at Elise, who sits cross-legged, leaning back in her seat with her face tilted toward the sun, completely unbothered. She's always like this, effortlessly graceful, as though the chaos around her is just white noise. And believe me, *there is a lot of chaos.*

Like right now as her dad jostles the boat, nearly capsizing it while I do all the work.

When she turns to look at me, her face is lit with a kind of joy that makes everything else fade away. The soreness in my legs, the ridiculousness of this outing it all disappears when she smiles like that.

ELISE

EPILOGUE PART THREE

"AHOY MATEY! It's my daughter's twenty-second year on this earth. Give a big round of applause for the lovely little cabbage!" he shouts to a man on a paddleboard.

I roll my eyes, but it's impossible not to smile. This is so quintessentially my dad, taking something as simple as a pedal boat and turning it into an excursion.

"This is how I die," Rafael mutters, sinking back into his seat. "On a plastic toy boat, in front of ducks, being yelled at in two languages."

"There's cake at the end of this journey. Doesn't that make it worth it?" I ask, whispering so my dad won't direct any more attention toward Rafa.

He gives me a look, the kind that says *only because of you*, and my heart does a little flip.

Even as I sit at this small rustic table tucked in the corner of a restaurant my dad took *Maman* on their twentieth wedding anniversary, I still find it hard to believe that we made it off of that pedal boat dry.

A waiter with two small lemon tarts and a chocolate mousse approaches the table, smiling as he sets the tarts in front of Dad and me and passes the mousse to Rafael.

"Thank you," I say as Dad digs around in his "murse." He's now on some man-purse kick thanks to Rafael's genius idea to take him shopping down the riviera after pedal boating.

He produces a cake topper that looks a lot like a closed-up flower. "Wouldn't be a birthday without a candle," he says, and his smirk gives him away immediately. He presses the plastic into the tart and grabs out a pack of matches. "You know, the one positive thing that came out of that pandemic is that I don't see as many people blowing out their candles on a communal dessert. That's just disgusting. I'm not sure why we ever did that. It really shouldn't have taken a global pandemic to help people realise that."

I chuckle, sucking in a breath, but before I can answer, he's lit the match and pressed it to the top of the candle. It starts to spin, opening slowly. Each petal has a candle leading to a sparkler in the centre. Each candle becomes lit one by one, and finally, the sparkler starts throwing off tiny flecks of glittery flames as the stupid piece of plastic starts to sing.

Rafael leans in close to my ear. "Make a wish, *mi vida*," he whispers softly.

But I don't need to.

I already got it.

RAFAEL

EPILOGUE PART FOUR

THREE YEARS LATER

MY FOOT BOUNCES at a million kilometres an hour against the metal stands as I watch in awe of my incredible wife.

My chest expands with a fluttering feeling, adrenaline rushing through my veins, and my throat feels so tight it's hard to get a good breath between each gasp and yell I let out.

Elise sprints down the pitch in the final moments of play, her dark ponytail swishing behind her as she pushes past Spain's defence. The announcer's words become muffled, my brain unable to keep up with all the extra stimulus as Elise narrowly escapes with the ball.

My breath leaves my lungs in a whoosh of air, relief flooding my still tight chest, but as the timer ticks down and her opportunity to win the twenty twenty-eight Summer Olympics for Argentina seems to be slipping out of her grasp, my blood is pounding through my veins.

Five.

She pumps her arm, gritting her teeth and gaining speed.

Four.

Spain sidles up beside her, nearly stealing the ball.

Three.

She takes the chance, kicking the ball with such force it physically knocks her on her ass. She was too far from the goal. There's no way that'll land.

Two.

I'm out of my seat, my fists balled, and my nails digging into my palms as the stands quiet, silence filling the space.

One.

The ball touches the inside of the net, slipping past the goalkeeper's glove by a literal hair's width of distance.

"YES! FUCK YES, BABY!" I scream, slapping my hands on my head, tearing at my roots as the emotions building inside me the last ninety minutes spill over.

Elise's wide-eyed expression turns on me. She pushes herself off of the ground and starts sprinting toward me. She's coming so fast she manages to run up the fence. I lean my bulk over the railing, grabbing her under her arms, and pull her sweat-coated body up against me.

She wraps her arms around my neck, and the flood gates erupt.

Tears are spilling out of my eyes as I ugly-cry into her neck, shaking our bodies with the rumbling from my chest.

"I did it," she whispers, her voice small and filled with disbelief.

"You fucking did it, mi vida," I tell her, pulling away to look into her pretty eyes. My lip is still quivering as I try to suck in a breath and calm myself down. "The best in the world, just like I knew you'd be."

Her lips pinch, and tears start to pool in her eyes, but Carlos taps her on the shoulder, dragging her attention away from me.

A low rumble leaves my throat at the intrusion, but I'll allow it, just this once.

"Look at that. A two-time World Cup winner and an Olympic gold champion, all by the age of twenty-five," he praises.

"Twenty-four," her dad corrects, leaning over us to press a kiss to the top of her head. "I've never been prouder of you, kid. Your mum and Rachelle are probably looking down on you right now with nothing but pride and stars in their eyes."

"Thanks, Dad," she says, her eyes flickering back to me. "I'm gonna need you to put me down now because my legs are going numb."

I press one quick, sloppy kiss to her lips that has her giggling before lowering her back down to run to the field and celebrate with her team.

As she rejoins them, I'm able to take a deep breath, some of the adrenaline wearing off enough that I can take a seat again.

"I have the coolest aunt," Valentina, Carlos's stepdaughter, whispers behind me.

I lean back, ruffling her hair. "You sure do," I agree.

And I have the coolest wife.

ACKNOWLEDGEMENTS

This book was long, but my gratitude is endless.

Thank you to every single person who played a role in the creation of Resilient Love, and has given me and my books a chance.

A massive shout out to Vai Denton for being the real MVP and dragging more out of me during edits when she knew I had more to offer.

And as always, the biggest thank you to my Unhinged Romance Slumber Party aka Evelyn Leigh, Cynthia Rodriguez and Kath Richards. I love y'all with every fibre of my being. <3

AFTERWORD

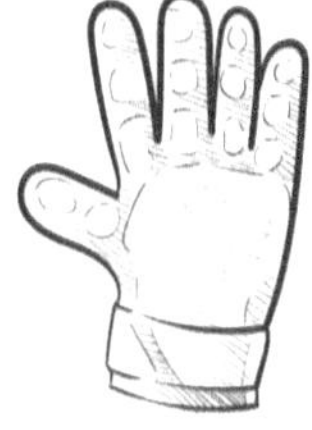

We still very much live in a world where mental illness is heavily stigmatised, regardless of how much positivity we see to the contrary on social media. Some mental illnesses are vilified more than others, and bipolar disorder (both 1 and 2) is one of them.

My hope when writing Elise was to remind everyone reading her story that living with bipolar disorder does not make you a villain.

If you're struggling with your mental health and well-being in any way, please ask for help. You matter. Always.

https//www.helpguide.org/find-help.htm

ABOUT THE AUTHOR

Giuliana Victoria is an author based in Pennsylvania who shares her readers' deep love of all things romance. She's a full-time physician assistant, whose passion lies in being there for her patients during their most vulnerable moments.

When Giuliana isn't writing swoon-worthy book boyfriends, she can be found yelling about human rights on Threads, hiking with her three large breed rescue dogs, and, of course, curled up with a good book beside her husband, the best "book boyfriend" there is.

She hopes you'll love **Resilient Love** as much as she enjoyed writing it, and she looks forward to sharing all of her future works with her incredible readers.

BIPOC AUTHORS I ADORE & YOU SHOULD CHECK OUT

In no particular order
    Evelyn Leigh
    Cynthia A. Rodriguez
    Ruby Rana
    Vai Denton
    Jada West
    Kennedy Ryan
    Nisha Sharma
    Talia Hibbert
    Shilo Kino
    N.M. Patel
    Natasha Bishop
    Janisha Boswell
    Deanna Grey
    J.S. Jasper
    Kristina Forest
    A.E. Valdez
    Miah Onsha
    Anna P.
    Varsha Chitnis
    Amy Oliviera
    Siren Crow

Mikayla Hornedo
Layna James
I.B. Solís
Britney S. Lewis
Danielle Brooks
Danica Nava
Ambar Cordova
Natalie Caña
Riss M. Neilson
Georgia K. Boone
MK Owens
Leigh Carron
AJ Alexander
Janiah Benitez
Nelle Nikole
Nouha Jullienne
H.M. Wolfe
Amber V. Nicole
Allie Shante
Santana Knox
Goddess A. Brouette
Ziye' Taylor
Tember Sapphire
Sophie Thomas
J.J. Greenaway
Ophelia Reign
L.M. Ramirez
Oona Arlo